LADY OUTLAW

"Kiss you again? I think not," Rowena shot back. Heat surged into her cheeks as she reached for the latch. With a swiftness that stunned her, however, the dark-haired man blocked her way.

"Leaving? I think not yet." Grasping Rowena, he held her in a tight embrace, his lips caressing hers again as his hand slid down the curve of her hips. From experience he knew that a woman liked a man to be strong and domineering. They liked to lead a man on a merry chase but always gave in once they were caught.

"Unhand me!" she ordered, unleashing a torrent of swear words, words unfit for a woman to say.

"What?" Kendrick's lips twitched in a smile as he regarded her. He held her tightly, refusing to give in to her plea. "Such language," he said playfully. "I ought to put you over my knee, wench."

Rowena did not stay to continue the conversation. With a curse she opened the door and fled into the hallway. She was running from a foe far more dangerous than whatever waited below; indeed, she was running from a man who was after a greater bounty—her heart and her virtue.

LADY OUTLAW

Kathryn Kramer

Zebra Books
Kensington Publishing Corp.

http://www.zebrabooks.com

ZEBRA BOOKS are published by

Kensington Publishing Corp.
850 Third Avenue
New York, NY 10022

First Printing: February, 1997
10 9 8 7 6 5 4 3 2 1

Printed in the United States of America

This story is dedicated to my friend Julie Munoz who shared in the creation of Kendrick d Bron and "Arrow."

And,
For Mark Penn, whose fascination with Robin Hood and Sherwood Forest inspired this story. At long last, the story we promised you . . .

THE FLAME OR THE ARROW

The Flame or the Arrow,
Which shall it be?
The flame pulls towards you,
The arrow towards me.

The flame of love
Burns with passion and fire,
Yet the arrow flies free
With my own soul's desire.

The Flame or the Arrow
Which shall it be?
Be it the flame or the arrow
The choice is for me!

AUTHOR'S NOTE

Robin Hood is said to have been a legendary outlaw who lived in the greenwood, dined on king's deer, was skilled as an archer, robbed from the rich to give to the poor, and teased and tormented both Prince John and the Sheriff of Nottingham. Ballads and tales tell of his band's compassion for the poor and oppressed, their narrow escapes from the sheriff's men, and their chivalry towards women. Robin Hood is first mentioned in the records of Yorkshire in 1230, where there is a reference to a "Robertus Hood fugitivus". The first literary reference to him by name appears in *The Vision of Piers Plowman*, written in 1377, when a drunken chaplain speaks about the "rymes of Robyn Hode". Unlike King Arthur, Robin was a man of the people with whom ordinary folk could identify.

Though details of the legend vary considerably, popular belief is that Robin Hood was particularly active while King Richard I was in captivity in Austria and John was in England plotting to steal his crown. Songs and legends of Robin Hood and his band of merry rogues have charmed readers for more than five hundred years. He was said to live in Sherwood Forest in Nottingham Shire, but tales also are related about his whereabouts in Barnsdale in southern Yorkshire.

A medieval outlaw was a man repudiated by the law, either for reasons of politics or because of a crime. He was cast out from the community, left with no defense against his enemies except his courage, strength and wits. Forced to hide away in the forests, he had to make his living by illegal hunting and by robbery. Often such outlaws surrounded themselves with other outlawed men to form a well-organized marauding band that blatantly rose up against the law. The medieval age was a violent time but, though he was an outlaw, Robin Hood was said to be adamently loyal to his king.

Richard I, often called "the Lionheart," is chiefly remembered for his exploits in the Holy Land, his quarrel with his ambitious brother John, and his association with the legendary Robin Hood. Richard shared some of his father's administrative capacity but his true skill was on a battlefield. His obsession with fighting led him to the Holy Land. Richard, a Norman by descent, upbringing and interest, was concerned with England only as a source of money and supplies for his crusading adventure. For this purpose he sold, often to the highest bidder, bishoprics, great offices of state, and claims to feudal jurisdiction. He also sold charters to towns. Despite his faults, however, he was popular with his subjects. He was a heroic figure, a determined leader, an educated man who could joke in Latin and embarrass the Archbishop, and at the same time a man who could while away the hours in his Austrian prison writing songs. He was a fierce fighter, a leader men could follow whose severity made him a king to be feared, yet he proved to have a generous spirit for forgiveness as well, as seen in his forgiveness of his wayward brother John.

Prince John (who later was to become a king) has furnished many a moralist with an example of an evil-doer. He was said to be a bad king, a false friend and a wicked uncle, faithless and untrustworthy. His treachery to his brother Richard was an ill omen for his own reign. History says that he was cruel and pitiless in the execution of his immediate will and lacked any conception of a far-seeing policy. Nevertheless, his legendary (or real, depending upon your point of view) fight against Robin Hood has made him one of the focal points of the legend of Sherwood Forest.

The tale of Robin Hood comes from the gathering together of many tales of brave deeds which over the years have been accredited to one man. In reality, however, the Robin Hood legend is a combination of stories of bold men of courage and the women who loved them. He is the symbol of good against evil and greed. The result is one of the favorite legends of all time—full of jaunty adventure and colorful history. And so it is that two young lovers are swept up in the legend; he a follower of Prince John and a knight hoping to reclaim his family's former glory, she a determined lady anxious to defend her country's rightful king by the only method she knows—by joining Robin Hood's men.

PART ONE:
A CHANCE ENCOUNTER

England—Winter, 1193

> "That power,
> Which erring men call Chance."
>
> —John Milton, *Comus*

Chapter One

It was dark in the forest. Eerie. The moon hovered high above, staring down at the earth like a gigantic eye, moving in and out of the clouds that threatened to snuff out its dim silver light. Gnarled tree branches reached out like mammoth hands from the shadows as if to grasp the three horses and riders daring to disturb the solitude of the night. The wind groaned as it whipped about Kendrick de Bron's face as if warning him not to approach.

"Go back! Go back!" it seemed to say. It was as if the forest had eyes, as if their arrival was being watched. But by who?

"I like this not at all, my lord."

"Nor I . . ." Kendrick replied.

"Shouldn't . . . shouldn't we turn around?" The voice of one of his servants quaked slightly with fear as he looked anxiously from side to side.

"Turn around?" For just a moment Kendrick *was* tempted to turn back, to forget this folly and return to France, the land that had sheltered him the last five years. Instead, he forced himself to say, "No, we will go on."

He was no coward. Moreover, this homecoming was long overdue. Prince John, who ruled during his brother's absence, had need of allies. It might well be Kendrick's only chance to regain the English lands taken from his family. If he was clever and able to align himself with the acting ruler he might well profit from this long journey.

"And King Richard be damned . . ." he mumbled. He had little reason to give him any loyalty after what he had done. Not content to wait for his inheritance, nor to allow his father, Henry II, to enjoy his declining years in peace, Richard had joined in an alliance against Henry not once but several times. Kendrick, his uncle Geoffrey de Bron, and every one of Kendrick's cousins had followed their consciences, aligning themselves with the rightful king. They had been rewarded when Henry was victorious in crushing the revolt of his sons.

The old, disheartened king had taken the field one too many times, however, and in the end was at last defeated when Richard and Philip of France united. Henry, who had at first put up a spirited defense, suddenly had taken ill. Accompanied by only a few retainers, he had left his army and retreated to Chinon, the heart of his Angevin lands.

Philip and Richard had overrun Normandy and Maine and forced the sick king to travel to Ballan where they compelled him to accept humiliating terms. He was to do homage to Philip for all his French lands and to place himself in Philip's hands while Richard was to inherit all the Plantagenet dominions, including England. Henry was carried back to Chinon in a litter, where the next day, he learnt that John, his favorite son, had likewise deserted him. He had become delirious. Shortly thereafter death ended an existence that was no longer endurable for the great and wise ruler.

"So much for his sons' honor . . ." Kendrick grumbled.

The de Brons' loyalty to Henry II during his fight against his rebellious sons was remembered by Richard when he took his crown. The de Bron lands, held since the Norman conquest, were deemed forfeit. Though Kendrick and his uncle had loyally served England in the capacity of advisors for several years, they now found themselves at odds with King Richard. Kendrick was particularly considered "dangerous" by the new king because of his outspoken views. The de Bron family had been declared unwelcome in England and exiled in disgrace.

"But Richard is absent now. England's cunning wolf has snapped at the crown like a bone and now holds the power . . ."

Would the prince likewise be as harsh as Richard or could his need for friends be used to Kendrick's advantage? Would he remember the family whose property was so cruelly wrested away? Could he be talked into giving the lands back? Or would he too offer retribution? Kendrick had to take the chance that the ghosts of the past had been buried. If he failed the results might well be harsh. John had imprisoned a great many men who angered him, men who did not see things exactly his way.

It doesn't matter. I have to take the chance. I must convince the prince that I am bound to him in loyalty! Kendrick thought as he guided his mount through the trees and up the rutted pathway.

Indeed, a great deal had happened in the last few months, threatening John's grip on the crown. Surely he must be more than just a little bit wary about his slipping power and the possibility of his brother's return. At first it had appeared that Richard would be gone for several years on his crusading adventure, leaving John in control, but the Siege of Acre had been accomplished much more quickly than had first been anticipated. Acre was reclaimed, the banner of the Cross once more floated over its walls. It appeared that total victory was in sight and with it would come Richard's return. John clearly had his back against the wall. Cornered men were easier to bargain with.

But can I pretend total comradery when I loathe the man who would be king? he wondered. Kendrick could not forget that John too had taken part in the rebellion against his father and had sided with his brother on the matter of punishing the de Bron family. In truth, Kendrick held no particular admiration for either of Henry's sons. Neither Richard nor John was fit to walk about in their father's shoes, as his Uncle Geoffrey would say. Despite his opinion of John, however, he had to do what he must. It would take a great deal of skill to work his way into John's favor, but Kendrick had faith that he was up to the task. Befriending John was the only chance he had of obtaining the de Bron lands again. His task must be accomplished before the return of Richard.

"I will succeed!" He set his lips in a hard line of obstinacy and squared his chin. He would not even contemplate failure. Bastard born or not, he was a de Bron, fully accepted as such. De Brons had always been winners. Feeling more at ease, he nudged his horse onward.

Suddenly a whistling sound tore through the air, tearing Kendrick's cap from his head. "BiGod!" He turned, startled, fully alert to danger as are those men forced to live in its company. With a swiftness that bespoke an athletic and well-disciplined body he gripped his sword. "Who's there?" His eyes darted left and right, lifting to the branches of a tree. There, perched on a limb, bow drawn and ready, was an archer, his form looking ghostly in the dim light.

"There is a fee for riding through this forest, my lord," called out a treble voice. Loudly. The mocking note matched the young man's insolent stance, Kendrick thought dryly.

"A fee?" Kendrick eyed the trees warily, wondering just how many lay in wait.

"Your purse. Forsooth let us hope it to be a fat one." There was a long pause, and when Kendrick showed no sign of budging even an inch, the voice called out, "Throw down your sword."

"No!" To do so would be the greatest foolishness. "I do not give in to thieves."

"Tut, tut, tut. What a shame that your stubborness will be costly." Immediately the young archer had restrung his bow and was now taking aim at Kendrick's short, rotund servant. "Methinks he will have little cause to thank ye when he feels the prick of this in his overpadded hide."

Seeing the look of stark fear on Humbley's face caused Kendrick to comply. He didn't want to see his servant harmed. Still, once it had clattered to the ground, he couldn't help but look at the weapon longingly.

"Good . . . good . . ." Not satisfied, however, with rendering Kendrick weaponless, the archer pushed on. "Now, get down off your horse, lest *you* want to feel the sting of my arrow."

Kendrick stared intently at the young outlaw, wondering if he should make his move now. The boy must be quite young, he reasoned, or a runt, for he was not overly large. In hand-to-hand combat he could be easily bested. Even so, he handled the longbow with a skill that had to be admired. Having handled bows quite often himself, he knew how heavily it must weigh in the lad's hands. "I *will* fight you!"

"And you will lose. My bow, you see, gives me every advantage. Now, down . . . down . . ."

When Kendrick still did not concede to the demand, the archer gave him a warning look, pulling ever tighter on the string. "I am true with my aim. And quick to restring my bow. I can and will shoot you all before you can even blink thrice."

Kendrick sincerely doubted that boast. Still, unless he wanted to put the others at risk, he had to be careful. The boy had little to lose by killing them.

"Oh, please, my lord, do as he says. I think . . . I think he means it." The second of Kendrick's servants was beside himself with nervousness. Hurriedly he jumped from his horse in a manner which sent him tumbling to the ground. The other servant seemed too petrified to budge.

Though primed for a fight, Kendrick slid from his horse. Perhaps it was the look in the archer's eyes which warned him not to trifle here. He was not afraid of a boy, but if arrows were unleashed one of his servants might come to serious harm. He didn't want that on his head. They had been good and loyal servants and deserved his consideration.

"God's teeth but you are annoying, boy. Nevertheless, I will obey." Flinging his leg over the saddle, he slid down from his mount. He stood glowering at his adversary, defiant and stubborn.

The sound of laughter teased Kendrick's ears. "You are obedient!" The archer put down his bow for just a minute, quickly taking it up again when Kendrick took a step towards his fallen sword. All trace of joviality was gone as he warned, "Don't tempt me, you jack-a-napes. Skewering such as you gives me great delight."

Kendrick wondered how young the lad was, for his voice had not yet changed and seemed rather high-pitched for one so daring. "And spanking wayward boys amuses me," he taunted. "Shall I?" He took another step forward, then another, but halted when an arrow went whizzing over his head.

"Next time I'll clip your ears. I warn you." The archer pulled another arrow from his quiver and positioned it threateningly. "Now stay where you are."

Kendrick complied, taking quick note of the archer. The boy's garb was a motley shade of brown, the hosen and tunic patched in several places. No doubt the lad was a peasant and as such more in need of his purse than he. Having come from Saxon, peasant stock himself on his mother's side, Kendrick felt a twinge of sympathy. It was difficult to tell what this lad had suffered.

"Boy . . ."

The word quickly caused the archer to stiffen. His voice

was shrill as he said, "I do not want to talk. I want your gold."

Kendrick shrugged. He'd give up the purse. In truth it held very little money. The bulk of his wealth was well hidden in his servant's tunic, a ploy well-seasoned travelers learned very quickly.

"There's little gold, but if you want my purse you shall have it," he said generously, flinging the leather pouch toward the tree where the archer hid himself. He was anxious to be on his way. "There, I have paid the fee."

"Not completely!" Swinging down from the branches of the tree by way of a vine, the lad moved into action before Kendrick even had time to react. Picking up the purse, he used it to give Kendrick's horse a slap on its behind, sending the animal galloping out of the woods.

"BiGod!" Anger raged through Kendrick's veins. "You overbold puppy!" The purse was one thing, the horse another. It was cold and he had a long way to go. He didn't relish the thought of walking, or worse yet riding double with one of his servants.

"A walk will do you good, my lord. It is pleasant at this time of early eve." Once again the young archer laughed, the sound spilling from his mouth with unrestrained gaiety as he seemed to imagine the scene.

"A walk!" Kendrick gritted his teeth, vowing vengeance. He'd seek this boy out and turn him across his knee. The lad was greatly in need of discipline.

"Aye, a walk." The idea seemed amusing to the lad for he laughed again, then recovering from his chuckling, bowed. "But lest I forget my manners, thank you for your purse and the people of King Richard thank you, too."

Kendrick's mouth grimaced into a look of complete disgust. "And I suppose you are going to tell me that it will be the people who benefit from this . . . this robbery." He sincerely doubted it. The lad would pocket every last coin.

"Believe it or not 'tis so!" Holding up the purse, the

archer shook it, listening to the jingle. "I rob from the rich and give to those in need."

"Ha!" Kendrick had heard that before. Crossing his arms across his chest he matched the lad's defiance. "No doubt all outlaws say that, but I call them liars."

For a fleeting moment there was a flash of anger in the eyes staring at him. "No man calls me liar, my lord." In punishment, Kendrick was ordered to strip. He gave up his cloak, tunic and boots into the archer's hands. "Also for the poor!" the archer exclaimed. "Now, start upon the pathway before I change my mind about being so lenient."

"Lenient!" Kendrick's parting words were unfit for gentle ears, a rumble of swearing. "Your father should have been gelded to prevent the spawn of such a son," he said over one shoulder before he and his servants disappeared through the trees.

By way of a vine the archer returned to his perch high in the tree and watched as the tiny procession left the woods. "My father sired no son, Norman, but a daughter. 'Twas the Lady Rowena who bested you just now, and no other." With a rustle as soft as the wind, *she* was gone, to bide her time until another day.

Chapter Two

"BiGod, barefoot and half naked. What an impression I will make on the prince," Kendrick grumbled as he clenched tightly to the horse's reins. He was still smarting from his humiliating encounter with the young archer, but he would not allow himself to be humbled. He would not!

"The prince, indeed!" Chadwick was indignant. "If you ask me, 'tis his duty to see that honest folk be able to ride through England's forests without being accosted by roguish thieves."

Humbley's long hair swished from side to side as he shook his head. "Such a thing would not have happened across the channel. *Mais non,* as the French would say."

"Aye, but it happened here," Kendrick exclaimed, "and that has changed our plans somewhat, I fear." Oh, how he regretted now his decision to travel on ahead of his baggage.

Indeed, they did find themselves in quite a quandry. Here they were deep in the forest, three men with only two horses. The servants understood why their lord was in a quarrelsome mood. Having lost his horse, Kendrick had no other choice but to ride with one of them, that being Chadwick, whose lean form would leave more room for Kendrick to comfortably sit at the front of the saddle. Humbley's poor horse was doing well, meanwhile, to support Humbley.

"It has changed everything. You wanted to make a grand entrance but now . . . Oh, what shall we do!" Chadwick's mournful wail sounded in Kendrick's ear.

"Wring that blasted lad's neck!" Kendrick answered as he stared broodingly across the River Trent. Nottingham Castle lay far to the south of this seemingly endless forest. Would he ever get there? At the moment it didn't seem so.

Humbley seemed to read his lord's thoughts. "Yon forest goes on forever . . ."

"Or at least it might as well," Chadwick observed.

Sherwood Forest stretched northwards for more than 20 miles from Nottingham and the Trent. It was a journey made even more cumbersome now considering the circumstances. Despite that fact, Kendrick's anger soon gave way to common sense. He had to think clearly, had to make the best of what had happened.

"Somehow, someway, I have to find some proper garments and footware, for I will not set foot in that castle looking beggarly." Nor in fact did he want to have to tell John the story of his fleecing. That would hardly be a way to earn the prince's confidence.

"Find garments?" Humbley cried out.

"And footware . . ." Chadwick echoed.

How were they going to supply their lord with clothing suitable for his upcoming meeting with John? Neither short, stocky Humbley, nor tall, lean Chadwick, owned anything suitable for such an audience. Nor in truth could Kendrick wear their clothes even if they did have anything suitable. Even though Kendrick was tall, he was not as skinny as Chadwick. His shoulders were broad, his arms muscular. Humbley's garments, to the contrary, would be far too large. Even so, because they desperately wanted to please him, they offered up their own clothes.

The generosity of his servants' gesture touched Kendrick. "Nay. 'Tis better to find another way."

The relationship between Kendrick and his two servants was one of complete devotion. Humbley and Chadwick had remained loyal to Kendrick and the de Brons throughout all of the past years' misfortunes. They too longed for the return of the lost power and prestige once claimed by the lord and his family and to the superiority that their own once well-lived lifestyle had provided.

"Another way." Humbley thought a long while then exclaimed, "Per- . . . perhaps we could do what that pesky lad did and . . . and steal some garments." He was proud of that idea.

"Steal?" Chadwick was indignant. "Steal from whom?" It was true. The forest seemed to be deserted. There were no travelers at this late time of night.

"Why . . . why from some fine lord or other journeying along this rutted road." Humbley looked Kendrick up and down. "Hopefully one who is close to my lord de Bron's size."

"Forsooth. Steal indeed." Chadwick looked down his long nose at his fellow serving companion. "Even if we were to come upon some nobleman or other, we dare not take a chance on such an action, lest we find ourselves in dire trouble."

"Well spoken, Chad." Kendrick gently chastised his other servant. "We must use caution, Humbley, and adhere to all of the prince's fine rules. We are no longer under the French king's jurisdiction. From now on all ways are John's way." He emphasized, "All ways."

Humbley chuckled. "What ye mean, my lord de Bron, is that from now on Chadwick and I will be kissing John Lackland's noble ass."

"A crude assessment, but true, I fear. If we do not want to spend the rest of our lives as exiles we might well have

to learn to be compliant." Though the de Brons had come
from Normandy, Kendrick felt a much stronger kinship
with England. He wanted very much to stay. If that meant
putting up with a few of Prince John's idiosyncrasies, so
be it.

"Most certainly we do not want to look like exiles,"
Chadwick exclaimed, getting back to the subject at hand.

"Most particularly we do not want ye to look like one,
my lord de Bron. We must find a cloak, boots and tunic."

"And a horse." Chadwick sighed wistfully, longing as it
were to once more be riding alone.

"Surely somewhere beyond this foul forest is a village."
Perhaps if they truly were lucky they might even find a
tailor. One who could work a miracle. Surely, that was what
was needed.

Kendrick and his men traveled all night, stopping peri-
odically along the way when it became necessary. It was a
slow and tedious trip but at last with the first light of dawn
they saw the village nestled along the east bank of the river.
Now they knew their haste was going to be rewarded.

Even at this early morning hour the village was a place
of bustle, clutter, and commotion. The squeal of cart
wheels, the clip-clop of horses, the bawling of hogs being
butchered, the shouts of peddlers and tinkers, the hissing
of geese, the crow of roosters, the barking of dogs, the
laughter and the high-pitched voices of children, were a
sharp contrast to the soft night sounds of the forest.

Stone construction was still rare in England, thus the
small houses were timber-framed with walls of wattle and
daub. The thatched-roofed dwellings stood at odd angles
with fences and embankments fronting the street. Near
the river was a small village green, the manor house and
the mill, which was powered by three oaken waterwheels.
Across the narrow dirt road stood a communal oven where
the villagers were obliged to bring their bread. It was the
stone stable, however, that immediately drew Kendrick's
interest. Besides housing cows, oxen, carts, tools and har-

nesses, it sheltered a few fine horses which belonged to the lord of the manor.

"I want the black one. See to it, Humbley."

Succumbing to the lure of the coins that the manservant had hidden beneath his tunic, the manor lord soon parted with that fine animal. Kendrick was pleased, yet because of the bargain made he did swear beneath his breath that he had been robbed yet again.

"Alas, I fear a tailor in this place is as scarce as hen's teeth, however, my lord." Though Chad and Humbley went from door to door they were met with either blank expressions or looks of suspicion. Sometimes they were even shown out-and-out hostility.

"An uncooperative lot."

"Poor and slovenly!"

"Aye, 'tis a far cry from the French court and the wealthy towns thereby," Humbley added. "Forsooth, even that manor lord looked a bit tattered and torn."

It was true. The villagers appeared to be far from prosperous. Undoubtedly they were suffering from difficult times. Perhaps that was why Kendrick's sorry state of undress had not even been gawked at. Dressed, or rather undressed as he was, he was still better attired than many of the villagers.

"I heard mumblings of high taxation," Chad whispered as the three men rode through the town.

"Because of Richard's crusade," Kendrick quickly concluded. "He needed a great deal of coinage to further the lust for his own vanity." He was scornful of the king's ferocious and savage warfare which had sucked the dominions almost dry of funds. All the while Richard had been an absent king. Meanwhile the venture had enjoyed limited success, for it had proven to be impossible to regain Jerusalem.

"Alas, the politics of the day which has benefited the few has impoverished the many," Chadwick said dryly.

"Thus . . . we will find no fine garments here."

But they did locate an old brewhouse where they stopped

for a drink of ale and a breakfast of pigeon pie. The murky wooden dwelling stunk of stale wine and recently brewed ale but after the long ride Kendrick, Chadwick and Humbley welcomed it. It felt good to be sitting on something besides a saddle.

"To the future here," Chadwick toasted, taking a seat beside de Bron on the hard bench. "And to John. May he be an understanding soul."

"And generous," Humbley added.

"To John." Taking a drink of his ale, Kendrick scanned the crowd, noting their worn Phrygian caps, hoods and faded dun-colored garments. Like all those who worked hard for a meagre existence, they were old before their time, their faces drawn and frowning.

"Not an overly jolly lot," Humbley observed.

"Not at all ..." Kendrick said beneath his breath. Though he had tried hard over the years to put aside all recollections of his own heritage, it all came cruelly back to him now. He was bastard born, the son of a Saxon villein and the brutal Norman feudal lord who had taken her against her will. He had been born in a poor village much like this one to people much like these.

Villeins. Peasants. Serfs. That was what Kendrick's once noble Saxon family had been reduced to over the years. Just like these people they had worked hard and died young, always giving to their overlords, taxed beyond their means. His mother had died in childbirth, a victim of her fate. Kendrick too would have died if not for his Aunt Kendra and the fierce pride and sense of rebellion that had burned inside her veins. A pride and rebellion that had goaded her to escape the sad reality of her fate and climb beyond. A pride he didn't want to forget ...

"They do not seem to welcome visitors." Chadwick's voice startled Kendrick out of his musing.

"Nay, I do not suppose that they would." And why should they? Strangers who came to the village undoubtedly came not to give but to take. Sadly, Kendrick let his eyes move over the men gathered under the brewhouse's roof.

In response the brewhouse's patrons were appraising Kendrick and his two men, doing little to hide the fact that they thought them to be intruders here. They were, in fact, openly hostile.

"God's teeth, they act as if their poverty was our doing!" Humbley wiped his mouth with the back of his hand.

"Not our doing but John's, or so I heard the villagers whisper." Chadwick pointed out the obvious, that unjust taxes, raised land rents and wrongful fines had taken a severe toll.

For just a moment something inside Kendrick wanted to cry out himself against the injustice of it all. It was not right that men could so mistreat other men and proclaim themselves lords and masters. Instead, he merely clenched his jaw and said, "What is done here is John's business."

Nevertheless, Humbley made it a point to let some of the villagers in on the injustice that had been dealt his lord. "Robbed he was, by as fierce an archer as was ever looked upon." Motioning with his hands he made it appear that the archer had been at least six feet tall. Kendrick's misfortune in the forest, however, was being heralded with little sympathy.

"Why, they seem to condone such thievery." A fact which gauled Kendrick, doubly so when he saw with his very own eyes why. "My cloak!"

Sweeping into the small room of the brewhouse, one of the villagers wore it proudly.

"BiGod!"

Perhaps had it been any other time, Kendrick would have allowed the poor man to keep his newly acquired treasure. As it was, the truth of his own desperation goaded him into action. Recognizing the fine woolen fabric, Kendrick rose to his feet and moved forward to get it back.

In response several of the villagers came up against him,

forming a protective wall. They might give in to those to whom they owed fealty, but they would not give in to him.

"That cloak is mine! Give it back."

"Nay, for it belongs to him now."

Despite his frustration, Kendrick was forced to back away lest there be trouble. Nor was the cloak the only stolen item that resurfaced. Kendrick's tunic and boots were likewise discovered adorning new and very thankful owners. True to his word, the young archer had given them away. In the end, the only way that the lord de Bron was able to retrieve his garments was to buy them back at a ridiculously high price. Was it any wonder then that as he and his servants rode out of the village he seemed to hear a voice within his head laughing at him?

"That damnable archer . . ." Looking over his shoulder he almost imagined that he saw him, hiding again in the trees. Ah, but to his relief as he traveled on his way, he realized it was naught but an illusion. Or had it been?

Oh, the excitement of it all! The exhilaration! Rowena laughed aloud as she climbed through the window of an old thatched-roof cottage in the village.

"Another Norman nobleman put in his place," she whispered to herself, taking great delight in knowing that the haughty stranger had been forced to buy his own clothing back. "What a wonderous turn of events." As to the stranger's purse, though it had not been as heavy as she might have liked, she knew the coins had brought comfort to the needy villagers. She had no regrets as to events. To the contrary, justice had been done!

Taking off her cap she sighed with relief and exhaustion, letting her long honey-blonde hair fall freely about her shoulders as she slowly collapsed to the ground. Laying full-length on the straw mat she closed her eyes, reliving her late night adventure.

"There is a fee for riding through this forest, my lord,"

she whispered. "Now, get you off thy horse lest you feel the sting of my arrow."

Motioning with her hands she pantomimed shooting her bow, then felt a surge of regret that such high moments of adventure and peril were so brief and all too rare. Alas, it was time to return to the constraints of her female clothing and to her father's side.

"Fie! Why could I not have been born a male?" Truly it would have made her life far more exhilarating and adventuresome, she thought, running her hands over her breasts, bound now to hide their alluring fullness. Were she truly a lad she would have been afforded far more freedom. As it was, the rules of her society dictated that she be under the governance of a man from birth until death, leading, as it were, a most tedious kind of sheltered existance.

Once again, Rowena ran her hands over her body, this time touching that place between her legs. It was said that a woman's body was a mirror image of Adam's body and that the female organs were similar in structure to the male's, but turned around, introverted. "More secret and thus more private." But like anything hidden, suspect, requiring a more vigilant guard. To man fell the "task of surveillance". Woman could not live without man and needed to be in a man's power, it was said.

"And why not, considering that it is men who rule the world!" It was an essentially masculine world, dominated by men's constant warring. A lord granted land to a vassal in return for services that were primarily military, thereby making women seem unimportant in the scheme of things.

Oh, there were a few women, like Henry II's queen, Eleanor, who had distinguished themselves in a man-dominated world, yet even they received patronizing credit. It was said that an able queen ruled "as if she were a man" or had a "man's courage". Only because of her father's lack of a male heir was Rowena deemed of an importance at all. Was it any wonder then that she so enjoyed dressing in male attire? Only then did she fully experience a freedom that could not be equaled when wearing skirts.

"In the forest, among the trees, I do not have to answer to anyone!" And best of all she could help all those who suffered from injustice far more than she. It was a hungry world, made hungrier by intermittent crop failures, a dismal existence that Prince John did little to better. With heartlessness he taxed the already burdened population far beyond common decency. Was it any wonder then how much Rowena loathed him and all those who followed him, or that she chose to torment them any time she could?

Reluctantly she rose from the mat and began to undress, tugging at her boots, pulling at the brown hosen that adorned her long legs. Removing her tunic she carefully bundled the garments together. They would be hidden along the way in a place that would not tie her in any way to the villagers.

Padding on her bare feet across the dirt floor, she poured water into a bowl to wash herself. This done she combed her long hair with her fingers, noticing at once how tired her arms were. They ached with tension and the soreness that always accompanied the use of her bow, yet it was a discomfort she did not regret. Last night had been well worth it.

Laughing again, she scurried to the corner of the cottage, retrieving yet another bundle. With renewed vitality she donned a chemise, kirtle, soft leather shoes and a fine woven mantle. Not bothering to plait her hair she hurried to the door. She had an appointment to keep, for she and her father had been summoned by the prince to a celebration.

"As if while he is in control we have anything to celebrate," she murmured, pushing through the door. Flinging herself upon her horse, she paused just a moment, then with a sigh headed down the very same road that the men she had so lightheartedly robbed had taken.

* * *

The rough stones of the castle walls stood defiantly against the winter sky as Kendrick de Bron rode forward. Like some stern, giant knight, the circular watchtower loomed in the distance welcoming him.

" 'Tis about time . . ."

Approaching the castle, crossing the drawbridge which reminded him of the open jaws of a snake, Kendrick forced himself to forget about his unpleasant experience with the villagers and concentrate on the matter at hand. Diplomacy was the answer. Diplomacy and a cool head. He must not let anger goad him into acting unwisely. Above and beyond all else, he must ensure the prince's trust. He must not act rashly, as had his childhood friend, Robert Fitzooth, only to find himself cast out as an outlaw. Nor could he let anyone or anything stand in his way. The de Bron lands would be reclaimed!

The hooves of the horses clattered loudly against the stones of the courtyard as he and his servants entered the outer bailey, blending with the barking dogs and the buzzing voices of the castle servants. Kendrick had been riding hard, and by the time he reined in his horse, the newly procured black animal was in great need of rest, as was he. Dismounting, he handed the reins to a groom, a grinning old man that reminded him of a monkey.

"Keep my horse well tended and fed until I return to claim him." Kendrick ordered sternly.

The man grunted in answer, judging Kendrick to be a man of little consequence, with his garments covered with the dust of the road. This was soon to be altered, for Kendrick was a man who always asserted himself. Seeking out a steward, he insisted he and his servants be shown to chambers that befitted him as the prince's guest.

Following the steward up the steep, winding stone steps Kendrick opened the thick wooden door and stepped inside the chamber assigned to him. A fire burned brightly

in the hearth, warming the room and casting light on the
inner walls of the chamber. It was a large room, the floor
covered with freshly strewn straw that smelled of herbs and
spices. A large canopied bed nestled in the corner and
looked inviting to one who had spent so long a time on
horseback. For a moment, he was tempted to bury himself
in the soft feathers and to forget about why he had come.
But instead, he waved all thought of comfort aside. There
would be time enough for sleeping just as soon as his plan
was set in motion.

Standing before the fire, Kendrick slowly stripped off
his travel-stained garments, thinking and planning silently
as he cast aside hose and tunic. Shaking out the dust from
his clothing, he was startled when the door behind him
opened. Ready to face any treachery, Kendrick reached
for his sword and whirled around.

"My Lord, I seek thee no harm," stuttered a short, stocky
man with deep-set eyes and a protruding jaw. His eyes
wide with fear, he added, "I am Hugo, your most humble
servant."

"My servant?" Kendrick scowled. Or was the man a spy,
sent by John to watch over him? "I already have servants.
I have no need of more."

The man was insistant. "I served your uncle well," he
hurried to explain, "and now look to you with fealty."
Hugo bowed as he spoke.

"My uncle?" Eyeing Hugo up and down, Kendrick slowly
sheathed his weapon and motioned for him to come inside.

"The most noble Geoffrey de Bron. We both served
long ago as clerics to the king."

Strange that his uncle Geoffrey had not mentioned
such a man. Measuring him sharply, Kendrick wondered
if this man could be trusted. He obviously spoke of having
served Henry, but just where did his true loyalties lie now,
with Richard or with John? Instinct told him to be doubly
wary. He would seek to find out the truth in time, but

for now, all he wanted was a hot bath and a change of clothing.

As if sensing his new lord's needs, Hugo quickly filled the large wooden tub, then sat down upon the bed to watch with piercing eyes as the young lord prepared to bathe. "There is a feast tonight, m'lord."

"A feast?"

"The prince is most generous in hosting his friends and servants."

Kendrick shook his head. "Nay, I am much too tired." He would choose to speak with John when they could be alone.

Offering Kendrick a half smile, Hugo advised, "it might be wise to attend . . ."

"A feast?" Kendrick quickly changed his mind. Why not? What better way to make new friends and further his interests?

" 'Tis the Christmas season and the household has been preparing for the celebrating all week. Tonight, the prince plans to make an announcement." A thick, dark brow was cocked in suggestion.

Kendrick nodded. "Then by all means, I must attend." Though Hugo seemed the faithful servant, Kendrick had not hidden from danger for so long to easily give his trust. The man was just too obsequious.

"Ah, good . . . very wise to bow to he who has the power . . ."

Carefully Kendrick chose his words, perceiving that what he said now would be reported. "John is a decisive and daring man, one after my own heart. I admire him and know that we will deal well together."

"I'm sure that you will."

Dismissing Hugo, Kendrick slid into the soothing warmth of the water. It enveloped him like a cocoon, taking away the stiffness from his joints. He leaned back, letting the grime of the road dissolve away with his apprehension. He had been suspicious about a possible trap, but clearly he was being welcomed here. Was it possible that all had truly been forgiven? Had John buried the past and forgiven the de Brons for siding with his father? For the first time in a long while, Kendrick held that hope.

Chapter Three

The large hall of the castle was bathed in light. Flames danced about the hearth, reflecting in its glow the many brightly colored tunics and mantles of the lords and ladies assembled for the festivities. Fires from the many candles twinkled along the tables, illuminating the richly threaded tapestries which hung from the walls. Fresh rushes carpeted the floors, crackling as both servant and guest walked to and fro. From bower to bower, mistletoe hung to usher in the holiday with rollicking good cheer, and to bring good luck throughout the following year. It was a time of celebration, the Christmas festival, a time when a man's heart was filled with the brotherhood of his fellow man.

The plunk of harp and lute added a sense of gaiety that was emphasized by the dancers and jesters. Babbling voices and boisterous laughter abounded throughout, yet one face at least was not smiling. Lady Rowena Fitz Hugh frowned as she and her father took seats at the table assigned to their station, above the salt yet a great distance from the reigning ruler. It was a reminder to them that they were but minor nobility and not yet entirely in John's favor.

"The prince has clearly outdone himself this year," a rotund, velvet-cloaked man declared aloud, appraising the doings with awe. Indeed, trestle tables were covered with bounty from the king's forest, including venison and pheasant. The plump browning flesh of a wild boar roasted on a spit over the fire, tantalizing the palate. For those who craved tamer meat, the trenchers were piled high with mutton and beef. The air was rich with the aroma of the sauces made from herbs, wine, and spices from the East. Fruit pies and tarts, freshly baked, tempted even the most jaded of palates. Servants hurried from table to table, their arms laden with platters. Wine and ale flowed freely from casks, bottles, and kegs.

Rowena leaned close to her father. "Outdone himself in his greed," she whispered, knowing well that the generosity displayed was at the expense of his subjects. "One would nearly think he fashions himself the king."

Sir William mirrored his daughter's dour look as he scanned the assemblage. Smiling sourly, he added, "In truth, he has everything *but* the crown. We would do well to remember that."

Richard the Lion Heart had been gone over a year now, to the Crusades, and his ambitious brother John assumed more and more power as time went on, despite the ever-watchful eye of their mother, Queen Eleanor. Slowly, so slowly, Richard's kingdom was slipping away and he was nowhere near so that he might guard it. Like dogs fighting over scraps from the table, John's followers were dividing England up and toasting themselves on their success.

Unlike the others, Rowena saw no cause for celebrating. Her loyalty was staunchly behind Richard the Lionheart, not his devious brother. She and her father had been ordered to Prince John's castle in Nottingham Shire to gather together with the other noble families of England,

and they could only be apprehensive as to the reason. Something was up the royal sleeve, but what?

Mingling with friends as well as those who were not so prone to offer friendship, Rowena pondered the question. Though the guests drank much ale and seemed contented enough, she sensed an underlying current of tension and suspected that she and her father were not the only ones who were ill at ease. It was no secret how fragile John's favor could be, nor that he hated those of Saxon origin and harkened to every opportunity he could to steal their property. What property they had left, that is. His schemes and treachery had reopened old wounds between conqueror and conquered, wounds that had once been laid to rest. For he rewarded his favored Norman knights with lands that had once belonged to others. Bitterness and hatred was John's legacy. As Rowena scanned the faces of all those bearing Saxon blood, she read apprehension and frightened curiosity upon their brows.

Rowena's mother had been a Saxon, the daughter of a prosperous London wool merchant. Lovely and gentle, she had stolen Sir William's Norman heart. They had married and born a child of their love, Rowena. But fate had not been kind to the lovers. Edwina had died of a fever shortly after Rowena's birth. Grieving and heartbroken, Sir William had refused to marry again, and had instead placed his steward's wife, Gwyneth, in charge of their home and the upbringing of his motherless daughter.

Gwyneth had had no easy task. Rowena, headstrong from the first and surrounded mainly by men, had preferred the freedom of the forest, climbing trees and practicing her skill with the bow and arrow over the working of tapestries and other ''women's'' activities. At first Gwyneth dealt strongly with her, but at last, realizing that Rowena would never bend to her will, she had accepted her ways and allowed her to be a happy and carefree child. Gwyneth had always understood that although some had called her wild, in truth Rowena was just a free spirit, an adventurer.

With the first swelling of her bosom and her ripening into womanhood, all had changed, however. Of late, her father had begun insisting she modify her attire and appear more ladylike, at least in public. After several arguments it was a wish she grudgingly obeyed. Thus, Rowena cared not how she looked this evening. She had dressed to please her father. She wore a gown of bright periwinkle blue and a mantle of velvet. The skirt hindered her movements, the bodice was so tight she wondered if she dared eat even a bite of food. But on the subject of the wimple, Rowena had firmly refused to wear that linen piece beneath her chin. It constricted her head movement and made her feel imprisoned, unable to move her head from side to side. Let the other women suffer this restriction; as for her, she had worn her blonde hair plaited and uncovered. Custom be hanged.

With a sigh Rowena put her elbows on the table, cradled her chin in her hands and watched the steady procession of servants bearing food. All sorts of exotic dishes were placed before her, heavily laced with spices. Wild swan with sage dressing, duckling floating in orange sauce, stewed and pickled vegetables of every kind. At least she would not go hungry.

"Hear ye, hear ye," warbled the page of the household, "our noble prince and ruler of the realm bids a word with his noble subjects before we sup."

"Merry-go-up! If I must listen to him I'll lose my appetite," Rowena whispered, only to be silenced by her father's stern look. "Ah, well . . ." Unlike Rowena, Sir William had no strong ill will towards John, had in fact been given some land in an obvious attempt to buy his favor. By her father's reluctance to speak out, it appeared that John had done just that. But not Rowena. Never would she pay a usurper homage.

"Hear ye, hear ye!" cried out the page again.

"Hear ye, hear ye!" echoed a tiny little man dressed in yellow and green, a three-pointed hat atop his head. The prince's jester turned a cartwheel before the table where Rowena sat, winking at her in merriment. For a moment her ire was gone as she watched his antics, but it was quickly replaced as the prince stood up and announced his intentions. From here forward, all taxes would be increased.

"It is to pay for my brother's campaign against the unholy heathens in the East," John proclaimed with a grin, trying to put the blame on his brother, the king. His left hand played idly with his dark beard, curling and uncurling the waxed hair as he spun his treachery.

A rumble went up in the hall. It was known by many that the monies that were supposed to find themselves in Richard's coffers went instead into John's treasure chests. Even the jester's antics could not calm the assembly, though the little man tried and tried. For once the prince had gone too far.

Rowena fought hard against her own anger, figuring in her head what this new assessment would mean. Something on the estates would have to be sacrificed. Did the prince not know that there was a limit to what burden he could put on even those loyal to him? How she would like to humble him as Robin Hood had a few months ago. He had made the prince an object of buffoonery by capturing him in Sherwood Forest and holding him for ransom. John would not be so haughty were he to find an arrow aimed at his brow!

"Like that haughty lord whose hat I sent flying . . ." she said beneath her breath. Anticipating this dull evening, she had wanted to do something fun and had therefore forced the confrontation with a Norman knight traveling through the forest. One of John's mercenaries, from the looks of him. "And John will be next . . ."

As if sensing her thoughts, Prince John's hypnotic eyes traveled to where she sat. Rowena looked hurriedly away

lest he set his sights upon her. The prince was well known
as a womanizer and despoiler of innocent young women.
He was known to seduce a woman one night and boast of
it openly the next. There were even those who swore he
had a sorcerer's power in those eyes of his. Rowena could
not control a shiver of disgust at the thought of finding
herself his victim, he with his large sweating hands and
bearded face.

"Excuse me . . ." A hand lightly brushed Rowena's arm.
She turned, opening her mouth to speak, but found herself
suddenly without voice as glittering brown eyes looked
deep into hers. Merry-go-up! It was the man she had
accosted in the forest. Her heart thumped wildly as she
sat perfectly still, fearing to even blink. For just a fleeting
moment Rowena lost her poise, and her face flushed, fearing recognition. He had taken note of her across the hall
and had come forth to denounce her before all!

"I hope this chair is not taken . . ." Gleaming white
teeth flashed in a smile of greeting. His hand touched the
back of her chair, lingering on her shoulder.

For a long moment Rowena just stared, then at last she
found her voice. "It is."

He seemed not to care, for he sat down beside her
anyway. The overbold buffoon! Undoubtedly he was the
kind who did exactly as he pleased, despite the consequences. Even in the forest he had proven to Rowena that
she might well have met her match. Remembering that
meeting, she hastily looked away, but did manage to study
him with a sideways glance.

Though she assured herself that he was much too arrogant to be handsome, her eyes appraised him anyway. He
was tall, much taller than she. His hair was so dark brown
as to be nearly black. Worn just below his ears, it brushed
his tunic as he turned his head. His shoulders were broad,
his waist trim. Grudgingly she admitted that he was well
put together. But though he was a strong and well-formed
man, he was nothing out of the ordinary—or so she told

herself. But his face! Now that she saw it clearly in the light, she had cause to stare. He had a face etched in strength, yet beautiful in a masculine way. His eyes were dark and penetrating, his nose . . .

"My lady?"

To her dismay, Rowena realized that she had turned her head and was staring at him. Nor had her gawking gone unnoticed. The newcomer studied her in a manner that made her blush and caused a curious stirring in her stomach. Something she ate, undoubtedly. She looked hastily away.

"I hope I am not unreasonably tardy. Has John spoken yet?"

The very mention of the prince unleashed her pent-up frustration. "Of a surety he has! But you have missed naught but donkey's braying if you are asking me." She kept her eyes focused on the trencher before her, wishing the splendidly muscled vision in green velvet doublet and gold hose would vanish. It was unnerving the way his very presence made her tremble. She, who could fence verbally with many a noble or swain. Now, suddenly, she was as tongue-tied as a simpleton, all because of this man she did not even know. Well, it hadn't been that way in the forest. Oh, to have her bow and arrow in hand again!

"Sounds as if you care not for John's rule. He is the true and rightful king in Richard's absence." Kendrick's eyes swept appreciatively over the young woman at his side, bedeviled by the very sight of her. So France was not the only country with lovely young women. This one's dark blonde hair was the color of honey, her wide blue eyes like the summer sky. Her slender form, with its impudent breasts thrusting firm and strong, partially hidden beneath the loose gown she wore, nevertheless hinted at the budding young curves underneath. She was lovely, with the warmth and freshness of a summer breeze, yet with a certain spice to her countenance. A spirited wench, Kendrick thought as he eyes swept over her.

"John is no king, he is—"

Quickly placing his hand firmly on Rowena's, her father leaned forward, looking around her to catch Kendrick's eye. "Sir, I fear my daughter often speaks from emotion and not sense when it comes to politics. She is but a girl that has grown up without a mother and is a little rough around the edges." Rowena's father, seeing a note of understanding in Kendrick's eye, relaxed a little.

"Have no fear, sir. Your daughter is but a child and I'm sure no one would take her seriously—though beautiful she is."

"Thank you, sir, for your understanding."

Rowena rose stiffly from her chair. "A child! You call me a child! I am a woman full grown, and as smart as any man. How dare you—" Rowena turned to leave.

Kendrick caught her by the wrist, detaining her. "My lady, please accept my apology. I had no idea you were serious. I thought you were only making light conversation, and wanted merely to caution you that your words could cause you grief. However, I would be happy to talk politics with you in the privacy of my chambers, away from listening ears." Kendrick smiled

Rowena glared at him. "Sir, I seek no man in his chambers. If it's *that* kind of company you seek, look ye elsewhere!"

"May I offer you a bit of venison?" a servant asked, leaning low over the table.

"No, thank you," Kendrick replied, thinking to himself that it was the young woman by his side that he wanted to taste of at the moment. His was a far different hunger. Her beauty was flawless and golden in the candlelight, as delightful to behold as an angel. He thought to himself that if he had one serious fault, it was his overwhelming attraction to beauty. But he had to remember where he was and his mission. He had not come all the way from Normandy to be swayed from his intent by one woman's beauty.

"Ah, but perhaps I will persuade you later," he promised himself with assurance. Kendrick had not yet met a woman he could not have if he so desired. He was certain that this fair flower, like all the others he had coveted, would blossom at his touch. At least the thought would make his stay in England a bit more enjoyable. A little something to look forward to during those moments when he was suffering John's company. An enchanting diversion.

Kendrick was a man sure of his prowess, as certain of all the ways to charm a lady as he was methods to conquer a foe. Both were skills that he took in his stride. He was arrogant, yes. But only mildly so. He viewed Rowena as a perfect match for him. A man could tell such things right at a glance, or so he had found from experience.

Rowena was aware of those heated dark eyes upon her, regarding her so intently, and was she more and more certain that he knew who she was and what she had done. He was playing with her, like a cat with a mouse. But when was he going to pounce? Nervously, she tugged at her gown, wishing she could read his mind.

"It is a costly campaign," John was saying, trying to placate the crowd. Rowena watched as he raised his hand for silence, his dark eyes sweeping over those gathered as if to seduce them to his wishes. A faint smile tugged at the corners of his mouth, as a thought seemed to flash through his mind. "I have seen fit to have it written that from hence forward, all Saxon lands are to be given to my possession, and those of you who favor their cause as well. He who honors me and swears to be at my right hand will profit by this edict of mine. I will reward loyalty richly and treachery with an iron hand."

Rowena seethed inwardly with her rage, knowing full well what the prince was saying, that those who offered resistance to his policies would be called traitor, that their lands would be swept from beneath their noses. Those who did John's bidding would profit from the villainy.

"Black-hearted bastard!" she swore silently. The hall

took on a deathly silence at John's words, and by the expressions written upon every man's brow, Rowena knew the assemblage echoed her own thoughts. Yet none among them spoke out. Looking from man to man, the prince issued forth a silent challenge, bowing his head in mocking tribute as he turned his back to return to his place at the head table.

The sound of wood upon stone suddenly shattered the deadly calm, as a chair behind Rowena was thrust back from the table. Turning, she looked to see who the would-be speaker was, as a gasp of surprise rippled through the crowd.

Expectation hung heavily over the room, as the fair Maid Marian and the scowling prince dueled silently with their eyes. He was warning her, but she ignored him, asking, "Are there none among you who will oppose Prince John on this matter?" Her eyes issued a challenge to the men of the hall to come forward despite the risk involved. Surely they were men and not mice to scurry to their corners to hide. Silence was her answer. "Are you all cowards, then? You know well that it is not King Richard's coffers which these taxes feed, but John's. Nor is it any secret that to even sneeze in John's presence if he does not will it, can cost a knight his lands." Holding her head high, she scanned the crowd. "Will not one of you come forward?"

Rowena started to rise, to echo Marian's words, but her father's strong hand upon her shoulder held her to her seat. His eyes urged her to caution, and she knew that he had read her thoughts. How it galled her to see John triumph because of the fear he inspired. She started to whisper a protest to her father, to plead with him to voice his objection. But before she could do so, she heard another voice cut through the silence.

"My dear *Lady* Marian," came Kendrick's deep voice, scathing in tone, as he rose to his feet. In stunned surprise, Rowena looked from Kendrick to Marian and back again. Expectantly, she awaited his words, hoping that this handsome knight would champion the rightful cause. Perhaps she had been wrong about him. For some unknown reason she hoped so.

Instead, his words poured forth disdain. "Women understand nothing of war and its cost, my prince," he directed at Prince John. Turning slowly in Marian's direction, he added, "Surely your father can spare an extra tuppence to support our noble king in bringing Christianity to the lands in the East?"

Kendrick stood with his head held high, and Rowena swore beneath her breath at the man's prideful arrogance. And to think she had seen such nobleness in his countenance. Her heart was pricked with disappointment. So she had been right about him from the very first. Another of John's weasels.

From across the room, Prince John's eyes challenged the Lady Marian to say more, insinuating that if she did, her father would be the one to pay dearly for her words.

Once Kendrick had dared to speak his mind and all it had gotten him was betrayal and punishment. Well, perhaps he could save the day and put himself squarely in John's favor at the same time.

Looking sadly into Marian's eyes, he spoke solemnly, "I fear that our lovely lady has partaken too freely of the grape." Kendrick smiled broadly in the prince's direction. "Please forgive her, sire. She is naught but a woman, after all."

"Naught but a woman!" Rowena seethed in outrage. Anger flashing in her eyes, she trembled with rage. Well, she'd tell him a thing or two! She started to stand up but once again she felt her father's hand tighten on her arm.

The room was oppressive with tension. All eyes were riveted on the prince in expectation of a potential tragedy. Instead of anger, however, he smiled. "We will forgive her *this* time," John mockingly replied. "She is, as you say, naught but a woman."

Rowena caught Marian's eye, silently urging her childhood friend to continue her argument. But the lady spoke no further. It seemed even she was afraid of the prince's ire.

"So that's the way it is," Rowena sighed, studying the lady intently. In truth, Marian had risked much to speak as she had. Rowena had always thought Marian to be beautiful, with her long, dark brown hair and eyes as green as the grass upon the hills. There was hardly a man in Nottingham who was not secretly smitten with her beauty. Even, she supposed, Prince John himself. But Marian's heart was true to a young man she had grown up with, a handsome young man who had alienated Prince John beyond consolation. Unlike those assembled here tonight, Robert Fitzooth was no coward. He had taken to the woods, inspiring Rowena with his daring acts against John's injustices.

"But the others are cowards," thought Rowena. If only she were a man, she would show everyone assembled here a thing or two about valor, about fighting for one's principles despite the danger. She'd not keep to a chair like a cowered schoolboy. She would come to Lady Marian's aid, shaming them all. And she would take particular pleasure in making a fool out of this dark-haired man sitting at her side. If only she were a man.

A sudden smile curved Rowena's lips. She might not be male, but that didn't keep her from acting like one. And perhaps, when all was said and done, she had far more courage than any gathered here. The outlaw Arrow would haunt the forest again. And this time Prince John himself had better beware!

Chapter Four

The chamber was dark and silent, a startling contrast to the revelry of the hall. Kendrick de Bron cautiously lit a wall sconce and entered slowly, feeling strangely ill at ease. All had gone well tonight. *Too* well, too smoothly. Dare he hope that he had earned the prince's trust by his play of words? Had his pretense of abiding loyalty been convincing? Had he been able to mask his true feelings behind his painted smile?

Kendrick had met with John after dinner in the king's chambers, an unpleasant meeting to be certain, yet one that he felt he had handled quite skillfully. He had played it to the hilt, mimicking the others loyal to the prince, likewise fawning over the grinning monarch. Boldly he had told John of the de Brons' justifiable anger with Richard and their wish to see John in his brother's place as king. Kendrick had promised to serve the prince with the unswerving loyalty he had shown to his father, Henry. He had vowed to help him win the throne. To fight for him. Die for him if necessary. To be his right-hand man. With every word he had uttered, he had pledged undying devotion to the prince and promised steadfast fealty. He had bowed his head to the prince in homage, swearing to faithfully serve him.

Though John had appraised him with furrowed brow, peering into his very soul, he had at the end of the meeting decreed Kendrick to be his faithful knight. The man who would be king promised full restitution of the de Bron lands and titles. As long as Richard's devious brother was in power, therefore, Kendrick and his family would likewise benefit. And yet the very thought of serving such a man deeply troubled him.

"I should be celebrating my victory, instead of hiding myself in my chamber," Kendrick exclaimed, discarding his mantle on a nearby chair. Why then had he retired to the silence of this room before the festivities of the evening were truly ended? Because tonight he had felt uncomfortably like a man who had just sold his soul.

"Bah! It does not matter," he swore. Ah, but it did. John's favor did not come without a price. That devil would have his due. Kendrick knew he would be called upon very soon to prove his loyalty. He could only hope that the task he was ordered to do would not bruise his conscience too painfully nor soil his honor too deeply. And if it did? He shrugged off a twinge of misgiving by telling himself that it was a cruel world. A man did what he had to do to survive and to prosper.

The de Brons' fall from grace weighed heavily on Kendrick's mind. Being back in England had brought back a host of memories. He remembered another night when the fog had been ghostly and grey, when the moon had fought its way through the smoky haze. Kendrick had been enveloped by the mists as he had walked along the path to his cousin's castle. Returning from the fair, his thoughts had been on a wager he had won concerning a cockfight, and he had jingled the coins in his pouch as he walked. Suddenly, some foreboding had touched him. A premonition that all was not well.

From the distance came the cry of a mourning animal, a low throaty moan as Kendrick had broken into a run. Unmindful of the fog, he had hurried, tripping from time to time over an obstacle in his path, falling to the ground. He had heard the sound of horses, the laughter and rumbling voices of men. Sheltered as he was by the fog, he had not been seen as they rode by, but the colorful hue of Richard's livery had been revealed to his eyes.

Casting a furtive glance over his shoulder, he had pushed through the door of his cousin's manor, taken the stairs two at a time, only to be shocked at the sight that met him. His cousin, as gentle a soul as had ever lived, lay face down on the rushes, a broadsword protruding from between his shoulder blades. It was obvious that he had been slain by the same men who had passed by Kendrick. But such cruel slaughter had not been the end of the story. A lie had been heralded throughout the land that Edward de Bron, a half-Saxon renegade, had been outlawed as a traitor to the crown. King Richard's henchmen had claimed that the young de Bron had tried to flee after committing an act of treachery and was therefore justifiably slain.

"Murdered!" Kendrick swore, trying to fight against the pain the image still brought to his mind. Then had come the pronouncement that all de Brons were likewise deemed traitors. Kendrick, his uncle, aunt and the entire family had been exiled. Led by a man named Fitz Hugh, they had been hunted down like dogs. There had been a terrifying trek over rocks, through a maze of forest land and on to the sea. Kendrick had left England an arrogant, spoiled man made vulnerable by circumstances. For the first time in his life he had experienced fear, not for himself but for those he loved. But those difficult days were hopefully over. Kendrick had returned to England a seasoned knight, John's ardent enemy, if only the prince knew it. And how bowing before that enemy tonight had rankled Kendrick.

Removing his tunic, Kendrick made his way to the bed, running his strong hands over the contours to test its softness. He was disappointed to find that instead of being comfortable, the mattress was lumpy and misshapen. He had heard rumors that John was miserly except where his own comforts were concerned; now he had proof of the whispering. Ah, well, tonight at least he was much too exhausted to notice. With a shrug he stripped off his garments, pulled back the blankets and got into bed.

Wearily closing his eyes, Kendrick was surprised by the image emblazoned there. Not John's face, but that of another. The lovely young woman who had been seated beside him, the young maiden who had worn no wimple. The haughty, outspoken, spirited one who had treated him as if he were a leper, indignantly turning down his invitation to meet him later in his chamber as if it had been the gravest insult. Envisioning a pair of wide blue eyes and honey-gold hair, he couldn't help but smile.

"Methinks she liked me far better than she was letting on . . ." he whispered, soothing his manly ego. Though she had incessantly frowned at him and acted the coy maid, he had sensed her attraction to him with her every stolen glance. "Aye, she liked me."

Though he was humble in many ways, Kendrick knew he attracted the fairer sex. It was not conceit, just an honest assessment of his prowess that made him so self-assured. Kendrick decided the young woman's pretense of disinterest had been just that—pretense. A ploy to fool her father, that gray-haired man who had been most protective of the young maiden, watching her intently as if fearing she might try to fly away. Well, if she wanted to try her wings, Kendrick was of a mind to help her. Closing his eyes, he vowed that he would do just that and that he would see her again.

The sound of two hounds fighting in the courtyard over table scraps was annoying to Rowena as she lay tossing and turning. She tried in vain to get some sleep, but the guest chamber of the prince's castle was cold and damp. The bed was as hard as a slab of stone, thus hindering her efforts even more. Still she burrowed her face in the pillow, determined to get at least a little rest before she and her father had to begin their long journey back home.

Alas, it seemed quite impossible, though she mentally counted more than a hundred sheep. There were too many distractions, too many things on her mind. The wheels in her brain seemed to be turning at a much too rapid rate to allow her to relax.

"Naught but a woman," she whispered, remembering the overbold nobleman and his words concerning Marian. "Naught but a woman. How dare he!" And no doubt he thought *her* to be "naught but a woman" as well.

Oh, she knew the way men like that one thought, that women were for a man's amusement, to be played with then discarded like toys. The way he had treated her tonight, for example. It had gauled her that he had treated her as if she were little more than an empty-headed bit of fluff with no right to opinions of her own. "A beautiful child," he had called her. One whom no one would take seriously.

Kicking off her blankets and bed linens, Rowena rolled over on her back and put her hands behind her head. She looked up at the ceiling, watching the shadows dancing about there as she contemplated her next move. Just what could she do to make that overbearingly bold man squirm? What could she do to humble him again? To give him his proper comeuppance? To teach him a lesson?

The rumble of growling, growing louder and louder, sounded down below again, disrupting her musing. This time Rowena rose from the bed, venting her anger for the moment on the unfortunate hounds. She looked out the tiny, slitted window to the courtyard with the intention of silencing the quarreling curs before they woke her father, but a sight below silenced any scolding she intended. Two men were standing in the shadows beneath her chamber, peering over their shoulders from time to time as if fearing they might be overheard. Instinct told her that something sinister was afoot.

Rowena had often been told by her nurse, Gwyneth, that "curiosity killed many a fine cat," but her curiosity was piqued nonetheless as she stood at the window watching. Dressing quickly in a light blue woolen tunic and throwing a gray mantle over her slim shoulders, Rowena made her way down the narrow spiral staircase. Ever so slowly she opened the door just wide enough to slip out, trying her best to keep it from creaking.

Hiding in the shadows, clinging to the stones of the wall in the courtyard, she moved as close to the two men as possible, taking a closer look. One man was big and burly, the other tall and thin. Though wrapped in a hooded cloak in an effort to shroud himself, Rowena recognized John at once by the manner in which he agitatedly stroked at his beard as he talked.

"Richard cares little for this business of being a king. He is happiest when roaming the shores of foreign domains playing crusader. I but want to insure his happiness."

"You ask me to betray my king? To be party to treason?" Rowena crept ever closer, straining her ears to better hear the voices. As she did so, she recognized the deep voice of Roderick of Herefore, a knight she had heretofore considered an honorable man. "Think you not that I value my head?" he was saying.

"If you value your head, you would do well to remember that it is I who decides if you keep it attached to your burly shoulders, Roderick, not Richard."

"You wouldn't!"

"Just try my patience and find out. You swore you would obey me."

"Aye, that I did." There was a long pause as the burly man thought the matter over carefully, no doubt juggling his loyalties. "You swear that no harm will come to his person?"

"Would I harm my own flesh and blood?"

Yes, Rowena thought, *if it would suit your purposes.*

"I will have no part in murder." On this the burly man seemed steadfast.

"Verily, I say to you that killing my brother is not a part of my plan. I have no need for bloodshed. All I need is time, and the Austrians can give me that and they will if the price is right. Money is powerful, my friend. It can often turn a son against his very own father."

"Or a man against his brother," came the grim reply.

Rowena was heedless of all else now except to find out what was being plotted. All caution fled from her mind as anger egged her on. The traitor! The cowardly, dastardly traitor! Angrily she moved ever so slowly, hiding behind a stack of boxes nearby from time to time as she moved closer to where the men stood scheming. Their voices were hushed now. She could barely make out what they were saying, thus she had no choice but to move even nearer.

"And Lady Marian presents a problem to me," she heard Prince John declare. This time he was louder as he voiced his irritation. "You heard the young chit speak out against me tonight. If I allow her to speak thus in my very own hall, if she is allowed to question what I do and go on her merry way, not only will I loose control of those faithful to me but my ambitions as well could be hampered. She needs to be silenced."

No! Rowena gasped silently.

Her thoughts were echoed by the knight's words. "Surely you cannot even dare to think of harming one hair on the head of the fair Lady Marian. I tell you, John, you go too far! She is but a young lass!"

Rowena could see the big man throw his hands up in the air and start to walk away, but the hand of the prince stayed him.

"Of course, I would not harm such a lovely lady. I merely

think that she would perhaps be better off staying as my guest in the castle, if you understand my meaning."

Rowena did. John was going to hold Marian captive. Certainly he had done it before when someone posed a threat.

"That way I will insure that she does not agitate those who do not favor me and thus bring danger to my person." The prince laughed softly. "I assure you, she will be most comfortable here." Rowena felt a shiver of fear run up her spine.

I must see that Marian gets safely away from here, she thought in alarm. Marian was her friend, a woman she admired. She would not sit by and let her be taken prisoner. Again she strained her ears to what the prince and his cohort were saying.

"Marian and her servant will leave at the crack of dawn to travel back to the lady's estates. I will give you a signal. You will merely escort her to my castle north of here. I have a guest chamber waiting. You will bring her to me there. One of my men will attend you to help you carry out the deed. I will send him to your room long before the cock crows."

"And just how will I know this man?" The knight's voice was filed with loathing, but it was clear he would do as his master bid.

Rowena was filled with urgency as she listened to the description of the scoundrel, taking mental note of all the details. Then, realizing she couldn't tarry, that there was much to be done if she were going to save Maid Marian, she retraced her steps quietly, stealthily. She was nearly to safety behind a wall when her foot became entangled in a mesh of ropes holding some boxes together. The boxes came down, crashing to the ground, giving her away.

"What the—?"

"Who goes there? Roderick, find out!" The scuffle of footsteps alerted Rowena that they intended to give chase. The hunt was on.

Chapter Five

Darting out of the shadows, Rowena ran for her life. If she could only escape, she would be safe from Prince John's revenge. Fleeing up the stairway she could only hope that with her agility she could leave the knight far behind. Alas, it was not to be so. Though she picked her feet up and set them down as fast as she was able, she could not move quickly enough to outdistance him. Her clothing weighed her down and got in the way of her feet and legs. With an angry oath, she hastily discarded her mantle, wishing she could cast off her long tunic as well.

"I must not let them catch me!" Thus avowed, she ran up the last ten steps as fast as her legs would carry her, determined to reach her room and safety.

"You! Wait!"

"Becket's saintly ghost!" Roderick of Hereford was too close to her heels to allow her an easy respite from his chase. Certain that he had not caught enough of a glimpse of her to know her identity, she decided against entering her own chamber. Of a certainty it would give her away. She had to look elsewhere for a hiding place. But where?

The heavy trod of the knight's footsteps set her heart beating frantically. Despite her effort, he was closing in on her.

With a sudden burst of energy Rowena lost him for just a moment. Hardly daring to hope, she tried one of the doors near the stairs. It was locked, offering no place where she could hide. Swearing beneath her breath, she went on to the next. It too was secure against her entry. On to the next and then the next she ran, but these too were bolted. All the while she heard the heavy footfalls coming closer and closer.

Rowena scolded herself for her lack of foresight in not bringing a weapon, any weapon, with her. Against the large man's strength she would be helpless, but she wouldn't be taken without struggle. Whirling around, preparing for a fight, she paused. She'd try one more door.

Running to the fifth portal she reached out, surprised when it swung open easily at her touch. Ducking into the room, Rowena shut the door tightly behind her. Her chest was heaving, her heart beating as rapidly as the wings of a bird, while her hair tumbled in disarray around her flustered face.

"Well, what have we here?" The voice was masculine and seemed to be one that Rowena remembered. "So, the lady is anxious for my company."

Turning around to face the occupant of the room, Rowena was mortified to see that it was the same dark-haired man who had sat beside her during the banquet. The handsome, overbold, swaggering one. She stood transfixed, looking into his brown eyes, trying not to lower her gaze to the broad expanse of his lightly furred chest, which was all too obviously bare. Horrified, she realized that he had very little on, only a thin piece of bed linen. The look in his eyes told her that he misunderstood her entrance.

"Be most assured that I welcome you."

"It . . . it's not what you . . . you think," she stammered, taking a step backward as he took several steps forward.

His hand touched her elbow with a firmness that seemed to tell her he wasn't planning to let her go. "Come in. I do not want to keep such a lovely young woman waiting." He grinned roguishly.

Kendrick stared into the young woman's wide blue eyes, thinking that they were just as blue as he had remembered. Her soft mouth was just as pink, though curled upwards instead of frowning it would have been more alluring. The soft curves of her slim form were plainly visible in the thin woolen of her blue gown. He thought again that she was lovely, as delightful as a wild rose.

"Lovely." Reaching out he touched the softness of her hair. It intrigued him, unusual in its tawny color. He smiled in anticipation. The fact that she had come to his room gave credence to the surety that the lady would quickly succumb to him. He had not misinterpreted her after all. His pride was soothed.

Rowena pushed his hand away. She didn't want him to think that she had wandered into his bedroom for a social visit. "I was trying to get away from a man," Rowena began, anxious to set his thoughts aright. She did not like the glint in his eyes. She was not so naive that she did not know what it meant.

"I'm certain that you *were* trying to get away from a man. A beauty such as yours must surely attract a flock of suitors, my lady. It is glad I am that you have chosen me."

"Chosen you . . . ?" The nerve of the man. Anger sparked in her eyes. She started to protest indignantly when a knock at the door silenced her. From beyond a husky, gruff voice called out, inquiring as to whether Kendrick had seen a young woman in a light blue gown.

"A light blue gown?" Impassioned eyes swept over her.

In quivering apprehension, Rowena waited for the dark-haired rogue to give her away, to hand her over to the brawny conspirator. Instead, he merely put his finger to his lips as he smiled, pushing her gently, but firmly, behind the door as he opened it.

"God's blood, cannot a man shave and go about his necessities without disturbance?" he shouted, feigning annoyance.

The knight was not intimidated. "I'm searching for a fugitive. A young woman wearing light blue or gray. Have you seen her?"

"Seen her?" Throwing back his head Kendrick roared his laughter. "My good man, had I seen a young woman roaming about I would now have her between the sheets, not be dawdling here jabbering with you. But the answer is no. The only face I've looked upon has been your ugly one, much to my regret."

This time there was a pause, then, "Are you certain?"

"As sure as I am of my own name, Kendrick de Bron. Now, if you have nothing more to say, my bath water is growing cold."

"Bath water? Fie! You men from across the Channel are a strange lot. Ugh . . . you'll catch the ague or at least a chill! But to each his own."

"Aye, to each his own."

There was another pause. "Well, if you cannot help me, good day."

"Good day!"

Rowena heard the heavy trod of footsteps and sighed with relief. Perhaps this dark-haired newcomer was not quite as bad as she had first supposed. "Thank you—" His mouth closed on hers before she could say another word.

For the moment, his firm lips molded against hers, Rowena was speechless. His kiss was surprisingly gentle as he caressed the softness of her mouth. So gentle that she somehow forgot to put up a fight. As his kiss jolted her with sweet fire, she yielded for just a moment. She had never felt like this. Never. It was as if he took her breath away, mingled it with his own. His strong arms reached around her waist to draw her closer against him and

Rowena did not want to pull away no matter how much reason told her that she should.

"It is as if you were molded just for me," she heard him say as he drew his mouth away. His words tickled her ear, sending another shiver of warmth up her spine. "I will show you delights you never dreamed of."

Again his mouth claimed hers and Rowena could only wonder at the feelings this man's nearness was igniting. It was as if a raging fire burned through her veins, as if she were standing on the edge of a precipice in danger of falling off. A breathless feeling, albeit a feeling heightened by a strange sense of fear. Somehow she was losing control and yet passionately she surrendered to her senses, shivering as his mouth and tongue traced the outline of her neck and shoulders.

Kendrick knew at once that the young woman in his arms was inexperienced but even so he continued with his lovemaking, surprised by the feelings she evoked. He had taken his share of women to bed, but never had a mere kiss so quickly ignited his passion. A strange feeling of protectiveness warmed him as he thought how she stirred his heart as well as his loins. Nonetheless he reveled in her response to him as he reached down the front of her blue gown to stroke the peaks of her breasts lifting so impudently to taunt him.

Rowena tensed immediately. The touch of his hands upon her naked skin with such familiarity brought her back down to earth with a thud. How dare this man she hardly knew be so familiar with her? She was no trollop sent to pleasure him. Breaking away from his embrace, remembering that he was Prince John's man and thereby a likewise devious bastard, she removed his offending hand from her gown, rasping her displeasure. This man presented a danger to her virtue. He was a womanizing scoundrel, that was obvious. Pulling away, she moved towards the door.

"Not so quickly, my lady." Kendrick motioned for her

to return to him. The lady was nervous about what he intended but he was confident that he could warm her again. She would be trembling with desire, as were most women he had encountered, after but another kiss or two. "Come, kiss me again. Ah, it was good . . ."

"Kiss you again? I think not," Rowena shot back. Heat surged into her cheeks as she reached for the latch. With a swiftness that stunned her, however, the dark-haired man blocked her way.

"Leaving? I think not yet." Grasping Rowena, he held her in a tight embrace, his lips caressing hers again as his hand slid down the curve of her hips. From experience he knew that women liked a man to be strong and domineering. They liked to lead a man on a merry chase but always gave in once they were caught.

Rowena could feel the hard, warm length of him as he held her against him and she stiffened in outrage. At that moment frustration and rage welled up inside to choke her. "Unhand me!" she ordered, unleashing a torrent of swear words, words unfit for a woman to say.

"What?" Kendrick's lips twitched in a smile as he regarded her. He held her tightly, refusing to give in to her plea. "Such language," he said playfully. "I ought to put you over my knee, wench."

Wench. The word infuriated her. Without thinking, she drew back her fist and hit him, not once but twice, with the speed of a striking reptile.

Rowena was strong. Years of stringing her bow and climbing trees had strengthened her arms and insured that she was no weakling. Now, as the handsome man stood sputtering before her holding his jaw, she stared at him in surprise. Fearing for her virtue, she had protected herself not by slapping his face as most young women would, but had reverted to her tomboy days and punched him as a lad would have done.

"BiGod!" Putting his hand to his jaw, Kendrick gently massaged his injury. Never had he been struck by a maid and he would not stand for this kind of treatment now. He stepped towards her, anger etched upon his face. "This is how you repay me? With a punch in the jaw, like some little ruffian? And after I lie to the guard for you?"

"I . . . I . . ." Unable to explain her actions, Rowena was speechless.

Kendrick delighted in her confusion, idly threatening, "Why, I have half a mind to turn you over my knee and trounce you soundly!"

"You wouldn't dare!"

Rowena did not stay to continue the conversation. With a curse she opened the door and fled into the hallway. She was running now from a foe far more dangerous than the knight who waited below; indeed, she was running from a man who was after greater bounty—her heart and her virtue.

Kendrick watched the girl scurrying away, not really knowing whether to laugh or curse. Truly she was a strange one. All passion and fire one moment and a fighting, sputtering kitten the next. One thing was obvious, however, she was in some kind of trouble.

"What has she done to cause John's guardsmen to chase after her?" Remembering her bold conversation at the Christmas feast he could well imagine. Undoubtedly she had spoken out before thinking and earned John's retribution. Ah well, it was none of his concern, he thought, retreating back into the room.

Then why had he shielded her? Why had he lied to the man-at-arms? As anxious as the guardsman had seemed to capture her, he might have earned John's gratitude had he turned her in.

"Was I that befuddled because of a kiss . . . ?"

Slowly, methodically, Kendrick got dressed, sorting out his thoughts as he tugged and pulled on each garment. He had wanted to bed the young woman, and why not? He was a man of strong hungers and she was a tantalyzing offering, sugar with just the right touch of spice.

Right from the first, the idea of being with her had crossed his mind. Tonight he had fantasized about holding her, warm and soft in his arms. This morning the reality had been even more stimulating than he had supposed. And now she was gone. The crazy heat and pounding of his body that she had stirred within him, however, was not.

"My lord de Bron?"

Looking up, Kendrick realized that Chadwick had entered the room. Though his servant had been talking to him he had been much too preoccupied for the moment to hear.

"Prince John has asked to see you."

"He has?" Kendrick was apprehensive, wondering if the time had come for John to test his loyalty. "Then of course I must hurry. One does not keep such a man waiting." Grabbing at the cloak he had flung over the bedpost, he started towards the door, then paused. "There was a young woman . . ."

Chadwick grinned. "The one with the dark blonde hair."

"Aye." Kendrick knew he had to see her again. "Find her." Slowly she was becoming an obsession, a fact that disturbed him more than just a little.

The hallway was cold in spite of the sconces sputtering on the gallery's stone wall. Kendrick tugged at his cloak, pulling it closer around him as he stood before the chamber room door, waiting for his audience with the prince.

"What does he want . . . ?"

He was apprehensive about having been summoned. His business with John had all been settled, had it not? Why then had John requested his presence at this ungodly hour? To question him again? Test his loyalty? Make idle conversation? Or was there a more sinister reason?

"The air is thick with intrigue . . ."

Kendrick sensed that there were plots and counterplots and men willing to switch sides in an instant were the monetary reward high enough. Why, even the women were involved in the sparring, he thought, remembering the Lady Marian's outburst. He would have to be cautious and just as calculating and clever as the prince and his cohorts, for one false move and everything could very well be lost.

"And I will find myself in exile again . . . or worse."

He had heard frightened whisperings about the torture chambers and dungeons below. Nevertheless, impatience goaded him. He wanted this interview over and done with, for waiting was not a thing Kendrick dealt well with.

Crossing his arms, shifting from foot to foot, he tried to make himself comfortable as the minutes passed by. Why was John making him wait? To keep him in his place? Or was something else going on? Remembering the young woman's flight this morning from the knight in the hallway, he was curious. More so when he heard the faint mumble of voices beyond the thick, closed door.

What is being said is none of my business. Perhaps not, but that didn't keep Kendrick from eavesdropping anyway.

"She escaped us, my liege. Somehow the woman in blue vanished right before our very noses."

"So I noted." There was a pause. "Alas, there are more fools than just Lankless abiding in yon castle, William."

"My lord, please let me explain . . ."

"No, let me. Allow me to talk of the hows and whys of such a failure." There was a long pause. "Now, because of your stupidity there is a chance that Marian will be forewarned."

"Then we will just have to change our plans—"

"I already have."

Kendrick quickly stepped away when he heard the shuffling of footsteps. He didn't want to be caught with his ear to the door. Taking several steps backward he pretended nonchalance as it was flung open.

"So, you obeyed my summons." The voice crackled with an icy tone, and Kendrick feared for just a moment that John suspected him of eavesdropping.

"Of course." Burying his pride, Kendrick affected a polite bow. "As I told you before, it is my intention to be at the beck and call of the next King of England. I, like you, always align myself on the winning side."

The beady-eyed John scrutinized Kendrick for a moment then, seemingly satisfied, he smiled. "If indeed you are as good with a sword as you are with your tongue, then I have no doubt that we will work well together, you and I." Roughly he pushed Kendrick into the chamber room, then slammed the door. "I will get right to the point. I am surrounded by bungling fools who alas have complicated the simplest task."

"And you want me to uncomplicate it."

With a grim nod of his head, John said, "Yes."

"What would you have me do?"

John's eyes stared straight into Kendrick's eyes as if somehow he could see into his soul. "I want you to act as guard dog."

"As what?" Kendrick's cheek twitched with irritation. He had no liking for being relegated to the position of a hound.

John tossed a log into the chamber room's small fireplace, then watched as the sparks danced up. "You heard the haughty babbling of my lady Marian."

Kendrick furled his brows. "I did."

John's face was an ugly mask of anger as he explained his plans for the lady in question. "She cannot be allowed to express her opinions so vocally."

"Nay, she cannot, but . . ." Kendrick shuddered, fearing

that John meant to see her put to death. He had never in all his life harmed a woman and he would not do such a thing now, even if it did mean the end to all his fine dreams.

"She needs to be put under lock and key until she can be made to see things . . . well, differently."

"Imprisoned, you mean." Kendrick fought hard against the smile that tugged at his lips. He had had dealings with Marian when they were both little more than children and he could well say that she was determined and exceedingly stubborn. Moreover, she had always loathed John. He doubted that Satan himself could make her change her views.

"Aye!" John wrinkled his nose. "Locked away until she can say a few kind words about me."

"As she did the other night," Kendrick teased.

The prince was not in a joking mood. "Do not mock me, de Bron! I am deadly serious." Looking down at the rings adorning his fingers, he toyed with the jewelry. "Once people laughingly called me John Lackland because my father had not yet secured lands for me, but now . . ." He swallowed hard. "Now, for the first time I have power within my grasp. I will not let anyone, much less a woman, interfere with my plans. Would you?"

Kendrick suddenly thought about the honey-haired woman who had so charmed him and shook his head. Not even for such as she would he risk his future. "No, I would not. As I said, Marian was naught but a woman."

"Naught but a woman." John's laugh was sinister.

"So, what is it you would have me do?"

John quickly explained his intention to allow Marian to leave the castle so that the inhabitants would see her go. Once she was well outside the castle walls, however, she was to be subdued, taken prisoner and secretly brought back to lodge in the rooms below.

"A simple scheme which would have unfolded without

any problems had it not been overheard. As it is, your part in all of this, de Bron, is to take any would-be rescuers unaware and to guard my lovely prisoner on the ride back to Nottingham.''

"I see." It was a mission that Kendrick did not like at all.

Chapter Six

Four travelers rode past the walls of Nottingham Castle and deep into the forest. It was a colorful band: a knight dressed in his best tunic and cloak, a lady dressed in her brightest finery, she too wearing a mantle, a servant dressed in gray and looking like a woeful pigeon, and last but not least a youth wearing boots, hood, cape and woolen tunic, carrying a bow and a quiver of arrows. All clutched their cloaks tightly about them to keep out the early morning chill, visibly expressing their hurry to end the journey and return to the warmth of hearth fires. Despite the haste, however, the lady stopped her horse and gazed upon the beauty of a doe foraging for food a short distance from the riders.

"Careful, little one, lest our mighty prince decide to levy a tax on you for eating the leaves on his land," she said bitterly. "He is so fond of taxes." As she spoke, the lady's cloak fell from her head revealing thick dark tresses that caught the dawn's faint glow.

"Aye, fond of taxes. That he is," echoed the servant accompanying her as he came to her side. "But Robin will show him. Methinks John will not end up as rich as he supposes." The little man was quickly silenced by his mistress but he kept on grinning.

"Is something amiss?" Roderick of Hereford was anxious to learn why she had paused.

"Nothing that Richard's return can't quickly rectify," she mumbled, then said louder, "I but needed to catch my breath, sir."

A grumble was her answer. "We have no time to rest here, Lady Marian." His gruff voice frightened away the deer and sent it scurrying. "I must be back to Nottingham ere nightfall." The knight's eyes scanned the horizon. He couldn't hide his nervousness, his agitation.

"Aye, back to do John's bidding, no doubt." Hastily Marian pulled her hood back up again. "Well, let us be off then."

The small band rode further on, the Lady Marian now taking the lead. Though her eyes were focused forward, the knight continued glancing behind him, as did the youth in the hood. The walls of the castle were becoming a speck in the distance, but not so small that the flickering fire of a torch could not be seen.

"The signal!" The preappointed sign that the prince and his men would soon be approaching. Pulling the reins of his horse, Roderick of Hereford brought the animal to a halt. "Now!" he commanded, beckoning to the hooded lad at his side. "Take them." With a stern frown he awaited the inevitable, raising his sword and slowly closing in.

Totally taken by surprise, Lady Marian tried to push her horse forward but found her path blocked. "What are you doing?"

"We go no further along this pathway, my lady. Instead, I must inform you that my intent is to escort you in another direction."

"What other direction?" Maid Marian was indignant. "What folly is this? I command you to get out of my way so that I may ride back to my home, back to Huntington."

"I think not. The prince has other ideas." Grabbing the reins of her horse, the knight kept her mount immobile. "You are to be the most honored guest of the prince."

"Guest! Fie, sir. You mean his prisoner." She shook her head violently. "I tell you I want no part of him . . ."

Looking first to her servant, then to the hooded lad, Marian couldn't mask her fear. It seemed to her as if the lad in the hood suddenly smiled, but why? Though the grin was meant to comfort her, to Marian who could no longer seem to trust anyone, that smile meant danger. Sliding from her horse she took to her heels, tripping over the long woolen skirts which were a woman's woe.

"Catch her, you blasted yeoman!" shouted the knight, turning towards the hooded youth. "Don't let her get away. Stop her!"

"Stop her?" Throwing back her head, Rowena laughed. Even Maid Marian had not recognized her, dressed as she was in the hood and clothing of Prince John's henchman. "I think not. It is you I came to spar with." Before the knight could react to her words, she had her arrow strung in her bow and pointed straight at the other man's heart. Loudly she ordered Marian's servant, "Go after your mistress. Tell her to come back, that I am a friend!"

Fumbling with his own weapons, the knight showed his outrage. "What goes on here?"

"A rescue, I would call it," Rowena retorted as she recalled how easy it had been to best the prince's hired kidnapper. A blow to his head, a length of rope to bind his hands and feet. Leaving the fool in naught but his under tunic, she had stolen his garments and taken his place. She had waited for the right moment. Now she congratulated herself that all had gone very smoothly. She had but to make certain that Maid Marian would reach her estate safely and then her mission would be at an end.

"Rescue?" The knight tried to scrutinize Rowena but she hastily turned her head. He took a step closer, halting

when she gave him silent warning. "What kind of fool has
John sent me? A traitor, to be certain."

"I am not a traitor." Her voice was husky for a woman's,
yet she sought to lower it even more, a ploy she had used
long ago when acting like a lad. The knight seemed no
wiser. "But *you* are."

"You dare . . . !" The knight reacted in anger, moving
forward with deadly intent, but his vengeance was thwarted
as the archer pulled back tautly on the bow.

"Aye, I do dare! Toss down your sword and get down
off your horse," Rowena ordered.

"No!" The knight responded stubbornly, enraged to be
outwitted by a mere yeoman. He grumbled beneath his
breath that he had not wanted this foolish, traitorous mission in the first place.

Rowena gave him a warning look, pulling tighter on the
string. "I will shoot you. Don't be so foolish as to test me,"
she warned. "Throw down your weapons and dismount."

Perhaps it was the look in her eyes which warned the
knight not to trifle here, for after but a brief show of
defiance he complied with her demand.

Giving the horse a slap on its hind quarters, Rowena
sent the animal back towards the castle. "That will slow
you down a mite." Ignoring the curses of the knight, who
swore beneath his breath most fouly, she ordered him to
strip. It was the same ploy she had used once before on a
dark-haired devil whose face she tried not to remember.
"I want your cloak, your tunic, everything but your inner
tunic and boots." She bowed mockingly. It had worked
before. She was certain she would be successful again.

"I would be the village idiot to do as you bid me," the
knight growled. "Take off my garments, indeed." He stood
with hands upon his hips in defiance.

An arrow whistled through the air, coming within inches
of his ear. "You would be the village idiot not to do as I
say." She reached for another arrow.

Quickly the knight held up his hands in defeat. "By our

Lord, desist. I will do as you ask. Prince or not, he is not worth dying for." Blushing furiously as he saw the figure of Maid Marian coming over the hill, the servant in tow, he nonetheless stripped. "But I warn you. I will avenge you myself for this act one day!"

"You and several others . . ." Rowena said beneath her breath. She nodded her head, sending the knight marching down the road.

Maid Marian stood viewing the scene with confusion clearly marked upon her face. One moment she was being abducted and the next moment she found herself looking after the retreating, half-naked form of her captor. "Whoever you are, you are very brave," she complimented. "Nearly as brave as another archer I know."

Rowena lowered her voice. "Thank you, my lady." To be compared to Robin Hood was a compliment. Rowena watched for any signs of recognition but saw none and knew that her disguise had worked. If Marian who had known her since childhood didn't know who she was, then she need not fear being recognized by others. It gave her just the confidence she needed. "Now come. To horse again. You have far to go still and cannot linger here. Prince John and his henchmen are not far off."

Marian pulled herself up on her steed, smiling at the young "man" who had saved her. "I thank you, kind sir, for your help this day. Perhaps someday I will be able to reward you for your act of bravery in saving me from the clutches of—" Her face paled as she looked back towards the castle. "Look! Someone is coming."

Whirling around, Rowena cursed beneath her breath as she recognized who was approaching. Even from afar she recognized the dark hair, the way he sat his horse, indeed the very arrogance of the man. "Kendrick de Bron," she exclaimed. Alas, he was not alone. Two other men rode with him.

"We'll be caught!" Marian hesitated, not knowing whether to stay or to go.

"No, we shall not." Rowena made a hasty decision to act as a decoy. "Ride. You must return to Huntington," she said a bit gruffly. "I'll lead them on a merry chase." When the Lady Marian refused, Rowena gave Marian's horse a slap on its rump with her bow. "I said ride!" Turning her horse around, returning her bow to the safety of its strap, she mounted, urging her horse onward. And just in time! The sound of horses' hooves echoed in her ears, coming closer and closer.

"The rogue robbed me. Catch him!" she heard Roderick of Hereford shout.

"Never!" she vowed. She would outride them all. Across the rocky hillside she guided her horse, moving towards the thickest part of the forest. The leafy branches beckoned her like the arms of a lover as she fled her enemies.

Feeling the pulsating rhythm of her horse's flanks beneath the high leather of her boots, she rode towards a clump of trees. Once there she could seek the shelter of the dense foliage, double back, make a large circle and emerge from the trees to take the opposite path back to the castle. A tricky maneuver but one she must complete successfully. To be caught would put not only herself but her father in danger.

Rowena's heart was beating like a drum as at last she reached the foliage. Reining in her mount she hid behind a tall, stout tree, scarcely daring to breathe.

"Where did the lad go?"

"He went to the right."

"To the left."

"Come, follow me."

From her position she could see the shadows of the men on horseback as they rode past her. She could hear their shouts, the plop of their horses' hooves, could nearly hear them breathe as they passed her.

Ride, you churlish bastards! she thought angrily. *But you will never capture me.* To assure that they would not, she kept her eyes trained on them, watching their every move. For what seemed forever she huddled behind the trunk, totally determined. Only when she was certain that they were gone did she come forth from her concealment.

"Had they but eyes in their heads they would have found me."

She was pleased with herself because of her cleverness, more so because she had outwitted the arrogant dark-haired knight who had been so certain she would anxiously jump right into his bed.

"Overbold knave!" Not for the world would she have admitted that his sexual virility had burned her like a flame, nor that in truth she had enjoyed the searing warmth of his kiss. "I have escaped you once again."

Rowena wasn't completely safe, however. She would have to take a shortcut back to the prince's castle, a dangerous one to be sure since it crossed through the wilder nooks in the forest, but she had to take the chance. She had to reach her father quickly and get him back to their own estates just in case the prince had any suspicions.

"Nay, it can not be!" Feeling a total surge of frustration, Kendrick rode hard in pursuit of the lad who had spirited Lady Marian away. "BiGod, even from a distance I recognized the scurvy bastard." It was the archer who had accosted him in the forest. So, once more the lad had gotten the upper hand.

"Gone, BiGod!"

"He disappeared into the trees!"

Kendrick's two companions were nearly as angered by the episode as he. In truth, all three of the men knew that this failure to bring Maid Marian back to the castle would infuriate John.

"He'll have our ears or worse . . ." Humbley shuddered.

"He will not!" Kendrick was determined. "If we have to look behind every tree, we will find the young scoundrel and take him back with us. That should appease the prince." He wondered just how cocky the lad would be once he found himself hanging in chains from the castle's dungeon wall.

"All well and good if we can find the boy!" Chadwick hugged his skinny arms around his horse's neck.

"Ha, we will find him, or my name is not Kendrick de Bron!"

It was to be an idle boast for although they searched high and low, looked behind trees, bushes and rocks they came up emptyhanded.

"Impossible!" Where had the boy gone? How was it possible to just vanish?

"Were I not a sensible man I might believe in magic," Chadwick exclaimed.

"Magic? I think not." Passing by a huge oak, Kendrick examined the yawning hole in its trunk. A small scrap of torn brown wool gave his fugitive's hiding place away.

"He was there?"

Kendrick answered Humbley's question. "Aye, the clever, clever lad. He used the indentation in the trunk to blend into the trees, watching as we rode by."

"And laughing," Chadwick added.

"Forsooth, not for long." Staring out at the horizon, Kendrick watched as the horse and rider galloped down the pathway that led back to the castle. "Clever perhaps, but not as clever as he supposes. Alas for him, he has been seen."

"And now followed, or so I would suppose." Hesitating for just a moment, Humbley was ready when the order came.

"Aye." Stuffing the piece of wool in his belt, Kendrick said only one other word. "Now!"

*   *   *

Rowena thankfully saw the wooden grids of the portcullis looming up ahead and sighed with relief, but the moment was ruined when she likewise heard the pounding of hooves and knew that she was being followed.

"Nay!" It could not be so. Ah, but it was.

Not even deigning to look behind her, she recklessly spurred her horse into a wild, mad dash. She couldn't allow herself to be taken. Far too much was at stake. Grasping the reins tightly, Rowena crooned in her horse's ear, urging the horse into a dangerous pace that visibly taunted, "Catch me if you dare".

Kendrick tried, muttering curses under his breath all the while. At last, because his horse was more powerful, he closed the distance between them. "Stop, in the name of the prince! Stop, I say!"

Rowena wanted desperately to tell him to go straight to hell, but she was much too busy concentrating on her horsemanship. Quickly she took evasive action, guiding her horse in the opposite direction. All she could manage to shout out was a breathless, "Nay!"

Angrily Kendrick continued his pursuit, changing direction so that he was able to come up alongside his quarry. "Stop," he ordered again.

Her heart beating painfully in her breast, Rowena reached out and struck at her pursuer. With a startling show of strength and agility she fought against the man who sought to subdue her. At last, once again, she broke free.

The hooves of her horse clattered loudly against the stones as she rode into the castle courtyard. Dismounting as quickly as she could, Rowena hid her horse at the far end of the stable. Tearing off her hooded cloak, loosening her hair, she ran frantically towards the castle.

Never had there seemed to be so many steps. Taking them two at a time, Rowena burst into her father's room. "Quickly, pack up your things. We must get out of here."

Eyeing her up and down, taking note of her dishevelement, Sir William said not one word in argument. He knew enough about the happenings in the kingdom to sense danger. Gathering together the meager possessions he had brought with him to Nottingham Castle, he was soon ready to go.

Chapter Seven

It was dark when Rowena and her father reached their own home, Grantham Manor. Rain and sleet from a sudden storm pelted the earth with a fury that caused her to shudder, bringing to mind tales and legends of spirits and ghosts that had roamed near here in days of old. Truly they were showing their anger tonight. Quickly tethering their horses, Rowena and her father ran to the door. Flinging it open they sought shelter inside.

Rowena quickly lit the five wall sconces one by one, smiling as their small flames illuminated the tapestries adorning the stone walls. The colorful pictures woven in thread told the history of the Fitz Hugh family, the villains and black sheep as well as the heroes, and daring exploits at the side of all the Norman Kings from William the Conqueror and beyond. Lovingly the story of her Saxon ancestors was portrayed there as well, reminding her that just like the splendid wall hangings, she was a blending of Norman and Saxon blood.

"Ah, there is nothing quite so welcome as a man's own hearth," Sir William exclaimed as he started a fire. With a contented sigh, he rubbed his hands together while the flames warmed him.

Rowena did not speak. She was still recalling her narrow escape. The next time she might not be so lucky. "Yon knight is most certainly a nuisance," she mumbled to herself.

"What did you say, daughter?" Sir William turned his backside to the fire, warming the other part of his anatomy.

"I said that Prince John is nothing but a braying ass!" As were the others in his entourage.

Nervously her father looked toward the door, as if fearing that portal had ears. He lowered his voice. "Have a care about your talk of John, daughter, lest you bring about our undoing." Pulling off his cloak, he hung it by the fire to dry.

Whirling around, Rowena couldn't hide her irritation. Once her father had been brave and strong but no more. Now he seemed all too determined to appease John's whims if it meant avoiding trouble. "We're not in the prince's castle now, Father. You needn't be so frightened that someone will overhear."

He was quick to answer. "Nay, but I cannot forget our frantic journey here, nor the look on your face when you pushed through our chamber door and bid me to pack my things. Something has happened. What?"

"I overheard John's treachery and . . . and I interfered!"

"Ahhh." Sir William woefully buried his face in his hands. "I feared as much."

"John was going to take Marian prisoner. I couldn't in good conscience abide such a thing so I—"

"You what?" His hands trembled as he imagined the worst.

"I came upon her abductors and frightened them off." She smiled sweetly. "'Tis all."

"'Tis enough!" Pacing the floor he wrung his hands. "All is lost. We are ruined. John will not waste any time in sending his men here." He looked towards the door.

"They will carry you off and blame me for your transgressions and—"

"They will not!" Coming up behind her father she gently laid a hand on his shoulder. "I was in disguise, Father. No one got a good look at my face. Not even Marian."

"Thanks be to God!" Plopping his girth down in a wooden chair, Sir William relaxed, then, looking up at his daughter, scolded, "Marian, she is the cause of it all. She should never have spoken up but should have remembered a woman's place."

"A woman's place?" Rowena rolled her eyes upward.

Sir William could see an argument brewing and hastened to get the upper hand. "Oh, I know full well what you intended to do during the festivities. To stand up and add your voice to Marian's."

"I didn't . . ." Ah, but she would have and in hindsight wished she had.

"Which was wise, considering the danger you would have put yourself in. I warn you that it would have been foolhardy."

"Nevertheless, I wish that I had. At least then one of us would have been brave." There was a long hesitation then she exclaimed, "How much longer are the men of this land going to hide their heads? How much longer are you going to let a tyrant sweep through the countryside taxing and terrorizing the people?"

"Hush!" Putting his finger to his lips he cautioned her again. "I said have a care, daughter, and mean it well. Servants have been known to tattle and with their errant tongues cause mischief."

"Have a care, have a care!" Rowena's patience was at the breaking point. "That's all you men ever say, while he whisks the land out from under your very noses. And taxes, there are so many that even a cleric is pressed to keep track. A penny to collect firewood, though it be in plenty and scattered about. Agistment for the right to graze animals in the forest. Chiminage for the right to carry goods through the forest. Bodel silver for the right to live in a house on the lord's land. Why, a poor villein even has to provide grain to feed the lord's horses."

Sir William defended a system that even he made use of. "That is the way things are, Rowena, the way things have always been."

"And yet I have heard you too complain." She took a deep breath. "Why, even upon death a family has to give the lord the dead man's best animal. And what of me? Were John to make a demand of my maidenhead, would you grant his request, just to keep peace?"

Sir William shouted out, "Of course not!"

"And yet he freely takes anything that suits his needs at the moment, money, sheep, land, castles." She took a deep breath. "When will he steal *our* home? Tell me that, Father."

His ill temper matched her own. "Soon, if you don't mind your tongue." Just as quickly his tone softened. "Oh, Rowena, I know you were disappointed that I didn't jump to Marian's defense, but we will fight John, albeit in our own way."

"Aye, in our own way." She longed to tell him about her escapades in the forest and about how she had fleeced one of John's haughty lords but the furl to his brows silenced her. Caution was her father's way. He was not daring nor bold and would only chide her for the danger she might have caused had she failed. But she had not failed

Going to the cellar for some wine, she heated it with a mixture of honey and clove. Sitting before the fire, she was silent as she brooded about all that had transpired at the prince's castle. Something was being planned. Something that went far beyond kidnapping the Lady Marian. But what? Just how far was John willing to go? Even so far as murder?

"By firelight you look so much like your mother. But

your temperament . . ." Sir William threw his hands up in the air. "Bah! It is all my fault."

Rowena turned her head. "What is, Father?"

"Your willfulness," he answered sourly. "I took no time to teach you how to be soft and feminine. Now it is time you found a husband and all you can think of is your hatred for Prince John."

"A rightly deserved hatred," she shot back, defending herself.

"Rightly deserved or not, I beg you to put it aside and think about your future." Moving closer to her he touched the tip of her nose. "Why, I would wager you were so busy being petulant that you hardly noticed that man who sat beside you at the banquet."

Rowena stiffened. "Man? What man?" she asked coyly, trying not to conjure up the memory of that man kissing her. Alas, it was impossible not to remember the softness, the fire. Touching her fingers to her lips she shivered, but not from the cold. Instead another emotion flowed through her body, a bewilderingly pleasureable tingle. It was because of the honey, clove and wine of course.

"A most eligible man, that's who. Dark-haired and bold." One booted foot tapped in agitation on the hard earthen floor.

Remembering his glittering brown eyes, Rowena blushed in spite of herself. "Oh, that man." She was quick to give her opinion. "He was naught but a vain and pompous braggert, one of the prince's hounds to follow at the royal heels." She stuck her nose up in the air. "I hardly even noticed him."

"Certainly he took notice of you. And I took notice of him." Rowena could sense a lecture coming. "He is the sort of man I would like to see you married to before I die. A man who could take care of you."

"Married to! Him!" Rowena nearly spilled her wine. "Marry, you say. I would as soon be thrust into the jaws of a dragon!" She shook her head angrily as she remembered the taste of his kiss, the feel of his fingers on her skin. Why, the man had brutely pawed her as if her wishes in the happenings had not even mattered. Marry a man like that? Never!

"A dragon, you say. Would you?" William's mouth tugged up into a smile. "Daughter you protest too—" A loud banging upon the door interrupted them. "God's blood, what is that uproar?" He soon had his answer as the door was thrust open and a woman pushed into the room. Her arms were outstretched, imploring help. A flash of lightning illuminated her tear-stained face. "Gwyneth!"

"What is it? What has happened?" Rowena hastened to the side of the old woman who had been her childhood nurse, friend and companion.

"They . . . they came. They took all," Gwyneth warbled, throwing her hands about like a wounded bird. She looked so pitiful standing there, her garments soaking wet.

It was obvious that the old woman was on the verge of hysterics. Rowena asked softly, "Took what?" Trying to calm Gwyneth, she put her arm around the distraught woman once again.

"Took everything. Ethelred tried to fight them, but . . . but . . . there were too many. Too many. And now his heart . . ."

"Let me help him." Compassionately Sir William followed Gwyneth to the rickety wagon just outside the door, bent down to pick up the wet and blood-covered figure of the white-haired Ethelred, and carried him gently inside. He placed him gently upon the reeds before the fire, then knelt down beside him.

"They came. Who came?" Rowena knew the answer before the words were out.

"The prince's men. They claimed the cottage, our poor little cottage and . . . and threw us out into the storm."

"Damn them!" Rowena's face flushed with anger. What kind of man would steal the cottage of an old woman and an old man? What kind of monster would want to harm two gentle old souls? "Is no one safe from that reptile's evil? No, of course not." Regaining control of her emotions, she sought once again to calm her old nurse, giving the woman a sip of the hot wine. "Here, it will be all right," she crooned, not believing her own words even for a moment.

"No! No! Nothing will ever be right again," Gwyneth gasped, casting her eyes towards her husband. His face was deathly pale, his features contorted in a grimace of the pain he had suffered, his hand still clutched at his chest. "They killed him. He had not the strength to do battle and yet he fought them for my sake." She seemed on the verge of collapse and Rowena could only guess at the furor they must have been engulfed in.

"I warned you, Father. Do you now urge me to 'have a care'?" she raged, gently mopping the damp from Gwyneth's brow. *Oh, if only I were a man I would show them all,* she thought sourly. But she wasn't. She was a woman, condemned by the skirts she was forced to wear. All she could do was to buzz around the prince's men like a gnat, annoying and humiliating them. She hadn't the power to fight, at least not hard enough to make a difference.

"Rowena, there wasn't anything that you or I could have done." Sir William's tone sounded as if he were talking to a child. "I know the world can sometimes be cruel but—"

"But nothing!" Though she knew it to be disrespectful Rowena muttered beneath her breath, "Cowards, every one."

This time she went too far and her words sparked her father's anger. "Daughter, hold your tongue!" For just a moment it seemed that William would strike her, but his raised hand fell uselessly at his side. "You . . . you are too young to understand."

"Too . . ." Rowena grew suddenly silent as she thought she heard a deep gurgle come from Ethelred's throat. Hurrying to his side she put her head to his chest, listening for the beat of his heart. There was no beat, only the steady gaze of Ethelred's eyes that frightened her, as if he was seeing beyond her into another world. "Ethelred . . ."

Not wanting to admit to the reality of Ethelred's death, Gwyneth threw herself forward, grabbing for his hand. "Husband. Husband, speak to me." Like a woman possessed she pushed at his chest, trying hard to make him come alive again.

It was no use. He was dead. There was nothing anyone could do.

"Poor old soul. He who never harmed a living soul." Sir William reached out his big hands, closing the old man's eyelids.

"Noooooooooo!" A shriek tore from Gwyneth's lips, such a mournful sound that Rowena's flesh prickled with goosebumps. Throwing herself upon her husband's body, the woman's sorrow was so agonizing that it was contagious.

Though she rarely cried, Rowena felt the sting of tears to her eyes. Ethelred had gathered the straightest twigs for her when she was a child. He had helped her form her first arrows. He had fashioned a small bow for her from the branch of a willow tree. Could she ever forget all his stories as she sat upon his knee? No. He was like the grandfather she had never had, like the image of what men could be—peaceful and kind.

"It . . . isn't . . . fair . . ."

"Life rarely is, Rowena," her father answered. "You will of course stay here with us, Gwyneth," he offered, turning away suddenly to hide his own misty eyes.

"Stay?" She looked towards the door, then to him, then back again. Where else could she go?

"Yes, stay," Rowena intoned, laying her hand upon the woman's shoulder. "I need you. You are like the mother that I never had."

Despite the sorrow of the moment, Sir William's face brightened. "Aye. Rowena needs you, I need you. You can teach my daughter how to cook and sew and tend the herb

garden. Forsooth, you can teach her your gentle ways."
He laid his hand upon her shoulder. "Please stay."

Rowena knew very well that her old nurse had nowhere
else to go. Even so, Gwyneth's facial features were a mask
of dignity as she raised her head. "If 'tis charity, then the
answer is no."

"Charity, no . . ." Rowena grasped the skinny fingers,
squeezing tightly. "I love you, Gwyneth. I always have."

"Aye, and I repeat, we need you." Exhibiting a rare
humility, Sir William knelt beside the newly-made widow.
"Our home shall be yours once again."

"At least until you are avenged for this dreadful evil and
your rightful property is restored to you," Rowena rasped.
She ignored her father's furled brows as she made her
own plans in the darkest corners of her mind. Let the
others whisper caution and hide their hands behind their
backs. She, Rowena, Lady of Grantham Manor, would
never again rest until she saw that this wrong was put to
right.

The inner courtyard rang with the sound of dogs, horses
and men. The castle carpenters, crossbow makers, blacksmiths and armorers were busy at their work. Everyone
knew his job and nervously sought to do that job well. In
truth, even the gong farmer who emptied the latrine pit
was busy with his bucket and shovel. Walking hurriedly
about Kendrick sought out each and every worker, anxiously questioning them about what they might have heard
or seen.

"I am searching for a young archer," he declared, making a guess as to the lad's height and gesturing with his
hand. "About this tall. He would have ridden through the
gate in a frantic hurry."

"Lad?" Raising his hammer and chisel, the armorer
thought a moment then shook his head. "Nay."

Approaching the carpenter at work with his ax on a

large piece of oak, he tried again. "I must find the young archer who rode into the courtyard this morning. Have you seen him and if so, where did the boy go?"

"Boy?" The air resounded with a loud thud as the carpenter's ax struck the wood. "Haven't seen one, unless you mean the boys playing with tops over there."

Turning his head, Kendrick was disappointed when he saw that the lads the carpenter spoke of were little more than babes. Nor did Chadwick or Humbley have any better luck. Seemingly the young archer was as elusive among a forest of people as he had been among the trees.

"How could he not have been noticed?" Kendrick kicked at the dirt in anger. "God's blood, he rode through the gate in the light of day, then just up and vanished."

"Aye, but how? We were following on his heels," Chadwick puzzled.

"And we didn't see him ride forth, therefore . . ." Humbley smiled. "He has to be within these walls somewhere."

Kendrick folded his arms across his chest. "Aye, he cannot have ridden out, lest we would have seen him." All they had seen was the departure of the frowning old knight and his spirited daughter. A departure that Kendrick had little time to mourn considering the circumstances and the precarious position he found himself in. He had come back to the castle emptyhanded.

"Soooo . . ." Chadwick grinned. "All that must be done is to ferret the little bow-carrying rat out."

A procedure that was carried out immediately. Guards were posted on the walls and at the gatehouse. Within the castle's sturdy walls these gates could become deadly traps. Only the most determined invasion force could enter the castle once the garrison had secured its stronghold, as it did now. Moreover, the gatehouse was also the castle prison. The towers' massive construction could keep prisoners in just as effectively as they kept invaders out.

"The lad has insured his own doom." A thought that

strangely gave Kendrick mixed feelings. He was angry, of a certainty, but enough so to long for the lad's death?

Involuntarily he stared up at the town gate where grisly sights greeted the traders and troops who passed through. Staring down from pikes high on the walls were the ghoulishly grinning heads of those deemed to be traitors. Below, in the ditch, stood the gallows and pillory, reminding the townsfolk of the severe punishments for breaking the law.

"I'll ask John to be lenient." Perhaps a mere stay in the pillory would teach the young archer a lesson. He could only hope that would be so. It was the punishment that Kendrick suggested as he put the scrap of brown wool into the prince's hands.

"Nay!" John had other ideas. Looking at Kendrick he raised one eyebrow in a gesture of displeasure. "I must catch him and make of him an example."

"An example . . ." The way John said the word gave him shivers. At that moment Kendrick deeply regretted having set the wheel of so-called justice in motion.

"Aye, a lesson to all the outlaws who so outrageously roam about my forests." His lips thinned as he grimaced. "Archer. Archer, so you say. No doubt he is one of Robin Hood's ragged band." Hissing with anger he enlightened Kendrick as to that hated outlaw's antics then, walking to the window of the meeting chamber, he opened the wooden shutter and looked out upon the courtyard.

"Perhaps the lad is but emulating this Hood fellow. From what you say he has established himself as the common man's hero."

"Hero!" For just a moment it appeared that John would lose all semblance of self-control. "He is a thief, a nuisance, and a traitor. One for whom I would give anything that I own. Ah, to see him hanged."

The way he said the word caused Kendrick to reach up and touch his throat. Once again he regretted having drawn attention to the bow-wielding lad. The boy had been annoying to be sure, yet had his mischief really done

Kendrick any real harm? Struggling with his conscience, he was about to plead once more for clemency on the boy's behalf when John craftily changed the subject.

"Ah, but let us not talk of punishments at the moment when we can speak of rewards."

"Rewards . . ."

"Your lands, de Bron. I promised you that they would be given back and so it is done. The usurpers have been driven off. A mistake has been corrected." He turned his head, waiting in expectation for an outpouring of gratitude that was not forthcoming, then said simply, "For, you see, I forgive you for the matter of Marian."

Kendrick's jaw tightened. He would make no apologies to any man, even a prince.

"Let us say then that you owe me, de Bron. Favor for favor. You owe me!"

The words rang hauntingly in Kendrick's ears long after he had left the chamber.

Chapter Eight

It was good to be home! Good to wake up in her own bed. Lying on her side, Rowena snuggled amidst the blankets like a caterpiller in its cocoon, thankful to have a soft mattress and peaceful quietude. Indeed there was only the crowing of a rooster to disturb her slumber. She was content, peaceful, that is until the events which had taken place the previous day snapped into her head.

"The cottage!" She sat up, so quickly that her head spun. How selfish of her to have put it out of her thoughts for longer than a moment. Swallowing hard she crossed herself. "Poor old Ethelred!" Poor Gwyneth.

She felt a physical ache at the finality of what had happened. It wasn't fair! Gwyneth and her husband had been kind and gentle people. They had not deserved such violence to shatter both their lives, death for the dear old man and widowhood for his wife. How had it happened? Why?

"Dear God!"

Rowena remembered how elated Gwyneth had been at the thought of having her own home. She had looked forward to the future with hope and gratitude, thankful to Sir William for his generosity. How was she to have known that her father's act would end up in tragedy?

The cottage and the land upon which it had been built was located between Grantham Manor and the neighboring Melburn Manor. For years its ownership had been in question, her father insisting it to be part of his land, the neighboring absentee lord determined to claim it for his heirs. The prince had been asked to intercede, cunningly using it like a carrot to dangle in front of her father's nose. For the last few years it had been under Sir William's control, and now without warning it had been wrenched away. But why?

Because of me?

Her face flushed with warmth as she reflected on her mischievous plotting and scheming. She had thought herself to be so clever, daring and brave. She had taken on the prince's men, provoking and ensnaring her quarry. Little had she realized that there might be a consequence to her deeds.

For a long while Rowena was as still as a stone, going over in her mind every minute detail of what had transpired. She had cautiously tucked her hair under a hat or hood, kept her face in the shadows, and lowered her voice when she talked. How then could anyone have guessed?

It *wasn't* possible. There was no way that her identity could have been discovered. Had the prince even a wit of suspicion as to who the mysterious archer was, he would have sent those men to the manor to capture her and take her back to Nottingham. Then why . . . ?

The more she wondered, the more the answer became obvious. John had sent his henchmen to the cottage to do just what he did. Steal it! "To reward some lord or other for obeying the prince's whims."

Maybe you will realize now, Father. The prince was evil personified and a man who had to be stopped before it was too late. As long as he was in power, no one was safe.

It was a chilling thought that shattered her false sense of peace. Rising from the bed, snatching up her clothes from a peg beside the bed, dressing hurriedly, Rowena moved to the doorway, strangely compelled to visit the scene of last night's crime.

Alternating between walking and running, Rowena reached the small dwelling, pausing as its thatched roof came into view. *Strange, how peaceful the cottage looks* she thought upon her arrival. Silhouetted against the soft pink glow of the sky, the cottage's wattle and daub walls, the trees surrounding it and the cool brook that babbled nearby, gave the semblance that all was well.

Pushing aside a branch, Rowena cursed when it snapped back and hit her in the face, then made her way to the cottage's small wooden door. Pushing inside she surveyed the scene, clenching her teeth in disgust as she viewed the damage.

"The bastards!"

Debris was scattered everywhere. There were broken chairs, splinters of wood, shards of broken pottery. A wooden chest had been pried open, the garments inside torn and tossed wildly about. With a sigh she bent down, trying as best she could to salvage at least a few of Gwyneth's belongings, cooking utensils, a wooden mug, a discarded hooded cloak, a mismatched pair of shoes, stockings, a tunic that had been Ethelred's finest, a woven basket, some ribbons bought on market day.

"Poor Gwyneth, what does she have now?" Very little to call her own. The woman had been uprooted as surely as if a bolt of lightning had struck her home. A lightning bolt that had a name—John.

Vengeance controlled Rowena's thoughts. How dare he do such a terrible thing? "Prince Loathsome, oh but you will pay." It was written, an eye for an eye.

With a gesture of defiance she clenched her hand into a fist and raised it high. John no doubt thought that there was no one to take retribution, that no one would care about the injustice dealt out to mere Saxons. Well, he was wrong. She cared and because of that she was determined to strike back.

"Perhaps sooner than I could have supposed!"

Turning her head she stiffened as she listened. Horses! Springing to her feet, she moved quickly to the door, peering out. Specks moved across the horizon. "A hunting party!" No, the prince was up to hawking today. Even from a distance she could see the birds of prey, clutching to their owners' wrists. Rowena counted the number of men—two, three, five, each with the type of bird that exhibited the owner's rank in society. A king hunted with a gyrfalcon, a lord with a peregrine falcon, a woman with a hawk.

"You are after small prey, John." Birds of prey were carefully trained to catch smaller birds, hares or rabbits. "As for me, I am after larger quarry!"

Did she dare? It would be five against one. Dangerous. Were she to be caught, the penalty would be severe. Even poachers who were apprehended were punished severely, either by hanging or by having their right hand cut off. What would happen to her for harassing the self-proclaimed ruler of the realm?

Hurrying back towards her father's manor in search of her bow, Rowena refused to even contemplate such a dastardly fate. She was far too clever to be caught.

The oak and pine trees were thick and brilliant green. Sparkling with moisture from a recent rain, they glistened in the sunlight as if bedecked with jewels. It was tranquil, deceptively peaceful. As Kendrick de Bron rode alongside the hunting party he felt mildly optimistic. And why not? John had promised to restore Kendrick's lands and titles and, BiGod, he had kept his word. Last night the usurpers had been sent packing, leaving the way clear for him to take possession of his rightful lands.

"Well, what think you, de Bron?" Prince John made a

wide sweep with his arm, pointing to his generous gift, acre upon acre of gently rolling hills and meadowland and a huge lake. Beside the lake was the manor that once belonged to Kendrick's aunt and uncle, and a small cottage.

The manor was quite impressive, consisting of a total of twelve hides of arable land besides sixteen acres of meadow and four acres of pasture. The manor house itself was of wood with stone foundations and a thatched roof that unfortunately was vulnerable to sparks. Built back a little from the banks of the water, midway between the fields but far away from the mud and dust, it was a blessed sight.

"I think that I am a most grateful man, your Grace." And he was, but also wary. Even so, it felt good to know that for once justice had been meted out, at least to him. "I had nearly forgotten just how beautiful it was here."

"Aye. Beautiful. And an excellent place for hunting and hawking." Because it was nestled at the edge of the forest, Kendrick's land was unfortunately also convenient to the Prince.

"An excellent place indeed," Kendrick replied. John was hinting none too subtly for an offer of hospitality that Kendrick could not refuse. Alas, he would have to lodge not only the prince but the two members of the royal party when the day's hunting and hawking was done. "And my home is your home."

The generosity was not twofold. John's laws forbade anyone to enter a royal forest with bow, arrows, dogs or greyhounds, save with special warrant. No one but the king and those authorized by him, not even the barons who held the land, could hunt the red deer, fallow deer, the roe or wild boar without John's permission. Indeed, no one dared, save one—Robin Hood.

There was something chilling in the prince's grin. "A kindly offer, though not unwarranted seeing as how it is by my hand that your property has been given back to you."

"I hope returning it to me did not create too much ill will." Pulling back on the reins of his mount, Kendrick straightened his back and sat tall in the saddle, affording his eyes full benefit of the magnificent view. Even if it had created hard feelings, what did it matter? This was his land again. His!

Shaking his head, Prince John insisted it had been no trouble at all. "The inhabitants were naught but Saxons," he exclaimed, forgetting for the moment that Kendrick was half-Saxon. "An old man and an old woman who were of little consequence to anyone. Indeed, they had no claim to the property at all. Trespassers is all that they were."

"I see." Kendrick felt a surge of sympathy he dared not show. He had assumed that some haughty Norman lordling or other had been given the land and that had filled him with indignant anger. Now, realizing that an old Saxon couple had been forced from the land wiped away any angry feelings. He could only hope that the pair had not been dealt with too harshly. He would not have wanted that.

"But come, let us have no more talk." The bells on the falcon jingled as John raised his padded glove. Special equipment was used to train and look after prized birds of prey. A leash stopped the bird from flying away, bells helped to find it if it became lost, a hood kept it calm, a leather purse contained a tasty reward for a hunt well done. "I want to show you something special."

For just a moment a serene stillness echoed through the forest, a stillness that was rudely shattered as the prince removed the hood of his gyrfalcon. "After him, Mordred!" he demanded, looking upwards as a wide-winged gray bird winged its way overhead. The four men watched as the hawk followed its prey, soaring and darting with a swiftness that spoke of death to the victim. The silence of the woods resounded with the shriek of the dove as it suffered a mortal wound.

Kendrick watched as the falcon and its victim swooped

down, the hawk dropping the dove at the feet of its master. It reminded him of how the Normans had come from beyond the seas, grabbing their Saxon neighbors by the throat.

"You have trained your hawk well, my lord," Kendrick assessed as he surveyed the scene. He decided quickly that he had no love for this sport of hawking. He preferred to do his own hunting, not leave it up to a bird.

"Ah, that I could train these pesky Saxons as well," John mumbled beneath his breath.

"Ah, yes the 'pesky' Saxons," Kendrick mumbled, barely keeping his temper in check.

The prince was peevish. "If you ask me, my brother has been much too soft on the lot of them. A few thrashes of the lash would do much to cool their haughty manners."

"They are a proud people," Kendrick whispered in his people's defense. They had been humbled, robbed and overrun, but they somehow managed to hold on to at least a shred of their dignity.

"Proud? Bah. They are fools. How else could we have so easily vanquished them?"

A slight breeze whispered through the branches of the trees, tingling Kendrick's angrily flushed face with its chilled breath, stirring wisps of his dark hair. There was a quiet all about, like the stillness before a storm, yet not a cloud marked the sky. At least until the blare of a hunter's horn shattered the reverie of the forest. Kendrick watched as a flock of birds, frenzied by sudden fear, burst forth from a nearby thicket to take flight.

"My lord, there is something in the underbrush," one of the prince's men insisted.

"Nay. However . . ." John motioned for one of his pages to investigate, muttering, "Aha," when the culprit was caught.

"A boy!" Kendrick rasped. A lad of not more than eight or nine. His hands were clasped tightly to a small hare he had snared and he was terrified, as well he should be. The penalty for catching the king's rabbit would be horrible, and all because of his hunger.

"You. Boy. What have you there?" Like a preening peacock, John paraded on horseback before the lad.

"I . . . I . . ." Turning, his wide eyes upon the mounted men, the boy gave in to his fright, setting his feet in motion with mindless terror. Stumbling over the root of a great tree, he fell with a sickening thud.

"Trapped, BiGod!" Nor was the boy alone. Nearby a young girl who looked to be his sister lay hidden. "Ah look, a pretty bird, to be sure."

"Pretty, but only a child," Kendrick said quickly. Immediately all his protective instincts were on the alert.

"Pray, do not touch me." This young girl's fears need not be as much for her life as for her virtue. It was well known that Prince John thought any Saxon maid to be his for the taking. That was why Kendrick thought the girl suddenly screamed, but as he looked in the direction of her eyes he saw there was a far different cause. A huge boar pawed the earth a few yards from where her brother lay. The massive, hairy creature was snorting and slavering as it glared at him. Paralyzed with fear, the boy could do little except stare into the cold, tiny eyes of the beast.

"Run, Wesley! Run!" the girl yelled.

"R-r-run!" the boy repeated, moving to obey.

"No, don't. Stay right where you are," Kendrick advised, knowing that any sudden movement would goad the beast into attack. If it did, it would be certain death for the child, for the tusks of the wild pig were like twin spears. "My lord . . ." He looked towards the prince, certain that even he wouldn't just stand by and watch the boy die, but he was to be disappointed.

"Looks like we won't have to punish that one, eh my lord," guffawed one of the prince's men. Leaning forward, he stared upon the scene as if preparing to watch a jousting tournament.

"BiGod, Sir Griffin, it seems we've been offered a bit of

unexpected excitement," John chortled, slapping his thigh with his hand. Likewise the other two men prepared themselves for the "entertainment".

Except Kendrick. He knew he had to do something whether John liked it or not. Unlike the others he could never watch such a slaughter. "Boy. Now listen to me. You have to move, albeit very, very care—" A whistling sound tore through the air before he had a chance to finish his advice, then before Kendrick could even react, another.

"BiGod! Who—?" Prince John swore loudly as the boar collapsed into a heap on the ground. His eyes darted left and right, looking for the boy's benefactor. "Someone shot those arrows . . ."

"Aye. Me!"

Kendrick's gaze lifted to the branches of a tree. Though the face was carefully hidden by a hood he could see the grin on the face that looked down at him. "You!" Oh, he recognized the little imp all right.

The archer was just as surprised. "I remember you!"

"You seem fond of lurking in trees." Well, if the lad had a thimble's full of sense he would soon get himself gone. Though he had done a noble thing in saving the life of a child, it was still true that the young archer had just killed an animal that was perilously close to the prince's forest. "Get you gone and quickly," he hissed, "or you will find yourself hanging at the end of a rope."

Alas, it was too late. His were not the only eyes that were turned in the lad's direction. "After him," John proclaimed. "After the poacher!"

The air resounded with the thundering sound of hooves. "Stop, in the name of the king!"

Only Kendrick resisted being drawn into the chase. His attention was focused on the two children, whom he promptly ordered to flee. It was an order that was quickly obeyed. Stumbling to his feet, jumping over the carcass of the bloody animal, the boy named Wesley grasped the girl by the hand and took to his heels. Meanwhile the young archer purposefully kept the prince's men occupied with a game of chase.

"For the love of Becket, can't anyone catch him?" Prince John put heel to his horse's flanks with thought in mind of his own pursuit of the culprit, but he too was unsuccessful. Laughter bubbled forth from the archer's throat all the while.

This time Kendrick wasn't angry. Nuisance or not, he admired the lad. Surely he had been on target with his bow. Moreover he had shown a courage that was surprising in one so young.

"De Bron!"

"Aye, my lord."

John's voice was a shriek. "He is on your land, albeit he is your poacher. It is up to you to catch him."

Catch him? Ah yes, Kendrick wanted very much to do that, but no, he would not turn the boy into John. Instead he would handle the young archer himself. Even so, he had to make a worthy effort at pursuit while John sat astride his horse watching.

In the tense moment that followed her daring rescue of the two Saxon children, Rowena thought of nothing but escape. Though there were a few harrowing moments, however, she outdistanced, out-maneuvered and outwitted her pursuer. Still, she knew that she would not really be safe until she reached the thick wooden doors of Grantham Manor. With that comforting thought in mind, she plunged directly into the thick leafy undergrowth.

Moving quickly, jumping over logs, ducking branches, swinging from limb to limb she was lithe, swift, skilled and graceful. At last, panting to catch her breath, she paused to look behind her.

"I've lost him!" She was surprised that her dark-haired adversary had so easily given up the chase, yet smug with the satisfaction of knowing that he would no doubt be in line for retribution. John hated defeat.

Chuckling as she made her way back to her father's house, she conjured up the overbold swain's moment of humiliation. John would yell, he would scold. He would take the haughty lord down more than just a peg. It would be a miserable ride back to John's castle. Well, he deserved it!

Stealthfully keeping to the shadows as she headed for the manor stables, Rowena tried to convince herself that she should be glad that she was well rid of the dark-haired lord who had accosted her in the castle. He was cold-hearted, a brute.

"And yet . . ." Had she imagined it or had there really been a look of concern on his face when those two Saxon children had been in peril? Was it possible that a follower of John's could have even a whit of empathy?

The stable was cool, pleasant at this particular hour. Hurriedly stripping off her archer's garments and hiding them beneath a pile of hay, then donning her "lady's" attire, she pondered the matter.

Suddenly one of the horses snuffled at the air and pricked up his ears, alert.

"What is it, Joust?" Instantly she was on guard, but not quickly enough to escape the hand that roughly grasped her by the shoulder.

"Well, well, well . . ."

Slowly she turned around, stunned to find herself face to face with the very man she had assumed would be out of her hair for well and for good. Her body taut as a bowstring, her senses tingling, she nevertheless fought against her surprise as she demanded, "Unhand me!"

"BiGod!" Slowly he trailed his fingers over her shoulder and down her arm, his touch melting through her flesh. Then he let her go.

There was a long moment of immobility as they stood frozen, silent, like figures woven on a tapestry. And all the while a knot squeezed in the pit of Rowena's stomach. Had she been followed after all? Had he seen her?

"What are yy-you doing here?" Was the tremor in her voice noticeable?

"I might ask you the same thing," he shot back, mellowing her concern. And all the while he stared. She was a pretty sight with her hair flying all about her face and shoulders, her clothing all askew, beads of perspiration dotting her forehead. He had forgotten just how pretty.

"I live here!" So, he hadn't any idea of her earlier escapade. She felt relieved.

He smiled, genuinely pleased by that bit of information. "Well then, I can only say that it is a small world." Wrapping his fingers in her hair, he took a step forward.

"Too small!" Rowena jumped back so quickly that she caused him to pull her hair. She winced but didn't cry out.

"I would say delightfully small." He laughed, a deep throaty sound that made her feel foolishly giddy. He reached out and took her hand, rubbing his thumb over her fingers. "I didn't think I would see you again."

She stared into his eyes, mesmerized by the shiver that rippled through her, a feeling that was strangely similar to the surge of excitement she had felt earlier in the forest when she had toyed with danger.

"But I am ever so pleased that I have." He stroked her hair, then gently cupped her chin in his hand. Raising her reluctant face to his he moved forward, intending to kiss her.

"Nay!" Remembering the other time, Rowena pulled violently away. "I am no kitchen maid whose favors are yours for the taking."

"Nor did I think you to be." Kendrick likewise remembered their previous encounter. "If I offended you at the castle then I sincerely apologize." Grabbing both her wrists he made certain she would not punch him this time, then he smothered any further conversation with his lips.

Rowena made a murmuring sound of protest, then answered the pressure of his mouth. In truth she couldn't have spoken even if she had wanted to. His mouth was gentle, strangely so. Rowena felt her heart race, then she feared it had stopped beating at all. She was breathless. Her mind was numb. Something was happening, something over which she had no control. Something frightening.

Kendrick felt her tremble. This time it was he who moved away. "Well, so much for neighborly introductions," he breathed.

"Neighborly?" She didn't understand, at least not at first. Slowly, however, it began to dawn on her consciousness. "Neighbor. You?"

He nodded enthusiastically, elated by the thought of such good fortune. His land restored and the lovely woman of his dreams living right next door. What more could a man ask for? "I'm the new resident lord of Melburn Manor," he said proudly.

"Melburn?"

"The property to your north side," he defined, just in case she didn't know.

She pointed. "There." Her anger surged all the way from her head to her toes. She should have guessed, should have known.

"Aye!"

Her eyes glittered with fire, yet at the same time they were so cold that he felt a chill. "So . . ."

Painfully Rowena closed her eyes, envisioning Gwyneth's mournful face, Ethelred's motionless body, and the mess that had been made of the cottage. In that moment she was certain that she truly hated the man standing beside her.

"Then 'tis you who are so cruel."

"Cruel?"

She didn't bother explaining, instead she merely wiped off his kiss with the back of her hand.

Kendrick winced at the vehemence of her action but ignored the gesture. "I came today to make introductions."

"And well you did!" Again she brushed at her mouth with her hand. "Now, get you gone!"

"Go?" He fought to somehow salvage his wounded pride. "Without giving my proper regards to your father?"

"Aye." Never had Rowena longed so for the blessed clout of a bow. How quickly then would he have scurried off! "For he has less tolerance for men such as you than I."

"Men such as me?" Now it was Kendrick's turn to be angry.

Rowena was not in the mood for a serious confrontation. Not now. She was anxious to get away. "Forsooth, you would not understand." He was a Norman, the so-called favored inhabitants of the land. He would never know what it was like to be part Saxon and part Norman, nor what it was like to have constant warfare going on inside your head. Unceremoniously she pushed past him, moving towards the stable door.

"Wait!" He was irritated and at the same time intrigued. "Come back!"

"Never!" With a toss of her hair she was gone.

Kendrick spoke to the door. "Run away then, but I will be back." Sooner than she might suppose.

Chapter Nine

It had proven to be a relatively mild winter with rain but little snow, the kind of weather that would have made it relatively easy for Kendrick de Bron to get his home in order had there been enough men on the manor to do the work. Alas, there were not. Although there were several dwellings that looked as if they had been lived in not long ago, there were only three men and their families here now. Those families left exhibited a mistrust that could be felt even from a distance.

"Something frightened the others off, but what?" Kendrick would have given a barrel full of coins to know.

"Ghosts?" Tramping through the ankle-deep mud, Humbley paused to look over his shoulder.

"Nay!" Chad had never been a superstitious soul. "I would say that whatever chased them away was a being of flesh and blood."

"You mean John?" Kendrick was more than a bit suspicious.

"Or his behavior," Chadwick insisted.

"Well, whatever it was it means that those of us left will

have to do at least twice as much work." Kendrick hadn't
come this far to let all of his dreams fall to ruin.

Picking up a carpenter's adze, Kendrick moved towards
the manor house. Chadwick and Humbley followed, carrying hammers, a gimlet to make small holes in the wood,
and a sack full of wooden pegs and nails. Together they
made much needed repairs to the timber-framed manor
house. Next the thatched roof was patched so that it would
be weather-tight. As soon as that had been accomplished,
they picked up shovels to dig deep ditches around the
garden to keep the animals out. Kendrick intended to
make improvements such as widening the stream, making
a fish pond, constructing a bridge and other structural
changes to the manor house once that was done.

"Work, work, work!" Wiping his sweat-beaded brow,
Humbley made no secret of his dismay.

All along the way to Kendrick's restored lands, Humbley
and Chadwick had tried to envision what their new manor
would be like, deciding in unison that it would certainly
be more elegant than their living quarters in France. After
all, they couldn't imagine their lord de Bron in any setting
which was not in keeping with his fondness for finery.

"Our lord does love his elegant life all right," Chadwick
grumbled under his breath, wiping his dirt-stained hands
on the hem of his tunic.

Kendrick sensed their peevishness but had no choice
but to prod them along anyway. He intended to be a resident lord at his own manor and wanted to oversee things
himself even if it did mean more than just a few blisters.
And after all, if hard work was good enough for him, it
was good enough for the men who served him. Was it not?

"Merry-go-up! You are so hard at work that you must
indeed be frightfully thirsty."

Glancing up, Kendrick hoped to see his lovely neighbor
standing there but saw a tall, red-haired, buxom young
woman standing there instead. Her smile exhibited a
crooked front tooth as she waved at Kendrick.

"And just who might you be?" Kendrick didn't recognize her.

"Allow me to introduce myself." She clutched at her dark brown skirt. "Maida. I . . . I am Rowena Fitz Hugh's . . ." She thought a moment before saying, "Companion."

"Companion." The white linen cap that covered her head, the plain cloth of her dress and the bucket she was carrying declared her to be some sort of serving girl. Nevertheless, he played along, thinking it a wise matter to ingratiate himself with the young woman. It might well give him a spying eye and ear inside his neighbor's manor.

"Aye." She crossed her fingers. "Rowena and I are as close as this."

"Indeed." Kendrick watched as she sauntered over to the nearby stream to fill her empty bucket. The water was cool and refreshing, quenching his parched throat and tongue. "Then I must suppose that you can easily tell me of her comings and goings." He suggestively raised one brow, then with a smile plopped a gold coin in her hand.

The red-haired woman was quick to catch on to his meaning and more than eager to be a tattle-tale. "I do suppose that I could."

So began their association, one which allowed Kendrick to bump into Rowena Fitz Hugh at every turn. Though Maida was clearly disappointed at first that the manor lord was not interested in her, her ego and pride were soon soothed by the attentions of Chadwick and Humbley.

Though it was winter and there were no flowers to pick, Humbley bought the young woman ribbons at the fair, Chadwick a bag full of fresh-smelling herbs to sweeten the smell of her underthings.

Maida responded in kind, baking pastries and collecting eggs for their breakfast, much to the amusement of Kendrick.

"Did you see the tart Maida baked just for me?" Humbley bragged, licking his fingers.

"Tart? Why 'tis surely not as tasty as the prune pudding

that she gave to me." Chadwick naughtily thumbed his nose.

"Th-that pudding was surely meant for me!"

Back and forth the two men verbally tussled. Kendrick watched as the two servants nearly got into a fistfight over who was the favored swain, then turning his back, began to chuckle. Leave it to a woman to turn a reasonably sane man into a stuttering fool. Well, that would not happen to him. He would court Rowena Fitz Hugh in such a manner that she would be the one stuttering over him. On that point he was determined.

Oh, what a small world it was! So small that it seemed Rowena was destined to bump into the irritating Kendrick de Bron over and over again, at the lake, the mill, and the fair. Oh, irony of ironies that he was their neighbor. Without even waiting for poor Ethelred's body to grow cold in his grave, the usurper had boldly moved lock, stock and barrel onto his ill-gotten manor house, digging and hammering. Oh, what a villain, albeit a villain who would be hard pressed to find workers for his manor. Poetic justice. A justice goaded on by Rowena, who had cunningly bribed and cajoled the Melburn workers to cross over to Grantham Manor's workforce.

"And, 'tis but the beginning, de Bron." Kendrick de Bron, she winced as she whispered his name, refusing to give even a moment's thought to the second kiss that they shared. De Bron must be repaid in kind for what had happened to Gwyneth and Ethelred. "De Bron, a most worthy puppet for John, the puppet master."

Nor was Ethelred the only victim of John and his cronies. All over England there were others of Saxon blood whose possessions were being stripped from them to give to John's cowardly crew. Well, John and the others had better beware. Rowena was determined to show him. She would show them all.

It was a matter that had been given significant thought. "Though my head will be in the hangman's noose if I am caught," she breathed, realizing that what she planned to do was no longer "child's play". From now on she was not going to go up against John's men whenever she had a whim. She intended to go up against him on a much larger scale. Her escapade when she had saved those two young Saxons, had made her realize how dearly she was needed. Robin Hood haunted Sherwood Forest, but there was no one to watch over the Saxons here at least until now.

Rising from her bed, Rowena took a linen chemise from her servant's outstretched hands, slipping the garment quickly over her naked body before the chill of the winter morning air could touch her. Washing her face in a basin of cold water, prepared by her servant, Maida, Rowena thought carefully. Should she join with other rebels or work entirely on her own? Strike at night or during the day? Should she tell her father or keep the secret to herself? Most importantly, how was she going to dispense with Maida's services so that she would be free to come and go without arousing curiosity? She dare not trust Maida with the truth, for the young woman often ran on with her tongue. Moreover, the young woman had been much too curious as to her comings and goings of late.

In truth, I can trust no one. It was a sobering thought.

"Maida."

"Aye, my lady."

Reaching for the towel the girl held out to her, Rowena attacked the situation as delicately as she could. "From now on I will not require your services in dressing. There will be no need for you to come to my chamber unless you are called."

"No need?" Maida was flustered, totally unprepared to be dismissed. "But, my lady—" She hung her head like an errant child. "Have I done something to offend you?"

Rowena shook her head, thought she could have sworn that the girl's face was marked by a guilty expression. "No, you have pleased me well. It is just that I am quite capable of dressing myself and . . . and there may be times when I will be up and about later than usual.''

"Later?" The young woman's eyes were slits of suspicion. "And just where might you be going?"

Rowena thought quickly. She could not take the chance of Maida discovering her climbing in the window dressed as a lad some fine morning, but what could she say? What reason could she give for her sudden need for privacy?

Maida, a lusty one to be sure, answered for her. "Oh, my lady has a knight."

"A knight?" Rowena recovered quickly. The more she thought about it the more convincing it sounded.

"Aye, that's it. A lover." Maida giggled like a child. A quizzical look came into the servant girl's eyes, as if trying to ascertain the identity of Rowena's nightly suitor. Then with a coy smile she breathed out a name. "Is it Kendrick de Bron?"

"What?"

Twittering at her very mention of his name, Maida made it obvious that she was well aware of that man's charms. "It is, I feel it in my bones."

"Aye." Oh, how such a lie galled her. The very name made Rowena stiffen with resentment; still, she managed to keep her poise. His name was as good as any other and in truth she could not think of another. That name would have to do. "De Bron!"

Lover indeed and de Bron be damned. Rowena was determined that she would be hung before romping about in some hay loft or succumbing to the likes of a man like her neighbor. Still, she played along. "There are times when I . . . I sneak out the window to meet with him."

"As well any woman would."

Being a lusty wench, always available for a toss in the hay, Maida was quick to believe the excuse. "I have an interest or two myself."

For just a moment Rowena felt a stab of jealousy as she

imagined that interest to be Kendrick de Bron. Between
gritted teeth she said, "You will not tell?"

Maida winked. "Nay, I will breathe n'er a word."

"And I will see that your silence is rewarded."

"I've seen him, you know."

"I might well suppose that you had."

Maida's expression took on the look of a love-sick cow.
"He's handsome." Rowena clenched her teeth as she
answered, "yes . . . yes, indeed he is." Anxious to be rid of
Maida's chattering, trying to control her ire she whispered,
"but how tired I am of hearing women tell me that. You
may go, Maida." She gestured towards the door with the
stern order, "do not rattle your tongue about it." Even as
she spoke she perceived that to be a futile command. By
tomorrow it would be the talk of the manor. Ah well. What
did it matter? She certainly had no intention of seeing that
haughty lord again. Why, even the mention of his name
put her in a foul mood. Her hands shook, her heart beat
irratically. Closing her eyes she seemed to see his arrogantly
grinning face staring at her.

Suddenly the walls of the room seemed to be closing in
on her. She was anxious to be out and about. Going to
her clothes chest, she picked up her kirtle and donned it
quickly, then tied her girdle around her waist. Kendrick
de Bron indeed!

The glow from the still lit wall sconces flickered on the
wall she ascended the stairs. Step by step she forced
herself into a calmer mood, a humor that was shattered
as she caught sight of a visitor to the manor. It couldn't
be. How would he dare! Not after what he had done. "De
Bron!"

"Ah, Rowena, so there you are." Her father, unlike
Rowena, was in a congenial mood. "Look, we have a
caller." He patted the interloper on the shoulder.

"So I see," she replied icily, running a nervous hand
over her rumpled kirtle. Why was de Bron staring at her
so?

"My Lady." Kendrick gave a nod of his head, enchanted by the vision she made with her hair slightly tangled and her eyes flashing daggers at him. Damn, but he was attracted to the willful little chit. She reminded him of a mischievous elf. So much so that he grinned.

That smile goaded Rowena into rudeness. "So, de Bron. Have you come to steal our land and manor from *us* too?"

The question took Kendrick totally by surprise. "I beg your pardon."

"Rowena!" Sir William was horrified.

Rowena tensed every muscle. Ignoring her father she said coolly, "My pardon you shall never have, sir. Never." Ethelred and Gwyneth were like family to me. I can never forgive you for being responsible for their being thrown off their land like beggers, she thought.

Sir William hurried to put himself between his daughter and the man she was insulting. "You must, pray tell, excuse my daughter," he sputtered. "I fear that being raised without a mother's soft guidance has left her a bit rough around the edges."

"A bit," Kendrick said wryly, remembering the way she had punched him in the jaw, but oh, so soft and desirable the other day in his arms.

"She does . . . does not mean any offense."

Kendrick was willing to let the matter rest. "Then none is taken."

Rowena was angered all the more at what seemed to be an alliance against her. Damn her father for being so obsequious! Because of this man and his desire to steal someone else's land, Ethelred was dead and Gwyneth left homeless. "None taken by you perhaps," she insisted, pushing the matter, "but as for me, I am not as eager to let bygones be bygones as my father. A great wrong has been perpetrated and I will not rest until it is righted."

"A great wrong?" For the love of him he did not know what that could be. "What?"

"As if you did not know." Rowena's next words sounded like a threat. "I give you fair warning."

"Is that so?" So, Kendrick thought, it is to be a war of wills between them. So be it. Rather than angering him, he found the idea stimulating. This young woman was challenging, interesting. He pressed on. "Then I suppose were I to ask you to go to the archery tournament with me you would refuse."

"Archery tournament?" Immediately she was curious. "What tournament?"

Playing her at her own game he took a long while to answer. "The Sheriff of Nottingham has proclaimed a tournament be held at the fair to celebrate the longing for spring. A golden arrow is the prize."

Rowena's eyes opened wide at this bit of news. "A golden arrow?" She thought immediately how proud she would be to win such a trophy from the hands of those who thought of women as weak and inferior creatures, fit only for their pleasures. Men such as this conceited oaf who had tried to seduce her, not once but twice.

"Aye." Kendrick could see her anger softening. "That is the first prize. The second, third, fourth and fifth are new bows and a chance to serve the prince as foresters."

"A job as the king's forester, indeed," Rowena shot back. Suddenly she broke out into gales of laughter. She would enter the tournament. No one could stop her. Not even her father.

"You laugh." Kendrick liked the sound.

"A private joke." One on the sheriff and his friends.

She seemed to be in a good mood, so he asked again, "Will you go with me to the tourney?"

Look at him, Rowena thought. So puffed up with pride and sure of himself. He thought nothing in the world to be as charming as himself. A man like that wouldn't fathom that a woman would actually say no. Perhaps that was why it felt so good for her to do just that.

"I would as soon go to the archery match with a weasel," she proclaimed loud enough for the entire manor to hear.

"A weasel." This time her disdainful attitude got under Kendrick's skin. A man's pride could only take so much. "And I would just as soon go with a shrew." He moved towards the door. "Good day, Sir William," he said, opening it and slamming it behind him.

Red-faced and blustering Sir William could barely keep his own temper in check. "Rowena! How could you be so rude?"

"To such as him it was easy," she answered, refusing to be intimidated even by her father. "Besides, I couldn't have said yes even had I wanted to." Her eyes sparkled with determination. "For I intend to enter that match, you see."

Chapter Ten

The buzz of human voices hummed in the air. There was always excitement whenever a competition of any kind was to take place and the archery tournament was no exception. Tired of winter and longing for spring, men, women and children from villages all over the shire came by cart, on foot and on horseback to watch the archers shoot for the golden arrow. Elbowing her way among the arrivals was Rowena, trying as best she could to blend in with the crowd. Despite her father's fierce objections of, "Rowena, it will not do", she was determined to take part in the contest. If that made her "pig-headed" as her father insisted, well, so be it!

"Oh, how I wish I could enter and win as a woman," she grumbled beneath her breath, adjusting her hosen. As it was, she had conceded to her father's opinion that it would shock the countryside to see a woman compete in so unseemly a manner. For the sake of her ego she couldn't afford to put herself in any danger, particularly when she had come up against Prince John so recently in the forest. Therefore, Rowena had conjured up a disguise.

Remembering poor Hugh Penny with his sightless eye covered by a patch, she had dressed likewise in the drab gray of a peasant. In her heart, however, she would know if she won that a woman had bested them all.

Rowena's thoughts were disturbed by the sound of a trumpet. Standing tall and proud a herald made an announcement that dampened the enthusiasm of the crowd. "From this day forward, Robert Fitzooth, son of Hugh Fitzooth, having murdered the forester of the king, is declared outlaw. A reward of one hundred pounds is offered to he who can capture him, dead or alive."

"Robert Fitzooth." She remembered hearing Marian talk of this man in terms of endearment. How sad. And how timely was this warning. She would take it to heart and use caution in her actions today lest she too end up on the prince's wanted list.

Hurrying to the archery field, Rowena passed a troupe of tumblers who had just formed a human pyramid, walked briskly by a wrestling bout, and barely took time to peek at a contest between two men who were armed with quarter-staves. There was no time to dawdle; she was here on business and that business was to win.

"Gingerbread! Freshly baked gingerbread," a pretty young woman called out. "Eat it while you watch the tourney."

"Wine! Cider! Ale," yelled out a rotund, gray-haired man, vying for passerbys' coins. " 'Tis wet and tart."

Though she was both hungry and thirsty, Rowena ignored their cries. Already several horns were shrilly announcing that all archers should take their places in line. Rowena drove all other thoughts from her mind except winning the golden arrow. Staring straight ahead as she ran, she was oblivious to all around her, that is until she collided with a man who stepped into her path.

"Methinks you be in quite a hurry!" boomed a husky voice.

Rowena looked up at the obstacle, so lean and handsome

in a tunic and hosen of scarlet, and muttered an oath as she saw that it was Kendrick de Bron. His gaze was steady, unwavering as he looked self-righteously down at her and for a moment she felt the apprehension of being found out. What if he somehow recognized her?

"Excuse me, my lord," she mumbled, forcing her voice an octave lower. Holding up her bow she exhibited her reason for haste. All the while her heart pounded so wildly in her breast that for the moment she could barely breath.

"Ah, another entrant for the shooting match." Dubiously eyeing her up and down, he shrugged. "The more the merrier, I would guess."

"Aye," she answered, anxious for him to step aside. It was always troubling to be in his presence, more so now. And yet dressed as she was, how could he possibly guess her identity? Rowena scorned her foolish apprehension. Even her own father wouldn't know her dressed as she was.

For his part, Kendrick was puzzled. There was something familiar about this youth dressed in gray with a patch over one eye, though he could not remember having seen him before. And why was there such intensity in his gaze? Resentment flashing from that bold blue eye?

"Strange . . ."

"What is, my lord?" Oh, how she wished to be quit of his company.

Kendrick shrugged. He was imagining things. "Nothing." This lad was a stranger, albeit a hostile one. But then, could he blame him? The way the common man was being treated by the prince was appalling. As Prince John's man he was therefore the rightful target of the youth's animosity. It was a sad fact of life.

Rowena was uneasy. What was Kendrick de Bron thinking? For what seemed like eternity he hovered over her, continuing to stare. At last he took a step to the right.

"Well, be off with you now." He sauntered off towards the stands.

"Be off with you now," she mimicked under her breath. She watched him for just a moment t but turned her head quickly when she realized that he had sensed that she was staring. Taking her place as the fifth entrant amidst twenty-two, she had no time for thoughts of the haughty de Bron as she readied her bow.

"Look, a pigeon and a peacock," someone shouted out, pointing towards Rowena and the beggar who stood beside her. Dressed in a tunic and cloak of several different colors of cloth patched together, the beggar did indeed resemble a brightly plumed bird. Rowena eyed the tawny-haired man with scrutiny. His hat was pulled down low upon his face as if he too was in hiding. It was curious. Particularly so, seeing as how Maid Marian who sat in the stands had her eyes riveted upon him. Who was he?

"A peasant and a beggar. Who told them that they could enter?" a swaggering nobleman chided, rudely pushing Rowena aside.

"This contest is open to all," she responded defiantly, watching as the beggar limped to his place in line. Could it be? Was it possible? Would Robert Fitzooth be so daring? Such a thought amused her. If she didn't make an ass out of Prince John today, then perhaps this "beggar" would.

Tension trembled in the air as the target was put into place. The riotous crowd grew silent as the first archer stepped up to take his turn. "Bull's-eye!"

As she waited to take her turn, Rowena took time to scan the crowd, wondering if her father had changed his mind about coming. Alas, she did not see him, but she did take note of someone else. The tunic and hosen of red made Kendrick de Bron stand out in the crowd. Surrounded by lovely, chattering maidens like some sultan in a harem, he looked anything but lonely.

"Shoot!" she heard someone command.

She did. Lifting her bow Rowena took careful aim at the target, imagining the bull's-eye to be de Bron's treacherous heart. She hit it dead center to the accompaniment of cheers from the crowd.

Next came the beggar who was made to suffer a taunt from the noblemen in the audience. Their jeers were silenced as he too was accurate in his aim.

"Well done," Rowena praised, wondering again at the beggar's true identity.

Another archer took his turn, then another and another, their struts revealing over-confidence. When all was said and done, sixteen archers were true with their arrows, including Rowena and the beggar. It looked to be a long, strenuous day, she thought as she watched the target being placed twenty feet farther away.

Again each archer took a turn and again Rowena was victorious. Laughter arose as the beggar limped forward, but he too hit the target right in the center. This time, in fact, only two missed the mark, including the over-confident nobleman. Angrily throwing his bow to the ground, he proved himself to be a poor sport as well as rude.

"Good riddance," she scoffed beneath her breath.

"Aye, good riddance," agreed the beggar.

A horn sounded as the archers prepared to shoot again. This time the target was moved to a distance fifty feet farther away, a tricky but not impossible shot. Fourteen arrows whistled through the air one after another. Only six found their mark, Rowena's being the last to hit the circle.

"Good shot!" The beggar seemed to have befriended her, for he patted Rowena on the back.

"As was yours," she said, returning the compliment. "Good luck," she whispered as the target was once more moved farther away. If she didn't win the competition today then she hoped that the "beggar" would.

This time Rowena shot first. Holding her breath she let it out in a gasp as she saw the arrow hit the small red circle. If anything was as exciting as this she could not imagine it, she thought as her whole body trembled. The feeling of success was very, very sweet. As she watched two noblemen go down to defeat, it was even more so.

"The beggar! The beggar!" The crowd shouted for the man in the multi-colored clothing to take his turn. They were not to be disappointed, for again his aim was true.

Again the target was moved and this time three archers took their turn. Rowena and the man dressed like a beggar hit the bull's eye, but the third archer was far to the left.

"So, it is only you and me," she heard the beggar say. Looking into his blue eyes she saw him wink. "May the best man win."

"Aye, the best man," she said with a smile as the two of them prepared to shoot, possibly for the very last time. She saw him gaze in the direction of the crowd and could have sworn she saw Maid Marian blow him a kiss. It proved to bring him luck.

"The beggar has hit the mark again!" shouted the onlookers, cheering at the top of their lungs. They issued a challenge to the gray-clothed archer to do the same.

From where he sat, Kendrick de Bron swore loudly. That archer. It had to be. No wonder he had seemed familiar. "The rogue of the woods!" The overbold young archer who had robbed him of his clothes upon their first meeting. He knew it now.

Rowena drew her bow, but as she was about to shoot she caught sight of Kendrick de Bron. Their eyes met, his seeming to penetrate to her very soul. He knew.

"Shoot. What stays you?" demanded the Sheriff of Nottingham, anxious to be done with the match.

Rowena let her arrow fly, knowing the instant it did that she had shot too soon. It missed the beggar's arrow by nearly a half inch to the left, grazing the feathers as it struck. Though it hit the target squarely, her arrow had not hit as accurately as his.

"Damn," she muttered beneath her breath. Still and all she was a good sport about it all, being as it were the first to congratulate the winner. "But I caution you, my friend,"

she added. "The next time it will be *I* who will best *you.*"
She turned then, purposely weaving in and out amidst the
flock of meandering onlookers just in case de Bron
thought to instigate her capture. From the safety of her
place behind an over-stout merchant she could see the
beggar standing before Maid Marian, the golden arrow
outstretched in his hand.

"I offer this to the loveliest lady in the land," he said,
confirming Rowena's suspicions that he was Marian's love.

Nor was she the only one to notice. The Sheriff of Nottingham and his men moved towards the young couple and
seeing the danger, Rowena had to make a move. Coming
between the two laughing lovers, she called out a warning.

"The fox is upon the geese."

"What?" Robert Fitzooth looked up to see the truth of
her words and in a blink of an eye had run away.

"You fools, get him!" yelled the sheriff. Answering his
command, several men-at-arms ran, shoving through the
crowd. They were almost upon him when the dwarf, Lankless, came between. Doing flips and handstands to enter-
tain the onlookers, it appeared that he purposefully got
in the guardsmens' way. At least so it seemed to Rowena.

"Out of the way, you simpleton!" Pushing Lankless to
the ground, the guardsmen sought to renew the chase but
it was too late. Robert Fitzooth had vanished into the
throng of bystanders.

"Thank God he escaped," Rowena whispered beneath
her breath. It was time for her to do likewise.

"Wait just a minute."

Rowena paled as a guardsman grabbed her arm. His
eyes scrutinized her suspiciously.

"Where did he go?"

"Where?" Rowena shrugged. "How should I know?"

"You were seen talking to him after the tourney."

Rowena shook her head. "I was, to offer my congratula-
tions on a shooting match well done." She cocked the

eyebrow over the eye not wearing the patch. "But what
has the poor beggar done that you should be after him?"

"What has he done?" The guardsman's sour look
seemed to tell it all. "He makes fools of us all. That was
no beggar, but Robin Hood. Robin Hood!" Clenching his
fists helplessly, he looked as if he was ready to explode
with anger. "Damn him. Damn him, I say!"

Wrenching herself free, Rowena made her own dart for
the safety of the crowd, smiling to herself all the while. So,
her most noble opponent had been Robin Hood. Oh, she
had heard of him and his daring exploits. What enemy of
Prince John had not? And thanks to her he had escaped.
That alone made her efforts today well worth the try,
though she had to content herself with being second best.

"Robin Hood." She had heard the troubadours warbling ribald tales of his bravery and life in the Forest of
Sherwood. Well, one day soon those same minstrels would
be singing tales of her escapades. That idea amused her.

"Wait! You!"

Kendrick de Bron's shout made it impossible to think
about such triumph ere long. Seeing him pushing through
the crowd in pursuit, Rowena took to her heels. As she
did she laughed, vowing that when all was said and done
he of all people would never forget her.

There could be no mistake! Despite the eye patch and
tattered peasant garments, Kendrick recognized the young
archer. How could he forget that swagger, that grin, that
flawless skill with a bow?

"Humbley, Chadwick, help me catch him!"

Thus said, he broke into a run, adroitly dodging the
Sheriff of Nottingham's men, who were also in pursuit.
Kendrick's motives were far different, however. His intention was not to imprison the young lad but to pin him
down and force the arrogant fool to listen to reason. The
boy was getting much too big for his boots, so to speak.

Toying with the prince and the sheriff was pure stupidity. Aligning himself with an outlaw as infamous as Robin Hood was insanity.

"He should be playing chess, or spinning a top, or expending all his pent-up energy on wrestling lads of his own weight and size, not entering into an archery tournament with such high risks. He is going to get caught!"

At least so Kendrick thought. His thoughts were assailed by visions of the lad's capture. The archer was much too quick and agile, however, and obviously as cunning as a cat. Pushing into a man selling apple tarts and spice cakes, he overturned the cart, vaulting over it to safety. Then he was gone.

"Like that!" Kendrick snapped his fingers.

"We've lost him. . . ."

"So I can see. . . ."

Humbley hung his head. "What shall we do?"

Kendrick shrugged. "There is nothing much that we can do. Go home, I would suppose."

"Home?" Chadwick was not yet certain that was what the manor house was. At least not yet.

"Aye." He started walking slowly in that direction, then changed his mind. Why return to his manor house when there was a much more interesting destination in mind— Grantham Manor. He wanted to see if a certain "lady" had tempered her bad manners and to relate the story of the exciting tournament she had missed. A tournament she too would have enjoyed had she not so haughtily said no to his invitation.

The smells from supper lingered, reminding Rowena how hungry she was as she slipped through the manor's front door. Hurrying to the kitchen, she picked up a large spoon and tasted the stew that was left over in the cooking pot, wrinkling her nose as she decided that it had too much pepper and too many onions. Ah, well, that was

Gwyneth's only fault. Because meat was so heavily salted for winter preservation, Gwyneth had a tendacy to use a bit too much spice in an effort to make the fare more palatable. Ah, well.

Ladling a large portion into a bowl, she hurriedly began eating without even bothering to sit down. Spearing a big piece of meat with a knife, she smiled as she thought about her performance at the tournament. "Splendid" was the word that she would use. Of course she must spend a few hours more in practice and not get too sure of herself. Nine out of ten times her arrow had hit the mark dead center, but nine was not ten. Rowena was disconcerted that she had never been able to learn to shoot against the wind, although she had tried and tried.

"Ah, but next time . . ." She was feeling exuberant and brave and absolutely proud. Though she had not won the tournament, it did her heart good to have come so close.

As she ate Rowena thought about the sheriff's embarrassment to have had both the beggar and peasant escape right out from under his long nose. Though his guards had searched high and low, they had not found any sign of either archer. Nor would they. Cautiously she had made a bonfire out of the garments she had used for her disguise, then put on her gown and kirtle. As for Marian's love, he had run back to the safety of the forest, far away from any prying eyes.

"My, my, my. Why, you smack your lips so hard one would think that you were starving."

Startled by the voice, Rowena whirled around, dropping the now empty bowl to the ground. "What are you doing in here?" That Kendrick de Bron would enter the manor uninvited infuriated her.

He shrugged. "Maida let me in."

"Maida!" Rowena clenched her jaw. She would have to tell the girl in no uncertain terms that the lord de Bron was not always a welcome guest.

"Aye. She was anxious to hear all about the archery

match today." His dark eyes shone with merriment. "Had I known she would have been so interested, I would have taken her with me." Making himself right at home, he plopped down on a kitchen stool at the nearby table.

"Taken Maida?" She was annoyed by the idea.

He nodded. "Aye. And been proud all the while." His tone held censure. "Unlike a certain lady, she at least knows how to mind her manners."

She took no offense. "And never call you a weasel even if you are?"

Kendrick scowled but didn't insult her back. "Never!" Anxious to avoid an argument he related the story of the two archers. "The tale of the pigeon and the peacock, or so it is being called."

"Pigeon? Peacock?" Reaching up, she toyed with her braid, pulling it down, then ran a nervous hand over her rumpled gown. Was there any chance that he might recognize her? If so, would he shield her once again or turn her in?

Kendrick detailed the two men's clothing, so vividly that for a moment she could see it before her eyes. "A strange duo, though a pair not particularly noticed among the other twenty and two, at least until they shot their arrows." He made a whistling sound, pretending to shoot a bow.

Rowena cocked her head. "They hit the target?" she asked with mock sweetness.

"Hit it? Both scored a bull's-eye." He laughed. "In truth they were both little more than magnificent!"

"Merry-go-up!"

Watching her intently he continued. "Not only once, but again and again."

Rowena averted his eyes. "Luck, no doubt." She bent over to pick up the bowl.

"Ah, no! T'was skill. Pure skill." He rose to his feet, moving closer to her. "Allow me to demonstrate." Taking the bowl from her hands he set it down on the table, then stood behind her.

Rowena could feel the heat of his body inches from hers. "What are you doing?" Oh, why did his nearness always make her feel so odd? So quivery inside?

He didn't reply. Instead he reached out and took both her hands in his. Positioning her one hand near her waist, drawing her other hand back, he mimicked the action of drawing the string on a bow. "It was like this . . ." Again he made a whistling sound. "First the peasant, then the begger."

She could feel his breath tickle her ear as he spoke and she shivered. "And then?"

Kendrick hugged her close and buried his face in her hair. There was something about this young woman that nearly made him lose his head. "Then they shot again." He slipped his arms around her waist and pressed himself against her. "And again, and again . . ."

He turned her around to face him, his eyes narrowing as he breathed in a deep, husky sigh. "Oh, Rowena . . ."

She pushed against his chest. "Don't!" Her stare was angry, challenging.

"Why?" Her continued cold reception of his advances was wearing on his pride. More so because the feisty chit was so damnably attractive to him.

"Be-because . . ." Something altered in the depths of her eyes. Her heartbeat accelerated. She shivered.

"Because why?" Bending down, he kissed her mouth with incredible gentleness. Then his mouth moved slowly down, tracing the slim line of her neck.

Rowena gasped, not with outrage but from the very pleasure of his sensual, delicate caress. She was in a haze, aware only that he was pressed tightly against her, his mouth warm and tantalizing. For just a moment she didn't know what to do or say. That is until she glimpsed the silhouette of Gwyneth standing in the kitchen doorway, reminding her all too painfully of what he was responsible for.

"Nay," she breathed, this time trying in earnest to escape.

He ignored her, inclining his head to take her lips. Ignored her, that is until she elbowed him roughly in the ribs.

"Get away!" Hurt and furious she tore herself out of his grasp, backing away as she verbally censored him. Her body tensed, her nostrils flared. "I will not abide the embrace of a thief!"

"Thief?" Now it was Kendrick's turn to be angry. "I will not abide such insult—"

"Ethelred and Gwyneth were like family to me," she breathed, inclining her head in the woman's direction. "I can never forgive you for being responsible for their being thrown off their land like beggers!"

"Thrown off—?" Kendrick was stunned. All too quickly, however, the truth of what had happened seeped into his mind. John had spoken of the Saxons he had cast out of the cottage. What irony that it had been someone Rowena held dear. "My dear lady, t'was not by my order, I assure you! And the matter can be easily rectified." He turned towards Gwyneth. "I have no need to be greedy. I invite you to go back to your cottage if that is your desire. It seems a simple matter to set things aright."

Rowena took a shaky breath, her voice low. "I tell you it is not. Unless you can bring the dead back to life!" Her eyes were bright with unshed tears as she told him of Ethelred's death, then because she was determined not to let him see her cry, she turned away.

"Rowena, don't go. I didn't know. I didn't want ... Please stay."

She paused, wanting to believe in his innocence, then without looking toward him again, she fled to the safety of her room.

Chapter Eleven

The hall of the manor was cold, dark and empty as
Kendrick de Bron opened the creaking door. Home. His
home. How then could it seem so unwelcoming? It hadn't
been that way once. He remembered warmth, light, love
and laughter, once so long ago.

"And it will be that way again," he vowed, hurrying to
light one of the wall sconces. Alas, that did little good.
Despite the flickering flame the place still seemed to be
filled with gloom. Stubbornly determining that it should
not be so, Kendrick lit every candle and lantern in sight,
stoking up the hearth fire.

"Ah, such a face!"

Kendrick looked over his shoulder but didn't see anyone
there, at least not at first. As he lowered his line of vision,
however, he could see that Lankless, Prince John's jester,
was standing in the door way. The "fool," as a jestor was
called, was a specially privileged entertainer whose colorful
outfits made fun of the noblemen's fashionable clothes.
Often his funny stories, antics and rude songs made fun
of wealthy and powerful people in such a subtle way that

those he was offending didn't even know it. Although Kendrick thought the jester to be amusing, he did not welcome him here.

Immediately he was suspicious. Had the prince sent the little man to the manor to act as a spy?

"Forsooth, I forbid any frowns, for I am the Prince of Smiles." The little man turned somersault after somersault making the bells on his colorful garments jingle, but Kendrick barely noticed. He was too deep in thought. Wondering. Pondering.

Be careful what you wish for, he thought, for you might get it. Night after night he had dreamed of getting his family lands and manor back but now that he had, his victory had turned to dust. He was troubled. Because of the old man's death? Yes. He couldn't forget the look of sorrow in Lady Rowena's eyes when she had spoken about Ethelred and how he and his wife had been forcibly thrown out of the cottage that had stood upon Kendrick's new land. Prince John had handled the matter in his usual hard-hearted way and Kendrick was seen by her as the culprit. Was it any wonder then that she looked upon him as a villain?

"Ah, still a scowl?" The little man stood on his head until his face turned red.

Kendrick motioned for the jester to stand up, applauding so as to appease him. "It is not you, little man. It is just that I have little to laugh about."

"Little to laugh about?" The jester shook his head. "Why, when you have all this?"

"This?"

"A whole village at your beck and call." Lankless bowed. "You are lord and master here. Why, you should be able to live quite well on the fees and rents you get from your tenants."

"Perhaps, had they anything to pay with. As it is, my tenants are quite poor, suffering from the effects of John's over-taxation."

There were other problems as well. The manor had been vacant so long that it was falling apart inside and out. Feed was so scarce that the skeleton of every animal on the premises was visible through its flesh. Crops hadn't been harvested in the spring and thus lay rotting out in the fields, wet from the winter's rain and snow. The furniture in the village cottages was broken and threadbare, the tapestries were torn. There were cobwebs on the ceilings, dirt on the windowsills, dust on the floors as if the inhabitants had just given up. Clearly Kendrick would have his hands full straightening it all up.

"But I will!" he vowed. The buttery, cellar and pantry were ill-stocked, despite all their efforts, but before they were through the manor would be prosperous again. He, Chad and Humbley would do all that they could to preserve the village and give aid to the villagers.

"You will what?"

Kendrick was cautious. "I will do my best to make myself worthy of John's generous bestowal."

"Worthy. Aye. As for those who look upon you as an interloper, they had best smile when you look at them or they will be gone. John will not stand for any show of defiance. There will be no rebels tolerated here."

"No . . ."

"No Robin Hoods!" Lankless shrieked, miming an archer drawing back on his bow.

"Aye, no Robin Hoods," Kendrick finished, giving vent to his frustration. That forest lad had better beware and know not to trifle with him. He had worked too long and too hard. Competing in an archery tournament was one thing, causing mischief was another.

"Robin Hood, Robin Hood, Robin Hood. And the poor gray pigeon." Lankless proceeded with an inventive and comical skit about the tournament, mimicking first the beggar's limp, then the peasant's eye patch. "Bull's-eye!" he shouted. "Again, bull's-eye!"

"Bull's-eye indeed," Kendrick was suddenly annoyed by

the reminder of how he had made such a fool of himself chasing after that imp of a lad. Well, if the boy wanted so badly to thwart injustice, why wasn't he doing something constructive instead of destructive? God knew there was much to be changed.

"Ah, but who were they, these archers so bold," Lankless whispered, doing a handspring to punctuate his question.

"Oh, that we knew," Kendrick grumbled. More than anything he was curious as to the boy's identity.

"Robin Hood one," Lankless stated. "But who the other? Who?"

"An irritating lad who needs a good wallop to the seat of his hosen."

With a jolt it had come to him. The archer dressed in gray and the lad in the forest were one and the same. The swagger had given the archer away. That and his skill with a bow. Having put that two and two together, he had been determined to capture the rogue, only to watch as the rascal had eluded him by merging with the crowd.

"Who is he?"

It was a question that bothered Kendrick, more so the more he thought about it. He remembered looking into those deep blue eyes and was shocked by another revelation—the startling resemblance the lad bore to the Lady Rowena.

"No!" Ah, but there had been something about the lad that had reminded him of the lady so fair. Coincidence? His imagination? "Have I been blind?"

A voice rose in his mind, silent but piercing. Of course. It all made sense. When he was at the castle the lad had been near by. So had the Fitz Hugh family. Now that they were here, so was the boy. No coincidence!

"BiGod!"

There could only be one explanation, that the lad and lady were related to each other in some way. A cousin? Or closer yet, perhaps the lad was some byblow of Sir William, bastard born like himself. Perhaps even Sir William's son,

born outside the bounds of marriage. The thought bothered him somehow. He wondered what Rowena would
think to see so clearly written upon this young boy's face
a resemblance to her own. Did she know about the boy?

Abruptly his mood changed as he remembered how
boldly she had shunned his invitation to the archery meet.
"Why should I care how she feels," he said to himself. As
to manners, that young woman had few. Her father had
been right when he had decried her arrogant and stubborn
ways. She, like the forest lad, needed a good spanking.
"Aye, a firm hand laid upon that comely bottom."

Lankless chuckled at that. "Her bottom, her bottom,
her bottom."

Slowly Kendrick walked to the window that faced in the
direction of the Fitz Hugh manor and, pushing aside the
shutters, looked out. "Rowena Fitz Hugh, be damned." If
he had the brains of a goose he would stay as far from
Will Fitz Hugh's daughter as he could.

"Fitz Hugh?" The jester's head bobbed up and down.
"De Bron and Fitz Hugh, Enemies two." It was then that
Lankless revealed that it had been a Fitz Hugh who had
chased Geoffrey de Bron and his family out of England.

"Ha, you are a fool, what do you know of it?"

"Fool?" Lankless tapped at his head. "'Tis no fool, I. I
know what goes on and all that has gone on." Sounding
more like a scholar than a jestor, the little man rattled off
the history of the de Bron and Fitz Hugh families and how
they had interfaced with the rulers of England.

"So, the de Brons and Fitz Hughs have been on opposite
sides in the past." But he wouldn't think about that now.
What was past, was past. Besides, it did seem as though
there could be peace. That is, if one didn't think too
hard about Rowena's bad manners. Manners that were not
entirely without warrant, considering the fate of her Saxon
friends. But he would make amends. From now on he
would. . . .

"BiGod!" The sight of smoke caught his eyes. Something

was on fire. His eyes scanned the horizon to discover the source of the smoke. Hearing the terrified whinnies of his horses, seeing them galloping every which way, he knew. "The stables!"

Instantly Kendrick took charge of the situation. If the fire wasn't quickly put under control, it would spread to the manor house.

"Lankless, there is a bell in the chapel. Go there and sound the alarm. We need water. Hurry!" Kendrick called out over his shoulder as he threw open the door and ran outside. Frantically, he looked around for Chad and Humbley, cursing to himself when he realized that the two were most likely off to the Fitz Hugh household to flirt with the red-haired young serving girl. It was left to him and a jester to save his property.

Running to the well he drew up two buckets full of water and heaved them on the burning wooden building, then returned to fill the buckets again. Over and over he repeated the procedure, frustrated that it seemed to do little good. The fire burned too furiously and too fast.

"Alas, I would do as well to spit at the flames," he swore as the silence of the countryside was shattered by the toll of the bell. Kendrick took out his frustration on a lazy-looking groom who crossed his path, walking with unhurried strides. Grabbing the unfortunate lad by the scruff of the neck, he none-too-gently set him to the task of filling two other buckets. And all the while the smell of smoke permeated the air.

"It's too late, my lord." Usually so cheerful, Lankless had a woebegone expression.

"Too late. Never!" Kendrick was not the kind of man to ever give up. "Lankless, take two men and go to the brewhouse. We'll use the water stored for the brewing of ale."

"The ale?" The tiny man grabbed at his throat. "Merry-go-up, we will all die of thirst if we waste even a drop." Nevertheless he complied. Soon the contents of the kegs were added to the steady slosh of water that was being thrown on the fire by all those who were gathering together at the stables. It was a unified effort that at last paid off and seemed to unify the inhabitants of the village.

In the end the stables were reduced to little more than ashes, but at least the manor was saved. "We will start rebuilding before dawn tomorrow," Kendrick proclaimed, assessing the damage done. Even so, he was angry. How had the fire started? There had been no lightning. A careless torch? Crooking one dark brow, he interrogated every villein who lived in the manor but only one small boy knew the answer.

" 'Twas done on purpose, my lord."

"On purpose?" Kendrick's brows furled as he stared down at the boy.

The child nodded. Tugging on Kendrick's sleeve he led him towards a far corner of what once had been a stable. There, stuck in the ground as if to purposely taunt, was an arrow. Wrapped around it was a note.

"What is this?" Kendrick's fingers trembled with his anger as he tore it off. "To he who takes what isn't his must come a reckoning," he read, knowing at once from where it had come. "The young forest demon," he hissed between clenched teeth. "Damn him to hell!" The fire had clearly been no accident then. Well, so be it. From now on it would be war between he and that bothersome lad. And when he found him, he would hang him by the heels from the nearest tree. By the name of the de Brons' he so swore. Fitz Hugh's bastard had better beware.

From her window Rowena stared out the window, taking note that the glow upon the horizon had vanished. The fire was out then. Just as well. She hadn't meant to do any real damage. All she had meant to do was teach the haughty de Bron a lesson. A poke in the eye for a poke in the eye, as it were.

"For Gwyneth and Ethelred," she said, raising her fist.

Still dressed in her short tunic of green, an under tunic, hosen, soft leather boots and the capuchin that had hid her hair, she felt triumphant. Still, it was not enough. The fire was but the beginning.

"So, de Bron. You think that a woman should sit at a spinning wheel all day or patiently work a tapestry in the corner of the room . . ." Or be at a man's mercy whenever he felt a twinge of desire.

Folding her arms across her chest, Rowena purposefully forced herself to remember what had happened in the kitchen earlier, angered by her own reaction to the passion that had sparked so fiercely. She had been unprepared for it. It had been so sudden, so strong. And so dangerous, to all that she stood for and all that she planned.

De Bron is poison. He would destroy her if she allowed herself to care. She knew his kind. He was incapable of loving any woman in return. His kind of passion was selfish. Shallow. Not at all what she had dreamed about. Above all she must remember that he was Prince John's man and thereby her enemy.

"Aye. Enemy," She wouldn't allow herself to forget that again.

Slowly, she tiptoed about the room as she made her plans. It was time to take a stand. Time to do more than talk and make mischief.

Moving to the door she made certain that it was locked securely, then looked in the large polished metal mirror hanging on the wall. Taking note of the wisps of hair that peeked out from the hood she made her decision— a sacrifice, as it were. Her hair would have to be cut. Though she had worn it securely wrapped around her head in braids, she couldn't take the risk of it tumbling down and ruining her disguise as it almost had at the tournament. Not now. Not when she planned to enter upon such a risky venture. Her honey-colored locks would have to go.

With knife in hand Rowena began, slowly cutting her long tresses. She would fashion a braid from the shorn locks to wear pinned to her head during those times when she would have to look womanly and ladylike. No one need know that her hair had been cut to just a few inches below the ear. Not even her father. It would be her secret.

Averting her eyes from her image, Rowena cut and cut until it was done, little realizing just how becoming the short hair was to her oval face. The honey-colored curls framed the beauty of her eyes. "Shorn like a sheep," she quipped, viewing her handiwork.

Picking up her long bow of yew wood and quiver of arrows she stared at her reflection long and hard, realizing in that moment that her child's play was over. What she planned to do now would take her into danger. Might well make her an outlaw like Robin Hood. Indeed, it might well mean her death.

There were only ashes where once a stable had stood. Ashes, blackened rubble and smoke.

"My lord de Bron, what happened?" Riding up to where he stood, Humbley reining in close behind, Chadwick was aghast.

"It seems we had a little visitor." Taking the arrow that had been left as a grim reminder, Kendrick angrily broke it in two.

"The archer?"

Kendrick couldn't answer. He was too filled with anger at the moment to put anything into words. Clenching his teeth in frustration, he did nod, however.

"The horses . . . ?" Humbley, a kind soul who was gentle with animals, studied the damage, sighing thankfully. "Well at least there is that to be thankful for. Methinks it could have been worse."

"And might be next time." Chadwick slid slowly from his horse. "Thus, what can we do?"

"Do?" The answer was obvious, although irritating for Kendrick to admit. "We must get reinforcements." With the act of arson the young archer had declared war. Besides, perhaps the arrival of guardsmen would frighten the young scoundrel off.

"From the prince?" Humbley wrinkled his nose.

"Aye." There was no other choice, although the very idea stung Kendrick's pride. He had to save the manor house, church and other village buildings at all cost.

Chapter Twelve

Three riders rode along the road, riders that Rowena recognized immediately from their helmets, hauberks and surcoats. "Prince John's rodents!"

Watching intently as they passed through a peaceful village of straw-thatched cottages, rode beyond the gnarled old oak, then splashed through a swollen stream, she didn't even have to guess where they were headed.

"De Bron's manor." So, he could not fight his battles alone but needed the prince's hounds. Well, so be it!

Rowena stared at the horizon as the men traveled another few miles, turning her horse around only when she saw them go beyond the waterwheel and pass over the newly built stone bridge that marked that spot where Grantham Manor and Melburn Manor touched boundaries. With a shrug she headed back towards the manor, pausing a short distance away to change her garments and hide them in an old abandoned well. Carefully she took the strings off her bow and put them in a dry pouch, hiding the bow and strings in a hole in the ground, then covering the hole with straw.

Riding into the courtyard, Rowena dismounted, handing her horse over to the grinning stable boy, and walked towards the manor house in hurried strides. It was much safer to be the lady again while John's men roamed about, she thought, reaching up to make certain her braid was pinned on tight. Then she entered the hall, smiling as she heard her father's voice.

Rowena's smile soon faltered at the sight of Kendrick de Bron's cloak hanging on a peg by the door. She swore, feeling not at all in the mood to suffer his company. She would never for one moment admit that she found him attractive. Oh no. He was her enemy. Worse yet because of his ties to Prince John, he was an enemy of her king.

Immediately the fire she had set on his property came to mind. *Does he know?*

Suddenly she longed to be out of these stifling woman's garments and away from the manor walls. She didn't want to come face to face with de Bron. Not now. Not ever! That is, unless she were to lock him in the stocks with her very own hands. Or make him walk barefoot and in his under tunic again. Or see that he got a good dunking in the pond.

"Why is he here?" For a moment Rowena felt uneasy. Was it possible? Could it be? Had Kendrick de Bron figured out that she was the one causing all the mischief at his manor? The fire in the stables, livestock let out of their pens, the beehives robbed of their honey combs. Had he come to accuse her? Warily she crept forward to eavesdrop.

"I know that we may not see things exactly the same, but you must agree this foolishness must stop! I would hate to see the destruction flow over to Grantham Manor."

Rowena stiffened. Was Kendrick de Bron threatening her father?

"As would I. I am a man who values peace."

There was a long pause before de Bron asked, "And can the same be said for your son?"

A strange question, Rowena thought. Worriedly she

remembered seeing the three men headed for de Bron's manor.

"My son?" Though her father seldom laughed he did so now. "De Bron, I have but one child, one who, female or not, can often be a handful."

Kendrick de Bron's tone was less jovial. "As well I know."

Though he could have said more, de Bron's comment was a subtle condemnation of Rowena's manners.

"I apologize for my daughter," her father was saying, a plea that struck a blow to her pride. Apologize. Apologize for her?

"Ah, the fairer sex," Kendrick answered, his voice so low that she could barely hear. "What do you do with them, but what could we do without them? They are a puzzle to ponder."

"Her mother was a feisty woman as well. No doubt my daughter gets her temperament from my fair wife, God rest her soul." Suddenly choked with emotion he paused, then confided, "I loved that woman more than life." There was another pause as Sir William got hold of his emotions. "As for Rowena, I take full blame for her willfulness, but I'm certain that you could soon tame her."

"Tame her?"

Rowena heard their "neighbor" chuckle and clenched her fists to think that she was the topic of conversation. Tame her indeed. That would be the day. Oh, if he only knew.

"Aye. Tame." Sir William cleared his throat. "I have been thinking of offering you my daughter's hand in marriage, to put the matter quite bluntly. It would be joining two of England's noble families and ... and be prosperpous to us both, considering that our lands now adjoin."

"Marry her?" The quiet was sliced through with the sound of Kendrick de Bron's laughter. "Marry her indeed. Now there is a thought." He laughed again.

That merriment was more than Rowena could bear.

Touching her face she felt the heat of her blush and cursed her father for humiliating her so. So that was what he had been pondering so diligently the last few days! As for de Bron, she hoped he choked on his chuckling. Oh, if only she could use her bow and arrow.

Goaded on by her temper, Rowena swept into the room. "So you think to offer me up to this . . . this . . . *traitor* on a silver platter," she said, her eyes sweeping the room. She saw de Bron standing by the fire and knew his eyes were riveted upon her as well. "Think again, Father."

Never had Rowena felt so estranged from her father. Oh, it was true that she and her father had seldom understood each other but never before had he been so callous about her feelings. Why, he sounded as if he couldn't wait to be rid of her. Was she really such a burden?

"A woman has but two choices, daughter." Raising his hand, Sir William put up one finger. "She can either marry—" he put up the second finger "—or give herself to God."

"I would as soon be sent off to a convent as to marry a fool like him." Just in case there be any mistake who she meant, she pointed a trembling finger at de Bron and continued. "I want marriage not at all. Particularly marriage to him!"

"Rowena!" Sir William coughed, sputtering on his ale. "And indeed you shall be sent to a nunnery if you do not hold your tongue."

Kendrick was taken aback. The pretty young woman's scorn was as powerful as her punch had been that day at the castle. He found himself wanting to reach up and touch his jaw as if she had struck him anew. And yet, instead of souring him on the girl, her spunk only served to add to his ardor. She had spirit, this one. He liked that. He wanted no milksop miss who jumped at his every command. His eyes swept over her. Would she be as bold in bed as she was when she was angered? Oh, that he could get her alone.

"Rowena, say that you are sorry."

"Sorry?" She looked de Bron over just as boldly as he had her. The trouble was, she liked what she saw. He had worn a leather tunic, brown hosen and a white linen shirt that was open to reveal a mat of black hair curling on his muscular chest. His muscles and that hair seemed to kindle an odd feeling deep inside her. She remembered his kisses and . . . felt desire? Heaven forbid! "Say I'm sorry," she said again, louder than before. "Indeed no, for I will not lie."

"Then neither will I." Kendrick's mouth compressed into a thin line. His words were clipped, harsh. The wench needed to be taught a lesson. "I understand your desperation in trying to find a husband for your daughter, Sir William, but count me out. As you can plainly see she is entirely unsuitable to carry the name de Bron. She is clearly no lady."

"Nor do I want to be," Rowena shot back. She should be pleased that he wanted no part of her. Why then wasn't she? Why did his words sting her pride? Irritated, she glared at him defiantly.

"That much is obvious." Kendrick's voice was harsh as he threw a final insult in her face. "But then take heart, Sir William. Perhaps you can find a husband for the wench after all." The incidents of mischief at his manor had taken a toll on his patience. Perhaps that was why he added, "Among the stable boys who share her common manners."

"A stable boy!" The old man was shocked. Humiliated. Even so, he seemed determined to change de Bron's mind, following at his heels as de Bron walked towards the door. As it was his effort proved to be useless, as the slamming door attested. Before he left, however, Kendrick had one more thing to say. A warning, as it were.

"I have always considered myself to be a reasonable man, but even a saint has his limits." Kendrick spoke loudly enough for Rowena to hear. "Mind me well, old man, I will not abide being made a victim. I will not tolerate any more destruction to my manor. Next time I will strike back and strike hard. Tell that to the perpetrator if you can." Thus said, he was gone, leaving Rowena behind to wonder at his words.

The sky was dark. Only a slice of the setting sun was visible behind the cover of clouds. As Kendrick rode back towards his manor his temperament was cloudy. Angry. There was no way he could soften the blow that saucy, boisterous chit of a girl had dealt him. He had been rejected, and not kindly.

"She said no to *me*. I was refused before I even offered for her hand. Never before have I been treated so foully." The Lady Rowena Fitz Hugh was like a flower, beckoning his touch only to prick him with her thorns over and over again. Why then was he so tempted to turn back? To try to make amends even though in this she had been the offender? Because he could well view the sweetness that dwelt beneath her barbs? Aye, that was it.

The lady in question was like a sputtering cat, an untamed colt, a wild bird that wanted to fly free. Deep in his heart he admired her spirit. But how was he going to get close enough to tame her, calm her, win her heart?

"All she needs is to be properly wooed and bedded," he said aloud, that being a duty he would welcome whole-heartedly. And yet in so doing, would he survive? Remembering their encounters in Prince John's castle and at her manor, he wondered. Surely she was the most incorrigible woman he had ever come across. At the same time she had enchanted him. Utterly. Thoroughly.

"But she will be mine." As he rode along, listening to the clip-clop of his horse's hooves he pondered how that was going to be.

It was but a short jog from one property to the other, thus it did not take Kendrick long to reach the wooden and stone building with its sod roof and tiny windows.

Dismounting, he gave the animal over to the stable boy, grimacing as he took a look at the lad and remembered his comment to Sir William. The young man was unkempt, grimy. Surely he would not want to wish this one on any unsuspecting maid, even if she did have a tart tongue.

"Be careful with him, Edmund. Do not curry him so hard this time. You almost tore his skin off last time. And water him sparingly. It is not my intent that you should drown him."

"Aye, aye, my lord." Though the stable boy's nod was acquiescent there was something in his eyes that warned he could be dangerous were he crossed. Unfortunately that was the feeling that Kendrick got from the three men who met him as he pushed through the door of his manor.

"John sent us, to make certain that there is no further trouble," one of the men with a scar on his cheek said. His tone was ominous.

Kendrick couldn't help wondering if these men intended to prevent trouble or to kindle it. Now he regretted his hasty decision to ask the prince for help. He feared he might have gotten far more than he had bargained for.

"Aye, we will soon show your villeins that anyone who dares to even sneeze without the prince's permission will be punished." Putting his hands around his throat the other man stuck out his tongue, mimicking the gruesome scene of a hanging.

Kendrick shook his head. "Nay, we will have no hangings around here, at least unless I will it."

"You?" The way the word was said mocked Kendrick's authority, as if to say that only John's "will" was to be obeyed.

"Mine!" Fearing that he might well lose his temper, Kendrick ushered the men to the door, offering them the comforts of one of the empty cottages. "Simple lodging for men such as you, but comfortable I hope." His smile was less than sincere. Watching as the three men strode across the road, Kendrick was tense and anxious for a solitude that was not to be allowed him.

"So, we meet again."

Turning, Kendrick recognized Hugo, the servant he had met at the castle who had claimed to have served Kendrick's uncle once. Stepping out of the shadows he made no apologies for his sudden appearance.

"Where are Chad and Humbley?"

"Who?" Hugo shrugged. "Ah yes, your servants from abroad. Let us just say that they were detained in Nottingham. The prince had a few questions."

"Detained!" Losing his temper, Kendrick grabbed Hugo by the front of his tunic. "So, I send two trusted men to the prince for help and he makes of them his prisoners. Well, I will not have it."

"Prisoners?" Pulling out of Kendrick's grasp, Hugo hurried to put his mind at ease. "Ah, no. John merely wants word of what improvements have been made to Melburn, that is all. Your servants will return very soon. Meanwhile, I am here to take their place, at least for awhile." He pointed to the fire where a large caldron of water was boiling. "But come, you seem tense and irritable. I will prepare your bath so that you can relax and think about things more clearly."

Eyeing Hugo, wishing he could look into his mind and soul, Kendrick made his way to his chamber and slowly disrobed. He would humor John's watch dog, at least for now. "No bath, but I would welcome a good night's sleep."

Hugo hurried to retrieve the garments his lord scattered on the floor as he undressed, then warmed the bed with hot stones that he took out of the just-extinguished fire.

Kendrick motioned for Hugo to go. Blowing out the fires of the wall sconces, he slipped naked between the covers of the bed. Staring up at the moonlight dancing on the ceiling he tried to sort out his emotions. Marriage. Imagine that! The very word caused every muscle in his body to stiffen, his throat to go dry. And yet, spending the rest of his life with Rowena Fitz Hugh might well prove to be an adventure. That is, if he could ever get her to stop resenting him so.

No easy matter. And yet, he had to win her over somehow.

Kendrick closed his eyes, then opened them again. Was he imagining it or was there someone in the room? "Hugo?" He held his breath, listening, and thought he heard the soft tread of footsteps. "Hugo?"

"Shhhhhhhh," whispered a voice. Before Kendrick had time to answer a hand clamped over his mouth. "It's me, Robert Fitzooth." Slowly the hand moved away.

"Robert?" Kendrick remembered hearing the heralds proclaim the man outlaw. And a shame it was. He had known Robert since boyhood and had always thought him to be honest and abiding. "What are you doing here?"

"Desperation."

"You are in trouble." Kendrick didn't have the heart to turn him away. There had been too many times that Robert had come to his defense when they were boys. Once he had even taken on three youths who had dared to call Kendrick "bastard" to his face.

"I'm not in trouble." There was a candle on a wooden stand near the bed which Robert lit now. "It is Marian."

"Ah, yes. I think I know all about that." Getting out of bed, Kendrick wrapped the bed sheet around him. He and Robert were of like height but he was solidly built, whereas the other man was of a more slender frame.

"Now that I have been declared outlaw I can no longer move freely about to gain information about John. Marian has been helpful in the past with her bits of news from the court but now 'tis no longer safe. John tried to take her prisoner."

"I know. I rode out that day trying to warn her."

"Some brave young lad beat you to it." The tawny-haired Robert grinned.

The memory of who it was irritated Kendrick. "How well

I know. I have a bone to pick with that bold youth." He was quick to promise, "But no matter. I'll do everything in my power to see that Marian doesn't fall into John's hands."

"I knew you would." Playfully Robert cuffed him on the arm. "Ah, but I have missed you. We have fond memories. Can you ever forget all the tussles we have had? You won every one."

"Yea, but it was you who were lighter of foot and won every race." Unspoken moments and events flashed through both their minds. "I was the swordsman."

Robert put his hands on his hips. "But I was the one swift with my bow."

"I drew the fairest women." Kendrick looked smug.

"But I won Marian." Robert sighed. "Ah, true love . . ."

"Love? Bah!" Kendrick's wrinkled brow gave him away, much to Robert's mirth. Throwing back his head he laughed soundly.

"A woman has caused you to scowl? Tell me all then, friend, before I go. What woman has so annoyed you?"

"Never mind." Kendrick didn't really want to talk about it. It bruised his ego to have to tell his friend that some young wench had scorned him.

Robert read his mind. "A woman has told you 'no'?" He clicked his tongue sarcastically. "Tut, tut, tut."

"It's not funny, Rob!" Pacing back and forth in his bare feet, Kendrick told Robert everything, including his first meeting with the lady Fitz Hugh.

"She hit you?" Robert roared with laughter, slapping his thigh with his hand. "And did you have it coming?"

Kendrick flushed. "I did, but that is not the point." Remembering the sting of her fist, Kendrick rubbed his jaw. "Damn it all, man, her father proposed that I marry the chit and she had the nerve to openly say she prefers a nunnery."

Robert's mood softened. "Ah, poor Kendrick. To be

struck with cupid's bow only to come up emptyhanded must have hurt indeed."

"It did." Realizing he was revealing too much, Kendrick affected bravado as he said, "But I'm certain I will survive."

Robert winked. "Give it time. It took me one full year to get a kiss from Marian. A full circle of seasons. But in the end she yielded and rewarded me thrice over for my patience."

"Patience," Kendrick grumbled.

"Aye, patience. Something you have little—" A thump outside the door caused him to be suddenly silent. Cautiously he moved towards the window. "John has sent his hounds here. I dare not be caught," he mouthed.

"I know." Kendrick blew out the candle, then hustled his friend out the window, aiding him to climb down a vine to the ground below. When Robert had safely descended, he waved. He had just turned around when the door opened. Hugo stood there. "What is the meaning of this intrusion?" Kendrick snapped. "I did not call for you."

The servant bowed. "Sorry, my lord, but I thought you should be aware of the outlaw who has been spotted lurking in the woods."

"Outlaw?" For just a moment Kendrick thought about the young archer, then realized that Hugo meant Rob.

"It seems Robin Hood himself is nearby."

"Robin Hood?" Kendrick raised his brows. Was it possible? Robert—Robin? He decided that it was. So, Robert was not just any outlaw then. He had chosen for himself a lofty alias. "Well, I'm certain that were he here you would be the first to know, Hugo." Acting as nonchalant as he could, he climbed back into bed. "As for me, I'm too tired to worry overmuch." Ah, but he was worried. For Robert. For Marian. And if it was known about his association with Robert, for himself.

Chapter Thirteen

A winter mist hung over the hillside and yet that did not dampen Rowena's good spirits. She felt invincible, she felt free. Roaming the woodlands disguised as a boy was what she so loved doing. She was making quite a name for herself as the avenging archer.

Oh, how surprised her father would be if he knew how and where she spent her days. During the evenings she was her father's proper daughter, dressed in her wimple and gown, her hair adorned with the braid; but during the time just after dawn and before dusk she rode about the nearby forests and countryside robbing from the rich, doing mischief to those who had done evil, helping the poor and those wronged by the Sheriff of Nottingham and Prince John. If she was mistaken for the famous outlaw Robin Hood, well, so be it. She laughed at the very thought, hoping that perhaps one day she would be able to let the truth be known and take credit for her own good deeds.

"I want de Bron to know that he has been bested by a woman." Oh, how that would wound his pride. Meanwhile, she would have to be patient and content herself with imaginary reprisals for de Bron's manor was of necessity off limits.

"Mind me well, old man," he had warned. "I will not tolerate any more destruction. Next time I will strike back and strike hard . . ." It was a warning that Rowena dare not ignore lest her father be harmed by her daring.

Rowena's restraint did not extend to the prince's men now living on de Bron's property, however. It was with the greatest delight that she taunted and teased them whenever she could. One had lost his helmet, one had lost his shield, gifts the blacksmith had quickly melted down.

"I will not rest until they have been chased back to the castle. They are not welcome here."

Whistling a bawdy tune, Rowena sat on a rock, contenting herself in looking up at the sky. It was a strange day. Fog floated across the sun, casting eerie shadows on the ground of the forest below, like witches or ghosts. Why, she could nearly imagine their shrieking.

"No." Rowena sat up with a start. It was not imagined. The sound was real. Frightened screams echoed throughout the forest.

Jumping to her feet, she vaulted onto the back of her horse, cutting short his peaceful grazing. Urging the horse onward, she rode in the direction of the sound, coming upon two figures silhouetted against the horizon.

"Please, spare me. Please." The voice was high-pitched like a child's, but though the owner of the voice was a mere three feet or so in height, it was no youth who issued the plea. The grey beard attested to that.

"Lankless," she whispered, recognizing the court buffoon. Clearly, as he was being poked and prodded by his attackers' swords, he was not laughing now. Like a trapped squirrel the small man's eyes darted back and forth looking for any means of escape.

"I will give you to the count of three to hand over your gold. If you do not, I will see that your size is diminished by another head. Do you get my meaning, dwarf?" boomed a voice. Taking a step towards the tiny man, a hooded figure looked as if he intended to give credence to his threat.

"Do as he says," commanded his companion. Stepping forward he began to search the dwarf as the other man kept him at sword's point. "I thought so." Withdrawing a large money pouch hidden in the jester's hood, he started to stuff them into his tunic but he paused as he felt his hat whisked from his head. "What in God's blood?"

Grasping her bow, Rowena showed herself. "Shame on you for seeking to harm one but half your size," she scolded. Robbing from the rich was one thing, but stealing from this little man was another. She knew Lankless to be good at heart no matter if he was in the employ of the prince. Nor was he rich.

Whirling, the man stared down at his hat which was pinned to the ground by a still-pulsating arrow. Sputtering, he bent to retrieve the object only to find it whisked from his head by a second arrow.

"Give the jestor back his coins." Arming herself with another arrow, Rowena pulled back on the string of her bow, eyeing the man in brown and green. "Robin Hood would be ashamed of you."

"Robin Hood be damned. It's each to his own." With a grunt the man held out the money pouch, but instead of returning it to its owner, he hurled it at Rowena, taking her by surprise. With a lunge he grabbed her by the foot, pulling her to the ground. She was forced to fight in hand-to-hand combat.

Rowena had spent several years wrestling with stable boys before she had grown to womanhood. Now her days of fighting and sparring came in handy. Rolling around on the ground, she felt the fingers of her attacker entwine around her neck, squeezing until she gasped, but she didn't panic. With a well-aimed blow to his manhood, she soon had the man groaning in pain.

Now it was Lankless' turn to come to the rescue. Turning

a somersault, he kicked the other outlaw in the jaw with his boot. Retrieving the man's sword, he held it threateningly against the man's throat. "Move one step and I will cut you down to my size," he threatened.

Picking up her bow and arrow, Rowena was once more in control of the situation. "Methinks we have caught ourselves two weasels, Lankless. Shall we send them back into the forest?"

"Aye." With a grin the dwarf gave each man a boot in their behinds. Brushing himself off, adjusting his yellow and green tunic, he grabbed his money pouch tightly and climbed up on his brightly painted wagon. "I can never repay you, archer." The bells upon his hat jingled merrily as he waved.

" 'Tis enough that you are safe." She turned away, then turned towards him saying, "I recognized them, no matter their disguise. I saw them at the castle. They were not Robin Hood's men, albeit it appears that's what they would have you believe."

"Little did they know that I would never have believed." He grinned. "For Rob is my hero." He took off his hat, exposing a rapidly balding head, then eyed her quizzically. "Why did you help me?"

"I have taken a vow to aid those like yourself."

"I see." He smiled. "Perhaps one day I'll be able to help you, too." He leaned over, confiding a secret. "Though the prince's jestor I be, I must confess that I have no love for the man. Long live King Richard."

"And God speed him back to England," she whispered.

"Only then will all be well." Bending over, the dwarf grinned at Rowena. "If you ever have need of me, merely whistle, like so, and I will come to *your* aid." Trilling his tongue, the dwarf made the sound of a lark three times.

"Like so." Rowena mimicked his sound.

He nodded. "I will consider you my friend from this day forth, archer. May God be with you." Pulling at the reins of his horse he guided the wagon down the road but he did look back several times.

"A friend," she repeated, pulling herself up on her horse's back. "No doubt I will have need of one before I am through."

Patience, Robert Fitzooth had advised. Well, patience it would be, Kendrick vowed as he appraised his appearance in front of the silver mirror in Sir William's entranceway. He had taken special care in his grooming and wardrobe, choosing black hosen, black boots and a tunic of black trimmed in silver. Having noticed Rowena's fascination with his chest hair, he had chosen the tunic because of the vee at the neck and because it emphasized his broad shoulders. A round amulet studded with small diamonds that had once belonged to his uncle, Geoffrey de Bron, seemed to add just the right touch of nobility.

"Rowena Fitz Hugh could not find a more handsome suitor," he declared somewhat vainly, running a hand through his hair.

Oh yes, her aloofness had taken a toll upon his self-assurance, Kendrick couldn't deny that. Being rejected was a new experience for him, but tonight his confidence was again restored. Robert Fitzooth's good-natured advice had egged him on. Tonight would be the beginning of his wooing, a courtship that was obviously favored by the lady in question's father, seeing as how he had issued a dinner invitation for this evening.

The scent of roast swan filled the air. Kendrick took note of the aroma and licked his lips. He had let it be known to Sir William how much he favored swan and he perceived it to be a good sign that it was going to be the night's fare.

"Ha! Too bad the daughter isn't as amiable as the father," he said to himself with a wry smile. He liked Sir William. And damned if he didn't like the winsome little witch, too. She had remained on his mind today, a disturbing and alluring presence. Closing his eyes he could see her nearly as clearly as if she stood before him. Her flawless skin, her mouth that always seemed to be mocking him, the tendrils of glossy honey-colored hair that curled around her pretty face. It was her eyes, however, that haunted him the most. Blue eyes. Eyes that could run the gauntlet from warm and kind to dark and stormy. He wondered how they would look tonight.

"Follow me this way, my lord."

A feminine voice behind him startled Kendrick out of his musing. Turning around, he was met by a friendly face that was thankfully recognized. "Maida." As he followed her down the long hallway he felt a bit of his cockiness returning.

"Look at him swagger," Rowena said to herself as she watched him from the top of the stairway. "Oh, how could Father do this to me?"

Why did Sir William encourage the man? She had made her feelings very clear. But then, what did it matter? According to the law of the land and the church, her father had the right to marry his daughter off to any man he might fancy. More than one noble daughter had been sold to the highest bidder. Some young women had even suffered beatings and near starvation in their fathers' efforts to break their resistance to an upcoming marriage.

It was a man's world when all was said and done. From the moment a girl-child was born her father had control of her life, making her little more than a puppet. Then she was pawned off on a husband who took over pulling the strings. If a woman had sons, they were the next in line to tell her what to do and when.

"Fie!" Her father had ordered her to dress in her finest for their guest, much to her protestations and willful frowns. Would she dare disobey him? Rowena paced anxiously, longing to be out of her stifling woman's garments and away from the manor's walls, for then and only then was she really free. "But why not now?" Why should she have to wait just because of an unwelcome guest?

Retreating to her room, she tore off her false braid and stripped off her bliaut and kirtle as if they burned her skin. She was outraged, but not at her father, for she did not really blame him. It was Kendrick de Bron's name she cursed. Had he not come, all would be well between her father and herself. As it was they had spent the last two days arguing over her haughty attitude and lack of congeniality. Well, if she wasn't at dinner tonight, then she wouldn't be tempted to fling insults at the man who had most certainly earned them.

Donning her archer's garb she swung one leg out the window and reached for the vine she used as a rope to climb to the ground. In mid-escape, however, she had a change of heart. She wouldn't run away. Not now, not ever. "Father wants to offer me to Kendrick de Bron. Well then, I will let my dear suitor see exactly what he would be in for." As she moved around her bedchamber choosing what to wear, her laughter was so spirited that Kendrick could hear it down below.

"Well, at least she seems to be in a jovial mood," he said to her father, looking upward.

"Rowena and I have had a long talk," Sir William informed him, clasping his hands together so tightly that his knuckles cracked. "I have made her see the error of her wayward ways. Tonight I am certain that you will see an example of the perfect lady." He gestured towards the chair which marked Kendrick the evening's guest. "The firm hand of a husband is all that is needed."

The table was covered with all kinds of dishes, a feast that might have been meant for Prince John himself. Not only were there platters of roast swan and duckling, glazed in their sauces of wine and honey, but dumplings and dressing to go with them. There were pies and pastries.

"Blankmanger!" The blending of chicken, rice and almond milk, garnished with fried almonds and anise, was

Kendrick's favorite dish above all. Sitting down at the table, he stared at his bowl, eager to eat.

"As I was saying," Sir William mumbled, tugging nervously at his beard, "Rowena has undergone a change of heart since last you visited us. Her walk is as graceful as a swan glides over the lake, her voice is soft and melodious, and her disposition is . . . is . . . well, you will see that she would make a very fine wife."

Kendrick looked in the direction of the stairway, wondering where this paragon of womanhood was. Certainly timeliness wasn't one of her new virtues. Or was this a sign of her rebelliousness? Would she refuse to come down? Snub him? If so, what would Sir William say to cover for his daughter's rudeness? "So, she has changed her ways," he said raising his brow.

"Oh, yes, yes, yes." Shaking his head in agitation, Sir William mumbled beneath his breath. Something about his regret at having spoiled the girl as he had. Chattering away he tried to keep his young guest occupied. "Perhaps she has a headache, poor dear. My daughter has . . ." He glanced up to find her perched like an elf on the serving table. "Rowena . . ." His mouth seemed to be open in a permanent "O" as he appraised her.

"Good evening, Father." Purposefully she had dressed in clashing colors. Nor was that the only fault with her grooming. She had left tendrils falling about her face as if she hadn't brushed or combed her hair. Her gown was wrinkled, her wimple askew. On her feet were mismatched shoes. "And good evening to you, my lord de Bron."

At first Kendrick didn't notice the flaws in her appearance. He was too busy taking in her figure. Hers was not a voluptuous body. She was slim, boyishly so, with a bosom that strained at the cloth of her gown. Pert, firm breasts as he remembered. How glorious they had felt beneath his questing hand.

Look at her now, he thought, poised as if she were ready for a fight. Her eyes were fixed unwaveringly on his with such intensity that he nearly shivered. He watched the way she moved, with all the grace of an animal who could explode into action if need be.

"Good evening, Lady Fitz Hugh."

His eyes clung to her slim figure. Oh, but she was a proud one, he thought. Her shoulders were squared, her chin tilted. She walked slowly, confidently. When she greeted him there was laughter in her voice, as if she were privy to some private joke. It made him extremely uncomfortable. He felt like a child having been caught looking through a peephole. It wasn't a comfortable feeling. Not in the least. Then all at once he realized the reason for her levity.

"You look lovely. Green, saffron, purple, scarlet and buttercup orange are my favorite colors." Though perhaps not worn all at one time.

"They are my favorite colors as well," she snapped without giving him even a cursory glance. Flattery, from him. He must be mocking her. Well, war it would be then. Plopping into her chair she positioned her elbows on the table in a definite display of discourtesy.

"Rowena!"

Sir William gave his daughter several warning looks but she wasn't glancing his way. She was too engrossed in eating a roast leg of swan which she promptly tossed over her shoulder as soon as she was through. With a plop it fell to the rush-strewn floor to be fought over by the hounds. "Good," she proclaimed, licking her fingers.

"Very good," Kendrick echoed after taking a bite of his own portion. Oh, he knew just what she was up to, but it wouldn't work. No matter what the little hellion did, he wouldn't be drawn into an argument. He wouldn't be sent scurrying from the Fitz Hugh household a second time. "My compliments to the cook."

"Aye, to the cook," Rowena shouted out. Picking up her cup she leaned across the table, clinking it against

Kendrick's. "Even if he is a whoreson." Putting her chalice to her lips, she downed her ale quickly and loudly.

"Even if he is a whoreson," Kendrick repeated. Oh yes, she needed taming all right, he thought, watching as she put her feet up on the table. Leaning back in her chair she tossed an apple up and down as if it were a ball, then tossed it at him. "Good throw."

"Good catch!" She looked back at him and had to admit that she liked what she saw. Oh, the devil knew how to dress to his advantage, she thought, staring his manly physique. How many women had he tumbled because of his good looks? Strange how such wondering spurred such a swift rush of emotion within her breast. The strange feeling was caused by the swan's leg, no doubt. She had eaten it much too fast.

"Kendrick tells me he likes dancing," Sir William blurted, watching as his hopes were dashed but still trying to salvage the moment.

"Oh?" Rowena smiled impishly, planning to step on his toes. "Then by all means." In preparation she wiped her mouth and hands on the tablecloth as the manor's two deft musicians hastened to pick up their lute and harp.

Alas, the dancing was to be her undoing. The moment he reached out and took her hand she was captivated, though she would never have let that be known. His touch was a shock. He clasped her hand in a way that was definitely a prelude to "other" things. Why, the way his index finger caressed the palm of her hand, it was nearly as if their hands were making love.

"Musicians, a slow dance . . ." she heard him say in that husky voice of his. Then for just a moment she was lost, mesmerized by his voice, his touch and the charmed circle of their closeness that seemed to block out all else. She could feel the muscles of his body as he briefly held her close against him.

Her breasts were crushed against his hard chest, his hand was around her supple waist and oh, the temptation was just too much for him. Kendrick stroked the fingers of his other hand through the soft hair at her temples. For a timeless, dizzy interval their mouths were only a whisper apart.

Suddenly Rowena's sense returned. "Don't you dare!" she warned, turning her back to him as she clumsily did the footwork of the dance, a pattern of facing each other, then moving back to back, then facing each other again. Twirling and whirling. She told herself that she was only too happy when it was through.

"Let me go back to my eating. I am starved," she insisted.

"As you wish." Kendrick smiled with self-satisfaction. Say what she might, he had sensed a response from Rowena Fitz Hugh that was anything but hostile.

Merry-go-up, I'm capitulating to him, Rowena thought as she picked at her food. That realization made her feel as if all the blood from her body was draining away. He was a man who was little more than Prince John's puppet. How quickly she had forgotten that Kendrick de Bron was a usurper when she was in his arms.

"Patience. Patience," Kendrick mumbled with a smile. It was a vow he might have been able to hold to had the subject of Prince John not been purposely brought up.

"And what have you heard from the prince?" Rowena asked out of the blue, knowing the subject would spark a squabble.

"The prince?" His eyes narrowed. It wasn't at all what he wanted to talk about.

"Your master," Rowena said under her breath.

"Only that he has mentioned that your lovely face was missing from his castle," Kendrick said, paying her what he thought was a compliment.

"Oh?" His words, far from flattering her, infuriated Rowena.

Kendrick pressed on. "Like myself, he is a man known for appreciating beauty."

Rowena looked from her father to Kendrick and back

again. She counted to ten, she held her breath, but it did little good. "The prince is a pompous, vain despoiler of women," she said letting her anger out. "I would as soon he found me wanting."

Shrugging, Kendrick hurried to make peace. Oh, how he wished that he could tell her the truth, that he too detested the prince, but he didn't dare. "'Tis no secret that the prince is a bit too fond of the ladies but—"

"And fools of a feather flock together." No doubt de Bron and the prince often talked freely about their conquests.

"I suppose that could be said," he answered, clenching his teeth and ignoring her purposeful insult.

"Oh, what's the use." Rowena felt the sudden need to be away from de Bron before she ended up infuriating her father again, thus she bolted for the door.

"Rowena, come back," her father demanded, a command that she ignored.

Without really knowing why, Kendrick found himself reaching out to grasp her by the wrist as she passed by him. Stubbornly he held her fast. "Were she my daughter I would lock her in her room and put her on bread and water until her anger cooled," he suggested.

"Indeed," answered Sir William with a look on his face that clearly said he was considering such an action.

"Bread and water." The reminder of the power and physical punishment that her father and all other men held over her was too much for Rowena. What's more, the subject of her anger was close at hand. Picking up the bowl of blankmanger, her nearest and seemingly only weapon, she dumped its contents upon Kendrick's head. "Father told me this is your favorite dish. How fortunate, for it does become you so."

"BiGod!" Stunned, Kendrick rose from his chair, the blankmanger dripping down his face. Ignoring his host's horrified apologies, he calmly and coolly wiped the blankmanger from his brow. Looking towards Sir William, he surprised himself more than the old man as he said, "I can see that you are right, sir. She does need a husband, who hopefully can survive such a marriage." The look on Lady Rowena's face as he said, "Let that husband be me," was priceless.

Chapter Fourteen

Sitting on the hard floor, her knees curled up to her chin, Rowena repeated for the hundredth time, "I will not marry Kendrick de Bron! Don't even so much as think upon it, Father!"

"You will not. So say you, when in truth you have naught to say about it. The marriage settlement will be drawn up quickly, before yon suitor has time to think upon it and change his mind." Sir William shuddered at the thought.

"Draw up the settlement if you will, but I warn you, Father, I will tear it up. I will not tie myself to a man like that. I would as soon spend the rest of my life languishing in the Sheriff of Nottingham's dungeon." Without realizing it she had clenched her fists so tightly that she had drawn blood. Now she looked at her wound.

"I am old. You need a man to care for you. You need . . ."

She was unable to hide the feelings of rebellion she felt. "I do not need anyone! Most of all a husband who monitors my every mood."

"You do. You of all people need caring for before you find yourself in trouble." He sighed. Reaching up, he tugged at the gray strands of hair on his forhead, what there was left of it. "Dungeon indeed. You might well end up there."

"Aye, I just might." She was tempted to tell him everything just then. What would her father's reaction be were she to tell him of her escapades with a bow? Opening her mouth, she was just angry enough to see but as she looked into his eyes he looked so old, so tired, so worried that she changed her mind.

"I want grandchildren, Rowena. Particularly a grandson. Is that too much to ask?"

"Nay, as long as the sire is not de Bron. Otherwise you ask too much of me."

"You will feel much differently after he has bedded you." Leaning against the wall, he rested his head upon the wood.

"Bedded me?" She blinked, then fearing that somehow her father might read the truth of how she really felt about de Bron, she hastily turned around. "Kendrick de Bron will never touch me, nor will I be his wife."

"I will have to see that you change your mind." It was the first time that he had ever taken such a tone with her.

"What are you saying?"

He came up behind her and took her by the arm, not forcefully but gently. "That I will have to initiate my fatherly prerogative and lock you up until you decide to comply with what I have asked of you."

Rowena followed her father out of respect and love, not out of fear. Let him believe that he was still strong, still in control of her. She knew differently. She was free, or at least she soon would be. Waiting only long enough to hear the door close behind her, she moved to the window, opened the shutters and disappeared into the bushes.

What a strange evening it had been, Kendrick mused as he tore off his cloak and hung it on a peg by his front door. Aye, strange. But his emotions and actions had been stranger by far. BiGod, what had prompted him to actually ask Sir William for his daughter's hand in marriage? Had it been a whim? Impetuosity? Insanity?

"My lord, your garments! What happened to your clothes? To your personage?" Hugo's questioning as he greeted him did nothing to lighten Kendrick's mood.

The blankmanger. "Don't ask. By my faith, don't say a word. Just fetch me water for my bath, Hugo and be quick about it. And heat it on the fire so my teeth don't chatter."

Hugo hurried to comply, eyeing Kendrick in a manner that seemed to indicate that he wished he could read his mind. What was it about the man that always unnerved Kendrick so? Made him feel uneasy? Spied upon? Well, on the morrow he would rid himself of the man, be he Prince John's retainer or no, he thought as he stripped off his clothes.

"You may go, Hugo." When the man didn't comply, Kendrick said a second time, "You may go!"

Kendrick stepped into the small wooden tub. The water was tepid but pleasing. As he sank slowly into the water he let it surround him. He sighed. All those who looked upon bathing as a strange custom just didn't realize how soothing it could be at times. Closing his eyes he was determined not to think about anything for the moment and just relax.

"What is this? Kendrick, tell me how it can be, that you have taken to wearing your dinner instead of tasting it?"

Kendrick opened his eyes with a start to see Robert, or Robin as he now suspected him to be, standing by the tub, hands on his hips. "You saw."

"I peeked in Sir William's window just in time to view the scene." He clucked his tongue. "Methinks you have met your match this time." It was obvious by the twitching of his lips that Robert was holding back a laugh.

"Not at all. What Rowena needs is a good spanking." Kendrick sat up, attuning his ears for any sound. "Your coming here is dangerous. Prince John is searching for you."

Robert's mirth evaporated. "Well I know, but I had to take a chance." His voice lowered to barely a whisper. "I fear that I must ask a favor of you, old friend."

"A favor?" One that would get him into trouble, no doubt. "So this is not just a social call." Kendrick shook his head. Things were going much too well for him to take a chance on spoiling it all. "I do not want to become involved in any of your schemes, Rob." Stepping from the tub, Kendrick dried himself and stood with a large linen draped about his muscular body. Like some ancient Greek, he thought.

"You must!" There was an edge of desperation in Robert's voice.

Kendrick eyed his friend warily. "What's wrong?" Usually Robert was so self-assured, so devil-may-care. Clearly he was worried.

"The king is in dire trouble. There is a plot afoot."

Unpleasant memories soured Kendrick's sense of loyalty to Richard. "So . . ."

"His life is in danger. He must be warned."

Kendrick angrily turned his back. "So, warn him." What happened to Richard was of no great concern to him.

"I can't. Now that I have been declared outlaw, I can no longer move freely about. I'm being watched."

The reminder did little to calm Kendrick's now pounding heart. He whirled around. "And because you are, have now undoubtedly put me likewise in danger."

"If I have, I am sorry." The tawny-haired Rob shrugged. "But I could not think of anyone else I could turn to. Or trust." For just a moment the years melted away and he reminded Kendrick of the young boy he had so openly admired.

"Trust," he repeated. He didn't have a care about the king, but Rob was in trouble. How could he just turn his back? Anxiously he ran his fingers through his hair as he thought the matter out. At last he asked, "What is it you want me to do?"

Quickly Robert explained. The king's brother was plotting to take over the crown he all but wore now, even if it meant imprisoning his brother in a faraway land. "I know that Richard has proven to be a negligent king who has spent little time in England. He left on his crusade with little thought to his duty to his people. He handed over his crown on a silver platter to John. I know that you and your family have suffered at his hands. But, Kendrick, he is king. However bad a king he might have been at times John would be much worse."

On that Kendrick had to agree. Power had gone completely to the younger brother's head. "Aye. And to think that Henry was such a good ruler. He would turn over in his grave."

It was as if all that had been done by Henry II was now all for naught. If not for Hubert Walter, Archbishop of Canterbury and Chief Officer of the Crown, Kendrick had little doubt but that John would indeed already have placed the very crown upon his own head. So far, the archbishop had suppressed John's treason, but he could not fight the prince's ever-growing ambition forever.

"Just tonight I found out that what we have so feared has happened." Robert took a deep breath, then let it out in a rush of words. "Richard has been thrown into an Austrian prison by his fellow crusaders as he was returning to England. Those who wear the Austrian arms."

"What? Prison?" Kendrick stood dumbfounded.

"It's true. Now you know why I am so desperate to enlist your aid. I am going to ride to London. I must inform all the nobles of what has come about. We must set forth to raise an army to rescue the king!"

"And me?" Already Kendrick was frantically tugging on his garments.

"You must ride to Canterbury to talk with Hubert Walter. Perhaps the church can aid in some way in the return of the king." Taking Kendrick's hand, Robert manifested their old boyhood secret handshake, then thrust a letter into his fist. "Hurry." Then he was gone.

Kendrick took no time to don his armor. Instead he rushed to the stables clothed only in tunic, hosen, shoes, mantle and gauntlets, a dagger and sword his only weapons. He was unaware of the traitor beneath his own roof or that he was being watched. Saddling his horse he made ready for his tedious journey, planning to stop at inns along the way. For the moment Rowena Fitz Hugh was forgotten. With his mantle billowing out behind him he rode. Richard was in danger. It was easy to pay an assassin to slay an imprisoned man. The king would be an easy target to aim for now that he was captive. An easy mark for the prince.

"John must never be king." It would bring havoc. Fighting. Bloodshed. Robert had been right when he had espoused the opinion that as unskilled a ruler as Richard had been, John would be much worse.

The forest lands loomed ahead of Kendrick, but he set aside his fear of outlaws. Robin was their leader. They would not do him harm. He would be safe in the wooded lands. Why then was his path blocked up ahead?

The men were dressed in hoods, much as the one he had seen Robert wear. "I come in peace," he said, raising his hand in a gesture of camaraderie. Alas he noticed too late that there was something in their manner to be fearful of. The way they sat their horses gave them away. They were no Saxon foresters, no outlaws. They were Norman lords. Prince John's followers.

Too late Kendrick spun his horse full circle to flee from the horsemen. "Don't let him get away!" commanded a voice. Three horsemen rode to the left of Kendrick, two to the right, one followed upon his horse's hooves.

"If you can't take him alive, kill him," shouted a voice familiar to Kendrick. He could not place it, yet he knew the man from somewhere. Hugo? God's blood, it was not possible. Yet it was.

Kendrick rode as fast as he could but it was useless to try and escape. Reaching for his sword, he turned to fight, meeting one man in arm-to-arm combat. The sound of their swords clanged through the forest, frightening the deer and woodland creatures away. Kendrick thrust out and felt the blade of his sword hit muscle and flesh. He saw a man fall.

"Kill him!" This time he knew it to be Hugo's voice. Fury overcame him, the desire to see the traitor die, but he had no time to attack the man who had played him false. As he swirled there were two other men at his side. He had wounded one man but five were in pursuit. It was a battle he could not win.

Kendrick fought on gallantly nonetheless, swinging his sword like a demon possessed, wounding yet another man. Being so outnumbered, however, he knew well what was to be his fate. He would die. As he felt a burning stab of pain sear his arm, felt a warm gush of blood, he knew that to be a certainty. Still, he fought on.

Blood seeped from his wound as he struck blow after blow. He was dizzy from loss of blood; the faces before him became little more than a blur. Another sword pierced his side, the force of the blow knocking him from his horse. He fell with a thud to the cold, hard ground.

"Finish him off and let's go. I want my money ere night falls," he heard a voice say, as if through a fog.

"Rowena!" Strange that as his agony engulfed him he should whisper her name.

"Kill him. Hurry."

Kendrick waited for the sword prick which would end his life but strangely it never came. He could hear horses' hooves and wondered at the sound. Why were the men leaving him now? It was puzzling, but he wasn't clear-headed enough to ponder the matter. Darkness overcame his senses, but not before he whispered a prayer for his king and one for his own soul.

Rowena's fingers trembled as she slipped another arrow into the bow and took aim at the fleeing horsemen. "Be gone with you all, you jack-a-napes! My men and I will see you in hell," she bluffed, hoping they would believe that there were others. The bluff worked and she reasoned that cowards such as they were always wont to flee when it appeared that their own lives were threatened. She could see the colors of their tunics in the distance—the greens, grays and browns looking like leaves of autumn. "Be gone, whoever you are."

At first she had reasoned them to be followers of the outlaw Robin Hood, but after recognizing one of the men as the knight she had bested near Nottingham, she knew at once that these were Prince John's men. But why were they disguised? Curious.

Running over to where these assassins' victim lay, Rowena bent down and examined the damage their swords and clubs had done. That she was too late to save the wounded man, that he was already dying or dead, troubled her, for he had fought bravely. Never had she seen a man of stronger mettle. Who was he and why had he been set upon so cruelly?

"Oh, please . . ."

The man was smeared with blood and grime so that she could not see his face clearly. Grasping his wrist she sought for a pulse and gave a sigh of relief at the faint flutter she found there. The man was alive!

"It does not matter who you be," she whispered, "for any foe of John's is friend to me."

For a moment she could see the man's lids pulsate like the wings of a butterfly as he sought to open his eyes. He began to struggle, no doubt thinking her to be one of his attackers. She held him firmly, all the while trying frantically to stop the ooze of blood seeping from his wounds. In desperation she removed her cloak, tearing it into strips to act as a binding against the red tide of his life's blood. All the while she whispered soothing words, telling him that she did not seek to harm him.

The man was mumbling. What was it about his voice that seemed to strike a chord deep within her? Did she know him? It was difficult to see his face with so much dirt and blood covering it but she stared nonetheless. He wore no armor. No knight then. A squire? An archer? One of Robin Hood's men perhaps?

"It matters not," she said, tugging him up to lean on her slim frame. He was heavy. His body threatened to topple her, yet she fought to maneuver him to her horse. Slinging him over the animal's back like a side of beef, she climbed up beside him. It was a testing of her horsemanship to guide her mount back to the stables with a man hanging over the horse, yet Rowena was up to the task. Nudging the animal into a swift though careful gallop that matched the beat of her heart, she headed for home.

Never had the familiar walls looked so dear. Heading for the stables, she reined her horse to a halt, pulling the injured man from her horse, and sought again for a pulse. For a moment she was fearful lest the frantic ride had done damage to his wounds.

"Easy. Easy." Looking anxiously at him she saw his chest move up and down, giving proof that he still breathed. But his wounds? The bleeding was profuse, threatening. Time was her enemy, this she knew. She could not take the time to change into her womanly garments. What then? Be discovered?

"Help me! Help me!" she shouted, feigning her best imitation of a male voice. When at last two of the larger stable lads had answered her shouts, she pretended to be a wandering bowman, telling the tale that she had happened upon the man in the forest, begging them to take the poor wretch to the lady of the house.

"And just why should we?" One of the lads was surly. Stubborn.

"Because I'll cut off your ears if you don't," Rowena threatened, leaning forward as if she meant it.

The lad jumped back, then quickly complied with her command, tugging at the arm of the injured man on horseback.

"Have a care! He's not a sack of barley!" She watched as the man was lifted up by the strongest of the lads and listened as he groaned. Suddenly she could have sworn she heard her name. Leaning forward she listened again.

"Ro . . . wen . . . a."

She had clearly heard it. "Who . . . ?" It was then he opened his eyes, only for a moment, but long enough for her to recognize their haunting depths. "No! Not him." Ah, but it was and the realization was shattering. "Kendrick de Bron."

Chapter Fifteen

In agitated apprehension and fear, Rowena looked down upon the pale face of the man lying on her bed. His face was so pale that he looked almost ghostly. He had lost so much blood that she knew him to be in great peril. Oh, dear God, he had to survive. She just couldn't bear it if he died.

Having quickly climbed up the vine outside her window, Rowena had changed into a gown and kirtle so that she could greet the stable lads when they knocked at the door of her chamber. She had ordered that Kendrick be placed upon her own bed then, kneeling beside him, had fitfully bound his wounds with torn pieces of her bed linen, seeking to save the life of the man she had so enjoyed sparring with. Oh, but she had wanted to see him brought low, but not like this.

"If only . . ." Oh, but she had been so hateful. Why? Had he really done anything so terrible? Was being handsome and attractive to women such a sin? "Gwyneth and Ethelred . . ." Even there he had not really been the guilty one, except by his association with John. It was not Kendrick de Bron who had ransacked the cottage, or thrown the two Saxons out in the cold. Why then had she so vengefully blamed him?

Rowena shuddered to think what might have happened had she not chanced upon that band of cutthroats. Kendrick's death, most surely. Yet he was not out of danger yet. He still might die. The very thought brought an ache to her heart, melting away any anger she might have once had. In the face of de Bron's agony, how could she feel resentment?

"Oh, my lord." Reaching for the cold, damp cloth beside the bed she gently wiped his brow then moved the cloth lower. And lower.

Kendrick felt the warmth of a body next to him. Everything was soft and safe. He could sense someone was with him but he hadn't the strength to open his eyes. Instead he gave himself up to the sensations. Bit by bit a refreshing coolness, an encompassing gentleness was stealing some of the anguish and pain from his body.

A voice was whispering in the darkness. A comforting voice, like an angel's. Fingers as gentle as a soft spring breeze were touching him. Up. Down. Along his arms, across his chest, down his side, across his hips and back again. All too abruptly, cruelly, the stroking stopped. In protestation he uttered a deep throaty rasp but the hands had left him.

Come back . . .

It was as if he were in a long dark tunnel, groping about, fighting to come into the light. To follow. He reached out to consciousness but it was like trying to walk a treadmill through a dense fog. Darkness was upon him and though he struggled to open his eyes, he could see only shadows.

His body hurt so very much and he was exhausted. Weary. He heard faint sounds, muted as if they were coming through deep, murky water. Gurgling. His voice? Yes. The sound of his own breathing became louder and louder until it was a roar in his ears.

He was lying in an awkward position but he couldn't quite seem to shift to a more comfortable one. Dull reverberations shot through his body each time he tried to move. Pain! He willed himself to awaken but it was useless. Something was holding him back. Those men! With a jolt, their faces popped into his mind and he remembered. Richard!

"The king. Danger."

As Rowena sat by his side she noted that Kendrick was mumbling again, the same thing he said over and over. It seemed as though he sought to warn someone of danger to the king and this surprised Rowena. He was John's man, was he not? How then did he seek to give warning? And if the king was in danger, what then?

"What about the king?" In a soft tone she sought to find out some answers. At the same time she crooned words of comfort to the wounded man, reaching for the damp cloth to wipe his face again and again. She had sought to see him humbled, had sworn a hundred curses at his head. Never had she desired to see him injured, though. Never like this.

"He has lost more of his life's blood than can be tolerated I fear, my lady." The voice of Gwyneth was tinged with grave concern. The old woman was well known for her knowledge of herbs and healing poultices, thus Rowena had requested her help in tending the injured nobleman.

"But he will survive!" That he would was an obsession with Rowena, for how could she go on day to day remembering the terrible way she had acted if he died? Rowena felt lost and forlorn. The sight of this dark-haired man lying so near death tore at her heart and her soul. Somehow she could not forget the feel of his lips upon hers no matter how hard she tried, nor the touch of his hands upon her flesh. "We must do everything in our power to save him."

"We will. But there is only just so much any mortal can

do." Gwyneth looked upwards as if calling on a more powerful presence.

Rowena bowed her head and spoke a silent prayer. *Please God. Let him live.* She wanted to see a smile touch his lips again, wanted to look into his eyes and see them sparkle, even if it was with anger. Silently she watched Gwyneth go about the business of working with poultices and sighed. *Admit it,* she thought to herself. Kendrick de Bron meant more to her than she ever would have admitted.

"It is his fever which frightens me, not so much the wound itself. Blood fever. That is what takes them to the next world and beyond. If it were up to me, I would burn away the reddened flesh and have done with it," Gwyneth was saying.

"Burn it away?"

Nodding, Gwyneth walked towards the knight's sword and thrust it into the fire. "Burn it."

"Nay." Rowena stayed her hand. "I would not see him suffer so." She had seen the cauterizing of wounds during jousting tournaments and knew the agony it caused.

"As you like." The old woman scowled. "I only thought to help. It would quicken his time of healing." When Rowena continued to block her way, Gwyneth busied herself with her herbs.

"What is that which you prepare?" The orange vegetable looked strangely like the food Rowena so hated to eat.

"Carrots for a poultice. It will help him, of that you have my word. Apply it to his wound every hour. Aside from burning the wound, it is the best that I can do." Handing Rowena the poultice, Gwyneth left the room, casting a glance over her shoulder to see if perhaps by caring for this man Rowena's heart would be softened. Indeed, Rowena noticed that Gwyneth actually seemed to like Kendrick de Bron.

"Every hour." Rowena was not used to tending the wounded, yet she bent over his form and gently applied the mixture, wincing as he groaned. He was still in a great deal of pain, lost in the world of his darkness. "Kendrick, open your eyes." That was what she selfishly wanted so that she could make amends, and yet perhaps because of his pain it was better if he was unconscious.

Remembering the scalding words she had thrown his way and the rude manner in which she had reacted to his compliments, she yearned for the chance to take those words back. All this time she had thought him to be the prince's man, and yet now she had her doubts. Just what was his game? What was Kendrick de Bron about? He seemed truly fretful about Richard. Or was it just pretense? No. Dying men did not act at charades. What then?

Her mind was in turmoil as she bent down and soothed his brow. She felt the same stirring, the same overpowering reaction to his nearness that she had that time before, but now she didn't fight against it. What would it be like to make love with him?

"Oh, Kendrick, why do you make me tremble all over at the memory of your touch? What is this magic you work so well on me even now?" Pressing her cool hand against his brow she sought for any sign of fever and was relieved that his forehead seemed to be cooling. Oh, but his skin was so smooth that she could not resist the temptation to run her fingers lightly over his face. His cheekbones were high, his nose finely carved, his chin firm and strong. He was as finely wrought as a statue. And just as still. "Oh, de Bron!"

Impulsively she touched his lips with the tip of her finger. So full. She remembered the taste of that mouth. "I wouldn't pull away from your kiss now." Forgotten was all the bitterness.

For a long while Rowena stared at de Bron's handsome face. His dark lashes shaded his face, casting shadows, and she reached out to brush them gently with her lips, then moved upward to kiss him on the mouth, lightly then with increasing boldness. Oh, how she wished he could respond, but nevertheless the sensation was pleasing.

Growing bold in her appraisal, she gave full attention to the physique that she had bared in order to tend his wounds. His arms were well-muscled, his waist trim, his shoulders broad. With a sigh she ran her hands over the hair on his chest, reveling in the sensation.

Once again Kendrick gave himself up to the wonderous stroking. Who? He forced his eyes open again but he could only see colors. A swirl of brightness. But nothing familiar. Where was he? How had he gotten here? In panic he pushed against the mattress in an effort to sit up, only to fall back down again. Then for just a brief moment he saw those eyes. Those wonderful eyes!

"Rowena!"

She was startled to see him looking at her. Flushing with embarrassment, she stepped away from him quickly.

"No, do not go . . ." He weakly raised his hand. Fighting to sit up, he gritted his teeth against the pain and soon gave up the effort, plopping back down among the pillows again.

"Lie back," she said more sternly than she felt. "You must save your strength. You lost nearly an ocean of blood."

He was confused. Why was he here? "You . . . you found me?"

"You were brought here." She tried to affect her haughty demeanor, but it was difficult in the face of his vulnerability.

He grimaced against a sudden stab of pain. "The . . . the king. I must get word." Thrashing about, he seemed to relive his battle. The effort sapped what little energy he had and he collapsed again. His eyes closed as he drifted off into a seemingly dreamless slumber.

Rowena scolded herself for not learning of the king's fate before he went out like a candle. Richard was in danger, that much she could tell. But from who? And when? Her eyes darted to the door and then back to Kendrick again. Damn, she was tempted to leave Kendrick's side,

don her lad's garb and be off, but what if something befell
de Bron while she was gone?

Struggling with her emotions, she longed to take to her
horse and carry her bow to help the king, but in the end
her attraction and concern for the man abed won out over
her loyalty to Richard. What devastating power was the
power of love, she wondered, knowing in that moment
that indeed she did love Kendrick de Bron. God help her.
With a resigned sigh, she adjusted the coil of her braid
and sat down beside him to hold vigil.

Chapter Sixteen

It seemed to be a never-ending cycle of the sun giving way to the moon as Rowena kept a constant vigil over Kendrick de Bron. Day turned into night and night into day three times as she watched over him and diligently tended to his wounds. In his defenseless slumber he brought out all the protective instincts within her and she vowed to do everything in her power to see that he was safe. When he moaned in his sleep she crooned to him and tried to bring him comfort, when he was chilled she pulled blankets over his nude, manly form. Hovering by his side she fiercely guarded him, determined to protect him from the men-at-arms who had knocked on the manor's door and were even now searching for him.

"Indeed, they will never find you. Fie on them if they think that they will," she whispered, stroking his thick dark hair. "Damn them for traitors."

At last Rowena had agreed with Gwyneth's pleas to burn the flesh of Kendrick's most severe wound. With relief she noted that the redness now seemed nearly gone. Remembering with admiration the way this dark-haired man had fought against crying out with pain, she smiled. Stubborn and arrogant he might be at times, but at least he was brave. That was a quality Rowena admired above all. She felt a new respect for him.

"Brave and handsome."

And definitely all man. Oh, that he would wake up and be no more a victim of the nightmares which so deeply troubled him. Tortured dreams that caused him to thrash about as he struggled with his assailants once again. Bending over him, Rowena sought to calm him as well as to find out once and for all what was going on with the king.

"Oh, de Bron, please wake up. Tell me what must be done to save the king. Please."

There was no answer. Kendrick hovered on the brink of consciousness, between sleeping and wakefulness. His mind floated freely in a dark, quiet wilderness where he could escape his anxieties, and his pained body was buoyed up by the soft surface on which he lay as he settled into that mindless netherworld devoid of pain and memory. Then an image disturbed his reverie. He seemed to remember swinging his sword, remembered falling. But what had happened then?

The glare of light troubled his eyes and he struggled to escape the black fog which engulfed him. Was he imagining it or did he hear Rowena Fitz Hugh's voice calling to him, pleading with him? The king? The king. The king. It echoed in his ears.

"The king," he murmured. It was just the catalyst needed to bring him around. He forced his eyes open.

Wisps of sunlight flickered through the half-open shutters, throwing shadows on the wall, images that teased his eyes as he slowly emerged from the darkness. From somewhere far away he thought he heard the sound of a bell. He was dizzy. The boundaries of the room alternately advanced and receded like waves against the shore. Back and forth. Up and down.

"BiGod!" Closing his eyes he reached out as if to steady

himself. He was as weak as a pup. With a groan he reached up to touch his arm. There was a pounding there, a dull, throbbing ache. And a bandage! He felt helpless. Foolish. He didn't like being at someone else's mercy at all. Particularly a snip of a girl's. No doubt she would as usual have some snide comment to unman him. A barb to prick his ego.

"You are awake."

Kendrick stared up at her, awaiting her sarcasm. "Aye." Alas, he was much too exhausted to be able to spar with her.

"I was so worried."

The soft tone of her voice caressed him, surprised him. In fact, he was stunned. Her sympathies were sincere. "You were?" And he had thought she hated him.

"I was." She pressed her hand against his brow. She wanted to tell him then and there that it was she who had saved his life, but she did not. She wasn't certain that she could fully trust him concerning her masquerade. And yet, oh how she would have liked to see the look on his face to know that a woman had come to his aid.

"How did I get here?" He pressed his mind into a semblance of coherency, remembering bits and pieces.

Her jaw tensed as she said, "A young archer brought you."

"A young archer?" He looked into her eyes, wondering why their sky blue should seem to swirl before him as if in a dream. He seemed to remember eyes such as hers looking down at him as he hovered between life and death. "Who?" He reached out and grasped her hand.

"A young forest lad," she answered, once again wishing she could hurl the truth at his head.

"Humph." He remembered now. The bothersome lad. The one who had taunted him right from the first. The thought that he owed his life to him was peevishly daunting. "Well, it would take more than . . . than a few churlish bastards to fell me permanently. As you see, I am too stubborn to die.''

"Aye, too stubborn." He looked so annoyed that she couldn't keep from laughing. A melodious sound.

"Rowena." Certainly her concern seemed genuine. If what he remembered was true, she had unselfishly brought him to her chamber to heal him. A noble gesture.

Never had her name sounded so beautiful, so feminine. As he spoke it a fire stirred deep within her. Strange, that always before she had taken no pride in her womanhood. Now . . .

"You are lovely when you smile." His fingers caressed the palm of her hand, sending a tingling sensation all through her hand. "Never again scowl."

"Never?"

Blue eyes met brown and it was as if suddenly there were no other beings upon earth, just the two of them touching for a moment in time. They looked at each other for a long, long while, achingly aware of the longing they felt. Then Rowena moved closer.

Oh, what a temptation her breasts were as they peeked over the cloth of her gown. Kendrick had no willpower at all.

She felt the warm, soft touch of his fingers, sending a shiver of desire coursing through her blood. His hand cupped the tender flesh, caressing the peak through the thin material of her bodice with infinite tenderness. The sensation was so stirring that, though she caught his hand with the intention of removing his fingers, she did not stop him.

"You like that?"

She nodded, sighing, then suddenly remembered the king. She had been so enamored she had let Richard's peril slip briefly from her mind. "You said something about the king being in danger. What has happened?"

"He is in an Austrian prison."

"Prison." So what he had said before was true. She

trembled at the very thought. Richard would be much like a trapped pigeon at the mercy of those who would profit by his death.

"I was on my way to Canterbury when I was set upon." The memory jolted him and he tried to sit up, only to fall back uselessly as dizziness engulfed him.

"Be careful. You will open your wound." Rowena was stern.

"Damn!"

"Methinks you will not be going anywhere. Not now."

"Nay, you are right." He felt so tired, yet even so he forced his eyes to remain open so that he could look at her. His eyes took in her beauty, so soft and golden. He admired her height. It added to her comeliness, making her seem regal, proud and graceful. "Lay down beside me." He wanted to feel the warmth of her body next to his. "Please."

How could she deny him? She wanted to be close to him "Well . . . perhaps for a short while." Carefully, so as not to disturb his injuries, she first sat upon, then lay down upon the bed, nestling into the crook of his good arm.

"There, you see, I am not a monster," he whispered, closing his eyes. It felt so good to feel her body lying close. He felt strangely secure and at peace. Later. He would figure out what to do about the king as soon as he had rested.

Oh, but it was pleasant lying beside Kendrick de Bron like two lovers on the grass on a summer's day, but the sensation was at odds with Rowena's anxieties. Richard was in danger. How then could she just while away the day? Kendrick had embarked upon a late-night ride because he had thought it important to get a message to the arch-bishop. Why could she not continue in his place? Undoubtedly she could ride just as well as Kendrick de Bron. Nay. Better!

"De Bron!" Rolling over on her side she gently nudged him. "De Bron!"

He moaned, mumbled, but at last opened one eye.

"You say that Richard is in danger, that you were riding to Canterbury. Let me help you."

"Help?" He looked bewildered. "How?"

"I will ride to Canterbury." Her words were uttered boldly. Too boldly.

He opened his other eye. "You?"

"Aye!" The more she thought about it, the more sense it made. She was most capable.

"No!" The thought of a woman, even a feisty one, attempting such an arduous journey was out of the question. She would get herself raped or killed. "No," he said again.

Instantly Rowena's temper came to a boil. How dare he tell her what to do! Oh, wasn't that just like a man? "It is the only sensible answer," she said, gritting her teeth to keep from swearing at him.

"Perhaps your father could go, or . . . or send one of his servants." Kendrick was so tired that he was having trouble focusing on the problem at hand.

"My father. A dottering old man." But still a male in a world dominated by the egotistical beasts. "I tell you, I would be much more likely to complete the errand."

Kendrick put his arm over his eyes, wanting to end the debate quickly. "You have not the strength."

"Have not the strength." Oh, how she wanted to tell him how wrong he was. Why, in a fair fight she could best him at quarter staff and with a bow. Had not the strength. Had not the strength. He would not be lying here alive if not for her strength, cunning and courage.

"Rowena, put it out of your mind. I will go. Just let me rest for a little while, then I will mount up and continue on . . ." Kendrick gave into his exhaustion.

"And fall in a heap by the roadside." Rowena grimaced at the stubbornness of it all. And all because of manly pride. Well, she would not give in to such foolishness. She would go and when she had completed the journey, she would make certain that Kendrick de Bron gave her a well-deserved apology.

Disentangling herself from his arms she opened the chamber door, hurriedly tearing at her false braid as she ran. Retrieving her archer's garments from her hiding place behind the stairs, she quickly donned them. They were still stained with Kendrick de Bron's blood, but she had not the time to clean them. Instead she merely pulled on one of her old mantles to hide the stains and slipped quietly out of the manor. Running to the stables, she drew her bow and quiver of arrows from the safety of a corner hayloft and jumped upon her horse.

Kendrick de Bron tossed and turned upon his straw bed. Oh, but it was aggravating being so helpless and weak. Kendrick didn't like it one bit. Still, there was at least one advantage to his predicament. Rowena Fitz Hugh's newfound devotion. Her presence beside him had calmed him as he slept and given him something to look forward to when he awoke.

"Something very good has come from treachery." Not that he would have willingly placed himself in the path of those men. But it had happened. And from the tragedy something very special had come.

"Oh, Rowena!" The name came forth like a benediction. She was everything he could want in a woman, beautiful, brave, and . . . "Stubborn!"

Even so, Rowena Fitz Hugh had become an enthralling obsession for him. Even now he fantasized about holding her, warm and naked in his arms. He wouldn't be injured forever. When he recovered, they had a great deal to talk about. A great deal, he thought opening the left eye just a slit.

"Rowena . . . ?"

She was looking in on him, her face haloed by the lantern light.

But what was this? Upon closer inspection, Kendrick was startled when his befuddled brain realized it wasn't Rowena at all but the old woman. "What? Where?"

"Lady Rowena has gone riding," he was informed.

"Riding?" And he had really thought that she cared. Obviously not enough to forgo her own pleasures. "Well, I have need of her." He was peevish, then as suspicion nudged at his brain, he was angry. The foolish woman had done it. She had ignored his warning and stupidly gone on what was supposed to be a man's errand. "BiGod! I have to go after her." He struggled to get up. He had to protect her before she got herself into trouble.

"You are not going anywhere." There was a strength in the old woman's voice that belied her age. Likewise her arms as they pressed against him were forceful.

"Don't you understand? She is no match for them." Once again Kendrick tried to get out of bed only to be thwarted most soundly. Oh, how humiliating!

Instead of looking properly worried as Kendrick knew she should, the old woman only smiled. "Lady Rowena is much stronger than you know. She'll take care of herself. Indeed, my worries are not so much for her as for he who incurs her retribution." The woman busied herself with changing his bandage.

"Ouch!" Kendrick's expression was accusing. "Certainly gentleness is not an attribute that you possess," he said. He damned Rowena anew for having left him alone with this unsympathetic crone.

"Nor gratitude one of yours!" Despite the criticism she continued her ministrations, calling the young woman named Maida into the room when he fought against her determined efforts.

"Alas, I am outnumbered!" Ceasing his struggle, he gave in to the inevitable, musing all the while. So, Rowena had gone. The troublesome wench had actually done it. Where was she now? What was she thinking? What was she doing? Was she regretting her overboldness? Well, perhaps a bit of a scare would give her her comeuppance. It would be good for her. Why should he worry? And yet he did. So much so that it nearly made him ill.

"There, that should do it." As the old woman tied the clean bandage securely in place she looked pleased with herself. "Now, behave yourself, my lord, lest I have to give you one of my sleeping potions."

"No!" Kendrick quickly pretended to be the most obedient of patients. All the while his brain buzzed with ideas of how he would escape from this place and follow after the headstrong lady. Then, just when it seemed hopeless, a chance presented itself.

"Watch after him for a moment, Maida, while I go get but a handful of some special herbs." Something to ascertain that he would behave, her manner seemed to say.

"Oh, I will." Batting her eyelashes at Kendrick the moment the old woman had left, Maida openly showed that guarding him would not be an unpleasant task. "Lady Rowena calls you the arrogant lord." Her voice was a breathy whisper. "But I know from having heard Chad and Humbley talk that you have a kind and compassionate side. If so, then tell me what has happened to them."

"Prince John has, as he has put it, detained them!"

"Detained?" She shivered, fearing for the two men. "Are they . . . are they . . . ?"

"We soon shall see, for I intend to get them back the moment I have regained my strength."

Maida sighed longingly, obviously regretting his injured state, imagining what mischief she could create. "You'll need more than strength to abide the mistress of this manor."

"What do you mean?"

"Lady Rowena has been acting strangely of late."

"Strangely." Kendrick was most interested. "What do you mean?"

"She won't let me help her dress any longer. She wants

to be free from prying eyes, or so it seems." She pouted
petulantly. "And she keeps the latest hours."

"Late hours?" He frowned. "What do you mean?"

"She roams about in the night like some nocturnal creature. I've been watching her." Maida's voice took on a
tattling tone. "She doesn't think that I know, but I do."

"So." Jealousy threatened to poison Kendrick. Was it
possible? Could it be? Had Rowena Fitz Hugh rejected his
wooing because she had a lover? Pondering the matter,
he decided otherwise. It had to be something else. But
what?

Maida soon answered. "She has taken to dressing like
a lad. I've seen her climbing up to her room by way of a
thick vine when she thinks no one is watching."

Dressing like a lad? Kendrick closed his eyes, seeing first
one face and then another. The lady, then the lad. Rowena
and the archer. Their features merged into the same face.

"Is it possible?" Could it be? No, it couldn't. Rowena
couldn't possibly be the same person as the bothersome,
unruly lad with the bow. Or could she?

Chapter Seventeen

Rowena rode at a punishing pace toward Canterbury without so much as a pause, all the while determined to prove her mettle once and for all. She would not be daunted in this mission, she vowed, for there was much at stake, her pride being just one of the reasons goading her. It was either reach Canterbury or be damned. She would show de Bron! She was no fragile flower in need of protection! She could manage quite well on her own, if you please. If the road was rutted and rocky, a far cry from the smooth pavement the Romans had instigated, she tried to ignore the fact.

The wind howled around her, rain from a sudden storm soaked her to the skin, but she continued on her way, shivering against the chill, gathering her mantle tightly around her body in a futile effort to keep dry. Push on. Push on. Push on. The fate of Richard, nay perhaps of all England, might very well rest on her accomplishment this night.

"Keep going! You dare not stop!"

A person could only push themselves for so long, how-

ever. After over eight hours in the saddle she was in misery.
It was the longest time she had ever been on horseback
without at least dismounting for a brief rest. When her
backside ached so intensely that she could not stand it,
however, when every muscle in her body throbbed and
begged for relief, she at last attuned her eyes for a tavern
or an inn. She had been riding hard. She and the poor
horse were in need of a rest.

"I will stop, but only for an hour or so," she told herself,
scanning the road ahead of her. The village just over the
hill was much larger than those in Nottinghamshire. Surely
there must be at least one tavern or inn.

At last she spied a likely resting place. If its thatched
roof looked in serious need of repair, if some of its shutters
were cracked and broken, well, it would just have to do.
Besides, one had to be suspect and cautious in the more
commodious and well-furnished establishments, for
thieves and spies were sure to abound. Sliding off her
horse, she hastened to the unpainted door and banged
loudly.

A tall man with shoulder-length, carrot-red hair and a
toothy grin opened the portal, beckoning her inside.
"Come in, come in, come in," he said. "It ain't fancy, but
it's warm and it's dry." He reached for her mantle but
Rowena shook her head. "A'wright then."

Following him into the murky wooden dwelling that
smelled of grease, sweat, stale wine and smoke, Rowena
looked around her. Hardly the place for a lady, but for a
"lad" it would do quite well, despite the fact that the
rushes were in dire need of a change and the benches
threatened to have splinters. After her hectic ride it would
be moderately comfortable. Far better a place to rest than
a stable.

"A mug of ale for the lad here!" boomed the tavern
keeper, motioning to the tavern maid. He took one look
at Rowena's green garments and winked. "A small reward
for wot yer did for me. I'll not soon be forgetting how

yer saved me hide and purse from the prince's thieving rascals."

"I . . . ?" Rowena stared into his face. No, he was not one of the men she had rescued. Who had rescued him then?

"Aye, you and your merry men . . ." He pounded her on the back most heartily, pushing her down on a bench.

Clearly it was a case of mistaken identity, the innkeeper mistaking her for someone else, one of Robin Hood's men, no doubt. Nevertheless, Rowena didn't correct the error, nor did she refuse the reward. She was thirsty.

"Thank you," she said to the tavern maid as she handed her a mug of ale.

"Is there anything else you be wanting?"

Looking up, Rowena found herself staring into the eyes of a big-bosomed woman who made it very clear she had much more than serving drinks on her mind. Much more. Had she not guessed the woman's intent, the bold hand reaching towards Rowena's crotch said it all.

"Nothing more," Rowena said gruffly, pushing the woman's hand aside. A woman like this would see through her disguise or force her to some rash action.

"Nothing . . . ?" The tavern wench was flirting, teasing. Obviously she was one of the prostitutes who frequented inns, praying on gullible patrons.

"Nothing!" It was women like this who gave all women a bad name, Rowena thought with a scowl, making it blatantly obvious that she wasn't interested.

"Well, I'll leave you alone then," was the reply.

"Good. Good." Rowena sighed in relief.

Scanning the crowd of patrons she quickly noted that as in most villages the favorite recreation here was drinking. Drinking and gaming. Huddled and hunkered down in the far corner, five men were playing at dice. The dicemaker's guild had strict laws against making fraudulent dice, but nevertheless there were some who managed to obtain a pair or two. Hopefully, there would not be any trouble.

Taking a hurried drink of her ale, then another and another, she didn't feel that she could relax for long. Standing up Rowena sauntered over to a table of dun and brown-clothed men. She would ask if they had heard any word about the king.

"Richard?" asked one of the villagers, casting her a wary glance. "Lionheart?"

"There is no other," she said tartly, sitting in the empty chair beside him. "Long live the king!"

Her words seemed to earn his trust and the trust of a seaman who quickly sought her out. She listened as he told the tale he had heard of Richard's betrayal. A seaman had access to such tattlings.

"Richard was thoroughly disheartened over his defeat in Jerusalem. He sailed on the ship I was on from Palestine in October. It was not possible for him to go by way of France, however, because his feud with King Philip had grown very bitter. Instead he decided to return by the Adriatic and across Germany."

"Germany?" A most unwise decision, Rowena thought.

"He had received reports of John's activities and realized no time should be lost."

"An astute observation," Rowena said softly. "But pray tell, what happened?"

The seaman sadly shook his head. "Alas, Richard's jeweled baldric somehow arrived at Rome and was offered openly for sale in that city."

"What?" Rowena had not heard this. "Surely not his."

"Queen Berengaria identified it herself, for there could be no mistake. It was a handwoven thing of blue velvet with the royal insignia and the letter 'R' embroidered on it in gold thread. At first 'twas thought the king's ship had gone down in crossing the Mediterranean and that the baldric had been among the possessions saved."

"Oh no!" For just a moment Rowena feared the worst. And if Richard was dead, then John would be king. A horrible thought.

"In truth it has been learned instead that the king landed on the coast of Istria and, disguising himself as a pilgrim, had ridden north into the territory of his most bitter enemies."

"The new German Emperor, Henry VI and Leopold of Austria," Rowena gasped. "So, 'tis already known."

"Aye."

None of those gathered doubted for a moment that Prince John had had a hand in the matter. All assembled got involved in what they had heard of the story. Richard, so it was told, had landed in Austria disguised as a pilgrim. He had ridden north into territory held by his enemies, the new German Emperor and Leopold of Austria. Coming to a small village, he had arrived at a dire time, when rumors of his arrival had already spread through the foreign land. Alas, he had been discovered.

"There he be sittin' before a fire in the kitchen of an inn," exclaimed an old man who recounted the tale as he guzzled his drink. "The mayor strode in as big as you please and said, 'Hail, King of England. Thy face betrays who thou art.' Richard was trussed up like a rooster for plucking and never seen again."

Rowena winced at the thought. "Poor Richard. Taken to Vienna."

"Ah yes, but the good prince hopes to raise a ransom to bring our good king safely home again," said another man, tottering on his feet, obviously in his cups.

"The prince has pretended that?" Rowena wrinkled her nose in disgust. How like John to pretend to be rescuer when instead he was at fault.

"John, indeed! The king had best look to his back," said another man. His golden hair bespoke of Saxon heritage.

Rowena asked about Hubert Walter, the archbishop. "Surely he will do all he can to free the king once he hears." She intended to be the one bringing him that message.

"The archbishop already knows and he is no fool. He

trusts John not at all. Hubert Walter intends to see personally to the collecting of the ransom."

"Oh?" Rowena turned her head to look at the man who had just spoken, a stout man who towered over her by nearly a foot and a half. He was clothed in a mantle with a hood and carried a staff, bow and quiver of arrows. "And just why are you so well informed?"

"Because I am returning from speaking with the archbishop." The big man crossed his massive arms across his chest.

"You?" She wondered it this could be a trap. Perhaps the archbishop was in danger. What would happen if that holy personage were to come to mishap? Would not John then have free reign? "And just *who* are *you*?"

"Who am I?" Throwing his head back, the big man guffawed.

"Aye, I ask again, who are you?" Though the man was a giant, Rowena refused to be intimidated.

"Little John," came the answer as the man lowered his head and looked at her nose to nose.

"Little John." Now it was her turn to laugh. "And just who is he?"

The man sitting next to her nudged her ribs. "The most important of all outlaws in England, except for Robin Hood himself."

Little John bowed mockingly. "So, lad, you see . . ."

"Little John, ha!" As if that one would be so bold as to show himself with the price he had on his head. "If you are Little John then I am . . . I . . . I am Robin Hood."

"Robin Hood?" A tiny little man in the corner looked at her with awe. "Really? Why, I thought that he would be taller."

"Robin Hood. Robin Hood." Little John tweaked her on the nose. "For a surety you are not, for I know him well." The description he gave was accurate, so much so that Rowena was convinced. She had seen Maid Marian's lover up close. "But methinks you be a brave lad nonetheless. Tell me, can you put your courage where your mouth is?''

"Aye!" She intended to say more, but the hum of voices interrupted her. Turning towards the men in the corner she heard accusations of cheating at dice. Suddenly havoc broke out in the tavern.

"I recognize that one. Little John," cried a voice, pointing his finger in the direction of the giant outlaw. "Get him."

"There is a reward on his head." Several men garbed in brown suddenly threw off their mantles, revealing themselves to be Prince John's followers. They came at Little John, outnumbering him at least two to one.

"Forsooth, I should not have been so foolhardy in revealing my identity," Little John swore, "but I thought I was among friends." He readied himself for a scuffle.

"And you are." The innkeeper joined in the ruckus.

Rowena didn't like the odds. It was too one-sided in John's favor. Picking up a large wooden chair, she threw it at the mob, joining in. If she had doubted Little John's identity or his loyalties, she did not now.

"Count me in," she shouted out. "It seems, big man, that you have need of another friend."

He laughed, despite the danger. "It seems that I do!"

Oh, what a fight it was! Little John fought with the strength of a wild boar, as good with his hands as he was with his staff. He took on two men at a time, three men, four, and still bested them. Indeed, he might have won an easy victory had it not been for the fact that the number of the prince's men increased steadily, entering through the windows and doors.

Rowena picked up a tankard of ale and struck first one of the prince's men, then another. "Take this, you usurper's hound. And this!" Wishing she had brought her bow and arrow into the inn, she had to suffice with what was at hand. Proudly she realized that even weaponless she held

her own. But only a fool was so stubborn as not to admit
when the odds were against them.

"Methinks it best we leave, my fine fellow," Little John
said at last. Grabbing her by the arm, he led her out the
door, taking advantage of the melee the inn's patrons were
creating as they threw themselves in between the outlaw
and the prince's men. Together they pushed through.

Rowena slammed the door in their followers' faces, brac-
ing herself against the wood to hold them off as best she
could. "Hurry. Ride," she ordered, calling out to Little
John. "I can only hold them so long."

"Indeed!" He mounted his horse. "You're a brave one.
We would welcome you in our band," he yelled out.

"Oh, you would!" She flung herself upon her horse's
saddle.

"Follow me. I'll take you to our camp."

Rowena chuckled at that, but shook her head. "Nay, I
am serving my king better where I am. I have a ride to
complete. But I thank you, Little John, for the compliment." She grabbed at the reins, but before she parted
company with Robin Hood's right hand man, she couldn't
resist yelling, "Say hello for me to your leader, though,
and tell him that when next we meet before an arrow's
target, I will best him."

"Best him?" Little John started to grin.

"Don't laugh. Robin will remember me. It was I who
nearly won the golden arrow. Had it not been for the wind,
I well might have done so." Not having time to wait for
Little John's reply, she rode off.

Kendrick tossed and turned upon the bed, besieged by
worry. How could he have allowed a woman to go on
such a hazardous mission? Why hadn't he guessed that she
would be so foolhardy and somehow stopped her? What
if she were caught? What if Prince John's men held her

captive at this very moment? He knew well what treachery they were capable of.

"Where is she? What is taking her so long?" His jaw was clenched as he thought about what had befallen him. Hugo! The traitor! Had it not been for Rowena, he would most likely be dead, or huddled along the roadside, dying. "Rowena!" She had saved him. Or had she?

Closing his eyes, Kendrick tried to remember exactly what had happened, but alas it was all a blur. He did remember a voice, however. Whispering. Caressing. "It does not matter who you be," the voice had said, "for any foe of John's is friend to me."

Suddenly Kendrick opened his eyes as he had another memory. "Help me!" a male voice had warbled.

"And just why should we?"

"Because I'll cut off your ears if you don't,"

He sat up so quickly that his head seemed to spin. Could it be? Rowena and the archer one and the same? If not, then why were there so many coincidences? How was it that Rowena and the archer merged in his mind's eye? First one and then the other?

Kendrick's head swam with a hundred angry questions that for the moment blotted out his pain. Was it? Could it be? How? When? Where? Why? Alas, he fell back down. Did it really matter? She was everything he could want in a woman, beautiful, brave and passionate despite her protestations to the contrary. She had felt so right in his arms. So very right.

That did not mean, however, that they did not have a score to settle, he reflected hazily. If she really was who he suspected she might be, she would need to be taught a thing or two.

Chapter Eighteen

Canterbury stood on a site that had already been occupied for over three hundred years when the Romans arrived. Now it was covered with a light dusting of snow which sparkled like jewels as the sun peeked from behind a cloud. Rowena walked along the cobbled streets, tugging at her mantle as she gazed at the city of Canterbury.

So much had happened here before she was born. Perhaps that was why she felt somehow as if the city were haunted. Looking at the town walls, the castle and the gray stone of the cathedral, Rowena could not help but be reminded of Thomas Becket. Twenty-three years ago he was murdered here by four Norman knights, making Canterbury a European center of pilgrimage.

"Who will rid me of this low-born priest?" King Henry II had cried out in a characteristic burst of rage. In all too eager response, four knights had volunteered, making the Saxon-born Thomas a martyr. Stepping through the wide wooden door, Rowena could nearly feel their presence.

It was quiet inside the gray stone walls. Though she trod softly, she could hear the sound of her footsteps echoing in her ears. She did not hear the cleric who came upon her, however, until she heard his voice.

"Are you looking for someone?"

Whirling around, Rowena was confronted by a tall, stern-looking, balding man all dressed in dark brown. "I wish to see Hubert Walter, elected Archbishop of Canterbury on the king's urgent demand."

"The archbishop." Eyeing her up and down and judging her to be inconsequential, he shook his head. "He is busy."

"I am certain that he is, however, I would think him not too busy to hear news concerning the king."

"The king?"

She stepped forward. "I have a message, one for which a man nearly lost his life."

The cleric was hesitant, then after staring at the "lad" for a long, long time, he beckoned her to follow him. "Come."

He led her in the direction of the Christ Church, a stone building with a red, black and blue roof whose turrets were topped with gilded pinnacles. From the apex of the central tower rose a cherub, riding high against the sky like a guardian. Nestled by the church's side around the great quadrangle of the cloister were the dark monastic buildings. It was to the archbishop's palace, a manor house, however, that she was finally taken.

Rowena took the stairs two at a time as she ascended into the main part of the archbishop's palace. The hall was dim and quiet as she entered and she paused in the doorway as she realized that those within were kneeling, saying prayers. Except for Hubert Walter, who was pacing up and down the room. He stopped as he noticed Rowena's presence.

"What is this, Henry? Who is this boy?" Dressed in a dalmatic, a richly embroidered robe with slits up the sides, a short tunicle and a sleeveless chasuble, he looked formidable and impressive. A worthy opponent for the prince.

Rowena hurriedly pushed forward, kneeling to kiss the

archbishop's ring before she answered. "Who I am is unimportant. It is what I have to tell you that is of consequence." In an even tone she quickly told him about Kendrick de Bron's ambush and her suspicion that in some way Prince John had been involved.

The wry-faced archbishop listened to all she had to say attentively and without interrupting. At last he did make a comment. "I am acutely conscious of the doings of that unscrupulous member of the royal family."

"Richard has been captured," Rowena breathlessly continued. "He was taken to Vienna. He must be rescued at all costs. I can gather up volunteers from among the villagers and I myself will go—"

"Impossible." His tone was curt and he made no explanations.

"Impossible?" Forgetting herself, Rowena allowed her voice to get shrill. "Nothing is impossible."

The corners of the archbishop's mouth turned down in a frown. "If Richard has vanished from sight, it is."

"Vanished!" Rowena's face paled.

"All that is known is that he is being kept by perfidious German rulers. Queen Eleanor is personally going to send a letter to the Pope demanding that the papacy compel the emperor to release her son. Other than that, all that can be done is to comply with the ransom demand."

It would be a hard task to raise the huge sum of money needed for Richard's ransom, for the country had not yet recovered from the drain of the Crusade, the archbishop said. He would make a radical experiment, placing a tax on the land. Twenty shillings on each knight's fee. In addition, he would make demands on the church. Even on monastic institutions, which had heretofore been exempt from taxation.

"Comply!" Rowena thought immediately of her father. This tax would hit him hard. Was it any wonder then that as she left Canterbury she was troubled?

* * *

Kendrick's wounds hurt. How then was it possible for a hot sweat of desire to run down his muscled chest and back and tickle his long, muscular legs? "Oh, God!" He wanted her. More than he had ever wanted anything in all his life.

The image of Rowena Fitz Hugh's slim, desirable form, her pretty face, in fact teased him unmercifully. He wanted her to hurry back, wanted to feel her firm breasts against his naked flesh, wanted to touch her all over.

He closed his eyes, reveling in the feel of the smooth linen sheets against his skin. "Mmmmm . . ." He imagined her body soft and warm, strangely magical in the power that her nearness had over him. Was that why he dozed off into a kind of throbbing, uneasy sleep, a sleep in which he dreamed of her?

She was in the room with him, her arms outstretched as she took a step towards him. "I love you, Kendrick de Bron. I want you . . . so much . . ."

Placing her long hands on either side of his face, she bent her arrogant mouth to his for a kiss. Her lips, so soft, like the touch of a cloud. Kendrick felt himself drifting, spinning, sinking.

He held her against him, his hands spanning her narrow waist, his lips traveling slowly down the soft flesh of her throat, tasting the sweetness of her skin. Murmuring her name he buried his face in the silky strands of her hair, inhaling the delicate fragrance of flowers in the luxurious softness. "I want you, Rowena . . ."

With impatient hands he quickly loosened her lacings, laughing softly as he realized how clumsy his fingers were. "I can't seem to manage . . ." Ah, but at last his fingers parted the fragile fabric of her chemise to cup one firm, budding breast, touching her, setting her body afire with a pulsating flame of desire. Rowena writhed beneath him, giving herself up to the glorious sensations he was igniting within her.

His hands moved along her back sending forth shivers of pleasure, he in the touching and she in being touched. Desire flooded his mind, obliterating all reason as he held her against his heart.

Wrapped in each other's arms, they kissed, his mouth moving upon hers, pressing her lips apart, hers responding, exploring gently the sweet firmness of his. Shifting her weight, she rolled closer into his embrace. His hands moved on her body, stroking her lightly—her throat, her breasts, her belly, her thighs. With reverence he positioned his hands to touch her breasts. Gently. Slowly. Until they swelled in his hands. He wanted to be gentle, but it took all his self-control to keep his passion in check. He wanted to make it beautiful for her, wanted to be the perfect lower.

"Rowena!"

He held her face in his hands, kissing her eyelids, the curve of her cheekbones, her mouth. "Rowena. Rowena." He repeated her name over and over again as if to taste of it on his lips.

Her hands caressed his chest, her wide blue eyes beckoning him, enticing him to enter the world of love awaiting them both. "Love me, Kendrick," she breathed. Arching up, she was eager to drink fully of that which was promised.

"Aye. Oh, I will my sweet, sweet love." Feverishly he clung to her. Their hearts beat in matching rhythm even as their mouths met, their bodies embraced in the slow sensuous dance of love.

"Kendrick!"

Kendrick gazed down upon her face, gently brushing back the tangled golden hair from her eyes. From this moment on she was his. He would never share her with anyone. Never.

From a distance, laughter, a piercing sound. Kendrick felt as if he were falling, falling . . . Reaching out he sought the security of his lover's arms, but she was gone. Hovering right above his head, however, was another visage.

"Oh, no!"

"There is a fee for riding through the forest, my lord," called out a voice.

"Fee?"

"Your clothes!"

Running his hands over his body, Kendrick found that he had already paid that price. He was naked. "You young scoundrel!" Clenching his hands into fists he lashed out, fighting, tossing, turning. "Where is she? What have you done with her?"

"Why, I am here, my love . . ." With an impish grin, the young archer cocked his head, warbling in falsetto.

"Nay!" It was but a mistake. He wanted his lady back, didn't want to believe.

Reality coursed through him as he felt himself hit the ground. Opening his eyes, Kendrick found himself lying on the floor, tangled in linens and blankets. Wincing against his discomfort, he propped himself shakily up on one elbow and looked around him. Just a dream. And yet . . .

The moon glowed like a golden coin through the haze of clouds but though Rowena wanted to rest, she prodded herself onward. She needed to hurry back home, wanted to tell her father and Kendrick all that had transpired in Canterbury.

"We must gather up the ransom money. Somehow . . ."

As she rode along, Rowena tried to figure in her mind just how many late-night rides she would have to make and how many rich noblemen she must "charge a fee" in order to give the archbishop sufficient aid in his quest for the ransom.

"At least a hundred nights . . ." But was that quickly enough?

Though she knew she shouldn't have eavesdropped, she had listened at the door as the archbishop had discussed the king's abduction with his clerics. A further worry had been added. It had been learned that the emperor had sent word to Philip of France about his plans for the royal captive. Philip had expressed interest in buying the king himself, declaring that Richard would never again see the sun shine on his own possessions. Refusing this, he had offered a huge sum if the emperor would refuse to release the prisoner. Moreover, the French king wanted John to visit Paris in order to get the matter settled, a request that Queen Eleanor had denied. Thankfully, her youngest son was still afraid of her. Still, it was not beyond John to let some other rat do the dirty work for him. Rowena could only worry.

Hoofbeats!

Rowena reined in her mount, hoping that she was wrong. Ah, but there they were again. She heard the sound distinctly now. She was being followed. No doubt John's henchmen had learned of a young "lad's" visit to Hubert Walter.

Fight or flight? Rowena decided to trap her pursuer. Leading her horse to a tree, she climbed upon a high limb, then gave the animal a gentle pat on its behind. Just as she suspected, a horse and rider exploded into view as they raced after her horse in pursuit.

"Only one?" She didn't know whether to be relieved or insulted. Still, she didn't have time to think about it long, for as the horse passed under the tree she dropped from the limb, grappling with the rider. Both fell to the ground, tumbling over and over. Rowena was winded and bruised. Gasping for breath, she called upon her inner strength to come to her aid. Struggling, she pinned her pursuer's arms to the ground, then quickly stepping away, she reached for her bow

"Oh, no! Oh dear!"

Something about the voice was recognizable. Staring

into a rotund face, Rowena drew in her breath with shock. It was Humbley. Kendrick de Bron's portly manservant.

"Please, let me go. I . . . I have no . . . no money pouch."

Rowena's stance was cocky as she was filled with renewed bravado. "You know there is a fee . . ."

"For riding through the forests, I know. But you see, I had to ride."

"You were following me . . ."

"Nay!" The man was terrified. "I . . . I escaped from Prince John, you see. Chadwick and I decided to ride in different directions. Home."

Were she not so tired, were it not so late, had he not looked so thoroughly disgruntled, she might have had a bit of fun with him. As it was, Rowena gave the man a hand up and pushed him towards his horse. "Then go. I will not detain you." When he hesitated she repeated, "Go!" Kendrick de Bron would have need of Humbley to do the work at the manor that he could not because of his wounds.

"Thank you!" The man was earnestly grateful. Smiling, he hurried to his horse.

Whistling for her own mount, Rowena climbed upon his back and continued up the road that would take her to Grantham Manor.

Chapter Nineteen

The sun peeking o'er the horizon and the cock crowing in the yard gave proof that Rowena had arrived back at the manor at a dangerous time of day. Scurrying up the vine, she hastily dodged through the window, only feeling truly safe when she had reached the safety of the guest chamber. Since she had relinquished her own room and housed herself in the chamber adjoining hers, Rowena had found another means of exiting and entering the manor by way of the window. Tearing off her lad's garments, she retrieved her woman's clothing. Then and only then did she dare to relax.

"Oh, what an adventure," she breathed. To think that she had helped the infamous Little John escape from the prince's men, then had galloped to Canterbury.

Standing in all her naked glory, her hands clasped around her body she relished her success like the finest of wines. Surely it had gone to her head. If she was filthy now, looking more like some stable boy than the lady of the house, well, that was the price that had to be paid. She wouldn't have traded one moment of her life up to now. Not a minute!

Walking on tiptoe to the doorway she peered out behind the crack and called loudly for Maida to bring her water for her bath. The young woman responded quickly, eyeing her up and down as if to wonder how a lady could get so dirty. Well, that would be Rowena's little secret, she thought with a toss of her head.

"Your bath, my *lady*."

Stepping into the tub, Rowena found it to be tepid. Even so she leaned back and closed her eyes, once again reliving the fight in the tavern. Little John had complimented her, saying she had courage and skill. He had asked her to join with Robin Hood and himself. She wondered what Kendrick de Bron would think of that!

"Ha, it is Robin who should join with me," she breathed. "I'm the one who stood face to face with the archbishop and not he." She felt outrageously bold. Lathering her body with the scented soap she had bidden Maida to buy for her at the fair, Rowena gave in to all her young dreams. She would perchance travel across the channel some day seeking adventure in a faraway land, or mayhap she would go on the crusades. At the moment nothing seemed impossible.

And Kendrick de Bron?

Unbidden, his brown eyes came to her mind. She could almost feel again the gentleness of his hand as it had gone searching, caressing. Sighing she felt a tingling between her legs, a longing. Though the water was cool she suddenly felt hot, uncomfortable.

"BiGod!" Quickly she sprang from the tub, nearly overturning it in her hurry. She would not allow herself to be attracted to the bold rogue. 'Twas folly to so dream of him. There would never be anything between them. Never. Rowena was unsure of her newfound woman's feelings and apprehensive of giving her affections, thus she forced herself to feel anger. "Perhaps he is not the villain I first perceived, but . . ."

"My lady!" Thinking there was something wrong with the water, Maida tested it, giving Rowena a puzzled look.

"I am troubled."

"Because of your future husband?" Maida could not hide her envy. It showed plainly on her face.

"Has Gwyneth . . . ?" She needed to know that de Bron's wounds were healing well. All too often a wound could be poisoned.

"She has watched over him nearly as diligently as she has always watched over you."

"Then . . . then he is well?" Rowena didn't want to sound too concerned. Ah, but in truth she was.

"Getting stronger with each passing hour."

"Good."

"Your father has been quite concerned about his future son-in-law," Maida tattled. "He has hovered over him nearly as much as Gwyneth, although he has not let de Bron know of his vigil."

"Father has watched over him?" And had no doubt noticed her absense. Rowena wondered if there was any excuse she could give that would soothe her father's ire.

"Perhaps he was afraid that de Bron would die before the wedding." Maida shrugged. "But he didn't and he won't. He is too strong and too stubborn."

"Stubborn," Rowena repeated. "But perhaps not as stubborn as I." Suddenly she felt the need to confide in someone. "Oh, Maida, what shall I do? How can a woman armour her heart?"

Maida smiled knowingly. "There is not metal strong enough to shield cupid's arrows."

"It would seem so." But loving was a weakness, one that she was determined to fight against.

"But if you speak of Kendrick de Bron, I would think you would not want a shield."

"I do!" Rowena felt something akin to fear as she asked, "What is it like?"

Maida, sensing her feelings and jealousy, said, "Ah, to be honest, it can often be painful."

"It?" Rowena wondered why then Maida was so frequently partaking of such "painful folly". But that was another matter entirely. Future husband indeed! Despite de Bron's redemption in her eyes, the very idea was infuriating. Two men had callously decided on her future without consulting her at all. "Marriage. Fie!"

Marriage was of a certainty something she wanted to avoid. Rowena had always been able to manage her father quite well. She had a great deal of freedom. With marriage, that all would end. A wife's life was a nightmare. She must get up early and say her prayers. She must dress suitably, without too much showing, taking care that her underdress did not ride up at her neck nor that her hair escape from her wimple. When she went out she had to be accompanied by her housekeeper or some other bothersome companion. She must walk with lowered eyes and speak to no one on the street. Worst of all, to her husband she must be loving, humble and obedient.

"Obedient and humble, ha!" Rowena knew that to be an impossibility. She had enjoyed freedom too long.

Rowena shuddered at the thought that a husband could beat his wife with full acknowledgement of the law and the church. Was she not his property? Then, when a woman was worn out from childbearing and wrinkled with age, the man suddenly in his dottering years found a younger woman to ease his urges, setting his poor wife aside for a mistress. Yet for a woman to do the same was enough for her to be put to death for adultery. Rowena's anger was as much for these poor hapless creatures as for herself.

Were she to marry Kendrick de Bron, her late-night excursions would be ended forever. No longer would she be carefree. A wife's life was filled with drudgery. Managing the garden, the servants, the steward, the housekeeper,

so that her husband's manor was suitable for his tastes.
Housework began early. All rooms had to be swept, stools
and benches dusted, cushions shaken into place. Grease
spots had to be removed. The kitchen kept clean. Proper
dinners prepared—like blankmonger. Rowena stifled a
laugh. Marry de Bron. Never! She would see to his health,
get him back on his feet then, before this traitorous heart
of hers succumbed to his manly touch, she would see him
gone.

Nevertheless she could hardly wait to look in on him.
Opening the door, she stood for a long while looking down
at the man on the bed. Strange how boyish he looked with
his eyes closed. Almost innocent. But then she knew better.
Her gaze wandered over him, capturing the memory of
his muscular strength nestling close in her arms.

"Rowena . . . !" Murmuring her name he flung out a
possessive hand, reaching for her.

"Oh, God!" Her insides turned to mush.

"You're back!"

"Of course I am. Did you fear otherwise?"

"I did." Lord, how pretty she was. Even twice as lovely
as she had been in his dream. Sighing, he remembered.

"The archbishop is going to put a tax on the land,
among other things, to raise the money for the ransom."
Proudly lifting her chin she related to him quickly all about
her hasty journey to Canterbury.

All the while she spoke, he looked at her. He could
nearly imagine it in his mind's eye, that is until his thoughts
turned to what she was wearing, a white gown and blue
kirtle that were tighter than what she usually wore. He
could fully appreciate the outline of her body. Her waist
was small. He could span it with his hands, and her breasts . . .
Remembering his dream the hot ache of desire sparked
within him.

"From the first moment I laid eyes on you, sitting beside
me at Prince John's table, I've wanted you," he blurted
out.

"Wanted . . . ?" As she stared into his eyes, Rowena's heart began to hammer. She read desire and something even more frightening. Possessiveness? "I will not marry you," she blurted out. "No matter what my father might have promised."

Once her attitude might have angered him but Kendrick was growing used to Rowena Fitz Hugh being contrite. "We'll see," was all he said.

"Indeed we will." Or at least that was what she thought, not counting on her father's stubbornness, nor the events that threatened the household. Upon answering her father's summons, Rowena learned that all had not been peaceful while she had been gone.

"Where were you, daughter?" When she did not answer, he simply shrugged, not in the mood for an argument. "Prince John's men were here again," he informed her.

"Looking for de Bron."

He nodded. "I insisted that we had not set eye upon our neighbor in quite some time."

"Is de Bron in trouble?" Strange how the very thought pricked her sense of protectiveness towards him despite her insistance that she did not care.

"They did not say." Taking her hand, Sir William furled his brows. "But I have been summoned to John's castle."

"You. Why?" The possibilities were chilling. Could it be that the prince knew what she had done? Was her father to be the victim of her rash boldness? Or was the "invitation" merely to be a social call?

"I do not know the why or wherefore, child, but I do know this! I have been afraid to speak out on Richard's behalf, have been a coward at times, but I know now where my loyalties lie. God bless Richard and God bless de Bron for his bravery." It was then that he explained his change of heart. Maid Marian had finally been cornered and taken prisoner on her own estate of Huntington. She was to live at the castle as the prince's legal ward, a move obviously intended to silence her outbursts while at the same time placing her wealth in John's own coffers.

"The prince is a scoundrel." Was there nothing too low for him to do?

"Aye, he is that." A pounding at the door announcing the prince's men-at-arms silenced him. "Ah, Rowena, so much happiness you have given me."

"Father." She was chilled by his tone. He sounded as if he were saying goodbye.

"My only peace of mind will come in knowing that I have left you in good hands."

"Good hands?"

"Kendrick de Bron's. I have made your betrothal to him official with the priest just in case—"

"You what!" It didn't make sense. De Bron was a wanted man, out of favor with the prince. "Father, what possessed you to do such a thing? De Bron is now viewed as the prince's enemy and—"

Sir William shook his head. "I will see to it that by what I say he is cleared." He kissed her on the top of the head. "Be happy, Rowena. I want that more than anything in this world."

"Father . . ." The loud banging at the door made her cringe.

"I'm an old man. The best years of my life are behind me. But you . . ."

Oh, dear God, she suddenly knew what her father was doing. He was going to sacrifice himself for her happiness, perhaps even confess to an evil he did not commit in an effort to clear Kendrick de Bron's name and make certain she would be safe. No. She would not allow it. "You have not done a thing. 'Twas I!" She started to make a confession about her late-night rides, but there was no time. The door nearly splintered as the guards called out Sir William's name. Then he was gone.

* * *

If ever an injury had been untimely, Kendrick de Bron knew his wounds to be so now. William Fitz Hugh had been forcefully removed from his own manor and that seemed to be but the beginning. A man would have had to be a fool not to realize that the manor was being watched. The roaming men-at-arms might pounce at any minute. He felt of a certainty that Rowena's freedom, perhaps even her life, was in jeopardy, but what could he do? Fight for her? Hardly. Though he was steadily recovering, he was not yet strong enough to fight a puppy. So much for saving his lady love then.

Tossing and turning upon the bed, he was frustrated. What if the prince's men came on the morrow to take Rowena away? Maid Marian had been imprisoned with the excuse of being made a ward of John, why not Rowena as well?

"Rowena." He glanced up at the rough ceiling and envisoned her face, and it was in that moment that he knew beyond a doubt that the feelings he held for her were real. His pursuing her, wanting her, asking for her hand in marriage hadn't been just a matter of male ego but a matter of deep affection. He felt a warmth inside whenever her name came to mind. Now his emotions were in turmoil as he realized he would be unable to protect her. From the sound of her pacing in the chamber adjoining his, he thought perhaps she was thinking the very same thing.

Up and down. Back and forth.

"Rowena." He called her name louder. "Rowena!"

Thinking perhaps that he was in pain she hurried through the door. "Aye, de Bron. What is it?" She was beside him in an instant. "Do you hurt? Are you chilled?"

He shook his head. "No. It's just that I heard you walking

about and since I cannot sleep either, I thought perhaps we might talk.''

She looked at him skeptically. "Talk?" Her gaze wandered over him, capturing the memory of his muscular strength nestling close in her arms, but she pushed such thoughts away. This man had already caused her trouble and promised to cause her more if she gave him but half a chance.

"Talk," he said softly, though seeing her in that angel-white gown brought other ideas to mind. Oh, to strip away the last vestiges of that loose-fitting garment and view what lay beneath. Lord, what a beauty she was.

"I do not think you are safe here."

"Nor do I." That was the reason for her inability to fall asleep. The question was what to do about it. To fight Prince John's men single-handedly was stupid. Flee, then? To go where?

"I think you should seek out the confines of a nunnery. The church will protect you." It seemed a logical suggestion.

"A convent!" Rowena nearly choked on her indignity. Better to be in John's darkest dungeon than that. "Never. I will not hide."

Oh, but another idea was coming quickly to her mind. Little John had asked her to join Robin Hood's band. Why not? Perhaps it was time to admit that she could not fight John alone. The outlaws would be her allies. With them she had hope of rescuing her father. Alone she did not.

"Besides, if I went scurrying to the sisters, who would take care of you? Who, de Bron?" She had meant to tease him, taunt him, but as she leaned closer her hand touched his leg. That touch was his undoing. How erotic it would feel stroking his manhood, he thought, shuddering with longing.

"BiGod!" The hot ache of desire sparked within him. He found himself reaching out, taking her by the shoulders, drawing her down.

"Let me go! Are you mad?" She was unprepared for his embrace.

"Mad for you." And he was.

"Oh . . . ?" She wanted to move away but something, the glitter of desire she read in his eyes perhaps, held her there. She remembered the firm gentleness and pressure of his warm lips against her own and swallowed hard.

"Shall I show you just how mad I am about you?" The soft material of her gown tightened across her breasts, making him fully aware of their tempting allure, but it was her mouth that fascinated him at the moment. It looked so soft. Her lips were moist, parted, inviting.

"No," she whispered, a futile protest. She didn't pull away as they moved together into an embrace. His mouth touched hers, coaxingly gentle at first, then exhibiting more pressure, forcing hers to open. His tongue eased its way between her lips and teeth.

Kendrick pulled her down beside him, ignoring the pain that blazed in his shoulder. Once a man so close to death, desire had given him sudden strength. He was completely ruled by his emotions. She was lovely, tempting and warm. Since that first time he had kissed her he had wanted her.

"Mmmmm . . ." Oh, but kissing him was so enjoyable. Rowena clasped her arms around his neck as they lay side by side. His body was completely bare, not even a loincloth covered him, yet instead of making her feel threatened, it only heightened her own passion.

"Rowena. Lovely, lovely Rowena," he breathed. His fingers parted the neck of her gown and he reached inside her bodice to feel the warmth of her, stroking and teasing the peaks of her breasts until she moaned low and whispered his name just as he had whispered hers. She yielded to his hands as they searched out the secrets of her woman's body.

Kendrick's hands pulled at the hem of her gown but when she might have protested, he silenced her with another kiss. Skin against skin, how would that feel? Curiosity got the best of her. "Take it off, de Bron," she invited, tickling his ear with her warm breath.

As he undressed her, Rowena was lost in the flush of sensations that swept over her. She felt wanton, aware of her body as she had never been before. If this was what it felt like to be a woman, perhaps it really wasn't so bad. So thinking, she answered him kiss for kiss, touch for touch. Her eyes met his and held and it was as if some primitive emotion was driving them.

Kendrick savored the expressions that chased across her face, the wanting and passion so clearly revealed. "Oh yes, you are a woman all right," he murmured. Slowly. Move slowly, he told himself. He didn't want to hurry or break the spell. He wanted to save all his strength for the right moment. Rowena Fitz Hugh was so unpredictable that he could fully imagine her changing her mind and suddenly swearing at him.

Rowena was totally immersed in her newfound passion, so much so that she didn't hear the sound at first, but suddenly it invaded her senses, blocking everything else out. "Listen!" She sat up in bed so suddenly that she took de Bron with her.

"Rowena . . ." Kendrick kissed the valley between her breasts with his tongue, then stiffened. He heard it, too. "Damn!" The sound of splintering wood gave warning that someone was breaking the door down.

"We have to get out of here! We'll saddle two horses and ride towards the safety of the forest." We, she had said. Rowena clearly realized that she could not leave de Bron behind. Not now. He was as marked as John's enemy as she, perhaps more so. The memory of his attackers was still fresh in her mind.

"Ride?" Making love was one thing, traveling another. "I cannot."

"You can and you will!" Not wasting even a moment, Rowena had hurriedly leapt from the bed and was now gathering up the necessary garments for de Bron as well as herself. "You thought to ride me just then, don't deny it, and if you had energy for such a tumble then I will not listen to any arguments decrying your lack of strength."

"Rowena! Be sensible." He thought of her. He would only slow her down. "Go alone. I will only be a burden."

She thought for just a moment. "Aye, a burden you will be." A nuisance for more reasons than one. What would he do if he learned that she was the forest archer? "I should leave you, but strangely enough I cannot." She thrust a bundle of clothing at him. "Get dressed, de Bron, and be quick about it." The violent noises below punctuated her anxiety. "Hurry."

Running stark naked to the adjoining room, she hurriedly retrieved her archer's garments, donning them with trembling fingers. Oh, but life had its odd twists and turns, she thought. She had wanted to seek out Robin Hood alone, now it seemed she must reassess her plans.

Tied to the saddle of his horse so that he would not fall off, Kendrick looked with anger at the saucy wench who rode beside him. She was dressed in lad's attire, a tunic, hosen and boots, similar to the garments he had seen the archer wear. Now beyond a doubt he knew her to be one and the same. The eyes gave her away, as did the way her shapely legs filled out her hosen. It was time for a confession.

As they rode Kendrick kept his silence, waiting for Rowena to explain and ask his forgiveness. Alas, such an outpouring of guilt never came. Instead she acted as if riding beside him dressed as a lad was not something out of the ordinary. Thus there was tension between them.

So that is the game that she intends to play. Oh, how she had made a fool of him, not once but several times. It was galling. Though he might have been amused had it been anyone else, though he might well have enjoyed such a prank, he was thoroughly annoyed. But he would not let her know. "Where are we?" is all he asked. She had led him deep into the woods. Though he had often hunted, he realized he had lost all sense of direction, at least for the moment.

"The forest to the north of my father's manor," Rowena answered. "Try to keep up with me if you can."

Try to keep up. Though he felt as dizzy as a fool and suffered a torturous agony where he had been wounded, Kendrick's pride dictated that he do just that, or die trying. He urged his horse onward, feeling the wind brush his face. He saw the trees speed by as he gave chase to the daring young woman.

They rode in silence through the thick foliage, Rowena glancing back at Kendrick de Bron from time to time. She knew he must be hurting, yet he somehow managed to stay just six horse's lengths behind her. Amazing. Either he was stronger than she had imagined or more stubborn.

"Shall we rest, de Bron?" she threw over her shoulder.

"Rest?" The very word was endearing to him at the moment, yet he shook his head. "No, let us press on."

Rowena's gaze took in his hands, grasped so tightly to his reins, remembering how they had felt upon her skin. She flamed with sudden desire at the memory. All she said, however, was, "Press on. So be it." And press on they did, at a murderous pace, their journey guided by the moonlight. All the while Kendrick de Bron did not utter even one word of complaint, or swoon in the saddle.

That did not mean he was not in agony, however. He bit his lip to keep from crying out. He would not let some chit of a girl witness any show of weakness. He would not! He would not!

"But I am only human . . ." he groaned. Then, just when he was about to admit defeat, it was Rowena who declared they stop. A welcome boon.

"It's going to rain. We'll take cover here."

"Rain?" Sliding from his horse, nearly falling on his face, Kendrick stumbled but somehow managed to walk

over to a log where he thrust his aching body. He looked
up at the sky. It was so dark. The moon had been covered
by thick clouds. A rumble in the heavens gave warning of
a storm. "Damn." The thought of a thorough drenching
was not a pleasant one.

"At least we know the prince's men will be as miserable
as we, if they are following," Rowena said as she likewise
dismounted.

Huddled together, using Kendrick's cloak as a tent
beneath the trees, both felt a rekindling of their earlier
passion. Rowena could feel the maleness of Kendrick's
body through the thin, damp cloth of his garments. She
could smell the scent of him, of spices and sweat, a strangely
pleasant and masculine odor. She could hear the intake
of his breath rustling in her ear. It sent shivers up her
spine. There was no need to deny that she had a strong
attraction to this man. Her senses flamed at his nearness.
Perhaps traveling with him was not such a good idea after
all. The hard patter of rain mingled with the beat of her
heart.

Rowena and Kendrick were soon soaked to the skin,
shivering against a sudden burst of wind which howled
around them. Despite the storm he was determined not
to complain, nor could he had he wanted to, for his teeth
were chattering so violently that he was not even certain
he could speak a coherent word.

Rowena felt a sudden twinge of conscience. "De Bron,
forgive me. It was not my intent that you should grow ill."
Her eyes mirrored her concern and for just a moment
Kenrick suspected that her feelings ran much deeper than
she knew. "Here, let me keep you warm."

Gathering Kendrick's cloak tightly about them, Rowena
tried futilely to warm him but the shaking of his limbs
would just not cease. Each quiver, each tremor was noted
by her, increasing her feeling of guilt. How could she have
forgotten the dangers of catching a chill?

"Rowena . . ." Drops of rain glistened on her thick lashes

and brows and he reached out to wipe them away. His finger moved over her cheek with a gentleness few such masculine men possessed.

Before she had time to think or to answer, his mouth was only inches from her own. Now it was she who shivered. "De Bron . . ." Her voice was husky as his lips drew ever closer.

"Rowena. Sweet, sweet, Rowena . . ." He was touching her, moving his hand slowly up her arm from elbow to shoulder as he explored. Caressed.

A flash of lightning crackled nearby, bringing Rowena instantly and disagreeably back to reality. Instantly she stiffened. What in damnation was she doing? Hadn't she any self-control? *Think, you fool. Think what you are doing.* With an indignant sniff she pulled away.

"Now is not the time for this, de Bron," she exclaimed. She looked him full in the face, but he was not looking at her. Instead his focus was transfixed unwaveringly on something else. "What is it? What do you see?"

"BiGod." He swore a vile oath as he saw silhouettes moving through the rain toward them. "Men." Their bows were strung with arrows and those arrows pointed straight at Rowena and himself.

"We have caught two weasels," came a low voice. As Rowena gasped and Kendrick groaned, the arrows were aimed right at their hearts.

Chapter Twenty

The light of the moon reflected on millions of raindrops, making it appear that the leaves were sprinkled with diamonds as Rowena and Kendrick marched along in front of the party of archers.

"Where are you taking us?" Rowena refused to cower. "Speak up, I say. Where are we headed?" She squinted her eyes, trying to pierce the darkness so she could distinguish the vicinity of where they were going. Deeper into the forest, it would appear.

"You'll find out soon enough," was the answer.

Kendrick's head swam with a hundred angry questions for the moment blocking out his urgent pain. "Who are you? Why are we being treated so rudely? Are you the prince's men? Or are you outlaws?" He felt an overpowering weakness in his legs, and a wave of dizziness sweep through his head. A man could only suffer so much.

The answer was the same. "You'll find out soon enough."

"They're outlaws." Rowena made her opinion known. She stopped walking, only to have one of the archers prod

her onward. The humiliation was not to be born. Clenching her fists tightly, she wished for just one moment to
hold her bow again. She would soon show these fools.

"Outlaws." On unsteady feet, Kendrick lurched ahead.
He was going to collapse at any moment. Then what? What
would happen to Rowena then? He had to go on, no matter
what.

"Did you hear that, men? Our identities have been discovered." There was laughter, then Kendrick was cornered. "And you, friend. You are dressed in the finery of
one of Prince John's nobles. What shall we do with you
then, enemy that you are?"

"I'm not an enemy." At least he hoped he wasn't. He
repeated a prior question. "Who are you?"

"Who?" One of the men puffed out his chest proudly.
"We're Robin Hood's men."

"Rob . . ." A ray of hope, Kendrick thought, quickly
saying, "I am a friend of his. I knew him when we were
both la—"

"Of course, ye were his boon companion." Gripping
his bow in his stubby fist, the archer scowled, then gave
Kendrick a shove that sent him sprawling.

"Leave him alone. Can't you see he's hurt?" Like a
protective mother bear, Rowena thrust herself between
Kendrick and the archer.

"Aye, leave him be." One of the archers at least showed
some sympathy. It was at his command that a litter was
fashioned with two tree limbs and Kendrick's mantle.
Despite Kendrick's protests he was forced to get on.

The party continued briskly through the forest, the men
seemingly anxious to return to their campsite. The frivolity
of Robin Hood's men was already legend. Despite the
circumstances of their capture, Rowena was anxious to
meet up with Robin again. To her mind came the moment
when she had nearly won the archery match. If not for the
breeze and her thoughts of Kendrick, it would have been
she who would have won the golden arrow. When she

proclaimed that fact, however, none of the archers would believe it.

One of the archers lit a torch and held it up in order to get a better look. "He speaks true. I remember him, dressed in grey. The pigeon."

"Aye, that's me." Rowena stared down into Kendrick's eyes, warning him not to breathe a word. So, the cat was out of the bag and he now knew. Well, so be it. "I am that *lad*, isn't that so, de Bron?" If he gave her femininity away, she would kill him.

A grunt was the answer. If she wanted to play such a game he wouldn't denounce her. But oh, how delightful it would be to have something to hang over her head.

"Well, whoever you are, we cannot take chances. If you are who you say, then we will make apologies." The tallest of the archers hovered over her. "And if you be foe, then you shall pay for your lies."

The night was filled with the sounds of the forest creatures, the howling of wolves, the hooting of owls. The archers led them over a rocky path, twisting and turning among the trees. Rowena's instincts told her that they were backtracking in order to confuse their captives. She wondered in which direction they were going now and looked up at the stars to try to better decipher their course. They were headed east, she decided, though she knew that were she to be forced to find her way again along this path, she would have a difficult time. The outlaws covered their tracks well.

"Watch your step!" barked an older archer, still distrustful of his prisoners. Rowena saw the reason for his warning as they came to a stream. A large dead tree acted as a bridge between the banks and the party was forced to walk single file to reach the other side. Glancing around, she nearly lost her balance and swore beneath her breath.

At last they were across the log and were led further up the bank where the current of the stream became swifter. Coming to a roaring waterfall, Rowena looked in confusion as the young archer bid her go on. To her eyes it was a dead end.

"Come," was all the young archer said, taking Rowena's arm and pushing her ahead of him. Rowena gasped in wonderment as her eyes beheld a cavern behind the waterfall. She was led through the splashing waters to the entrance of the hideaway. Several torches and campfires glittered, reflecting in the waters. In all her wildest dreams she could never have imagined such a sight.

"Merry-go-up! No wonder no one has ever been able to find Robin Hood." She was thankful now that she was not an enemy of the outlaw for, having witnessed the secret entrance, if she were foe she surely would not have been allowed to live with such knowledge.

There was not much time to marvel at the wondrous sight, for again the archers pushed them forward. Walking a short distance she could see that around the fires sat several archers. One man stood from the rest because of his great girth and height.

"Little John!" Never had she been so glad to see anyone. The large outlaw looked in her direction with puzzlement. Rowena realized that when last she saw him she had been garbed in her archer's clothing.

"Little John. The inn. Remember?" Reaching up, she yanked at her hood, exposing her cropped hair. Now recognition flooded Little John's eyes.

"Lad!" he cried, striding quickly towards her. He shook his head at the archers. "Put down your arrows, this young lad is friend to me. Saved my life and fought bravely he did."

Rowena could see Kendrick's eyes riveted to her and thrust back her shoulders in pride. Perhaps now he would realize that she wasn't just some silly female. "So it seems that I at least am safe," she chided to him. The archers were still pointing their arrows at him, however.

Kendrick looked anxiously around for sight of Robert

Fitzooth, but could see no sign of his childhood friend. "Where is Robin?"

"Playing a trick upon our dear sheriff," came the reply from a round-faced outlaw.

"Aye, he pretends to be a butcher. Little John here is soon to join him," said another. He winked boldly at Little John.

"Which reminds me. I must be upon my way if I am to be the first one at the fair." Little John held up his staff. "I have this ready."

Rowena watched as Little John left, overcome with curiosity. Oh, what fun it would have been to join in on whatever prank was to be played.

"Show the lad here proper hospitality until I return," John called back over his shoulder.

At his words a tankard of ale, no doubt stolen from some rich man's table, was thrust into Rowena's hands. She drank the contents quickly, then turned her attentions to Kendrick. Since there was no one to vouch for him, his hands were being tied behind his back lest he escape. He looked towards her, pleading with her to help him. Impishly she took her time, but at last nodded.

"He is a friend." She winked at him, then settled down by the fire.

It was several days before Robin Hood returned. When at last he did, he and Little John brought with them the Sheriff of Nottingham's own cook.

"Kendrick!" Robert Fitzooth was stunned to see him among his men. "What are you doing here?"

"It's a long, tedious story."

"And one that you must tell, for from what is being bandied about, you are being called a traitor to England. There is a warrant out for your arrest." Robert shrugged. "So you see, we are both outlaws now."

"So it would seem," Kendrick shot back, wondering how his carefully laid plans had gone so awry.

"Well, perhaps it is for the best, at least for me. I have need of a man with your courage and skill." He toasted him with a mug of ale, then Robert looked towards Rowena. "Who is he?"

Rowena's heart quickened. Once again she wondered if Kendrick would give her away. Clenching her fists, she waited.

"A bothersome lad I met along the way," Kendrick said wryly. Oh, but Rowena was going to owe him for this.

Robin stepped closer, pulling the hood from Rowena's head. She tossed her head back proudly and stood with shoulders back, head up. "Why I think I recognize him. The one who shot with me at the fair."

"Yeah, it was I." She strode forward. "As I told you before, I will win next time."

Robin threw back his head as he laughed. "We shall see. We shall see." He looked her up and down. "Meanwhile, come join my band."

There was danger in the venture, for whoever was caught would have their neck stretched by the hangman's rope. Even so, the thrill of joining with this man chased away all Rowena's fear. "I will, with pleasure."

"Not so fast." The archer who had taunted her all along the way declared that the newcomer should prove his prowess.

Reaching for her bow and an arrow, Rowena was anxious to. "I can shoot strong and true, as you know," she said confidently.

Robin shook his head. "No, it will be with quarter staff that we will meet. I did same with Little John and the others in this band." He looked towards Kendrick. "You too will have your turn, once you heal."

Little John came forward with a hearty laugh. "I knocked our good Rob into the water when first we met. I have the honor of being one to have bested him. Let's see if you can do as well, lad.'' His wink told Rowena that he was on her side. "It would do good for Rob to meet his match.''

Taking up her quarter staff, made from the stout branch of an oak, Rowena prepared herself for the match. It would be a matter of her skill matched against the outlaw leader's. Looking upon Robin's broad back and the well-muscled arms, she knew this would be one match she would never forget.

"Be prepared for a fall,'' she challenged, leaping forward.

Robin picked up his own staff, making ready. He braced his strong legs slightly apart. Rowena heard Little John counting. "One, two, three!''

Robin swung his quarter staff, missing Rowena by only the width of a fly as she ducked just in time. She was nimble of foot and smaller than he. Striking out quickly, she threw a blow of her own that struck Robin soundly on the shoulder. He winced in pain, but quickly parried another of her blows.

"Good for you, lad.''

The air was rent with the sound of wood upon wood as the two fought. Robin was much stronger than Rowena, being a man, but what she lacked in strength she made up for in wits and mobility. The crowd of archers gathered tightly around the two, forming a large circle.

"Go, Robin!''

"Show the lad!''

Rowena sidestepped another of Robin's blows but her attention was diverted for just a moment—long enough for Robin to catch her unguarded. He gave her a resounding stroke to her elbow.

With a sharp cry of pain Rowena drew back, ready to concede the match, but a look in Kendrick's direction prodded her to fight on. He looked so smug. Well, she would show him.

Kendrick wasn't as smug as he looked. Damn, but he was impressed with Rowena's fortitude and skill. There were few who could give Robert a merry fight. Even he had been bested often enough. He watched as again and again she struck out and parried, swinging her quarter staff.

Sweat beaded Rowena's brow and her arms ached from the thrust of the blows. She was doing well, but she was tiring. Still she bluffed. "Do you concede, Robin?"

"Concede? Never." Thus said, his fighting became fiercer. Strike, parry, strike, parry and so on.

"Enough of this." Little John came between the two combatants with arms outstretched.

Rowena and Robin threw down their quarter staffs, laughing. Breathing hard, they collapsed upon the ground. "We will call this a draw," Robin decided.

It wasn't as good as winning, but Rowena felt she had held her own. As she rose to her feet to take a drink of ale, she smiled at Kendrick, whose eyes mirrored his admiration.

"You are certainly worthy to join with us," Robin was saying loudly. "But first we must give you a name just as we have the others." He thought a long moment. "What say you to Arrow?"

"Arrow." Rowena said it again. "Arrow."

"The name will suit the one who so nearly bested me." Robin Hood put his hands on his hips. "Arrow."

"Arrow! Arrow! Arrow!" chanted the assembled band of outlaws.

"So, now you will be known as Arrow, *lad.*" Kendrick put his hand upon hers and Rowena felt the old flames of desire fan through her. If only she could conquer these feelings his nearness brought forth. Alas, what did it matter? Kendrick's attempt at seducing her was certainly out of the question now. For as long as they were among Robin Hood's men, he couldn't and wouldn't. Not unless he wanted to look strange to the others. For that she should feel relief, and yet she didn't. For the first time in her life she felt trapped by her lad's clothing.

PART TWO:
THE FLAME

Nottinghamshire, England—1193

Your love is all consuming, like a flame;
Blazing forth my heart, my soul to claim.
Not ocean, river, nor earth's waters
Can quench this fire.
You are and always will be,
My love, my heart's own desire.

Chapter Twenty-One

Rowena knew if she lived to be a hundred she would never forget what it was like being one of Robin Hood's "men." It meant enjoying the ultimate freedom combined with a comraderie that put a whole new meaning to the word friend. Indeed, living in the forest with a price upon one's head meant that each and every outlaw depended upon the other. Just one mistake, one slip of the tongue or bit of foolishness, could mean disaster, thus they were loyal to each other to the point of obsession.

That did not mean that everyone got along, however. The outlaws were much like a group of siblings with Robin at the head as father. It was up to him to settle disputes, keep the peace, enforce the rules of the band and generally govern. All this he did with a fairness that Rowena greatly admired. Because of him, life in the forest retreat usually went smoothly and followed a strict code. Strict, that is, but not too strict. Above all, the outlaws never seemed to forget their penchant for having a good time and poking fun at Prince John and his favorite henchman. This evening, it seemed, was to be no exception. As Rowena watched a group of her friends arrive back at camp in their brown hoods, Lincoln-green tunics and hose, she sensed that some mischief had been in the making.

"Little John, what have you been about?" she asked, tagging after him as he started a fire and readied the spit. Whatever it had been she wished she had been included. Sitting around camp all day or being forced to do chores was the part of living among the merrymen that she abhorred.

"About?" He grinned like a boy, hefting up the hind quarters of a large deer, antlers and all. "Just roasting the prince's cow."

"Cow?" For a moment she feared something had addled his wits, but as he winked at her merrily she knew he was making a pun. "Of course. Cow." Whatever he wanted to call it, cooking over the fire it smelled delicious. Soon the aroma of roasting venison filled the air of the forest. Around the crackling fire crowded the group of hungry outlaws, Kendrick included. Just like Rowena, he seemed to be thriving on forest life. He was now nearly healed, his color had returned, most of his strength was revitalized, and above all his good humor was present at least half of the time. From across the fire he grinned at her now, an irritating smile that seemed to remind her that she had a secret, one that he could hold over her head.

"Ale all around." Little John's voice thundered over the other outlaws' chattering. He raised his own tankard high in the air, motioning towards a man who stood at the back. "Bring our guest forward."

"Guest?" Rowena quickly noted the blindfold wrapped around the man's face, but recognized him the moment the cloth was removed. It was a very angry Sheriff of Nottingham. As he turned his beady eyes in her direction, Rowena flushed and turned away, hoping he would not recognize her as the Lady Rowena.

"What treachery is this?" he was asking, seemingly amazed to find himself surrounded by his worst foes.

"Why, noble sheriff, you are to be our guest." Robin Hood motioned towards her. "Arrow, get our guest a cup of ale."

Rowena poured the brew from the wooden keg, all the while keeping her head down and her eyes to the ground, hoping her identity would go unnoticed. It did, for the sheriff was much too angry to notice anything except that he was being made a fool of. Like a wolf he snarled and growled.

"Killing the prince's deer. You will all pay for this," he threatened. "You are thieves, all of you." He started towards Robin Hood, but Kendrick blocked his way.

"Nay, sheriff, it is you who are the thief," Robin countered. "I merely am trying to do a good deed. To take from those who rob and give back to those who in truth are the real owners." Rob pushed the sheriff down upon the ground to sit at a huge split log which acted as banquet table. "But no more of talk, let us dine."

All of the outlaws likewise sat down, some on makeshift chairs, others on logs, a few on the ground. For just a moment Kendrick's eyes met Rowena's and he beckoned for her to sit beside him. She shook her head "no." Since joining the outlaws she had carefully avoided him, determined to rid herself of the power his nearness had upon her. Instead, she sat beside Little John.

From behind a thick cropping of trees came the sheriff's own cook, bringing with him a set of silver dishes and cups. Placing the plates and cups before the sheriff, the cook bowed mockingly.

" 'Tis you. Here!" sputtered the sheriff. His eyes blazed anger. "Rascals. Rogues. You take from me my servants and silver as well."

As the outlaws dined, the story was told that Robin Hood had gone to Nottingham dressed in the blouse and apron of a butcher, having also purchased the man's cart and horse. A merry disguise.

"He made his way to our dear sheriff's own house to

dine at a banquet, babbling like one simple of mind. Robin talks about his herd and asks twenty pieces of gold for five hundred of the creatures," John whispered in Rowena's ear. "Thinking our Rob to be a fool of a butcher, the sheriff agrees and offers to go with him the next day."

"A herd of five hundred?" Rowena didn't understand what John thought was so funny.

"Aye." John laughed so hard that he was unable to speak for a moment. "Not cows, you see. But the prince's own deer is the herd he was talking of." Again he laughed. "You can imagine the fury our sheriff felt to find that instead of fleecing the sheep, he instead was fleeced by the butcher into having given twenty gold pieces for that which was not Rob's to sell."

"And serves him right, too." Rowena looked towards the sheriff, who sat cross-legged upon the ground, his sharp teeth devouring the venison. It was a proper jest to play upon him. How she wished it had been her idea.

As they supped, John told her of his own mischief-making, that of entering the employ of the sheriff. "I vowed to be the worst servant he had, thus I proceeded to eat the sheriff's best bread and drink his best stock of ale and wine." After jousting with the cook, who at first tried to protect the sheriff's supplies, Little John had persuaded him to join Robin's band. Stuffing the sheriff's silver plates and cups into a sack, they had both taken off for the safety of Sherwood Forest.

Little John's tale was interrupted by the sound of a horn signaling a merry bout of skill between the men of the band. Rowena was quick to finish her slice of venison and down her cup of wine. As a small target was set up, she readied her bow. "Well, de Bron, will you enter too? Or are you afraid of being beaten by a woman?" she challenged in his ear. "He who misses the target will get his comeuppance, or so I have heard, and be target for the outlaws' jests."

"Oh, is that so?" While no one was looking, he whacked

her on the behind, laughing softly at her gasp of indignation. "Well, I shall soon prove that it won't be me."

A wreath of evergreen branches was set far into the distance. Each of the archers took turns shooting. Rowena's aim was true, as was Kendrick's and Robin's, but there were those whose arrow was short of the mark and who had to face condemnation. As the outlaws formed two lines, the outlaws who had failed to hit the bull's-eye had to walk in between, suffering the humiliation of being spanked by paddles. The Sheriff of Nottingham, having missed the mark as well, was among them.

"Well, de Bron, you were lucky this time," Rowena taunted.

"As were you," he responded, wishing he could take her over his knee and spank her as soundly as she deserved. Oh, how she had been teasing him of late, keeping just out of reach yet looking at him every chance she could. Oh, she still cared, he thought, as he would prove were he to get her alone. For just a moment their eyes met and held, communicating his inner thoughts.

"Never," Rowena retorted, reading his mind. Thank God for the safety of the outlaws. He wouldn't dare try anything. Quickly she turned her back on him, but before she could get away they were both pushed forward by the suge of outlaws who had volunteered to accompany the sheriff back to Nottingham.

"I swear by my patron saint, St. George, that I will n'er seek to cause ill to befall the outlaws in Sherwood Forest," the sheriff was saying as Robin held him at dagger point. "But out of Sherwood t'will be another matter," he shrieked as soon as Rob put the dagger away. Blindfolded again, he was taken kicking and screaming from the hideaway.

Rowena felt a tap on her shoulder. Expecting it to be Kendrick, she whirled around. "Get away from me— Robin."

He recoiled. "Lad, I was but going to tell you that you shot very well."

"Oh." She tried to make amends. "As did you," she couldn't help blurting. "So when are you going to let me do more than just stay around camp? I want adventure. I want to help in getting the monies necessary to bring our king back to England. I want—"

"Calm yourself." Robin laid a hand on her arm. "You chatter on like some female." At her frown, he laughed. "You will get your chance." He eyed her up and down. "Perhaps now."

Reaching for her bow, which she always kept nearby, Rowena was enthusiastic. "I'll do anything."

Robin grabbed her wrist. "Nay, not the bow. I have other things in mind." He left and came back with a small bundle. Rowena took the package from his hands, a look of puzzlement on her face. Opening the bundle she found women's garments inside. A flash of fear struck her. Robin knew.

"What would you have me do with these?" she asked, her fingers grasping the fine cloth tightly.

"Wear them," Robin answered.

"No!" She threw them on the ground defiantly. "Damn de Bron!" He had told on her. Angrily she sought to find him in the crowd. She would tear him to bits with her bare hands. She would—

"De Bron hasn't anything to do with it," Robin said, trying to calm her. "I merely thought that you wanted to go with us."

She was careful in what she said next. "I would, but not dressed in skirts. I want to fight."

Robin gathered up the clothing. "Then you refuse."

"I do!"

He walked a few feet away, then paused. "You must learn to obey my orders, lad. My loyal men never question what I ask of them."

Lad. He had said *lad*. Rowena quickly recovered her poise. "And I will. I will."

"That's better." Robin explained that they needed a decoy, a young woman dressed in finery to lure the prince into a trap. "You are slim and therefore of the right build to fit into these clothes," he added, thrusting them into her hands once again. "Put them on." He waited as if expecting her to dress right there in front of him.

"No . . ." She couldn't take off her garments while he was watching. More than her modesty was at stake. "I . . . I . . . well, I . . ."

It was Little John to the rescue. "Methinks our young lad is a bit shy. He will soon learn." Taking her by the arm, he led her to the bushes. "Dress here if you must."

Rowena's hands trembled as she stripped off her tunic, leaving on only her hose. The binder which flattened her breasts was still secure. She longed to remove it if only for a moment and let her breasts free, but didn't dare. Instead she slipped the kirtle over her slim body. Tying the belt securely around her waist, she headed back towards the men.

"What in heaven's name?" Kendrick was totally stunned as she walked by him.

"Shhhhh." Putting her finger to her lips, she silenced anything he might say.

"We're going to use Arrow as a decoy," Robin explained, "though we must do something to cover his hair. That mop would give him away immediately."

"Mop?" Self-consciously, Rowena ran her fingers through her hair, which was shorter now than it had been. "Does it really look that bad?" The criticism stung.

"Aye," taunted one of the archers. "If you ask me, no one would stop for this wench."

Seeing the hurt in Rowena's eyes, Kendrick quickly defended her. "I would."

From the bottom of her heart she thanked him for that.

"Oh, you would?" She affected a defiant stance. "Well, little good it would do you."

"Here." Robin reached inside a large pouch, pulling out a veil and wimple from among other confiscated goods. "This will work the magic we need upon our lady's head." He draped them over her hair, then stood back and looked at his handiwork. " 'Tis a fetching wench you will be now."

"Fetching," laughed Little John.

"Best show our lady how to act as one," shouted one of the archers. "Arrow walks like a man. He should walk like so." The archer walked about, swinging his hips slightly in a graceful movement.

All the outlaws joined in. "Oh, dear lady, let me kiss your hand." Rowena promptly gave the man a shove that sent him sprawling as he reached out. Hoots of laughter followed.

Robin put up his hand to silence them. "Leave the lad alone. Don't make fun of him. We have much to do and far to go. We have to get started."

Rowena was relieved. Being made sport of was annoying. Worse yet, someone might accidently stumble upon her secret if they thought about it very long. "Aye, we had best get started." Before they did, however, they were interrupted by an out-of-breath archer.

"Robin! Robin! You must hear this," he was sputtering. Excitedly he told of what he had heard in the village, that Kendrick de Bron had abducted the Lady Rowena Fitz Hugh out from under the nose of her own servants. "They are crying out for his head."

"Abducted the Lady Rowena. Absurd," Kendrick fumed. "It is but an excuse to have my head. Why, the lady is right—"

Rowena silenced him with a kick to the shin. Now wasn't the time for a confession, were he contemplating one. "Come, de Bron, escort me to my horse," she commanded in a high falsetto voice amidst loud chuckles from the outlaws.

"Perhaps Arrow does have promise after all," Little John exclaimed, gently tweaking Rowena's nose. "At least he sounds like a woman when giving orders."

"Aye, perhaps you do have promise," Kendrick whispered in her ear as he walked beside her.

With a laugh "Arrow" was pushed forward, surrounded by the merry band, then led to a horse. The band of outlaws set out from the forest, some disguised as townsmen, tinkers, tailors, carpenters, butchers, and even a farmer or two. Rowena was at the head, riding on a gray mare. She had escaped detection this time, but would she again? It was a troubling thought as the small band left the security of the forest.

It was bothersome riding in skirts but Rowena made the best of it, determined to follow Robin's orders to the last detail even if it killed her. To earn his respect and trust was of the utmost importance. She had to prove herself. Then and only then could she hope that he and the others would help her rescue her father.

The plan was a simple one. She was to stand beside the road holding the reins of her horse, pretending her horse had gone lame. It was well known that the prince was fond of female company. He would, of course, stop to offer assistance to a woman in need. Those of the band who were in disguise would be scattered, looking like harmless travelers upon the road. Others would be hidden behind the trees, fully armed and ready to spring out at the hapless prince and his entourage. Robin had learned from reliable sources at the prince's own castle that John would have with him several sacks of gold, money collected from the landowners. Supposedly, the money was to go to the archbishop for the ransom of Richard. Robin intended to make certain that indeed it would go for that cause.

"Above all, hold your temper," Rowena warned herself.

She tried; the taunts she suffered from some of the bolder outlaws nearly unleashed the full measure of her anger.

"Oh, fair lady . . ." Playfully one of the merrymen waved at her.

"May I pledge thee my troth?" called out another.

"I think I love you . . ." yet another cried out, even going so far as to blow her a kiss.

"Go to the devil," she shot back.

Daring to be a bit reckless, she urged the mare on to a faster and faster pace, soon leaving the others behind. Make fun of her, would they? She would soon show them. A mischievous gleam sparkled in her blue eyes and a smile was etched on her full mouth as she loosened her hand on the reins, giving the gray mare free rein. She raced like the wind, reveling in the sheer pleasure of the wild, mad ride.

"BiGod, she'll get herself killed," Kendrick swore beneath his breath as she burst from the forest. With another grumbled oath, he dug his heels into his stallion's side and darted after her. Ego demanded that he catch up with her. It goaded him into closing the distance between them.

Rowena wasn't conscious of anything but the enjoyment of the ride, but the instant the strong hand made a grab for her horse's reins she was alerted that she was no longer alone. "Let me be," she demanded hotly, but one look at the intruder softened her mood to laughter. "De Bron?"

He had mimicked the disguise she had worn at the archery tournament, dressing as a begger with a patch over one eye. "Aye." Wisps of white bird feathers stuck out from beneath an old hat so that he looked like an old man.

"You look silly."

She, on the other hand, made a charming picture, he thought as he took in the enchanting face framed by the wimple and veil. Hers were the most beautiful eyes he had ever beheld. And her mouth . . . It challenged a man to taste its sweetness. He wanted to tell her that, but instead he simply said, "You look pretty, no matter what the others say."

"Pretty?" She made a face. "I don't want to be, for 'tis bothersome."

Seeing that her wimple was askew he reached out and straightened it. "You are bothersome, Rowena. Lord, do you have any idea how much you tempt me?"

She pulled away. "I don't intend to." Then she smiled. "But what are you saying, de Bron, that you secretly lust after—"

"A fiery chit of a woman who thinks it a lark to masquerade as a man. Yes." Once again he looked into her glorious eyes. "I can be patient, Rowena. You will soon come to your senses."

"Come to my senses?" Somehow she managed to suppress the urge to slap his face. "And then do what? Marry you and content myself with womanly chores?"

"Aye," he answered, being fooled for just a moment into hopefulness.

"Never!"

Compulsively his hand tightened on her shoulder. "Never is a long, long time." He regarded her questioningly, then with an exasperated sigh bent his head down to align with hers. Fiercely he kissed her, as if by doing so he could change her mind.

The touch of his warm, hard mouth engulfed Rowena in a maelstrom of intoxicating, well-remembered sensations. Ah, but it was sweet to have his lips touch hers, even briefly. Too briefly.

"I love you, Rowena Fitz Hugh. When is that going to be enough to satisfy you?" Oh, how he wanted to sweep her off that horse and carry her away, but that he would never do. The choice had to be hers. "Well?"

She hadn't the time to answer. As the others caught up, the warning of "He comes!" alerted all that the prince's caravan was in view.

"Hurry, Arrow," Little John called out in a high-pitched voice. His voice, like his person, was disguised as a woman. A heavy veil hid his beard from sight, his arrows were concealed beneath the heavy folds of his skirt, his bow beneath a heavy cloak.

Sliding down from the gray mare, Rowena quickly affected the mannerisms of a helpless woman. "I'm ready." She turned her eyes in the direction of the prince's caravan. John, dressed in a bright blue tunic embroidered with pearls and threads of gold, sat astride a fine black stallion. His hose were of white, a startling contrast to the darkness of the animal beneath him. Belted to the prince's waist was a large purse.

Pulling the veil across her face in an effort to hide her eyes from the prince's sight lest he recognize her and take his wrath out upon her father, Rowena purposefully stepped out on the road, blocking his way.

"Well, well, well, what do we have here?" John exclaimed upon seeing the lovely vision before him. He swung his legs from the horse to dismount, but one of his retainers put out a hand to stop him.

"Nay. We cannot stop here. Sherwood Forest is only a mile down the road and it is there that the outlaw Robin Hood lurks."

Ignoring his guard's words, Prince John slid down from the stallion. "I do not fear that loathsome cur," he said. "Besides, it bids me ill to see a fair damsel in distress." Coming upon Rowena he reached for her hand. "What misfortune had befallen you?"

In an attitude of coy shyness, Rowena answered, "My horse has gone lame, sire." His hand was cold and clammy and she suffered a twinge of revulsion as he kissed her fingers one by one.

"Lame. What a pity." His manner seemed to say that he was anything but sorry. "But an opportunity for you to ride with us. We travel to Nottingham."

"Then I will likewise go and thank you from the bottom

of my heart for rescuing me in time of need," Rowena said with sugary sweetness, nearly choking on the words. The cad. It was likely more than one young woman had been caught by his pretense of being a gentleman.

Cautiously Rowena measured the odds here. There were nearly thirty men with the prince and only fifteen or so of the outlaw band. The odds were two to one. Could they hope to be victorious over the prince? Yes. Somehow she knew that they would. Wits would win out over brawn any day. As to John, she wanted him all to herself. He had a sword, but she could unarm him and thus even the odds at least by one man.

"We will ride together, you and I," John was saying as he enfolded her small waist in his left arm and drew her with him towards his horse. "Will that not be delightful, my sweet?"

"Delightful." From the corner of her eye Rowena could see the forms of the outlaw band, disguised in their colorful clothing, creep nearer and nearer. Thought to be little more than villagers, they went ignored by the men-at-arms. Meanwhile those garbed in their Lincoln green were stealthfully crawling about on hands and knees.

"What is it?" Suddenly John seemed to hear a sound.

"The wind," Rowena answered. Knowing she had to distract him she fought her dislike for him as she leaned against him. "Imagine, being escorted to Nottingham by the prince himself. It is enough to make a lady swoon." She made as if to fall and felt the prince gather her close against his chest.

Little John tugged at his ear. The signal!

It was as if everything moved in slow motion. Rowena reached out as if to put her arms around John but her nimble fingers had found his scabbard instead. He was stripped of his sword as easily as a baby is of its playthings.

"By God's teeth!" he exclaimed, stepping towards her as if to strike out.

Poising, the sword in her hand, Rowena thrust out with

the weapon. "Take not a step further if you value your life. Prince or no prince, I will unman you," she threatened.

"You wouldn't." Though his tone of voice was confident, the fear in his eyes clearly told her that he wondered.

"I would."

The clash of sword upon sword, the whistle of arrows in the air, the sound of grunts and groans, sounded a tune by the roadway. Here and there a serf had stopped working and watched in wonder at the sight of the fighting men.

" 'Tis Robin! 'Tis Robin Hood!" they shouted, taking note of the men in green.

Kendrick wielded his sword with all his knightly prowess, proving that at last his wounds were healed. He ran through one man in front of him, wounding that one in the arm, then turned quickly to the man at his back. He recognized him in an instant. "Hugo. You bastard." It was the servant who had betrayed him.

"Bastard? That is a name for you and not I," came the reply.

"Then traitor is what I will call you." For just a moment Kendrick stood still as though he couldn't move. "Why, Hugo?" Kendrick didn't see the swordsman creeping up behind him.

Rowena did. "Kendrick! Kendrick!" It was as if her heart stopped beating in that moment. She watched as the swordsman struck a blow to Kendrick's head.

Kendrick could perceive the sound of the sword whistling through the air and ducked just in time to avoid his beheading. The sound of splintering wood told him that the blade had found a tree trunk instead of his neck and for that he whispered a prayer to God. But Hugo was still to be reckoned with. With a growl of anger he threw himself against Roderick, charging like a mad man. He was joined by another swordsman, then another.

"De Bron . . ." Pushing the prince into Robin's able hands so that he could divest John of his purse, Rowena ran to Kendrick's side. She couldn't let him be killed. He meant too much to her.

"Get back!" Kendrick was horrified to see her joining in the melee.

"You need some help." Stubbornly she stayed put, swinging the prince's sword as she joined the furious battle that tested strength and skill.

Rowena had little experience with blades, but she made a good show of thrusting and parrying. Reacting to the warning of her senses, her sword arm swang forward again and again, turning the odds in Kendrick's favor. At last with a strong thrust she knocked her enemy's sword to the ground.

"Good show, Arrow." Someone was cheering her on from the sidelines.

Then, it was over as quickly as it had begun. A horn blast from Little John signaled the end of the fighting. Prisoners were gathered up and stripped of all that was of value.

"We will meet again, John," Robin Hood said with mock politeness, going so far as to bow. "Thank you for your contribution to our coffers. I'm certain your brother will thank you as well."

"You dog! I will see your head put on a pike to decorate London bridge!" The prince watched as the weapons of his men and other valuables were loaded on an old cart.

"We have need of these," Robin said. The cart was harnessed by John's own stallion.

"Ah, you are a horse thief as well."

"It is a fine animal," Kendrick responded.

"You." Only then did John notice that he was among the outlaws. "Your head will reside next to your leader's upon my bridge."

Kendrick wasn't upset by the warning. "I don't think so. I've survived your treachery once and will do so again. But if you are wise you will look to your own head. Richard will return, and when he does it will be your head on the scaffold.''

For just a moment Prince John paled. "We will see," he said as he regained his composure, then he was pushed and shoved towards his companions.

"Come lads, the fight is over." Robin was zealous in his triumph but Rowena was not as cocksure.

"Not over, but just beginning," she said, coming to Kendrick's side. "At least for you, de Bron, for I fear that John sincerely hates you now. He will never forget nor forgive."

"So be it." Kendrick was in a fine mood. Rowena cared! She had proven it. No matter what she said or did, he would always remember the look on her face when she had feared for him and the way she had risked her own life to save his.

Chapter Twenty-Two

Streaked with the moon's silver, the small lake was mesmerizing, inviting. Rowena gazed at it with longing as she and the outlaws passed by on their way back to the hideout. Her garments were covered with mud. She smelled of sweat and horses. Oh, how she wished for a dip in the cool water, she thought, wiping at her face, but it was out of the question.

"Tut, tut, tut, your vanity will be your undoing."

Turning her head Rowena saw Kendrick de Bron grinning at her and knew he had read her thoughts. Worse yet his eyes seemed to strip her naked.

"I . . . I was but thirsty, that's all," she said quickly. "Verily, it has been a hard ride."

"Aye, in truth it has. But if it is your thirst you need to quench 'tis ale and not water you have need of." The thought of seeing her "in her cups" was amusing. Hopefully a bit of ale would soothe her inhabitions. "Unless you cannot hold your liquor, *lad*." He emphasized the word with a wink.

Seeing that Robin had ridden up to ride three abreast,

Rowena stiffened her back. "I can match you tankard for tankard, de Bron," she bragged. Alas, it was a boast she was forced to live up to as Robin's men arrived back at camp and prepared to celebrate the success of their raid on Prince John.

Fires were sparked, meat prepared for the spit and wooden kegs opened so that the golden ale could be shared all around. The night air rang with laughter and chatter as each of Rob's men tried to outboast the other.

"May I fill your cup?" Determined to hold her to her words, Kendrick de Bron hefted one of the kegs as he passed in front of Rowena.

"Aye, do so," she answered, holding the tankard high. The drink was stronger than the watered-down wine and ale she usually drank, so strong that she nearly choked. Somehow, however, she managed to empty the tankard. Likewise, de Bron drained his cup to the bottom.

Rowena no sooner drained one cup before another was poured for her, and another, and another. And all the while Kendrick de Bron's grin mocked her, dared her, infuriated her.

"Tankard for tankard," he cheerfully reminded her.

"Tankard for tankard," she repeated, trying not to slur her words. Oh, but she felt so lightheaded, so unsteady on her feet. Even so, she stubbornly held out her tankard to be filled again, then moved toward the central fire.

Oh, how she wanted to slip away.

"The lake . . ." she breathed, longing again for its cool water. It's chill would clear her head as well as bathe her. Should she? It took only a moment to decide.

Kendrick watched as Rowena left the glow of the fire, slithering off like someone up to no good. He saw her look around to make certain that no one noticed her departure, then slip into the trees. Likewise sneaking from the circle of the outlaws, he followed.

Rowena pushed through the foliage, walking at first, then running. It took several minutes to reach the bank of the lake. The night air was calm, not even the hoot of an owl could disturb the peacefulness. Quiet. Blessed, blessed quiet. How good the silence seemed as she reveled in her solitude.

A soft whispering breeze caressed Rowena's face as she viewed the untamed woodland of tall, slender silver birch trees. It was a natural wonderland, a haven with a mossy floor hidden from view by a drapery woven of hundreds of leaves. It was so achingly lovely here. More so because of the ale that imbibed her senses with tranquility, perhaps. Whatever it was, something made her feel as if this magical spot somehow belonged to her.

Rowena stood for a long time on the bank, then testing the waters, she decided to take a dip, in spite of the chill. Stripping off her garments one by one, she hung them on a nearby bush then splashed into the water, unaware of the man who crouched behind a nearby bush watching her.

"So lovely . . ." Kendrick murmured softly, staring at the beauty so openly presented to him. The moonlight reflected upon her bare back and buttocks, making her skin gleam like marble in its light and emphasized the slim curve of her long, lithe legs. Fools the others were to think for even a minute that Rowena Fitz Hugh was a boy. Why, that delightfully curved bottom of hers should have given her away. "And her breasts," he breathed as she turned around. Those womanly mounds with their rosy tips were so perfect. What a shame it was to have to hide them.

Desire threatened to suffocate him as he watched her enter the water up to her waist, then splash about. He wanted to rip off his own clothing and join her, to feel the softness of her body against him and lie with her upon the mossy bank but he held his hungry yearnings in check, contenting himself to just feast on her with his eyes.

Suddenly the hoot of an owl shattered the quiet. Rowena turned her head. "Who is there?" she asked, fully submerging her body. If it was one of the outlaws, then she was in for the devil's own time explaining her femininity. Heart thumping, she waited. No one answered.

Feeling secure in her aloneness again, she began to swim about, letting the cool, smooth water splash over her body as she closed her eyes. Somehow she felt safe here, assured that no one knew of this secret haven. That was why she was doubly surprised to look up and discover that she was not alone. Someone stood silhouetted in the trees, looking her direction.

"Who are you? What are you doing here?" Her voice had a sharp edge to it as she asked the question. "Show yourself!"

Knowing that he had been seen, Kendrick moved slowly and sinuously in his grace, coming at last to the water's edge. Somehow this moment seemed fated, as if it had been destined to occur right from the first moment he had looked upon her haughty little face.

"Relax, it is only me," he announced softly.

"De Bron?" Rowena was so relieved that it was him and not Rob or one of the others that she sighed, little realizing that Kendrick took this as a sign of acceptance of what was to come.

"You seem to be in need of some company. Mind if I join you?"

"No," she tried to cry out, but somehow the word was choked, unintelligible.

The air crackled with anticipation. A shiver danced up and down her spine as she looked wide-eyed at the masculine perfection of the body he was baring to her view. She had almost forgotten how broad his chest was, the flatness of his stomach, how muscular his legs were. He looked invincible, dangerous, strong. Somehow she knew that the image of his broad, bronzed shoulders, wide chest, flat belly and well-formed legs would forever be branded in her mind.

Again she tried to cry out, knowing well what would happen if he entered the water, but her voice came out

in a rasp. "De-de Bron . . ." she somehow at last managed
to say. Then it was too late. With a splash he dived in.
Rowena held her breath in expectation as he swam towards
her. Slowly he reached for her hands, pulling her to him.

Rowena floated on the water, feeling strangely as if she
were flying instead. The buoyancy of the lake made her
seem weightless, the ale made her feel dreamlike and contented. Without protest she let him grasp her by the shoulders to pull her close. With the tips of his fingers he traced
the line of her cheekbones, the shape of her mouth, the
line of her brows.

"You will never know how you have tortured me . . ."
he whispered.

"Tortured?" Had she? The thought made her smile
impishly.

"Aye, tortured."

At first he simply held her, his hands exerting a gentle
pressure to draw her into the warmth of his embrace. Then,
before Rowena could make a sound, his mouth claimed
hers in a gentle kiss, one completely devastating to her
senses. She was engulfed in a whirlpool of sensations.
Breathless, her head whirling, she allowed herself to be
drawn up into the mists of the spell.

Leaning against him, Rowena savored the feel of his
strength, giving herself up to the fierce sweetness of his
mouth. Her lips opened under his as exciting sensations
flooded through her. Kendrick's lips parted the soft yielding flesh beneath his, searching out the honey of her
mouth. And all the while the water swirled around their two
entwined bodies. Heaven. Pure heaven, Rowena thought
hazily.

Then, all too soon, the kiss had ended.

"De Bron . . ."

Her heart skipped a beat as he brought his head down
and traced the bare curve of her shoulder with his lips.
Long and languorously he explored the soft flesh, moving
to her neck, his tongue searching her ear in a way that

made her whole body tingle. A near madness seized her and she found herself thinking the most dangerous thoughts.

"Ah, Rowena," he breathed as his lips nuzzled against the side of her throat. He uttered a moan as her hands moved over the smoothly corded muscles of his shoulders.

It seemed as if Kendrick's breath was trapped somewhere between his throat and stomach. He couldn't say any more. The realization that she was finally to be his was a heady feeling that nearly made him dizzy as he brought his lips to hers once more. Such a potent kiss. As if he had never kissed her before.

In fact, Kendrick had the feeling that he was doing everything for the very first time as he made love to her. All memories of other women faded from his mind. Hers were the only arms he wanted around him, hers the only mouth he wanted to kiss, her softness the only reality in this hostile world of warring.

Their bodies were crushed together as both simultaneously reveled in the delight of the texture and pressure of the other. The water whipped around them, intensifying the sense of pagan abandonment. Two lovers in the moonlight, Rowena thought. Lovers. Once the word had had a tawdry ring to it, but tonight it sounded glorious somehow.

"It seems so right, being here together like this," he whispered, letting her know that he was feeling the magic of the moment too. Burying his face in the soft, silky strands of her hair he breathed in the fragrant scent of her hair and was lost to any other thought.

Rowena's arms entwined around Kendrick's neck, her fingers tangling in his thick dark hair. Fascinated, she let her hands explore his body as his had done to hers. He uttered a moan.

"Kendrick . . ." Closing her eyes, Rowena awaited another kiss, her mouth opening to him like the soft petals of a flower as he caressed her lips with all the passionate hunger they both yearned for. Rowena loved the taste of him, the tender urgency of his mouth. Her lips opened to him for a seemingly endless passionate onslaught of kisses. It was if they were breathing one breath, living at that moment just for each other. Mutual hunger brought their lips back together time after time. She craved his kisses and returned them with trembling pleasure, exploring the inner softness of his mouth.

Desire that had been coiling within Rowena for so long only to be unfulfilled, sparked to renewed fire and she could feel his passion likewise building, searing her with its heat. They shared a joy of touching and caressing, arms against arms, legs touching legs, fingers entwining and wandering to explore.

"Rowena!" Desire writhed almost painfully within his loins. He had never wanted anything or anyone as much as he did her at this moment. It was like an unfulfilled dream just waiting to come true. Now she was *his*. Bending down, he worshipped her with his mouth, his lips traveling from one breast to the other in tender fascination. His tongue curled around the taut peaks, his teeth lightly grazing until she writhed beneath him. He savored the expressions that chased across her face, the wanting and the passion for him that were so clearly revealed.

The cool night air caressed Rowena's skin, yet she caught fire wherever he touched her, burning with an all-consuming need. She shivered in his arms and, fearing it was from the night air, he gathered her closer as he lifted her from the water.

"I'm not cold!" she whispered. Still, she made no protest as he lifted her up in his arms and carried her to the bank. Finding a soft spot covered with leaves he warmed her body with his own.

"Better?" he asked with tender concern.

She nodded, trying hard to control the shudder that passed through her, a desire that coiled and writhed almost painfully within her loins. Now she knew how he had felt.

If she had known then what she knew now, she would never have pushed him away.

Kendrick pulled her closer, rolling her over until they were lying side by side. Rowena felt a great pleasure in the warmth and power of the firmly muscled body straining so hungrily against hers. Secretly she had to admit now that despite her quarreling with him, this was what she had wanted all along, to be naked against him. Her only fright perhaps was in the provocative feel of his stiffened manhood that brushed against her leg from time to time.

"Oh, Rowena . . ." she heard him breath.

Looking up at his face she saw that his eyes were closed. How strange that his expression made him look as if he were nearly suffering, yet he was smiling all the while as if in sweet torment.

"De Bron," she whispered, all of her fear vanishing as she suddenly realized that it was she who had the power to hurt right now and not he. But she wanted to give him pleasure, not pain. "Kiss me again."

He did, his knowing, seeking lips moving with tender urgency across hers, his tongue finding again the inner warmth and sweetness of her mouth. His large body covered hers with a blanket of warmth. Rowena felt the rasp of his chest hair against her breasts and answered his kiss with sweet, aching desire. But kisses weren't enough. His lovemaking was making her far more intoxicated than the ale. She wanted. She needed.

"Kendrick . . . love me . . ." she breathed, feeling intensely sensitive to his slightest touch.

"In due time . . ." Sensuously he undulated his hips between her legs and every time their bodies caressed, each experienced a shock of raw desire that encompassed them in fiery, pulsating sensations. Then his hands were between their bodies, sliding down the velvety flesh of her belly, moving to that place between her thighs that ached for his entry. His gentle probing brought sweet fire, curling deep inside her with spirals of pulsating sensations. Then

his hands left her, to be replaced by the hardness she had
glimpsed before, entering her just a little, then pausing.

"Take me, de Bron. I'm not afraid," she said, clenching
his neck feverishly. And she wasn't. Not now. To prove it
to him she reached out and guided him into her softness.

Kendrick's size made her ache, but there was only a
brief moment of pain. The other sensations pushed all
discomfort away. Rowena was conscious only of the hard
length of him creating unbearable sensations as he began
to move within her. Capturing the firm flesh of her hips,
he caressed her in the most intimate of embraces. His
rhythmic plunges aroused a tingling fire, like nothing she
had ever imagined, she thought as she arched herself up
to him, fully expressing her love.

Kendrick groaned softly, the blood pounding thickly in
his head. She was so warm, so tight, that he closed his eyes
with agonized pleasure. His hold on her hips tightened as
the throbbing shaft of his maleness possessed her again
and again. It had never been so good for him before. Ever.
Because of love? He knew it to be so.

"Rowena, my love . . ." he sighed with sensual tenderness.

Instinctively Rowena tightened her legs around him,
certain she could never withstand the ecstasy that was
engulfing her body. It was as if the night shattered into a
thousand stars, bursting within her. Arching her hips, she
rode the storm with him. As spasms overtook her she dug
her nails into the skin of his back.

A sweet shaft of ecstasy shot through Kendrick and he
closed his eyes, whispering her name again and again. Even
when the intensity of their passion was spent he still clung
to her, unable to let this magical moment end. He touched
her gently, wonderingly.

It was a long, long time before either of them spoke.
Propping herself up on one elbow, Rowena looked at Kendrick de Bron long and hard, deciding quickly that she
had no regrets. Still, she would never let him know how

deeply he had shaken her. Instead she said simply, "I must admit that what happened between us was decidedly pleasureable, de Bron."

"Oh . . ." Playfully he bent his head to her breasts, his tongue flicking and teasing. "Shall we do it again?"

She thought a moment, remembering all that he had done, but before she could answer the forest was shattered by the pierce of a horn and the moment was lost. "Alas, I fear we have no time," she exclaimed. The fear of being caught and found out to be a woman sent her scurrying for her garments. Likewise Kendrick sought for his clothing, then like two conspirators trying to feign complete innocence, they headed back toward the camp, though not without looking at each other from time to time.

Chapter Twenty-Three

Love. Just a word to Rowena before. An emotion for fools. Something to avoid. Now as she walked back towards the camp with Kendrick de Bron, it had a new meaning of warmth and joy. Tonight she had become a woman. Was that really so bad?

"No," she breathed. Quite the contrary. What had happened between de Bron and herself at the lake at last made her realize that her femininity was not a curse but a blessing. Her body was capable of enjoying such wonderous feelings that it was staggering. Desire and its fulfillment were unequaled by anything she had ever experienced. Anything!

Not that she was going to change herself in any way. Oh, no. Just because she gave in to her passion didn't mean she would give up her freedom and content herself with being the proper little wife. It was just not in her nature to be dominated, not even by such a magnificent specimen of manhood as de Bron, she thought, glancing at him now. No, she was what she was. Hopefully he would respect and admire that.

"De Bron. . . ." She wanted to ask him so many things, but as he turned his head she didn't really know where to begin, thus she asked merely, "What are you thinking?"

He answered truthfully. "That I am going to have the devil's own time keeping my eyes and hands off you now." He shook his head. What had passed between them had changed everything. Now, having possessed her, he could never turn away, never give her up. He had to accept the truth for what it was. He loved her. "I fear I just might give myself away."

"And in so doing, me as well." And yet, having felt the touch of his hands, the softness of his lips, the hardness of that which made him male, how could she even think to tell him to stay away? She loved being Arrow, one of Robin Hood's "men," but in her heart she knew she cared for him even more.

He mistook her expression. For just a moment he knew fear as he asked, "Are you sorry about what passed between us, Rowena?" If she said yes, he knew it would be agonizing.

"Sorry?" Once she might have toyed with him, teased. Instead she answered from her heart. "Never. Tonight was the most wonderful of my life." Without even thinking about what she did, Rowena stood on tiptoes, closing her arms around his neck.

"For me as well," he exclaimed.

His mouth descended upon hers, kissing her with a passion that rekindled the spark of desire that had flamed so brightly. Wrapped in each other's arms in the shadow of the trees, they kissed and fondled each other, giving in to the fierce emotions that raced through them. It was as if they wanted to memorize the feel of each other for those moments when they would be forced to keep at least an arm's length apart.

"Oh, Rowena!" he groaned, his mouth roaming freely, stopping briefly at the hollow of her throat, lingering there, then moving slowly downward to the skin exposed at her shoulder. "How can I stay away from you? How can I bear it?"

"I don't know." She could feel the pulsating hardness of his manhood and wanted desperately to be naked against him again, to feel the warmth and power of him. Lost in the flush of sensations which swept over her, she held him tightly against her, forgetting all reality for the moment, that is until she heard the sound of a twig snapping beneath someone's foot.

"Kendrick. Arrow."

Instantly they pulled away from each other.

"We have been looking for you two. Where have you been?" The voice belonged to Little John, much to Rowena's relief.

"De Bron, here, had too much to drink," she said with a sly smile. "I followed him into the woods to make certain he didn't get lost." She fought the urge to look into Kendrick's eyes for fear their passion would be mirrored in the depths of that glance.

"Aye, he did," Kendrick explained quickly, making a great show of staggering as he walked to add credence to her explanation. "God bless the lad."

"It's drunk that you be?" Little John threw back his head and laughed. "Well, this should sober you up." Before Kendrick had time to even think he found himself thrown over the big man's shoulder. Then he was being carried and lastly thrown into the waters of a nearby stream. He came up sputtering. "Feel better now?"

Though his temper flamed, Kendrick held it in check. "Aye. Much," he said between clenched teeth. He stood up, brushing at his soggy clothing.

Little John threw back his head and gave vent to his merriment. "Ah, but you hardly look at all like the man with such a high price on his head now," he said.

"Price on my head." How could Kendrick have doubted it? "And just what are my many sins?"

"The usual. As well as for having abducted the Lady Fitz Hugh."

"Abducted the Lady Fitz Hugh!" Kendrick and Rowena spoke in unison.

Little John grinned. "Aye." Then he asked, "Did you?"

"Of course not," Kendrick replied, then turning towards Rowena he winked. "Besides which, I hear that lady in question is said to be quite a handful. Hardly the kind of woman a man could run off with."

"Then add it to the prince's many lies. No doubt he imagined that decrying such a thing would give him an excuse to make of you an outlaw."

"No doubt."

Little John nudged Kendrick in the ribs. "As it is her father has offered a small fortune for her return, as well as a reward for your head upon a platter."

"Sir William?" Kendrick's eyes caught Rowena's. Something was very wrong. They had left after her father had been summoned by the prince. Moreover, Sir William was favorable to a match. He would never make such an accusation.

"He would never!" Rowena blurted out, then amended, "Or so I would suppose." Ah, but she was so worried. Prince John must surely have forced her father to make such a decree. If so, then surely it meant that he was a prisoner. But where? She had to find out.

"I know what you are thinking." As soon as Little John left them alone, Kendrick gently touched her arm.

"I am."

"But you must not take a chance on being caught yourself. No heroics, dear 'Arrow'. Your father would not want you to be caught." He emphasized, "You are *safe* here."

"For the time being perhaps, but what good is that when I do not know the fate of my own father?" She went in search of her bow and arrows, intent on a rescue, but Kendrick held her back.

"We'll send a message to Chadwick. Far better for him

to inquire about your father than for you to leave the hideout." He made her a promise. "Once we learn what is happening, I will aid you in your rescue."

Searching for parchment, quill and ink, Kendrick soon found what he sought among Allan-A-Dale's belongings. The minstrel was often writing down ballads and songs or love poems, that is when he was not strumming upon his harp.

"Here."

Rowena stared down at her hands feeling suddenly helpless and foolish. "I can not read or write," she confessed. In truth, few women could. It was not deemed important that they learn.

Kendrick's eyes were gentle. Writing was just something he took for granted, having been taught by his Uncle Geoffrey, once a cleric. "Then I will write the message for you."

It was a short message, seeing as how Chadwick's vocabulary was limited. In it Kendrick explained that the Lady Rowena was safe and in good care, warned Chadwick about the danger they were all in, and asked Chadwick to try and find out the whereabouts of the lady's father. He set up a meeting at a bridge in Nottingham for Chadwick and himself so that he might set the lady's mind at ease.

Folding the paper in fourths, Rowena stuck it down the front of her tunic to be held safely within the straps of her breast binding. She wanted to find a messenger in the abbey nearby, someone whose presence in Nottingham would not be questioned. Overhearing Will Scarlet and Robin Hood talking about a portly friar gave her just the opportunity that was needed.

"I have seen him. I say that he is the match for both you and Little John."

"A friar, you say? By our Lady, I would want to meet such as he. BiGod, we will ask him to join us." Rowena had learned that it was Robin's way to seek out those who could give aid to his band of merry men. "Come lads, who else would like to join us?"

Rowena was the first to step forward. "I will." Kendrick was second. Three other outlaws likewise decided to venture forth. The small band set forth through the waterfall, over the rolling hills, winding through pathways until they came to a stream. Cautiously they paused.

> "Well, 'tis folly to love a young maiden,
> Or to follow the ship to the sea,
> 'Tis well to be jolly and well fed,
> And to have freedom to lay 'neath a tree."

The voice singing was deep and warbled more than slightly off key. Allan-A-Dale wrinkled his nose in dismay. "Hopefully he is better at fighting than at singing."

Rowena took a hesitant step forward, anxious for a look at the singer, but quickly stepped back as she heard a voice say, "I shall have a bite of meat pie. Truly it is tasty."

Another voice, higher of pitch, answered, "Nay, nay. T'would be much better to ease your hunger with a bite of mutton."

"There are two men," she whispered to Kendrick. "Surely we can persuade one of them to carry forth the message."

Daringly Robin Hood pushed through the trees to encounter the two men. Rowena, Kendrick and the others followed. What they saw was amusing. Sitting all alone was a portly friar talking to himself, using a different pitched voice to answer, turning his head from side to side as he spoke to denote two different personages.

Rowena studied the friar. His head was bare except for a fringe of brown hair where it had been tonsured, his cheeks were red as two apples, his nose bulbous, his plain brown habit tied by a rope around his corpulent stomach. He wore a sword, which peeked from beneath the folds of his garments.

"We will have some fun with this one, eh lad?" Robin poked Rowena in the ribs, then grabbing up his bow, confronted the holy man.

"Good friar, I demand that you act as my donkey. Come hither that you may carry me across this stream, ere I wet my fine leather boots."

"Carry you?" The friar looked up with anger in his beady dark eyes, but seeing the arrow pointed at him soon put down his food and did as he was bid. Rowena watched as her outlaw leader climbed upon the back of the friar.

" 'Tis cruel to play such a jest on the poor friar," she said aloud. She did not feel sorry for him for long, however. As he reached the other side the holy man took Robin unaware and brandishing a sword held Robin at bay.

"Do unto others," the friar said with a laugh. He motioned for Robin to act like the beast of burden and Rowena could hear Robin Hood's groan all the way across the stream as he struggled to carry the friar back to the spot where he had been enjoying his supper. Surely the corpulent friar was a heavy load.

"Thank you my son." Sitting back down, the friar picked up his mutton, obviously considering the jest to be at an end. Robin, however, seizing the friar's sword, continued with the playful joust.

"Turnabout is fair play." Once again he climbed upon the friar's back.

Not to be outdone, the friar bent down and sent the hero of England flying over his head, into the cold water of the stream. Sputtering, Robin moved his arms about as he began to swim.

"Need a hand?" Kendrick gave his friend a hand out of the water, pulling him upon the grassy bank. "I can't remember another time when you have been so outwitted."

"Outwitted?" Reaching for Little John's sword, Robin fell upon the poor friar. The forest echoed with the sound of their battle. Rowena held her breath, fearing that one or both of them would be wounded. When at last they were finished, however, and each lay laughing upon the ground, their energies spent, the two acted more like small boys than the fierce fighters that they were.

"Friar Tuck, I am,"

"Robin Hood!" Bolting to his feet, Robin grasped the friar's outstretched hand and helped him to his feet. "Your reputation is well deserved." Robin invited the friar to join them. "It is whispered that you would like to see the prince humbled."

"I would."

"Then come with us. You would add a great deal to our band."

Scratching his head, Friar Tuck thought over the offer. "Ah, but let me eat. I cannot make such a decision on an empty stomach." He tore at the leg of mutton as if he were a starving man, eating while all watched. His enjoyment of the food made Rowena hungry. The friar did not offer anyone food, however, then when at last all the food was gone, he picked up his sword. "Let us be off."

"Not yet!" Grabbing hold of the friar's sleeve, Rowena made her plea. "I have a message that must get to Nottinghamshire. Will you help me?"

The friar's eyes were sympathetic, as if he sensed her desperation. "Nottinghamshire. Nottinghamshire, you say." He put his stubby fingers to his head as he thought. "Why, as it is I seem to remember that they have an excellent bakery and ale house there." Cheerfully he agreed.

Without a second thought, Rowena thrust the parchment into the goodly friar's hand. "Do you think that he can be trusted?" she asked Kendrick as she watched the friar walk away.

"We soon shall see."

The hum of voices droned in the air as the townspeople moved in and out of the fixed stalls and small shops of the marketplace. The air was rent with the odors of cloves, garlic and fish. True to his word, Friar Tuck delivered the message to Chadwick and arranged a time for the meeting between Kendrick and his servant in Nottingham. Now, winding down the cobbled streets, Kendrick hurried to the bridge.

Dressed in the garb of a common labourer, thick hose of coarse gray yarn, a Phrygian cap of red wool, and dun-colored tunic, he tried to blend with the crowd as he looked over his shoulder. He was wary of being followed, not just by enemies but by Rowena Fitz Hugh. Only after a fierce argument had he at last convinced her to stay behind. Now as he pushed through the crowd he had a funny feeling that she was not too far behind.

"Troublesome woman!" Spotting her, dressed in garments similar to his, he swore beneath his breath. Her presence would put them both in danger, for now he would have to worry about not only himself but her as well.

Darting out from behind an old rickety cart, Rowena made no secret that she had ignored Kendrick's advice. "My hosen are coarse. They make my ankles itch," she said as she greeted him.

Pulling her cap down as far on her forehead as he could, Kendrick's protective action belied his gruff words. "What are you doing here?"

"I came to watch over *you*," she replied.

He swore beneath his breath again, but took her gently by the arm, leading her past a brightly garbed juggler, towards the old gray stone bridge. Thankfully he could see Chadwick's lithe figure there. His back was towards them as he gazed towards the other side of the bridge.

"Hurry, de Bron! Why are you slowing?"

Kendrick hadn't realized that he had, but now as he looked towards the bridge he understood that some inner voice deep inside his head was warning him. Something was in the air that smelled rank and it wasn't the fish or the garlic. Every nerve fiber shouted out a warning.

"Run, Rowena!"

"Run?" Stubbornly she refused, that is until the man she thought to be Chadwick turned around. It was not Chad at all, but someone she supposed to be one of Prince John's men. Accompanying him were three men-at-arms who brandished their swords as they ran forward. "Merry-go-up!" How quickly they had been surrounded. Looking to the left, then the right, Rowena had to admit to herself that there was little chance of escape. That is until a tinker's cart came rolling past with a smiling Humbley at the reins. So Kendrick's servants had not let him down after all.

"Humbley!" Never had Kendrick been so glad to see anyone. Particularly since he had brought weapons. Grabbing a sword, Kendrick wielded it skillfully, felling two men-at-arms who blocked their path. He watched as one man fell into the waters below, then taking Rowena by the hand, he jumped into the wagon.

"Hold on to your cap," Humbley commanded, pulling at the reins of the one-horse cart. The wagon burst into motion, its wheels grinding on the cobblestones. Like the wind, they flew by several of the townspeople, knocking over barrels of mead and suffering the curses of the wrathful owners.

"What has happened to my father?" Rowena had to know.

"He is a prisoner! As is poor Chadwick now."

Breathlessly he told of how the Sheriff of Nottingham had locked up Sir William, under John's orders, then forced the unfortunate man to sign a warrant making Kendrick an outlaw. Spying at the castle, Chadwick had learned Sir William's whereabouts but before he could meet Kendrick at the designated spot, he had been captured, the message had been ripped out of his hand, and he had been taken back to the castle, there to languish himself.

"Father!" It was just as Rowena had feared.

Veering to the right, Humbley only narrowly managed to bring the cart under control as it threatened to capsize.

They could hear the rumble of horses' hooves behind them and knew that the men-at-arms had called for added reinforcements.

"Hold on to the side of the cart!" Kendrick shouted as they headed straight for a pile of straw. Crashing through the middle, the cart soon came to a stop as Kendrick lifted Rowena down from the wagon. Pulling her along behind him he ran through the streets and into an alehouse. Peering out of the window, they could see their pursuers brushing off the straw from their garments.

Rowena fought against a mist of tears. Her father was Prince John's prisoner and she could not help but feel responsible. Sir William had feared all along that to go against John would bring dire consequences. Now circumstances revealed that he was right.

She had selfishly given in to her yearning for adventure without a thought to her father's safety. "I was tired of listening to all the people who only talked of doing something about Prince John. And I must admit I wanted excitement." She did not add that she had always been rebellious. "It's my fault!"

"No!" Gathering her into his arms, Kendrick kissed her forehead. "You cannot fault yourself for following your heart and doing what you believed in. Nor can your father."

"We have to save him!"

"Aye."

"Do you think Rob . . . ?"

Kendrick nodded. "He owes me a favor. Besides, I cannot think of a time when Robert didn't enjoy a lively scuffle." He squared his shoulders. "As do I."

His bravado was taken more than a little aback, however, as they heard the town crier shouting out a proclamation. "Citizens of Nottingham, know you that Kendrick de Bron has been declared outlaw by our noble prince for treason against the crown and for unlawful abduction. Hear you that a reward of two hundred pounds has hereby been offered for capture of said Kendrick, alive or dead."

"Alive or dead. Dead." The word echoed over and over in Rowena's brain. Suddenly what she had thought of as an adventure had turned ominously serious. "You cannot stay here!" His very life was in danger. "Kendrick!"

"I'm not afraid." Oh, but in truth he wasn't nearly as unconcerned as he sounded. It was as if he could already feel the sting of the headsman's ax slice his neck. More so as he heard the alehouse door give way and realized that they had been discovered.

"Show yourself as a woman, Rowena. They will give you mercy then," Kendrick commanded. Suddenly it was not himself that he worried about but her. He could not bear to see her wounded or slain.

"No!" This time it was she who took the lead, ducking in and out of the shadows as she tugged at Kendrick's arm.

"Quick, follow me!"

At first Kendrick thought that it was Rowena who spoke, but as he looked around he found himself staring at a wide-eyed boy. One who was strangely familiar. "Who . . . ?"

"Shhhhh!" He pointed at Rowena. "I recognize your friend, the archer. He saved me from a wild boar out in the forest. Now I can repay the favor. Come."

The boy led them to a trapdoor concealed in the alehouse's floor that led to a tunnel below which, during the Norman Conquest, had been used to smuggle goods into the city. Tugging the trapdoor open, he held it firmly as Rowena and Kendrick pushed their way inside.

The air was chilly and damp. It was dark. Still, as Rowena wrapped her arms protectively around her body, as she fumbled through the darkness, bumping into obstacles and brushing against spiderwebs, it was a most glorious haven. They had escaped. Taking hold of Kendrick's hand, she whispered a thankful prayer as they broke into a run, putting Prince John's men far behind them.

Chapter Twenty-Four

It was an exhausted Rowena and Kendrick who rode into the camp of Robin Hood. Having ridden nearly night and day, they had taken little time to eat and rest along the way. Only once had they given in to their longing for each other upon the soft grass beside a bubbling brook. Now they fought the urge to cast their eyes upon each other, fearing that their passion would be mirrored in the depths of a glance or a look.

It was Little John who met them as they rode in. "We were worried about you two," he said in his deep booming voice. "Robin learned that the price upon your head nigh equals that put upon his own, de Bron."

Kendrick bounded off his horse to greet the large man, nearly giving Rowena away by helping her down from her horse as he had so often the last few days. Only by his wits did he save the day. Reaching up towards Rowena, he pretended that it was for her longbow that he came towards her. Grabbing that weapon, he examined it as if for a loose string, then handed it back to her as she got off her horse.

"So tell me where you were." Little John put a friendly arm about Rowena's shoulder.

"We went to Nottingham."

"Nottingham?" Little John grimaced. "To pay a social call on our dear sheriff?"

Rowena told the truth. "To find out about Sir William of Grantham's whereabouts." She couldn't keep her voice from trembling. "It seems that the prince has gone berserk. He has imprisoned that most noble knight because of a mere suspicion."

"Suspicion? Sir William?"

"We must save him. We must!"

Fearing that Rowena was perilously close to giving herself away, Kendrick stepped in between. "Arrow was once Sir William's stable boy. He treated him just like a son!"

"Hmmmm, is that so?" Little John cocked one brow, then smiled.

"He was always most kind to me. And always loyal to the king." Though she tried to keep calm, her heart was booming. They had to rescue her father!

"My servant Chadwick has been made a prisoner as well."

"Then of course, we cannot let John go about locking up men who see things our way." He paused, then asked, "Where is he?"

"In Nottingham Castle."

"Nottingham Castle."

Rowena watched as Little John made his way to the fireside where Robin Hood sat in discussion with the jolly Friar Tuck. She could not help but feel apprehensive about the holy man, fearing that it was he who had given her message into enemy hands. Would he seek to betray them all now as well? How could she trust him?

As Little John returned and touched upon Robin Hood's rescue plan, she found out that she would have no choice. Friar Tuck was to give them aid in shielding the rescued prisoners in his old abbey once they were out of the castle.

"Sir William will be disguised as a friar. That will amuse him well," she murmured, thankful that in such a disguise he would be safe. Deep in thought she followed John, joining with him, Robin and Allan-A-Dale to discuss the plot in detail.

"The Castle of Nottingham will be a difficult fortress to siege, so we will have to act by our wits," Rob was saying. "I will disguise myself as a barber. We will get a message to Sir William to pretend to have a toothache which causes him great pain. Even John must be sympathetic to such a plight."

"Let us hope," Rowena whispered.

"John will have to let a barber in to pull the offensive tooth," Robin continued. "Me!"

"No, Robin. It is much too dangerous for you to do," argued Will Scarlet, joining the group. "Your face is too well known among the prince's men. Let me act the part!"

"No, I am not a coward."

"Yes, you are likewise not a fool."

For quite a while they argued between themselves but, having thought a moment and seeing the wisdom of Will Scarlet's argument, Robin at last agreed. "All right." He patted Kendrick on the back. "You and I, old friend, will wait patiently until they can let us in the castle walls." He looked at Rowena. "How be it if Kendrick and I dress as old women? We should go undetected then, eh? I will leave it up to Kendrick to rescue his manservant."

Rowena smiled. "Dressing in foolish skirts worked for me. Pray tell we will see if you make as good a woman as did I." She waited, and when Robin did not include her in the scheme, asked, "But what of me?"

"You, lad, will accompany Will as barber's apprentice. It will be your duty to lead Sir William safely through the gates. How like you that?" The "lad's" smile was his answer.

Robin picked up a twig and drew upon the ground. Rowena could see that it was a map, no doubt of the castle.

"I have been in Nottingham Castle many times upon one mischief or the other. The door is thick and sturdy. We could never drive it down, but look here." The outlaw leader pointed to what appeared to be a long shaft that reached nearly to the ground. " 'Tis the latrine shaft. We have only to climb up here to acquire access to yon castle."

"The latrine." Rowena wrinkled her nose in disgust. She did not envy those whose duty it would be to enter the castle thus. Glad was she to be able to accompany Will Scarlet through the door. "And just who might those fortunate climbers be?"

There were no volunteers. In the end straws had to be drawn, the owners of the short straws the unfortunates. For a long time they and the company of archers crowded around Robin Hood as final plans were hatched and fine-tuned. They would leave long before dawn's first rays touched the earth in order to reach Nottingham Castle before the servants and lords were astir.

Nottingham Castle looked gloomy and forboding. As Rowena walked beside Will Scarlet towards the wooden doors, she eyed the mammoth fortress with apprehension. Would the plan work? Would Allan-A-Dale in his guise as a minstrel be able to smuggle a message to her father so that he could aid them? For that matter, was her father even alive? Was he well? These questions played heavily on her mind as she set one booted foot in front of the other.

"How do I look?" Will Scarlet stroked the beard of which he was so proud and smiled with gleaming teeth.

Turning her head, Rowena surveyed him. He was a handsome man if a trifle effeminate for her liking. His looks, however, were misleading. She had heard that Will most certainly did not lack in courage and that he was skilled with both bow and sword. Somehow, though he did not look like she imagined most barbers would look, she tried to give him confidence. "You look just right."

"I certainly hope so," he said with a shrug, touching his garments with disgust. "These garments smell of sweat." The clothing as well as the instruments he carried with him had been borrowed from a barber in the village who was loyal to Robin and his band. "The odor of my person offends me."

Rowena laughed, pointing to the archers whose job it was to climb up the latrine. "Perhaps, but consider how lucky you are, my friend. At least you need fear no sudden surprises." Since the latrines were cleaned with rainwater from time to time, there was the danger that the archers would find themselves met with a waterfall.

"Water, we hope," Will whispered, knocking loudly upon the castle door. They were met by a stern-faced, red-haired man-at-arms, swathed in armor, who eyed them up and down with nary a trace of a smile.

"State your business," he growled, looking as if something had soured his stomach.

"I am a barber and this is my apprentice. We come from the village to offer our aid, if it is needed."

"We don't have need of you," the guardsman answered, making as if to slam the portal closed again. Will Scarlet risked his well-being as he hastily thrust his foot in the space between door and frame.

"Not so quickly. I want to talk with someone of higher rank than you."

"My master can offer his services as bloodletter, dentist, and surgeon as well as trimmer of hair," Rowena hastily added. Humbly she bowed. "Please, sir. We are in need of work. Won't you let us in?"

The man-at-arms touched his sword in a threatening manner, looking at the several other armed men who stood nearby, but instead of being aggressive he at last stood aside. "I'll ask about," he barked angrily. "But if no one has need of you, I expect you to be off on your way."

"Of course, sir." Rowena's smile was all innocence. She watched the man walk away, crossing her fingers all the while.

"Pleasant fellow, isn't he," Will Scarlet hissed, nervously tapping his fingers upon his arm as they waited.

At last the guardsman returned. "Come with me." He led them towards the lower hall and then to a stone stairwell which no doubt led to the cells of those unfortunate enough to find themselves to be the prince's "guests". "This way." The guard gave them a push. The thought came to Rowena's mind that perhaps this was a trap.

"Where are you taking us?" she asked, keeping her eyes upon the stone steps in case she had to flee.

The man-at-arms words set her at ease. "There is a prisoner inside who pains with a toothache. It is for him that you are here." He took out a large ring of keys and fitted one of them in the lock of a small wooden door.

Rowena looked in the cell and saw her father clinging to the bars. It took every ounce of self-control she had not to cry out his name. Instead she merely said, "We have come for your toothache, my lord." Her eyes silently communicated with her father.

"Well, 'tis about time, too," Sir William scolded. "I feared I would nearly die of the pain." He pointed towards the back of his mouth at a lower tooth.

Rowena followed Will Scarlet inside the cell and were thereby followed by the guardsman, who tapped his foot impatiently.

"Let me have a look," Will said, inching his way closer. Meanwhile, Rowena reached inside her apron and brought forth a dagger. Springing upon the guard she held it at the guard's throat.

"What the devil?" He struggled at first, but as the point pressed at his jugular vein all fight quickly evaporated.

"Cry out or make one move and I will kill you," she threatened. To save her father she might have to. "Now remove your clothing."

Will Scarlet too had a dagger. He pressed in close to the guardsman, forcing that man to remove his garments one by one.

"Sir William, take off your clothing and dress in these." Rowena handed him the clothing of the man-at-arms. "Hurry."

Sir William donned them in great haste as Rowena secured the guard and stuffed the hem of her apron in his mouth to keep him from sounding an alarm.

"Hurry," she called out again, beckoning Will Scarlet and her father to follow her. Climbing the stairway, they looked about for any sign of pursuit, but there was none. It was the time of day when the other men-at-arms seemed to be more concerned with their stomachs than in guarding the prince's prisoners. Only when they came to the hall did she hear any sound of a scuffle. Robin was tussling with a handsomely dressed lord, stealing the rings off his fingers and a golden amulet from around his neck. He would make certain the jewelry would go into the coffer for Richard's return, a much better use than to adorn some arrogant buffoon, he said.

"Stay here with Sir William," Will Scarlet bid his young apprentice. "I must help Rob." Thus said, he plunged into the fighting, wielding his barber's tools as lethally as he did a sword. Rowena made use of the distraction to squeeze her father's hand.

"I was so worried!"

"But not so much so as to keep from traipsing off." His tone was stern. "An outlaw, BiGod."

"No, John is the outlaw. I but align myself with those who are actively trying to save Richard." For a moment she felt defiant, but her anger quickly faded. "Father, try to understand. I am fighting for the rightful king in my own way."

"Cavorting around with a band of irresponsible men. Dressing like a man." He shook his head. "I wanted better for you."

"You wanted me to be happy and safe and content," she whispered. He nodded. "And I am." As they walked along she tried to briefly tell him about all that had happened to her since last they had seen each other, but there was no time. The other outlaws had entered the castle, turning it into a battlefield. It was dangerous to be distracted. Grabbing her father by the arm she gave up any attempt at explanations, saying merely, "Come!"

Their escape wasn't as easily attained as their entrance, however. As Rowena and her father tried to leave through the gates, they were suddenly confronted by a dark figure coming as if from nowhere. Standing in front of the door, he blocked their way.

"John!" Rowena eyed the prince with distaste but without fear. He didn't frighten her in the least. If she couldn't get the best of him then she didn't deserve to be a member of Robin Hood's band. Brazenly she hefted her sword, daring him to stop her from leaving.

"Anxious to duck away without thanking me for my hospitality, Sir William," he smirked. "Shame, shame, shame."

"Hospitality. Is that what it was?" Sir William bristled, angry that although once he was known for his prowess, he was as helpless now as a gelded lamb. "Fie on you, John, and shame it is on *you*. Your brother trusted you and yet you betray him again and again."

"Betray?" Though his tone was mocking, John kept a careful distance from the lad accompanying Sir William. "No, my father Henry wanted the crown for me, not for Richard. I but want to assure that he can rest well in his grave."

"The crown belongs to Richard and you are a traitor," Rowena challenged. The gates were beginning to close. Though Robin and the others were putting up a valiant fight, they could only hold the castle guards at bay for so long. If she and her father didn't get out right away, they would be trapped inside. "But I will not argue the point. Let us pass," she exclaimed.

"Let you pass?" An evil chuckle escaped the prince's lips as he motioned for aid. Three large men-at-arms answered his signal.

"BiGod!" Rowena was outmatched and she knew it. It looked as if she and her father would be sharing the same cell. So much for valor. Even so, she couldn't allow herself to just give up. Grabbing her father by the arm she chose another way out. To run. They were followed, just as she hoped.

"Get them!" John's command thundered through the courtyard. Furious, he joined in as his three guardsmen went in pursuit. "Capture them or take Sir William's place in the dungeon!"

John's voice was so loud that Kendrick could not help but hear. Though he was safely beyond the gates he turned back, knowing of a certainty that if Sir William was in trouble Rowena would not be far behind. Running back through the gate, he hastened to come to her aid but stumbled and fell. The skirts of his disguise as a widow hampered him. Cursing, he wondered how women ever got where they were going when they had to bother with gowns and skirts. Was it any wonder she chose lad's attire, he thought, hurriedly getting to his feet. In anger he ripped off his skirt, gripped his sword, then proceeded into the melee Rowena was creating. The clanking of sword upon sword sounded in the courtyard as Kendrick wielded his weapon.

"De Bron!" Rowena had never been so glad to see anyone in all her life. Now the odds were more even. Three to two she could handle, especially when her father seemed to suddenly spring to life. Hefting up a barrel, ignoring the ache in his back, he threw it at one of the guards, sending him tumbling. Now it was two to two.

"The gates! Close the gates!" shouted the prince.

Swinging her sword like someone gone mad, Rowena

soon bested her opponent. Likewise Kendrick de Bron made a good show of his skill with a sword. And all the while Prince John shrieked his outrage at being foiled.

"The gates!" The creak of aging wood and metal gave Kendrick warning that they had to leave now. Acting as a shield for Rowena and her father, he herded them through the opening just a moment before the gates banged shut.

"Open the gates! Open them at once!" the prince was yelling now. But by the time his order was obeyed the outlaws were gone.

PART THREE:
ARROW

Sherwood Forest—1194

Three cheers for the lad named Arrow,
Wise and brave and strong.
With our cups raised up,
We drink and sup,
And offer him this song.

Chapter Twenty-Five

The roar of the waterfall welcomed the weary but victorious band of outlaw archers back to their camp. One by one they stepped onto the rocks behind the foaming water and through the archway, disappearing much like the fairy folk that children are told about while sitting on their mother's knee.

"What is this?"

Rowena laughed at her father's shocked look. "Magic, Sir William. Magic," she answered, feeling more at peace than she had in quite awhile. Her father was safe, the outlaws had been successful and Kendrick de Bron had proven his deep affection for her by coming back through the gate to help her. Though of course she hadn't really needed his aid, she told herself stubbornly.

"Magic. Of course." Sir William tried to be as light afoot as the others but nearly slipped as he stepped across the rocks. Still, he was in good humor. "BiGod, what a clever concealment. No wonder Prince John cannot find the infamous Robin Hood no matter how hard he tries."

"Aye, but t'is nature's cleverness. I cannot take any of

the credit," Robin threw over his shoulder as he took his turn to vanish.

"Perhaps, but after all you did find it," Will Scarlet shot back. Mischievously he gave a push to two of the archers who had entered the castle by way of the latrine. They fell in the water with a splash. "If you ask me, you had best stay in that water a very, very long time."

"Says you?" In answer to Will Scarlet's prank one of those forced to go for a swim tugged at his leg, sending him into the stream as well. Resurfacing with a sputter, he insisted that was no way to treat a man of nobility like himself, but he was smiling all the while.

"Nobility," Sir William said with a sigh. "How long ago it seems that I could make that claim." He brushed at his soiled tunic. "I fear since being in John's prison I will never really be the same." He shook his head. "God grant that our beloved king is returned safely to us and that our loyalty will not be for naught."

"Richard is a fair man. He will soon see that your lands are returned," Rowena said with more conviction than she felt. Would it all be put to right? Once she had been so certain. Now she wasn't so sure. Oh, they had won today, but would that be the case tomorrow, or the next day, or the next? She purposefully pushed her misgivings aside as she stepped inside the cavern and was assaulted by a tantalyzing aroma. Friar Tuck, who had stayed behind, had prepared a veritable feast for his companions. Always one to appreciate good food, the friar looked upon each meal as an adventure.

"Come, come," he beckoned with his pudgy hands. "See what I have wrought for you." Noticing that Sir William was reluctant, he took his arm. "Mutton soup with thick pieces of bacon, roast swan with raisin and brown bread dressing, roast hare cooked with almonds. All to make your mouth water."

"As it is." Sir William mumbled under his breath about

John's meager rations, "Too long have I been on dry bread and ale."

"Then come. Don't be shy," Friar Tuck cajoled.

"No, don't be shy, Fath—" Quickly Rowena put her hand over her mouth, realizing how she had nearly given herself away. She looked around to see if anyone had noticed and was relieved to see that the archers were too preoccupied with filling their plates to have noticed her near slip of tongue. Kendrick de Bron had noticed, however. As she looked his way he winked at her.

"I'll have the duckling," Sir William hurried to say. Taking a large portion, he then set about seeing what vegetables were offered. He chose spinach, boiled with vinegar and lettuce leaves. Ripe strawberries and a mug of wine finished his feast.

Rowena chose the mutton soup, a mug of ale, a leg of swan, some lettuce leaves and the ripe strawberries. Finding a secluded spot by the fire where they would not be over-heard she sat beside her father. Robin had decided that on the morrow Friar Tuck would take Sir William to the abbey, so tonight was her last night to be with him for awhile.

"Outlaws though we all be, we did at least save you," she said softly, beginning the conversation. "Do you still scorn me and the others?"

Wearily Sir William shook his head. "No. Not after what I have seen here." Was she imagining it or did his eyes have a faint glow of admiration? "Besides, knowing you are in Kendrick de Bron's care relieves my mind," he whispered softly.

"De Bron? In his care." Rowena laughed. "You have it all wrong. It is he who is in mine." Without knowing it, her eyes traveled to where Kendrick de Bron was sitting and the look gave her away.

"So, you do not think him so arrogant and hateful now do you?" When she didn't answer he pushed her on the matter. "Do you?"

"Perhaps not." She lowered her eyes, fearful her father might see into her mind. "But I still refuse to marry him," she added stubbornly.

That did not mean that she didn't find herself longing to be near him again, however. Just the sight of his broad shoulders was deeply unnerving. How she longed to feel his body pressed close against her own. Whatever hunger had lain dormant within her, Kendrick de Bron had brought it to life. Now she doubted that she could ever truly be content to be celibate again. His arms were a haven of comfort, his lovemaking the spark that flamed her soul. It was as if with the first thrust of his manhood within her he had unleashed an undying ember. But what was she to him?

Rowena was soon to learn. When all the outlaws had bedded down for the night, and were sound asleep Kendrick came to claim her. "Care to go for a swim?" he whispered in her ear, nuzzling the soft flesh of her earlobe.

"We cannot!" For just a moment she regretted her masquerade. If not for the fact that the others thought her to be a young man, she could have done just as she pleased. As it was she had to force herself to stay away from Kendrick de Bron.

"We can't? Why not?" Teasingly he tugged at her hand.

"I cannot be discovered. We cannot be seen together. Rob, Little John, Friar Tuck and—"

"Are all asleep." He paused. "Listen to their snoring." Had she any doubts, the gentle rumble that stirred the silence was proof of the outlaws' slumbering.

"My father . . ."

"Is also sound asleep. Moreover he would welcome a tryst between us, not scold because of it."

The warm evening breeze gently caressed Rowena's face, likewise tempting her. "A short swim, perhaps." Stealthily following him, she ducked out of camp. Running through the woodlands hand in hand, they were like two naughty

children. Reaching the bank of the lake they knew the risk
to be well worth it.

"The night is beautiful and so are you," Kendrick
breathed in her ear.

"Am I?" Noting the gleam in his eyes, she couldn't
doubt it.

"More so without your garments," he added with a roguish smile, tugging on her sleeve.

Rowena gave in to his urging. Looking about to make
certain that no one would take them unaware, she removed
her clothing then dove into the lake. The slight chill took
her breath away, but after a few moments of swimming
she felt nearly warm again. Kendrick stripped off his
clothes and soon had joined her. Playfully grabbing her
ankle he pulled her under the water, locking her in an
embrace. Surfacing together they fused their mouths in a
kiss, his lips and tongue probing, hers opening to accom-
modate his quest. There was a roaring in her ears, but there
was no waterfall. Familiar sensations stirred her, urged her
to embrace him and bring him closer.

Kendrick's hands slid over her wet body, cupping her
breasts in his hands. Rowena responded, touching him,
caressing him. Her legs brushed against his, arousing him.
In that moment swimming was the farthest thing from
their minds.

Impatiently Kendrick pulled her toward the shore.
Reaching the mossy bank, he covered her naked body with
his own and she sighed at the feel of his hard, lithe body
atop hers. A flicker of arousal spread from her mouth to
the core of her body. Being with Kendrick encompassed
every emotion she had ever known.

Hungrily, eagerly, his lips devoured hers over and over
again. Rowena felt a mounting passion surging through
her body as their eyes met and held. An unspoken commu-
nication passed between them. He was ready for lovemaking and so was she.

Slowly, sensuously, Kendrick let his hand slide up her

thigh, his fingers questing, seeking that most intimate part of her. Rowena responded in kind. She caught his throbbing staff between her thighs, longing for the pierce of that sword. She reached for him, grasping his manhood and opening her legs to sheath it gently at first, then with passionate urgency.

"Rowena," he whispered as he was met by her velvety softness. Slowly he began to move within her, stroking her hair, whispering words of love. Rowena lost track of time, forgot who and where they were as she gave in to her desire and longing. She was filled with an aching sweetness, wishing this pleasure could go on forever. Then it seemed as if the night shattered into a thousand stars, tumbling the world around her.

"I love you," she heard Kendrick proclaim and found herself saying the same vow. Suspended in time they clung to each other, parting only reluctantly as they realized they could not risk being together for very long.

"We have to get back," Rowena declared, picking up her scattered clothing.

"Not yet." Kendrick was mentally making plans, mapping out his life and their future. "We'll have Friar Tuck perform the ceremony and we'll—"

"Ceremony?" Rowena paused in tugging on her hosen. "What ceremony?"

Kendrick blurted it out, feeling sure of himself and cocky. "Why, the wedding ceremony, of course." He stiffened as he took note of the stubborn tilt to her chin. "Rowena, it is only right."

"Because you lay with me?" She shook her head. "I feel no shame in what we have done. You don't have to make our being together legal."

"But I want to." More than anything in this world he wanted to make her his wife.

"No." Rowena was adamant on the subject. "I will not give up my freedom. Even for you."

"What!" He could not hide his frustration.

"I will not be anyone's property, to cook his bread, keep a goodly ledger and bring forth the fruit of his seed again and again until my body is old and worn. I want to be a person in my own right, to be judged for the skills I possess."

Kendrick bolted to his feet and caught hold of her, determined to argue her to reason. "It won't be like that between us. I—" A rustling sound from the bushes caused him to quickly let her go.

"Get dressed," Rowena breathed. "We cannot let anyone see us." She fully expected Robin or one of the outlaws to bolt out of the foliage but it was only an owl taking flight. Even so she urged him to hurry. As soon as they were dressed, they silently, separately made their way back to the camp, their tryst in the woods ruined by the conflict that had risen between them.

Covering herself with several woolen blankets, Rowena lay staring up at the stars. Slowly her thoughts took shape and she tried to sort out her emotions. Just how did she feel about Kendrick de Bron? Certainly his lovemaking made her feel vibrant and alive, but was the passion she felt with him really love? And if it was love, were her feelings strong enough for her to tie herself to him for life?

"No!"

The very idea was much too frightening. Marriage strangled love, it didn't nourish it. Hadn't she seen that over and over again? "I cannot marry him. Nay, I cannot." Somehow she had to make him understand. But how? As she looked across the camp to the lone lit fire where he was pacing, she knew she had to find a way, for though she didn't want to marry him she didn't want to lose him either.

"Oh, de Bron, what are you thinking? What are you feeling?"

Kendrick was at the moment deliberating his alternatives. He could reveal Rowena's identity to Robin Hood and hope that in so doing he could force her to his will; he could leave Robin's camp and travel on his way; or he could bury his pride and hope that by his patience he could win her heart and eventually her hand in marriage as well. He opted for the latter. She was worth waiting for. But oh, being a man with little patience to spare, it was going to be difficult.

Even now he fantasized about holding her, warm and naked, in his arms. Waking up beside her. Looking across the table and seeing her face. Holding the fruit of their love in his arms. Sharing his life with Rowena Fitz Hugh would be a wonder beyond compare. Certainly she would never be boring. Oh no. Kendrick laughed as he remembered their first encounter. She had forced him to strip, had held him captive with the power of her bow. She was willful. Stubborn. Wild.

"And the woman I love." Who had denied him over and over again but who, when she had at last given herself to him, had done it so openly, so completely that he had been shaken, stunned. She was a woman he could never give up.

"I did not think you one to fancy boys."

"What?" Kendrick was startled as Robin Hood stepped out of the bushes and took him unaware.

"Arrow," the outlaw leader whispered. "I would have to be blind not to know that something is going on." Robin looked at his friend with searching eyes. "I saw you walking through the woods together, hand in hand."

"Oh." Roderick clenched his jaw, wanting to tell Robin the truth but at the same time loath to give Rowena away. Being in Robin Hood's band meant so much to her. How could he spoil it all? "So, now you know."

"The truth is as plain as the face of an old maid at her spinning." Robin was sullen. Silent. Then he laughed. A sound so loud that it threatened to awaken the entire camp.

"What amuses you so?" Kendrick was incensed. Raising his fists, he prepared himself for a scuffle, for no one, not even Robin, would be allowed to ridicule him.

"The truth," Robin answered. He jabbed Kendrick in the ribs.

"You have no idea just what that is," Kendrick answered. Picking up a handful of dirt, he threw it on the fire.

"Ah, but I do." He quieted, then said so softly that Kendrick could barely hear, "Certainly Arrow looked fetching dressed as a lady when we encountered the prince. Much too lovely for a lad."

"Arrow is not—"

"Ah, but you lie." Robin affected his jaunty air. "And quite a woman at that. Imagine that. Why, I was nearly beaten at the archery tournament by a female." He clucked his tongue. "But do not worry. I can keep a secret."

"Can you?" Kendrick was relieved, but wary as well. "And will you?"

"Aye." Robin wistfully lapsed into loving words concerning his own paramour, Marian. He longed to see her again. "And perhaps I will see her. Sooner than I think."

"What do you mean?" Kendrick was immediately curious.

"This." Reaching into his boot, Robin brought forth a handbill. "By order of his highness, Prince John, let it be known that on Friday next, an archery tournament will be held at Nottingham Castle," he read. "The winner will be crowned King of Archers."

"King of Archers," Kendrick repeated. It sounded like a trap. "Why would Prince John announce such a contest so soon after our entry within his castle walls?"

"Because he has a fondness for archery?" In curiosity, Rowena had gotten to her feet and joined in the conversation at the sight of the handbill fluttering in Robin's hand. She read on. "The hand of Lady Marian will be given in marriage to he who shoots straightest and truest." Mentally she repeated, *the hand of Marian.* And her whole life as well. How terrible to face the prospect of being given to a stranger? She looked Robin in the face, and seeing the anger there she knew he would be the first to go to Nottingham Shire.

"Damn John's soul to hell." Robin pounded his fist into his palm. "I will not let another touch her. Marian is mine. I love her and she loves me."

"No." Knowing well what was in his friend's mind, Kendrick grabbed him by the arm. "You cannot even think to go there."

"Nothing can keep me away." In a battle of wills, Robin Hood was unbeatable. "I will go to Nottingham and it will be I who will win the title as well as the hand of Marian. She will be my wife and no other." And there was no dissuading him. He was too wrapped up in being the knight that saved his lady fair.

Rowena threw up her arms. "It seems there is nothing that can be done unless . . ." Her mind was instantly made up. If she were to shoot the winning arrow, all would be well. It was all so very simple. Being a woman she could not claim the lady's hand in marriage, yet she would keep any other contender from winning Marian as a trophy. It was all so simple. "Unless *I* be declared the winner." The thought of being crowned "king of archers" caused her to smile. It seemed she was going to meet Robin Hood in an archery tournament once again.

The outlaw camp began to stir much earlier than usual. One by one Robin's men rose to their feet, rubbing their eyes and stretching their arms. After a hearty breakfast of mutton and goose eggs, several men set up targets to practice with bow and arrow. It seemed that Robin and Rowena were not the only ones who wanted to make a good showing at the tournament.

Rowena was awakened by the thump, thump of the arrows as they hit a tree, but although she was anxious to join in, she had more important things to do. "Would you like some breakfast, Sir William?" At his nod she gave them both a hefty helping, then sat down beside him. Something was troubling him. Curious to know, she asked what it was.

"I want to go home."

"So that you can be taken prisoner again? Think."

He did think, at least long enough to make the startling proposition that if he could not go home he should stay among the outlaws. "I am not some doddering old man who has to be hidden away in an abbey. I can still wield a sword with the best of them," he complained.

"Nay!" She wouldn't have it! He was her father. She had to protect him. "Life here is not for you. Sleeping on the hard ground would bother the ache in your bones."

"It wouldn't—"

"It would!" Though she didn't want to hurt his feelings, Rowena could plainly see that Sir William was getting old. Too old to be an outlaw. But how could she convince him without a quarrel? "You will be more comfortable at the abbey for now. Once Richard returns, we will all be able to go back to our homes where we belong . . ." She let out a long shuddering sigh. "Please . . ."

Sir William tensed but didn't argue. "I will miss you."

"And I you," Rowena answered. She looked searchingly at him for a long time. Sir William looked so tired, so old with the deep creases on each side of his mouth and around his eyes. "Sir William." *Father.*

"Say no more." Slowly he rose to his feet. "If it is your wish that I be put out to pasture while you roam about, then so be it."

"It is not my—" Looking up she was confronted by Friar Tuck's girth hovering over her.

"My good lord, are you ready?"

Sir William nodded. "As ready as I will ever be." Haltingly he got to his feet.

"You will be safe where I am taking you," Friar Tuck announced with a smile, urging Sir William down the path.

Rowena watched with a lump in her throat, feeling for just a moment like a lonely child. This was not the kind of parting scene she had wanted. Was it any wonder then that as she watched Sir William walk away she felt her eyes sting with tears?

Chapter Twenty-Six

Undoubtedly it was a trap. Nevertheless, each and every outlaw had opted to follow Robin Hood to Nottingham. Disguising themselves as foresters, ploughmen, townsmen, bakers and tinkers they rode on horseback, wagons or went on foot down the road that took them towards the shire, joining in among the procession of judges and contestants.

Rowena had chosen to don the garments of a shepherd boy with loose tunic of dun-grey wool and a brown leather belt. Her pointed hood of brown wool covered her neck and shoulders and hid her face from any who might be looking for her. Robin too chose the same disguise, carrying a brown leather pouch at his belt, a hiding place for gold in case he found himself close to the Sheriff of Nottingham's full purse. Kendrick was garbed in the green of a forester with a red feather stuck in his cap. Allan-A-Dale dressed as a minstrel, clinging to his harp. His tunic was of many colors and he made a colorful sight amidst the drabness of the others.

"Seek the safety of the crowd," Robin had advised, thus Rowena mingled amidst the merrymakers as they pushed through the open gate. Though tournaments were officially for nobles, everyone who could elbow his way to a advantageous viewing spot watched the doings.

The contest was to be held in the lower baily where tier upon tier of seats had been erected for the spectators. Those seats were filled in the blinking of an eye by those anxious to witness the show of skill. Had they known that all of this was to capture their beloved Robin Hood, Rowena had no doubt but that they would have stayed away or sought to aid the outlaw leader instead of ogling. As it was they were buzzing excitedly like bees, pointing at the gaily colored tents that dotted the field like flowers. Each was the domicile of a different knight and was distinguished by the coat of arms that floated aloft on a pennant in the breeze. Yellow for the Duke of Buckingham, white for Sir Griffin, blue for Hubert Longsley, the Prince's favorite.

In and out among the crowd went those selling pies, cakes and wine. Voices hawked mugs of ale and turkey legs as well baubles for a fine lady's pleasure. Many a serving wench and lady of means brushed elbows as each strolled about the grounds. Rowena frowned as she saw one over-eager young maid boldly clinging to Kendrick's arm. Sauntering to his side, she boldly thrust the woman aside, then lest she give herself away, she pretended to an interest in the maid herself, much to Kendrick's amusement.

"But alas, too skinny," she declared, pinching the serving wench's hip, then sending her on her way.

"No, she was definitely not as comely as you, Rowena my love," he breathed in her ear as he passed by on his way to the archery field.

The blare of horns summoned all to their seats or to take their places. Rowena scanned the crowded seats as she likewise walked to the field. She could see the grinning face of the Sheriff of Nottingham, his beady eyes scanning the crowd anxiously and she knew at that moment this was indeed a trap. Resolving to win this archery contest and save Robin no matter what, she continued on her way.

A herald garbed in red and yellow stepped upon a high platform to announce the archery match, naming the prizes to be won. "Third prize will be a purse of silver. Second a purse of gold and first prize—"

Rowena watched as Prince John stood up from where he sat in his royal, canopied box. He held up a silver crown for the crowd to see. "The King of Archers will also receive a great honor. The hand of the Lady Marian in marriage," he proclaimed generously. As if it was his right to give her away.

"The bastard!" she said beneath her breath. Women were believed to be inferior to men and could show their abilities only in a restricted way. Even so, John had gone beyond the bounds of decency even for a scoundrel. Looking towards the royal box, she took note of Marian's pale face as she sat next to the grinning prince and her heart went out to her. Surely Marian had guessed the reason for her hand in marriage to be given as the prize. What must she be thinking at this moment?

"Ha. For the hand of so fair a lady," she heard Hubert Longsley say, "I would shoot at the very stars themselves." Arrogantly he pushed by her, giving her a deliberate shove. Well, let him exhibit his conceit. It would only make his fall that much harder when she beat him at this game, she thought as the shooting began.

The match was much like that other contest had been. Twenty targets, easy ones at first, were placed about fifty feet away. Even so there were two entrants whose arrows veered short of the bull's-eye. Rowena, Robin, Kendrick, Little John, Will Scarlet, and Allan-A-Dale all found themselves huddled together with the prince's favorites to await the second round. This time the targets were placed at twice the distance, their dark black bull's-eyes looking like eclipses as they loomed ahead.

"Now, remember. Shoot well but not too well," Robin

instructed his men. "I would not take kindly to any of you marrying my lady." His strut was cocky. Bold. If he feared that winning the tournament might be his undoing he did not show it. Perhaps because he had gotten out of dangerous situations so many times before without being captured. But there was always a first time.

Each archer took his turn, determined to weather this round, but there were several misshots. Amidst boos from the crowd, they departed the field looking with envy upon the successful archers. But the success was short and sweet. It was just the beginning of the competition. Four rounds of shooting proceeded. Rowena gritted her teeth, determined to last to the bitter end. And she did. She had, in fact, never shot better. Under pressure her aim was faultless.

"Bravo," Kendrick whispered in her ear, as the crowd cheered. "But do not carry your masquerade too far."

It was a warning she ignored. Winning had become an obsession, more so as she noted that the targets were coyly being moved away from the gates of the castle baily, making it more difficult to escape. From the corner of her eye she could see the prince giving orders to his men. She watched as the men-at-arms formed a half circle around the archers, which had been narrowed down to Rowena, Hubert, the knight of the Duke of Buckingham, Little John, Kendrick, Will Scarlet, Allan-A-Dale and Robin Hood.

The crowd was stilled as each took his turn. The Duke's archer, Allan-A-Dale and, much to his shame, Kendrick were eliminated this time. Rowena noted how Kendrick lowered his eyes, his pride hurt by having missed the mark. Onced she might have goaded him, but as the crowd stirred with anticipation she instead centered her concentration on one thing. Winning.

Rowena watched Little John take his turn, planting his feet firmly on the ground as he took aim. The shaft struck true to the black of the bull's-eye as a cheer rang out from the crowd.

Will Scarlet was next, though his shaft swerved downward, a hair's distance from the black of the mark. A silence followed and Rowena could see disappointment upon the brightly arrayed man's face. Will hated losing.

Hubert shot next, his arrow hitting but a finger's width closer to the center of the target than Little John's. The nobles in the crowd cheered loudly as one of their own scored well. The haughty man looked upon Little John with a smirk. "It takes one of noble stature to win the hand of a lady," he declared.

"Which leaves you out," Rowena remarked as she gripped her bow. She held her breath as Robin's arrow whistled along, striking dead center on the dark of the bull's-eye. She could see the men-at-arms coming closer to Robin, certain now that any moment they would have their prisoner. Only one man could shoot like that, their expressions seemed to say. Meanwhile the crowd was on its' feet as the air was rent with cheers.

Rowena stepped forward, her stance bold and sure as she tried to throw the men-at-arms into confusion. With a manly stride she stepped forward. Drawing back her bowstring she took aim, murmuring a prayer beneath her breath. As soon as the arrow left her bow she closed her eyes, and it was only by the tumult of the crowd that she knew that she had won. Rowena looked to see that she had split Robin's arrow in two with her own.

"BiGod!" Robin couldn't believe it. "It cannot be." Ah, but it was, and in the next moment Rowena paid the price.

"Grab him!"

She felt one man-at-arm's hand on her arm, another guard's grip upon her leg, one more reaching to hold her by the neck.

"No!" Kendrick cried out. He tried to reach her but his path was blocked by several more guardsmen.

"Aha!" The Sheriff of Nottingham was overtly gleeful. "I have you at last."

"I denounce you as an outlaw, the vile Robin Hood,"

Prince John accused, pointing his finger at Rowena. "To the dungeons with him."

Rowena looked over her shoulder and was moved to tears to see how valiantly Kendrick de Bron was struggling to reach her side. He was pushed back over and over again by the crush of bodies all eager for a look at the infamous Robin Hood. "No, it's not true!" he shouted. "Tell them who you are."

Indeed she might have done that were she a coward, but in that moment Rowena Fitz Hugh was content to be the sacrificial lamb in order to save Robin's skin. Slowly her eyes looked into Maid Marian's and she saw a mixture of confusion and relief, yet also pity. No doubt Marian was joyous that her love, Robin, had not been captured, yet also sorry for the one caught in his place.

"You . . ." she heard her say. "The one who saved me from Prince's John's henchmen the day after the feast."

"I am Robin Hood," Rowena said loudly. Looking straight into her friend's eyes, she warned her not to give away the truth. Even Prince John would never dare to hang a woman of nobility. That thought gave her some peace of mind as she was dragged away. Still, as she felt herself being pushed towards the gated castle doors, she wondered at her fate.

Kendrick fought like a man possessed, lashing out at those who held him as he watched Rowena being taken away. He had planned to guard her, protect her, but he had failed. All he could do was watch helplessly as she was carted away to the cold, dark prison cell of the castle.

"You fools! You idiots! That was not Robin Hood!" he yelled. "That was a woman who just won your foolish tournament. A woman!"

"A woman?" A crowd of onlookers looked upon him warily, certain he was touched in the head. "A female win the match?" Several of those standing nearby chuckled at that. "No woman could have done such a thing. It takes strength to shoot a bow."

"It was a woman. Rowena Fitz Hugh!" Though Kendrick tried to keep control of his temper, he snapped as the men in the crowd hooted in merriment. He struck one particularly obnoxious man in the stomach, then put up his fists. "You laugh. Well, I will change your mood."

Kendrick didn't notice that he was being observed by those trying to decide who among the crowd were followers of the outlaw leader. "Look there. He was with the outlaw!" Slowly they closed in on him.

"Kendrick!" Robin hissed a warning but it was too late. He hesitated but realizing that his friend was about to be captured, Robin motioned to the others. One by one they escaped beyond the wall, making use of the distraction Kendrick was creating. And all the while Kendrick fought on, aware only of Rowena's peril. Too late he realized the danger he was in as he was grabbed and thrown to the ground.

John came forward to take a look at the man creating such turmoil. "Well, well, well, de Bron. So, an unexpected boon to this little snare I set up."

For just a moment Kendrick broke free. His eyes darted back and forth, searching for any means of escape. The gates were shut, the bridge up, the walls too high to scale without a rope. For a moment he wavered, wanting to be put in prison with Rowena so that he could be of comfort to her and at the same time realizing he would do her little good if he too were taken.

"Catch him!"

Hearing the command he ran, only to be cornered at the gate. His only satisfaction came in knowing that it took eight men to hold him to the ground.

"Captured like a common outlaw. So much for the house of de Bron," John taunted, hovering over him like a bird of prey. "I would have thought better of you, Kendrick. Ah, but it is too late. You will hang like the traitor that you are."

"Traitor? I?" Kendrick was defiant despite the knot in his stomach that formed at the word "hang". "You are the traitor, and a tyrant and a coward as well. 'Tis Richard who is the true ruler, but you have betrayed him." He wanted to yell out the truth to the crowd, that Richard had been imprisoned because of his brother's actions, but he didn't have the chance. A hand was clamped over his mouth.

"Take him to the tower. We will make an example of him." John paused, then added, "Put him in a separate cell than Robin Hood. I want no chance of their working together to escape."

Kendrick felt ropes bind his hands and legs as he was dragged away from the castle wall. In that moment, far from his worries being about himself, it was Rowena's fate that consumed him, tormented him.

Chapter Twenty-Seven

It was dark and silent in the prison cell. The only noise was the scurrying of the rats. That and the drip, drip of water from the outside wall that made it cold and damp. The stale odor of rotting hay assailed Rowena's nose as she sat hunched in the corner. She looked about her at the cracked stone walls in disgust. "John's hospitality," she grumbled, shivering. Hearing the trod of footsteps, she stiffened.

"Gallows bait, that one. Said to be Robin Hood himself."

Looking through the tiny grille of the mammoth door, she could see the shadow of two men. The guard and the jailor no doubt, talking about her fate. In that moment she didn't know whether to laugh or cry. She wanted to be free again, to roam the forests, to put her arms around her lover. For just a moment her courage faltered. What foolishness had made her go through with this scheme? Why had she traded her freedom for Robin Hood's? Why had she made herself a martyr?

"Because I had to!" It was the only way to save Robin Hood, the only hope to see that Richard was put back upon the throne. But oh, now that it was done it seemed a hefty price to pay.

"Kendrick!" Her need to be with him right now was nearly an obssesion. Escape. She had to get out. Rising to her feet she walked around and around, prodding and poking at the stone, pulling at the grate. Alas, John's prison was well built, thus she sat back down again.

Time moved slowly. Because Rowena wasn't used to being closed in, the walls seemed to be closing in on her. She jumped at the creak of the door. Turning she saw the burly guard grinning at her from the doorway. "Here's your dinner, outlaw," he said, thrusting a piece of dry bread and mug of water at her. "Eat heartily." His eyes were filled with mocking, his voice taunting. "A meal fit for a king—eh, archer. King of Archers." Laughter boomed through the room.

The water was slimy, clouded with a greasy film. Though Rowena was thirsty she poured the contents upon the stone floor. She was hungry too, but not so hungry that she would eat moldy bread. In disgust she handed it back to him, her manner haughty. "Please, take this away."

"Please, is it?" He clucked his tongue. "My, aren't outlaws polite?" Angrily he threw the bread upon the ground and Rowena watched as a rat ran to it, gobbling up the morsel as if it were a feast. The guard guffawed. "Your companion here is not so fussy about his fare as you, but then he is not a king."

"Not a king, but if you look closely that rat resembles he who rules in the king's place." She turned her back.

"You dare talk so of the prince?" There was a moment of silence, then he walked back towards the door, opened it, slammed it shut and locked it again. "Well, before too long you will be begging for what you just refused."

"Beg? Never!"

The air from a crack in the wall chilled Rowena and she wrapped her arms around her body in an effort to keep warm. It was a losing battle. She shivered, her teeth chattering. Again she longed to have Kendrick's strong arms enfolding her. Was he safe? She imagined him sitting before the campfire plotting ways to save her. Well, she had a few schemes up her own sleeve.

Rowena smiled and that smile erupted into a laugh. Of course. That was it! But she would need help. Who? "Lankless." The jestor's name popped into her mind. He had told her that he would help her if she needed him. Most certainly she needed him now.

Kendrick's accommodations were not any better than Rowena's. He also lay in a small, dirty prison cell. His hands were bound behind him, so tightly that he had to keep moving his fingers to keep his blood circulating. One leg was shackled and kept him chained to the wall. He was bruised, battered and bloody. The bastards! They had enjoyed every minute of abusing him, taking great delight all the while in reminding him that in three day's time he was going to hang. The cold chill of fear coiled him through at the thought. He had no doubt that Prince John would do as he threatened.

"A fine ending," he mumbled, "to dangle from a rope." And Rowena? There again his jailors had been cruel, refusing to tell him anything about his "companion," whom they insisted was Robin Hood.

Kendrick had insisted just as strongly that it was a woman they held and not the outlaw leader, but again had received laughter in response to his declarations. "We can hang a woman from a rope the same as a man," one of the guards had said. That threat Kendrick was tormented by now. What was going to happen to Rowena?

"So, one of Robin Hood's men you be." A whisper in the darkness sounded raspy, gruff. Squinting, Kendrick assessed his jailmate, a gray-bearded old man who was sprawled near him. Muttering to himself from time to time, he seemed to be somewhat content drinking the ale one of the guards had given him.

"One of Robin's outlaws and his friend," Kendrick answered, straining the chain on his leg as he tried to move closer to the man.

"Me too." The old man scratched at his head.

"You too what?" The jail was brimming with vermin. Kendrick felt suddenly crawly. His own skin seemed to prick at the thought of the bugs and he was bothered that had he the need to scratch, it would be impossible. It would drive a man mad.

"I be an outlaw. Was before Robin Hood was even born." Finishing the ale, he wiped his mouth and Kendrick found himself envious of the man's lack of shackles.

"An outlaw." Kendrick doubted it. Obviously the man was in a drunken fantasy. Or perhaps he had been an outlaw once. Certainly they roamed about England in huge numbers, Robin's band being only one of many but by all odds the most famous.

"Not only an outlaw. I was the smartest this land has ever seen." For a moment the old man was lost in reminiscing. "Roamed with a bow, I did. Hiding in the forest. Ah, but we had such adventures."

"I've no doubt but that you did." Maybe so, maybe not. Kendrick would not argue it. If the man wanted to imagine he was the King of England, what harm would it do? At least he seemed harmless.

"Helping prisoners escape is my specialty . . ."

Kendrick started to laugh at that. If that was true, then what was the man doing here? He didn't have time to ask. The cell was suddenly flooded with light. A big hulking guard strode into the room. Thrusting the torch in front of Kendrick's eyes he gave a grunt.

"Looks like you be still safely secured."

The sudden light blinded Kendrick. He closed his eyes to escape the flickering glare. "How could you think otherwise?"

"It was feared you might escape." He looked over at
the old man as if to say he had worried that the old man
might have given Kendrick aid. His concern caused Kendrick to look anew at his gray-bearded cell mate. Maybe
the man wasn't as befuddled as he appeared.

"Well, as you can see, I didn't." But perhaps there was
a chance. That hope was dashed as the guard motioned
with his torch for the old man to follow him.

"You. Come with me. Just in case you have any ideas."

"Don't want to." The old man was stubborn. Belying
his frailty, he struggled with the guard, giving nearly as
good as he received. In the end, however, he was subdued.

"I have my orders, old man." Pulled and pushed along,
the old man was soon beyond the door.

"BiGod!" As the door slammed shut and the key was
turned in the lock, Kendrick had never felt more alone in
his life. The brief hope he had of getting free was dashed.
Destroyed.

Was he going to die? No, somehow he could not imagine
his own death. The thought of never holding Rowena in
his arms again was just too devastating, thus he forced
himself to calm. Somehow, someway, despite all the odds
he was going to get away. It was just a matter of time.

Chapter Twenty-Eight

Rowena listened to the thump, thump, thump of the rain as it fell from the ceiling above to the stone floor. That and the high-pitched shrieks of the rats as they scurried about in the night made it impossible for her to sleep. She hated being locked up. Hated it more than anything. She was caged like some animal and there didn't seem to be anything she could do about it. The dungeon had been built to keep prisoners in. And all the while the ghostly clang of closing gates, the rattle of keys and heavy trod of footsteps were constant reminders of the lack of privacy she had.

"Well, well, well. And how be our king of the archers?" asked the guard from the door, peering through the grille. All through the night he had made it a point to goad her with jeers and sarcasm. Now he seemed to be at it again.

"Go away!" She sat up. "I already told you I'm not hungry or thirsty. At least for the fare you offer."

"Is this more to your liking?" He dangled a leg of mutton through the opening in the grille, laughing as she got to her feet and tried to grasp it just as he pulled it away. "Ah, no. I'm sure it is undercooked. Not at all up to your fine tastes."

Angry with herself for allowing her gnawing, hungry stomach to rule her head, Rowena sat back down. "As you say." Determined to ignore him, she drew her legs up to her chest and turned her back. At last the guard left, but only for a short while. All too soon he was back. This time to tease her with a mug of ale.

"Forsooth. You again?"

"Thirsty?" Deliberately he poured it on the floor. "Well then, lap it up."

"I'm not a dog," she retorted. "If you expect me to beg you are wasting your time. I will not grovel."

"Even for your life?" He put his hands at his throat and mimicked the gasping sound of a man being hanged.

"Not even for that." She would only hope that once it was discovered she was not the infamous Robin Hood that she would be spared.

"Then you will die." With that said he left again, but after a time he was back. "Up on your feet. Daylight is fast approaching. It's not time to sleep." He rattled a stick over the grille. "Awake. Awake. Awake."

"I wasn't asleep." She held her temper in check, knowing that an argument was obviously what he wanted. "I've stayed awake, anticipating your fine company."

"My company?" For a moment he showed surprise, then he laughed. "So you will miss me when I give you over to the day guard?" he taunted.

Rowena's spirits lightened. She got to her feet. Of course. There would be a changing of the guards at daybreak. It was common practice. Why hadn't she thought of that? And with the changing of the sentries would be her one chance of escape.

"Of course I will miss you," she said in a forced affable manner. "You have been so *kind*. Besides, I've gotten used to the rhythm of your boots as you pace up and down. Makes me want to dance."

The guard grunted, angered by her apparent cheerfulness. "Makes you want to dance, does it." He kicked at the door, making a frightful noise. "Well, Edgar's trod is twice as loud because he is twice as big."

Rowena smiled. "I'm looking forward to meeting him." Certainly he couldn't be as big a lout as this one. Or could he? Settling back down on the hard stone floor and closing her eyes, she could only imagine as she drifted off to sleep.

"Pssst!"

Her eyes flew open at the sound. A rat? Instantly she was wary, for the disgusting creatures were not unknown to nibble at human flesh. She was always on guard against them.

"Psst!" she heard again.

This time she suspected that the sound was human.

"Who's there?" The thought occurred to her that perhaps the change of guard was earlier than usual.

"Lankless!"

"Lankless." She could hardly believe her good fortune. He was the one person in the castle that she trusted. Still she was cautious. "How do I know it is you? Let me see you."

"It is I." She could see the brightly colored shoes with their pointed toes peeking through the door. The bells on those shoes jingled as he moved closer. "I heard by way of the castle grapevine that you had been captured. I've come to help you, Robin." Because he was so short, just the top of his hat showed through the grille.

Instantly Rowena was on her feet. "Thank God!" Running to the door, she stood on tiptoe looking out. "I'm not Robin, but will you help me anyway, considering that you made a promise?" Quickly she revealed their meeting in the forest when she had come to his aid.

"The lad! But how—"

"Shhhhh. What I told you is a secret." In a hushed whisper she told him about her successful plan to save Robin Hood. "Now it is time to save myself and Marian.

I need your help." Rowena waited for a reply and was dismayed to see the jester's hat disappear. So that was her answer then.

As quickly as he had disappeared, the little man reappeared. "I thought I heard someone coming," he explained. "I wanted to wait until the guard moved to the other side of the cells." His hat bounced as he hurried forward. "But tell me. What can I do?"

"I need women's clothing. A chemise, robe, mantle and head covering, and I need you to take a message to Lady Marian to instruct her to be ready to flee the castle ere dawn."

"Women's garments?" He laughed and in that moment she knew he sensed what she was about. "It might work. By the Lord, it just might." He was silent a moment, then his voice was very spirited. "And I will keep yon guards distracted with my tomfoolery."

"It will work!" As she watched the jestor's hat bobble away, it was as if she could see the open skies above her, smell the fresh air. This time when she heard the rustle of hay as a rat scurried by her feet she was not afraid.

Rowena's fingers trembled as she fastened a belt about her kirtle. Straightening the folds of that gown she looked about her for any sign of the guard. "Is it clear?"

"All clear."

"Bless you, Lankless," she whispered, adjusting her headdress, a circular hat-like garment called a fillet. It was the latest style, Lankless had told her, shoving it through the grille with the other garments. "How do I look?" Unruly strands of her hair stuck from beneath the chin cloth, but she had not the time to tary. Soon it would be time for the changing of the guard.

"Lovely. Were you really a woman I would woo you unswervingly." His bells jangled as he made a bow.

"Good." Stuffing her man's garments with straw so that

it appeared that the scarecrow was huddled upon the hay, Rowena thought over very carefully every detail of her plan. Then, hearing the shuffling steps of the guard she stiffened. If it was the old guard, all was lost. She could only pray that it was the new one.

She heard the sound of keys. Looking around the cell she lamented that there was not even a stool to use to bang him on the head. What then? As she heard the sound of the grille hatch being opened further, her heart sank just a little.

"Hey you, wake up! King of the archers, it is time to rise." The guard had seen the scarecrow and thought it to be her. So much the better. She heard the key in the lock and braced herself for attacking him if that was the only way out. "I'll wake you up!"

Rowena waited for the door to open but it remained closed. The silence was eerie and for a moment she wondered if the sadistic fool was playing some kind of game. A moment later the riddle was answered, however, as she heard the boom, boom of footsteps. The other guard. No doubt her antagonist was anxious to be off duty and had thus abandoned all thought of tormenting her further.

"I thought I heard you coming. You're late. Do you think I like to stay down here, BiGod?"

"Sorry, but I found a wench in need of my wooing outside the scullery. Can't blame a man for having a bit of fun, now can you?"

"Nay! I would do the same." Rowena could hear the footsteps again and hoped that it meant the old guard was leaving. Crossing her fingers, she waited. In a few moments the sound of the outer prison door told her that her wish had been granted. She counted to twenty beneath her breath, then adjusting her garments, stepped away from the door.

"You. Guard!" she called out with all the authority her nobility had taught her. She held her head erect in a haughty manner.

A pair of eyes stared at her through the grille. "Who are you? And what are you doing in here?" He had not expected to see a lady in an outlaw's cell.

"I want you to let me out of here at once," she commanded, refusing to answer his question.

"Let you out? Who let you in?" He was puzzled. This one was much younger and to her relief seemed far less intelligent than his predecessor.

"The other guard," she lied. "I came to say goodbye to Robin Hood, yet since he lies there and sleeps I say let the gallows have him. He sleeps when he could be in my arms."

"A fool he," he complimented. Still, he hesitated. "You say Edgar let you in?"

"Aye. But I must admit I bribed him. I gave him several gold coins."

"Gold coins?" The mention of money made him more pliable. "And would you likewise give me gold to let you out?"

Rowena nodded. "Of course."

"Give them to me." His greed was obvious.

"First let me out." She walked to the door. "Or shall I give it out that it was you who let me in and see you flogged to within an inch of your life."

"Don't be doing that!" His voice was tinged with fear.

"Well then . . ."

Rowena heard the key in the lock, then a jingle as it fell to the floor. He picked it up and put it in the lock again. She heard the key turn. Then the door was open. Rowena stepped through to freedom.

"My gold?" He blocked her way, he the only barricade to her freedom.

"Your gold?" She reached inside the folds of her kirtle as if fumbling for her purse, then taking him by surprise, kneed the guard in the groin. As he lay writhing in pain she wrenched his nightstick out of his hand and hit him hard upon the head, not once but thrice. Then picking up her skirts she fled.

* * *

Rowena retreated into the dark shadows of the castle corridors. She had to find Lady Marian and wisk her away to Robin's camp, else she could be used as bait for Robin again. But where was the lady? It seemed a hopeless task to locate her. Like looking for a needle in the hay.

"Psst. Arrow."

Like a welcome boon, Lankless popped out from behind one of the doors, pointing towards the top of the stairs. "She is in her chamber. Third door to the left." A key dangled from his hand and he grinned. "Which soon will be unlocked."

"Thank you, Lankless." Suddenly fearful for him, she asked, "And what of you?"

He shrugged.

"Come with me," she urged. "Join Robin's band. Methinks it might not be safe for you now. John will know that I had inside help to escape."

The little man thought only for a moment before making his decision. "Agreed." Wielding a large club he promised to defend her if need be.

"Then come on!" Together they ran up the stairs, taking them two at a time. At the top Rowena paused, listening. Being met with silence she proceeded on, coming at last to the bed chambers. She counted three doors and was just about to knock when she heard the sound of voices coming from within. Shrinking back, she waited anxiously.

"You will marry Sir Guy of Gisborne, I say. Your lover Robin Hood will decorate my gallows. I fear he will not have time to pay his respects to you, my lady." It was the voice of Prince John.

"Never! I would as soon marry the devil as to marry that evil lout. I'll marry Robin, or none at all. You promised me to the winner of the tournament and Robin was the winner."

"BiGod!"

"You cannot make me marry!"

"Ah, but I can. Just wait and see."

Rowena pressed tightly against the stone wall as she heard the door open. Footsteps descended the stairway. Waiting until the count of twenty, she then approached the door. "Lankless . . ." Feeling behind her, she felt the cold metal of the key grace her open hand. Fitting it in the lock, she turned it slowly, silently, then opened the door.

"I already told you I wouldn't—" Marian stared at Rowena, open-mouthed. "Rowena?"

"Hurry. We haven't time to chatter. It's a long story. I'll tell you on the way." Pushing Marian none too gently, she prodded her along.

"What of Robin?"

"He's back at camp. You'll see." Taking her by the hand, she pulled her down the stairs with Lankless tagging along behind. Past the buttery and the pantry they ran until they had reached the front door of the castle. Only then did they stop to catch their breaths.

"How are we going to get past the men-at-arms?" Marian was fearful as she noted the two guards looming in their path.

"Leave it to me," Rowena answered. With her most seductive smile she walked towards one of the men, her hips swaying provocatively. Acting as if it were her intention to seek him out, she came before one unusually tall guard.

"What are you about?" the man asked with a lift of his brows. His eyes roamed over her lithe, young body.

"Looking for a tumble," she purred. "You look so handsome that I have picked you for the honor." She inched closer, running her fingers up and down his chest in a suggestive manner. Suddenly, with the swiftness of a striking snake, she grabbed for his sword, taking him completely unaware.

"What the—?"

"Open that door or I will use this, you jack-a-napes,"

she threatened. When he faltered she said it again. "Open it, I say."

The other guard, seeing his companion was in trouble, came quickly to offer aid, initiating Rowena into combat. Thinking a woman to be easily bested, he lunged at her again and again. "Such a pity to have to kill a woman so pretty," he cajoled.

"Pretty is as pretty does, my nurse used to say," she responded. Wielding her sword well despite the encumbrance of her skirts and long, full sleeves, she soon had him on retreat. The odds were two to one, however. The tall guard also came into the fight, closing in behind her.

"Watch out!" With a frightful shriek, Lankless rose to the occasion. Bounding up, he crashed his club down upon the guard's head.

Rowena at last knocked the armed guard's sword from his hand. Holding the point of that sword at his throat, she repeated once again, "Open that door."

This time he did as he was bid and Rowena and Marian pushed through together. Lankless paused for just a moment, as if regretting to leave the comfort of the castle, but in the end capitulated.

"Come, come, you two. We have no time to dawdle," he said with a laugh, pushing in front of them. "We have to be on our way."

"How?" The idea of walking was not particularly appealing to Marian.

"Why, we'll travel in style in my jestor's wagon." He motioned to them. "Come along."

The inner courtyard rang with the sound of dogs, horses and men. Unlike their lords, the servants had work to do and could not stay abed. Roused from their pallets they lighted fires and prepared for the coming day. Thankfully they were much too busy to notice the threesome that scurried towards the stables. Lankless ducked inside. When he came out he was sitting atop a brightly painted little wagon, holding the reins tightly in his hand.

"My ladies . . ." Giving them a hand he helped them up. "Away we go." Then they were off, clattering over the drawbridge which had been briefly lowered in order to bring in supply wagons loaded with food. "Perfect timing."

"Indeed!" Rowena felt the wind in her face as the wagon rolled down a path that led into the woods.

Misery was being Prince John's prisoner, Kendrick thought as he shivered at the cold of the cell. It was uncomfortable. Tedious. Boring. Frustrating. "Freedom," he whispered. "A word taken far too for granted until . . ."

At first he had fought against his captivity, determined that somehow he was going to get free. He had tried every way to escape. Trickery, force, violence. As time passed, however, he had to at last come to an acceptance of being cooped up. The realization that he might be doomed was jarring. It was possible that he was going to die. Certainly his guards had threatened so.

"Death." Contemplating one's own demise was beyond description. It was frightening, even to the bravest of souls. "By hanging." He swallowed hard, almost feeling the noose around his neck already.

Kendrick had always been one to appreciate life. He relished it. Had enjoyed it. Now to think that he might see the dawn of only a few more days was tormenting. To never see Rowena again seemed beyond belief. It wasn't fair. To have been allowed to love each other so briefly seemed the most ludicrous of punishments.

"Rowena!" He thought of her during the day and dreamed of her at night, aching to hold her in his arms. The thought that most pained him was to never see her again. Even so, if he were certain that she was safe he knew he could have born even that. Raising his eyes towards the heavens, he whispered the prayer that had consumed him since seeing her taken away. "Please, save Rowena!"

How quickly prayers were answered.

"I tell you truly Robin Hood has escaped," Kendrick heard one of his guardsmen say.

"Oddsbody, what? Escaped? How? When?"

"He stuffed his garments with straw, leaving them behind—"

"And so we have a naked man running about the castle? It would seem he would be easy to notice."

"Nay, but how he escaped remains a mystery. The man on duty insists he saw naught of the man. He saw only a light-haired woman leaving the cell, a lady of some rank by her appearance."

"A lady? In the prison cell?"

"Who obviously helped him escape."

Kendrick didn't know how, but he knew who. Rowena! Oh, she was such a clever one. "Run and keep on running, my love."

"What did you say?" The sound of the creaking door interrupted Kendrick's spoken thoughts.

"I heard what you said about Robin's escape and freely celebrate," he answered.

"Celebrate?" Folding his arms across his chest, the guard stared him down. "Well, have your fun. At this time tomorrow you will be swinging from the gallows."

"Tomorrow?" Kendrick felt his heart leap up to his throat. "I was told my hanging was to be in three days." What kind of cruel jest was this?

"The prince has decided otherwise."

Kendrick listened to the guards in shock.

"You are to be taken to the courtyard at dawn tomorrow to dance upon the gallows."

It was mid-morning when Lankless, Rowena and Lady Marian arrived at the entrance to Robin Hood's camp. They had left Lankless' wagon with a farmer in exchange for three horses, which they now dismounted.

"A waterfall . . . ?" Marian looked surprised, more so when Rowena bid her to walk through the water. The jestor, however, was the first to step through, being as he was of an adventurous nature despite his size. Rowena followed, then Marian.

They found the outlaws sitting in a circle, obviously in the midst of some kind of discussion or other.

"Poor Arrow. The lad is a brave one to risk his life for you, Robin," Little John was saying.

"And what of Marian? What will become of her now?" asked Will Scarlet. "Will she be married off to the lad before he is hanged?" He looked at Robin to see his reaction to another marrying the woman he loved.

"The lad will not marry the Lady Marian," Robin answered with conviction. "At least of that I can be sure."

"How?"

Allan-A-Dale stroked the strings of his harp, making up a song about the incident.

> "The sheriff and prince held a tourney,
> All on the castle green.
> 'Twas as fine a match of archers,
> that ever was to be seen.
>
> Robin and Will Scarlet,
> Roderick and Arrow, too,
> Took each their turn, shooting strong,
> The maiden's hand for to woo.
>
> But treachery flooded the morning,
> The crown was but a tarnished one.
> 'Twas with evil thought the deed was wrought,
> and with the horn a trap was sprung.
>
> Sing therefore for the brave lad Arrow,
> Praise him, so daring and good.
> With courage and care he reached into the snare,
> And took from the prince, Robin Hood."

Allan-A-Dale finished and shook his head. "But alas for poor Arrow."

"Perhaps not," Rowena said as she led the others into the camp. It was quite a vision they made, the little man and two young ladies. Enough of a vision to make Robin choke on his ale.

"BiGod!" Jumping to his feet, he was just about to rouse his men when he recognized his visitors, one in particular catching his eye. "Marian!" With long strides he ran towards her, gathering her in to his arms.

"Oh, Robin! Robin! When I saw them surround the victor of the tournament I . . . I . . ." She wound her arms around his neck, so tightly that it appeared she would never let go.

"Don't cry, dear heart."

The men of the outlaw band swept forward to take a look at their guests, taking special note of Rowena. "Who have we here?" asked Will Scarlet, bowing low to her and taking her by the arm.

Rowena was coy. "We have met before," she chided. All the while she was searching the camp for Kendrick.

"Met before? Oh, no. For surely I would remember."

"Would you, sir barber?" Taking off her headdress she smiled at him.

"Arrow!" He looked with puzzlement upon her curves which were unfettered by her breast binding. "But where did you get such padding? Why, you could have fooled me. I thought you really were a lady."

"Did you now?" Rowena toyed with him, but a more important matter goaded her to ask, "Where is Kendrick?"

"Kendrick?" Will Scarlet looked down at the ground. "He's not here."

"Not here?" A feeling of apprehension tugged at her heart like a beggar in the marketplace. "Where is he then?"

Robin stepped towards her to give out the news. "He was captured at the tournament."

"Captured? How?" In that moment her whole world crumbled.

"Trying to save you," Robin explained. "When he saw you being taken away he went wild with fury. He was fool-hardy and fell into the sheriff's hands."

Little John intruded. "We tried to save him but alas, could not."

Rowena put her hand to her mouth. "No!" Though she had never cried in front of the outlaws before, she did so now. It was all her fault. De Bron had thrown himself into danger because of her. How could she live with that?

"Arrow . . . ?" Friar Tuck looked at her quizzically, setting the other outlaws' tongues into motion.

"Why did Kendrick go so beserk?"

"What is Arrow to him?"

"What is going on?"

It was Robin Hood who strode forward to answer the question. "Gentlemen, we have had a lady in our midst for quite awhile, haven't we, Arrow?"

Looking up through her mist of tears, Rowena knew her masquerade to be over. Slowly she nodded her head.

"Lady!" They all gasped. "A woman!" Pandemonium broke out as the outlaws argued among themselves. Most of them wanted Arrow to be driven from the band. She had betrayed them, they said. She was a fake, a charleton. Their verbal battle was silenced by Robin's uplifted arm.

"Order. Order." He patted Rowena on the arm. "Aye, Arrow is a lady. But after the tournament and after what she has been through, I would think not one of you could question Arrow's courage." His eyes looked steadily at her, mirroring his respect. "Be she woman or lad, there is no one who is her equal. If it were up to me solely, I would let her stay."

Rowena felt like a mare at market as they all circled around her, looking at her with appraising eyes. At last Will Scarlet spoke. "I say Arrow stays."

"She stays," Allan-A-Dale agreed.

"Lady or lad, she is a brave one," Little John added. "She stays. I will challenge anyone who says nay."

One by one, each of the outlaw archers said the same. Rowena had won their hearts, every one, with her courage and her bravery. She smiled her gratitude, but quickly gave up her smile for a look of determination. "Thank you, friends, but I cannot bask in your adoration ere long. Not when Kendrick's life is in jeopardy." She roused them to action. "We must go. Now! We must set him free." Picking up the nearest bow and quiver she was prepared to set out at that very moment.

"Wait." Robin blocked her path. "We will try to free him . . ."

"Try?" Rowena stiffened. "What say you, *try?*" His reluctance angered her. "You, a coward, Robin? Well then, have no doubt but that I will rescue him if I have to do it all alone."

She started off, but he grabbed her by the sleeve. "Cool your temper. I only meant that we had to use caution. The prince will be expecting us to try something foolhardy, something daring. We have to think."

"Think." Rowena took a deep breath to calm her nerves. She would not act like an impetuous woman. Yet every fiber of her being called out a warning that they could not wait. "When is he to be hanged?"

"On Friday before the sun reaches high noon," Robin answered. "We have planned to act that same day before the sun rises. We will have a little surprise in store for the prince and the sheriff."

Rowena shook her head. "No! We cannot wait. I know it. I feel it. Call it woman's intuition if you like, but I am determined on this."

The outlaws conferred on the matter, some agreeing with Robin, the others with Arrow.

"We do Kendrick no good from behind bars should we likewise be captured."

"But we do him no good if we wait until after he is dead!" Little John exclaimed.

"Aye, they will hang him!"

"We must get him out of the prince's clutches."

"We must use caution and clear heads."

"Clear heads be damned. Bravery will win the day. Or are we cowards?"

Tempers ran high as some of the outlaws were all for marching that very minute to the castle to free Kendrick.

"No. We cannot act impulsively and rue the rescue," Robin insisted.

The argument went back and forth. Indeed the outlaws might have argued the matter for a long time had not a messenger arrived on the scene, a spy sent into the castle disguised as a tailor. What he revealed determined the matter, for it was learned that because of "Robin Hood's" escape, Kendrick de Bron was to be hung much earlier than planned.

"Tomorrow right after sunrise. The prince fears that if he waits, the noble Robin Hood will enact a clever plan that will not only free de Bron but make John look like an ass."

"Then we must act tonight," Robin exclaimed. He put his arm around Rowena. "And so, my brave girl, it is I who will repay your good deed. Now I will help you save the man you love."

"Tonight!" came the echo of all.

"And pray to God that we are not too late."

Chapter Twenty-Nine

Kendrick watched through the cracks in the wooden door as the first rays of the new day dawned. Sunshine. Warmth. Light. But to him a curse. Never had he been so dismayed to see the beginning of a new day, for this day would be his last to breathe in the sweet air of life.

It would not be a pleasant way to meet his end. He had seen many men hanged before, had heard their cries and taken pity upon them. Now it was his turn to feel his tongue hang out as he gasped for the precious elixir of life.

"Dear God, let me be brave."

Kendrick's hands were numb, his back ached and his feet felt as if they were being pricked by needles as he lay upon the straw in a cramped position. The guards had been cruel in their treatment of him, taking delight in seeing one of the nobility meet the end in a state of humiliation. They had brought his last meal, setting it upon the floor. Refusing to untie his hands they had told him to lap up the food from the bowl like a dog. He could still hear their laughter at his efforts at dignity. But how could one feel any pride when in such a position?

"He is not so lordly looking now," one guard had jested.

Now Kendrick was all alone with only a spider to keep him company. Seeing it hanging from its web, he shuddered as he was reminded that soon he would be hanging thus.

The jingle of keys announced that he was soon to have company. Was it time already? Kendrick felt a rush of fear. Would he die quickly? Or would it be slow? Oh, God help him!

The door was thrown open. Bright light blinded Kendrick and for a moment his eyes, which were used to darkness, squinted at the light. He heard the trod of heavy boots and looked up, but his eyes could not see and it was a helpless feeling.

"You must let me see a priest before I die," he said with more bravado than he felt. "Surely even a condemned man has the right to save his soul. Even the Sheriff of Nottingham cannot be so cruel."

His answer was silence as he fought to look upon the person who had entered the room. Who was it? What did it matter? All he knew was that he was being forced to his feet. He tried to stand—it was impossible at first. He was as weak as a babe, having lain in one position too long.

"What does it matter?" he thought wretchedly. An arm steadied him and he wondered at the kindness of the jailer. Or was it just that the guard was in a hurry to send him on his way up to heaven?

"We must hurry," said a gruff, raspy voice.

Kendrick laughed to himself. "Hurry? I'm in no hurry to meet the hangman."

He winced as he felt a dagger sever the ropes about his wrists. He was free, at least for the moment, but what good did it do him? There was no place to go. No place to run.

Clenching and unclenching his fists, he sought to bring blood back into his hands. If only he had a weapon. Anything. He would put up a fight. Alas, it was too late. With horror he felt rough cloth engulfing him. He was going to suffocate!

"And so my time has come," he mumbled, then felt himself maneuvered about like a blind man. Pushed to the ground like a sack of wheat, he could only hope that God would be merciful.

Dressed in loose white woolen robes, white linen wimples and black woolen veils, the nuns moved with graceful strides towards the site of the gallows. As they glided like heavenly messengers, they kept their heads bowed in reverence to the condemned man who was about to make his appearance. Following close behind the sisters, clothed in his coarse brown wool, his cowl over his head, strode the friar.

"God have pity upon the poor condemned man's soul," Rowena prayed aloud, crossing herself. As she looked at Friar Tuck she winked, then blended in with the various townspeople—tailors, tanners, blacksmiths, laborers, their drab aprons and caps at odds with the bright tunics of the nobility. To all it was as if a festival were to be held, not a hanging, for there was revelry and jesting as the onlookers milled about.

How ghoulish, Rowena thought, cautioning herself to act pious at all times as she dodged the carts and wagons rumbling through the courtyard. The wagons stopped and their occupants, a miller, a mason and a traveling troupe of actors, paused to witness the spectacle. The sound of harp and lute filled the air and the crowd gave themselves up to the music. For just a moment Rowena nearly forgot herself as she walked in time to the rhythm, but Friar Tuck's frown reminded her.

All about, men-at-arms and men known to be the sheriff's followers formed a circle about the crowd just to make certain that there would not be any "last-minute" rescues, thus Rowena and her little band of followers had to be doubly careful. But one face was missing in the crowd. That of the Sheriff of Nottingham.

"Where in heaven's name is he?" asked a nervous guard as he watched the sun rise in the sky. "I thought he would be the first to be about this morning."

The other guard wasn't interested. "Who cares? Am I his keeper?"

They both watched the cart that was wheeled under the gallows. It would be jerked from beneath the prisoner, causing the poor wretch's neck to be snapped like a twig from the tree which hung over the stones of the courtyard.

Some in the crowd were curious. "Do you think Robin Hood will rescue him?"

"Nay. He'll swing. Just like a fish on a hook."

All looked up as the sound of a horn announced a noble spectator.

"John," Rowena whispered. The prince had elected to view the day's proceedings. Riding upon his white horse between the rows of soldiers and royal archers, his face showed that he too was wondering about the outcome. From time to time he glanced towards the south, as if expecting to see someone there. But who?

"Do you think he suspects?" Friar Tuck mumbled.

"Let us hope not."

"And where is the Sheriff of Nottingham?"

That seemed to be a question asked frequently over the next several minutes, for it was the sheriff's duty to initiate the details of the hanging. At last the prince seemed to lose all patience.

"Enough of this dallying," he commanded. "We will go about with our business, sheriff or no sheriff."

Rowena and the others stopped in their steps, mentally preparing themselves. Crossing her fingers, she could only hope that all would go well as her eyes, like all the others, looked towards the tower as the prison door was opened. Out stepped a hooded figure.

"De Bron!" Rowena gasped, wincing as Friar Tuck stepped on her toe to silence her.

Oh, dear God, look how he fought against the ropes which bound his hands behind his back, she thought. He seemed to be yelling curses, but his words were muffled by the hood which was worn over his head. That hood was meant to be a kindness, but Rowena wondered how it must feel to be pushed and prodded along, stumbling all the way.

"My prayers are with you," shouted out one old woman. "You and Robin's band have given us hope."

Indeed, instead of celebrating the hanging, it appeared that the crowd assembled had actually come to cheer on Robin Hood, in defiance of the prince.

"May God save you, Master de Bron," shouted out another.

There were curses uttered too, for not all were in favor of the outlaws. The nobles gave vent to their anger at one who had betrayed his rank. "Die, de Bron, outlaw that ye be. Meet your reward."

"To the gallows with him," shrieked one bejeweled lady.

Rowena watched as the condemned man was shoved onto the cart just as a cloud passed by the sun. For just a moment the earth was darkened as if in an omen of doom. Just as quickly, however, it passed, shining once more upon the tragic scene below.

Rowena and the other "nuns" and the friar reached beneath their robes, assuring themselves of what lay beneath. Pressing forward they made as if to offer comfort to him about to die. Their way was blocked by the guards.

"We have been given orders that no one come near the prisoner," said one burly guardsman, holding up his sword.

"Let me pass, my son. I come to save that one's soul from eternal damnation," said Frair Tuck softly. "As you can see by my robes, I am a friar. It is my duty to my God and to God's children to see that this one's soul is saved."

The guard shook his head violently. "No. The prince himself has ordered that no one step closer."

"But we must!" Rowena cried out, pushing forward. An arrow aimed at her heart caused her too to hold her place. Looking at the rope, she mouthed a silent prayer, then looked wildly about her to seek aid.

"Now see here." Not to be stayed by the words of a lowly pikeman, Friar Tuck sought out the prince himself to issue his plea. "You must let me hear his last words, sire," he pleaded.

"Let him die like the dog that he is," came the reply.

"No!" Rowena was close to losing all self-control. They had to get near Kendrick in order to save his life.

Desperately her eyes searched the crowd. In that moment she saw a wagon rumbling and only narrowly missed being hit as she hastily stepped back. A miller, dressed in his white garments, rode through the town splattering dirt on the onlookers. Forgetting herself, Rowena raised a fist at the impudence of the fellow, then turned her attention to the proceeding.

"We must do something!" She watched as the man she loved was secured about the neck with a rope, feeling utterly helpless. Their plan had gone awry. It would be certain death for them all to move one step further. And yet . . .

"Calm yourself," Friar Tuck's pudgy hand pressed into the small of her back.

"Calm myself?" Was she to be forced to watch de Bron die? The thought was too brutal to bear. Feeling tears trickle down her cheeks, she let them go unheeded as she watched the rope tied around Kendrick's neck. She had the wild impulse to throw herself forward and grab for the guard's sword but before she could a bloodcurdling yell sounded from the prison doors.

"No! Wait! You have the wrong man," came a voice.

Looking towards the direction of the sound, all eyes watched as the rotund figure of the chief jailer, clad only in his loincloth, flung himself forward. Like a quivering bowl of custard, he fell at a heap at the prince's feet.

"What is the meaning of this?" Prince John's face was flushed.

"It . . . it . . . is . . . is not Kendrick de Bron that . . . that . . . you . . . you are about to hang but our noble sh-sh-sheriff," the man stammered.

Rowena's eyes met those of Friar Tuck. Was it possible? But how? Looking about she could see Robin in his disguise as a harper, Little John as a mason, and the others, too. Who then had worked this miracle?

Striding forward, Prince John sought to learn the truth as well. Making his way towards the prisoner he yanked at the hood as a gasp rent the air.

"It is the sheriff!"

There was a gag secured in his mouth. Babbling, he sought to make himself understood.

"Let him loose," John commanded. He pulled off the gag and prodded at the sheriff, showing little concern for the man's ordeal. "How did this happen?"

"The miller . . . not a miller. The old coot . . . really Edwin Greybeard . . . outlaw . . . fooled us."

Rowena could not contain her joy. Hugging the friar, she felt as if at that moment she had been reborn, given a second chance at happiness. She wanted to laugh, to cry, to shout aloud, but instead quickly gained control of her emotions. They must all get away and quickly now, before they were discovered. Meeting Robin Hood's eye, she nodded her head in the direction of the road, but not before the prince's voice rang out.

"Close the gates! Block all roads! I do not want anyone to leave here until I find the culprits responsible for this."

Rowena watched as the soldiers scampered forward. She, Robin and the others were hopelessly trapped.

Chapter Thirty

No one dared utter a sound as the archers and knights formed a barrier to keep everyone within the walls. Rowena looked at Friar Tuck and he at her. With a nod of his head he silently communicated with her not to move a muscle as the prince wove in and out among the townspeople on horseback, looking at every face. She didn't move but perspiration beaded her brow as he rode within inches of her, trying to recognize any outlaw among the crowd.

"You, sister!"

Rowena reached beneath her gown, touching the handle of her dagger. If she must, she would wield it. "Aye, my lord."

He was instantly suspicious. "What have you there?" He had seen her movement, much to her regret.

She thought fast. With her head held down in an attitude of meekness she answered, "My rosary. I was whispering a prayer that the Lord would intervene this day to see justice done." For a moment she feared she would be recognized.

"Then if your prayers are answered, we will soon have

that scoundrel within our grasp to hang as he deserves."
Belying her apprehension, the prince moved on, intent
upon seeking out the men in the crowd. Seeing Lankless,
he approached him. "You. Where have you been? Last
night you were gone from the castle when I would have
had you cheer me."

The prince's fool grinned wickedly. "Even a little man's
blood runs hot, my lord. 'Twas in the hay, I was. With a
comely wench, not looking for a needle." He chuckled,
then turned a cartwheel.

Behind Lankless stood Robin and Allan-A-Dale, dressed
brightly as musicians. The Prince beckoned toward them.
"Who be these minstrels?"

Lankless hurriedly stepped forward. "Friends of mine,
my lord. From the court of the French King. I plan a
surprise for tonight that I know will please you."

Rowena held her breath.

"Friends?" For a moment his expression mirrored suspicion.

"Remember I told you of Andre and Pierre a few weeks
ago? But then perhaps your thoughts were elsewhere."

"Perhaps." The prince moved forward, but threw over
his shoulder, "See that you are back tonight or I will have
your head, little man."

Rowena's heart pounded violently as John continued his
search. Would he recognize any of them? It appeared that
he would not, for he passed several of them by. Then all
at once he stopped before where Will Scarlet stood.
Dressed as a tinker, the foppish outlaw was wearing a bright
red hat.

"The fool!" Rowena breathed. His vanity was going to
be the end of them all.

"I recognize this one." John motioned to the guards.
"Arrest this man. We may have a hanging here today after
all."

The guards surged forward, but Will Scarlet was quick
on his feet. He dodged in and out among the crowd dodg-

ing his pursuers. Climbing atop the very same wagon that had been meant to carry Kendrick to his death, he set about to urge the horse forward, but a shower of arrows from the prince's archers kept him from escape.

"Catch him!" Urging his mount to block the wagon's escape, the prince was determined.

"We must do something!" Though she was not particularly fond of Scarlet, Rowena couldn't just stand by and see him hung. Nor was she alone. Seeing that one of their own was about to be captured, the outlaw band flung back their mantles, cloaks and gowns to display the weapons and garments beneath.

"Lord Prince, tis I who you want and not that poor fellow," Robin shouted, sacrificing himself for the life of his friend.

"No, I am Robin," Rowena cried, moving forward.

"No, it is I whom you seek," shouted Little John.

"I am Robin Hood," shouted another, anxious to join in the charade.

"No, I am Robin," shouted an archer.

Even Lankless got into the game, running in and out amidst the legs of the guards so that they were hindered in their pursuit. Even the townspeople joined in, each claiming to be Robin Hood. In confusion, the sheriff's men and the prince's guards didn't know which way to turn.

"Seize them all!" The prince was anxious to show these surly rebels.

Trying to soothe his injured pride, the sheriff ran to and fro issuing his orders, but the townspeople, who had long hated him, felt sympathy for the outlaws. They blocked the way. With fists flying, tanner, tinker, tailor, mason, butcher, merchant and beggar alike joined in the fracas.

"Enough of this!" The sheriff pointed at Robin, who had bested several of the sheriff's men in his bid for freedom.

Recognizing him, he gave the order. "It's him! He's the real Robin Hood! Hang him!"

Rowena watched in horror as one end of a rope was placed around Robin's neck, the other around the gallows.

"Hurry, you fools!" The sheriff smiled triumphantly towards John. "See, I have your outlaw for you. Justice will be served this day."

All fighting ceased. Everyone stared at the sight. The most famous outlaw in England, the hero of them all, was about to meet his death.

"Pull the rope. One, two . . ." shouted the sheriff.

"No!" Rowena grabbed a bow from out of the hands of one of the prince's archers. Heedless of her skirts or wimple, she placed an arrow in the bow and pulled.

"Three!"

Shooting at the rope, Rowena hit that target just as the cart was yanked from under Robin Hood's body. He fell to earth unharmed.

"God's teeth!" Prince John was in a state of outraged shock, but he wasn't going to accept defeat. Spurring his horse forward he plunged into the crowd, only to be pulled off his horse by Friar Tuck, who used his robe's girdle to aid him. Seeing their prince fall, several of the soldiers stopped in their tracks, confused as to what to do.

Robin's men followed Rowena's example, raining arrows at the sheriff's and prince's men. Those who did not work magic with a bow fought in hand-to-hand combat.

"Like bees we will give them a feel of our stingers," Rowena declared, shooting again and again.

Then Robin took a hand in the matter. Grabbing the sheriff from behind, he held a knife to his throat. "Call off the hounds!"

"No!" The sheriff paled as the knife was placed closer, but still he was stubborn. "I will not issue such a command." A line of red appeared at his throat as Robin pressed the knife into his skin. "Well, maybe . . ."

Meanwhile, as Prince John sought to mount his horse

again, Rowena threw herself against him, tumbling him to the ground. Slipping the dagger from her gown, she followed Robin's example and held the prince at peril.

"Let us go. Tell them to retreat."

John, known to be a coward, didn't even falter. "Put aside your arms. Let them leave!"

The signal from Robin set the outlaws into a hasty retreat, running, jumping and scrambling to get to their wagons and horses.

Rowena felt a hand about her waist and looking up saw that it was Little John. "Come, Arrow. Methinks you will find Kendrick safely sitting before the fire ere we reach the camp." Mounting the prince's stallion, they rode away from the town—looking back only long enough to see that several guardsmen were streaming out of the doors of the tower to follow in pursuit of the outlaw band.

The boughs of the trees and the roar of the cascading water beckoned Rowena as she approached the encampment. She looked like a pilgrim, one of those travelers to the holy land, dressed as she was in her nun's habit, which was now in tatters. She hoped the kindly sister who lent it to her would not be too angered that she had not been able to take better care of it.

Dismounting from her horse, giving the animal a pat on the rear to send it home again, she ran as quickly as her legs could carry her. Surging through the waters into the cavern, her eyes sought out only one man. Seeing him, her heart took flight as well as her feet. Then she was in his arms.

"De Bron! I thought never to see you again. Oh, my love. I died a hundred deaths . . ."

Kendrick thrust her from him, thinking to save her from betraying her disguise. "The others—"

"Are privy to my deception. So . . ." She wound her arms around him. "So, kiss me. Have no fear." Hardness

against softness, they strained together. Rowena kissed his
cheek, his chin and then his lips. Her hands wound in the
tendrils of his hair. They would have stood like that forever
but a cough sounded behind them, drawing them apart.

"Ahem!"

Rowena stiffened as she saw an old man with a wrinkled
face and gray beard. "Who are you?"

"Edwin Greybeard." The old man bowed gallantly. "'Tis
pleased I am to meet such a beautiful lady. You be Rowena
Fitz Hugh, no doubt."

"I am." Impulsively she squeezed his hand. "How can
I ever thank you for saving my love? I have so many questions."

He grinned. "And I many answers. Shall we begin?"
Taking her arm, he drew her towards an old log and beckoned Kendrick to sit beside her.

"I thought my last day had come," Kendrick began. "I
could not see Edwin clearly when he came to rescue me.
I thought him to be the hangman."

Edwin Greybeard explained it all. He had long ago been
a forester in the king's service, that king being Henry.
Being kind of heart and having mercy upon those who
stole the king's deer to feed their starving families, he had
turned his head when they had trangressed. His kindness
had soon put him at odds with the king and rendered him
an outlaw. "King Henry was a powerful man, but I fear
not a merciful king."

"It was Edwin who took an interest in a young lad, Robert
Fitzooth by name, and taught him the ways of the forest
and how to shoot straight." Kendrick looked apologetic.
"When he told me that he was one of Robin Hood's men,
I thought him to be just an old man in his cups, yet he
proved himself today."

Cocking one eyebrow, the old man bent near Rowena.
"The sheriff thought me to be an old drunk, fond only of
my ale. Now, I'll admit that I like my drink now and again,
but I always keep me wits." He tapped his temple. "When

I heard tell of the trap the prince and sheriff were planning, I arranged to get into their dungeon.''

Rowena folded her arms across her chest and leaned forward. ''But if you are an outlaw, wasn't there danger there for you?''

''No.'' He sighed. ''I was pardoned when I grew old. They didn't think I was any danger to them.'' Pulling at his beard he seemed to be remembering his younger days. ''But they were wrong. My hair may be frosted with winter, but I've given aid to any who need a friend.''

''The poor and the needy,'' Rowena whispered. ''But how was it that the Sheriff of Nottingham and not Kendrick was brought to the gallows? And where was de Bron? In the wagon?'' She was enthralled.

Kendrick answered. ''I was hidden in one of the flour sacks. Edwin dressed in a white miller's apron and thus we rode out of town beneath the very noses of those who sought my death.''

Rowena remembered the sight of the miller's wagon splashing mud as it rattled on. ''But the sheriff?''

Edwin raised his brows. ''I am not as old and feeble as one might suppose, my lady. It took only a matter of wits and skill with a club to persuade the sheriff and his two guards to sleep for a while. I put him in young de Bron's garments, gagged him, then put a hood over his head. When the hangman's apprentice and the men-at-arms came for de Bron, they got him instead.''

''And the Sheriff of Nottingham was taken to the gallows by mistake. A clever but slightly devious plot,'' Rowena complimented.

''Aye, clever.'' Kendrick patted the old man on the back. ''But what of you now? Will you join us?''

Edwin Greybeard thought a moment, then slapped his bony thigh with his hand. ''Aye, that I will. Methinks there will always be a need of loyal men of stout heart no matter their age.'' He winked at Kendrick. ''But perhaps for now I will leave you two alone. Eh?''

Taking Rowena's hand, Kendrick took the matter into his own hands, pulling her towards that part of the forest where they had enjoyed such tender moments of ecstasy. When they were at the side of the lake, he lowered his head and kissed her gently at first, then with a hunger that only she could assuage.

The world blurred at the touch of his lips. Rowena couldn't think, couldn't breathe. Her ears were filled with a sound like the waterfall. She felt her heart thump wildly then seem to stop beating entirely. It had been much too long since she had felt his lips against hers.

How long he kissed her she didn't know, but when he drew back their lips formed smiles at the very same moment. "I have never kissed a nun before," Kendrick teased, bidding her to loosen her gown.

"Nor I a sack of flour," she answered, laughing as she gently wiped a smudge of flour from his chin.

"Ah, Rowena. Rowena, how I love you!" His breath was warm in her ear. Taking her hands, he placed them inside his tunic so that she could feel the beat of his heart.

Rowena began to tremble. Her breath was coming faster, he had ceased to breathe at all. "De Bron . . ."

"Shhhh." Putting her hands behind his back, he laced her fingers with his. "No more words." Kendrick set about to ignite the blaze of her desires with a veritable feast of kisses.

Rowena's hands traced his spine. She had thought never to be able to touch him again, but here he was and she was so thankful. Savoring him with hands and lips, she forgot all else but this man whose life was so very dear to her. If her behavior was wanton, then so be it. This day had proved to her how precious was every hour.

Rowena cherished her lover as expertly as she had her bow, until Kendrick was taut with his need of her. He in turn played upon her curves as tenderly as a harper plucks the strings of his harp. She felt an aching longing as their bodies touched full length. She shuddered.

Kendrick tugged her down to lay beside him, helping her undress, peeling off his own clothes. They lay motionless for a minute. Rowena felt her mind racing, was caught up in a trance of unforgettable pleasure. Then, slowly, he began to make love to her, molding her, shaping her, enfolding her in a web of desire. She felt her heart move. This was what she had been born for. To be Kendrick's mate. To love him, cherish him, to be at his side for the rest of her days. How could she ever have thought anything was important compared to being with him like this?

"Marry me, Rowena?" he breathed.

"Marry you?" She closed her eyes, trying to think of something coy to say. Instead she merely whispered, "Yes, I will."

Chapter Thirty-One

Wreaths of mistletoe and pine bedecked the outlaws' hideout. A wedding uniting Kendrick de Bron and Rowena Fitz Hugh in holy matrimony was to be held amidst the boughs of the trees.

The hum of lively talk and robust laughter were carried through the forest by the breeze. Friar Tuck bustled about making preparation, singing as he worked. Not only would he conduct the ceremony, but he had promised to see to the wedding feast as well. Robin, who had agreed to be Kendrick's best man, was in an unusually romantic mood, picking a bouquet of wild flowers that he presented to Lady Marian, who had been asked to be Rowena's maid of honor. As Marian looked into Robin's eyes, it was plain to see that soon there would be another wedding.

Maid Marian had aided Rowena in finding a proper dress for the occasion, sewing a magnificent creation out of a lace tablecloth and a large piece of white satin which had been stolen from a very rich merchant in league with Prince John. Kendrick would be married in his hose of green and a new tunic which was likewise of pilfered cloth.

If the bride and groom were not bedecked in elegant attire of brocade, if jewels did not adorn their persons, nonetheless they made a handsome couple whose glowing eyes and smiles made them as regal as any king and queen.

Only one thing marred the happiness of the day, that the King of England was still in danger of losing his throne. Word had been bandied about that Prince John planned to have himself crowned king before his brother could set foot upon English soil again. It was even rumored that although he was already married, John would seek the hand of a foreign princess as his queen.

"John goes too far, if you ask me," Edwin Greybeard declared. "Methinks even his own followers will turn against him soon. Why, he has agreed to give away a large part of Normandy to the French King if that monarch will aid him in his quest for the throne."

"Then God speed the rightful king back to England," Rowena declared. She had no doubt but that the path back to his rightful realm would be strewn with many rocks and pitfalls for Richard.

"Aye, God speed him." Kendrick brushed her hair back from her ear, nibbling that pink shell gently.

Rowena leaned against him. "If only Richard were on the throne we would not have a care in the world."

"I know, but we are helpless to aid him. It is in God's hands." He hugged her tightly against him. "Our new friend Greybeard says that Philip of France has tried desperately to prevent Richard's return."

"Philip?" The news was disappointing. "So poor Richard has more enemies than he knows."

"Aye. And John is ever the clever fellow who knows that the clink of coins can soon turn friend against friend." A look of worry crossed his brow. "While in my cell I learned of John's cunning. Though the ransom has been sent, he finally persuaded the Austrian emperor to change his mind about letting our king go. Orders were sent to bring the king back to the emperor. But luckily the ship had already sailed."

Rowena's eyes held hope. "Then Richard is on his way?"

"Let us pray so, but anything can happen."

Rowena reached up to gently caress Kendrick's face and found that it was slightly stubbled with a beard he had not yet had time to shave. She teased him about it as he gathered her into his arms and kissed her, but as his tongue found the softness of her lips she forgot all else except his mouth. For a moment, thoughts of the king were forgotten.

"I wish we were alone," Rowena sighed, looking in the direction of the lake.

"Yea, but we have a ceremony to think about. We must prepare ourselves, my love." Kendrick cupped her face in his hands.

She smiled. "I do not need any ceremony to feel married to you. Perhaps in truth we have been married these past weeks just as surely as if the good friar had spoken words over our heads. We were married in our hearts that first time we made love."

They had forgotten the presence of anyone else in the world, that is until Edwin Greybeard sneezed. Quickly they pulled apart, but he reassured them. "It does me good to see two people so in love. Reminds me of my Margaret."

Kendrick gave Rowena over to Marian. "Make haste with my future bride's preparation. I do not like to be parted ere long."

Seeking the shelter of a grove of trees near the lake, Rowena stripped off her garments, her hands trembling as she pulled her hosen and tunic over her hips and legs. She was unprepared for Marian's playful push that sent her tumbling into the water. Laughing, she sputtered as she came up, brushing the hair out of her eyes.

"Here!" Marian had procured some soap from Robin's stock of stolen merchant's goods.

While the two women talked "women" talk, Rowena gave herself up to the joy of her bath, lathering her arms

and legs, washing her hair. When at last she stepped out
of the pool, Marian helped her dry, then helped her slip
a soft chemise of white linen over her body. The lace and
satin wedding dress was next, belted by one of Marian's
own sashes.

"Let me do your hair, Rowena."

She felt the tug of a comb through her short tangled
curls as the young woman arranged her hair atop her head
in a froth of curls. A wreath of leaves held a sheer veil in
place. Rowena had entered looking like an outlaw, now
she left it looking like some woodland princess.

"The lady of the lake," Kendrick dubbed her. Had he
looked beneath her gown, he would have had to stifle a
laugh. Having no shoes to put on her feet, Rowena wore
her archer's boots. She resolved not to pick up her skirts
too high lest she reveal to all her only manly apparel.

Kendrick was handsome, Rowena thought as her eyes
moved over his rugged features and broad shoulders. His
black hair shown like ebony. His roguish grin promised
many delights when they were alone. Oh, how she wanted
to be his wife and yet at the same time she felt a twinge
of apprehension. No matter what anyone said, marriage
would curtail some of her freedom. Was she ready for that?
Her heart answered for her. *Yes.*

The forest rumbled with the sounds of revelry. A wedding was a wonderful excuse for a celebration. The outlaws
had great fun telling ribald stories, but their voices faded
to mere whispers as they looked towards the somberly
dressed monks that were now entering the camp. With
them they brought a tall, well-muscled man in the guise
of a wanderer. He hid in the shadows, content to watch
the proceedings from there.

Rowena looked towards the stranger, wondering why
she had the feeling she had seen him somewhere before.
Her eyes questioned her father, who was among the monks
and friars. He merely nodded his head to tell her that all
was well and that the man could be trusted.

The harp of Allan-A-Dale strummed a processional as Rowena walked upon her father's arm towards the man who was to be her husband. In her hands she carried a bouquet of early blooming forest flowers which blended with the fresh scent of spruce and pine. She could see the eyes of the archers upon her as they stood tall and straight, holding their bows of yew erect in a sign of respect. She felt the touch of Kendrick's hand upon her own as she knelt before the oak log which was to be their altar.

Stepping forward, Friar Tuck began the words of his Latin mass, uniting Rowena to Kendrick for all eternity. When the blessing of the couple was completed, Kendrick took from his own finger a ring of gold and emeralds which held his family crest. Putting it upon Rowena's finger, he kissed her gently to seal their vows. Then they drew apart. Friar Tuck held forth the bridal cup. They sipped from it to cheers of approval from the outlaw men.

"Oh, that I had seen her first," shouted Drawbow.

"Long life," shouted another.

"I wish you happiness," exclaimed Little John. "And long live King Richard. We must remember him."

"Aye. Long live the king."

It was then that the stranger stepped forward. The shouts of the archers stilled as they eyed the man warily. Who was he and why was he here?"

"Why do you toast King Richard, when it is John who rules England?" the dark-clothed man asked.

"Because Richard is our king now and always will be," answered Little John. "We will never bend our knee to another."

"Our loyalty is to Richard," Robin added. "We would ride to the realm of hell and back for our king."

The archers crept closer to the man who wore wanderer's attire. Suspicion reigned that he was a spy for Prince John. Tempers were on edge. Hands were poised at swords and bows.

"Who are you?" Rowena asked what the others pondered.

"A man who has come to you for help in ridding this land of the king's enemies." The man stepped forward. "What do you say to that?"

Robin answered for them all. "If you are loyal to the king, then our arrows and bows will be at your command."

"Then come. Your king has need of you in Nottingham where the Prince of England holds the shire and castle without thought to yielding it to the rightful owner." As he spoke, the wanderer slowly removed his hood. His blonde hair gleamed in the light of the day, his blue eyes flashed like fire. With stately grace, he held his head proud. The Plantagenet profile was shown to all.

"The king," came the whisper.

"It is the king."

Falling upon their knees they paid their homage.

Rowena looked into the proud yet kind eyes and remembered the first time she had seen Richard at his castle when she was a tomboy child. It *was* Richard.

The king was welcomed with wild acclaim throughout the land. Church bells rang out, people filled the streets and the air was rent with shouts of joy for the return of the rightful king. It had been an easy matter after all for the king and his loyal followers to recapture the castle of Nottingham. With his knights on his left hand and the archers of Sherwood Forest on his right, Richard, King of England, took back what was rightly his.

Rowena and Kendrick rode on horseback behind their king and delighted in the pomp and pageantry of the welcome. Richard was going to have himself crowned a second time just to prove to his adversaries that he was King now and forever more. Until death parted him from his crown.

When at last they arrived at Westminster, Kendrick

helped his lady off her horse. "It will take some time for me to get used to wearing skirts again," she confided, practicing her womanly grace.

"You don't have to wear skirts for me," Kendrick teased. "Methinks I prefered you in hosen anyway. Skirts do not divulge your nicely rounded—"

"Kendrick!" She blushed as his hand sneaked a pat at that beloved flesh. Oh, how could she ever have thought not to like married life? Or have thought that Kendrick de Bron would be a typical husband? Most certainly he was not. He was surely more passionate, considerate, loving and exciting than any other man could be. But most importantly, he accepted her for the way she was. He didn't want or plan to change her. More importantly he was the consumate companion, even going so far as accompanying her when she was in one of her "wilder" moods and wanted a daring dash through the forest.

"I hope Rob and Marian will be half as happy as we." He delighted in patting her on the behind again, grinning roguishly at her when she might have scolded.

Robin Hood and Lady Marian followed closely behind Kendrick and Rowena. The outlaw and all his archers had been given a pardon by the king. They had aided the poor, befuddled the prince, and thwarted evil at every turn. How could he not grant them abstinence? With their help, his ransom had been gathered and his realm guarded from his brother's evil hand. From this day forward Richard declared they would be the king's men.

There was a feeling of anticipation now as the king bid them enter the doors at Westminster. There in his throne room with all there to see, he reached for his sword. "Kneel, Kendrick de Bron," he said solemnly. "Swear that you will serve me faithfully from now on."

Kendrick's voice trembled with emotion. "I do, my king. God as my witness, I do."

"Then rise, Earl of Nottingham."

"Earl of Nottingham?" Rowena's eyes misted at the

honor given her husband. He was an earl, though she
loved him just as much as when he had been an outlaw.

"Robin of Sherwood." The king beckoned him. "Swear
that you will serve me faithfully."

"I so swear, my lord."

"Then rise, Earl of Huntington." The king looked about
at the archers of Robin's band who had crowded in to
watch. Each of them was knighted in turn with a merry
order to be royal archers. "And you, jestor," he added
with a wink at Lankless. "It will be Sir Lankless from now
on."

The little man knelt before his king in homage. What
he lacked in height, he made up for in spunk and bravery.

Kendrick returned to his wife's side. She felt his strong
arms enfold her and heard his whispered words of love.
"You are my love, my life," he whispered tenderly.

Rowena placed her hand in his. They had a long life to
look forward to together. "Our love will endure forever."
And from that love would spring forth future generations
to listen to the stories of Robin Hood and the outlaws of
Sherwood Forest. Already she had felt the seed of this
future begin to grow within her.

"Come, wife. We have yet to celebrate our wedding
night." Secretively they slipped away.

As they felt the breeze of the out of doors upon their
faces, walked in the light of day a dove flew across the sky
carrying in its mouth a leaf.

"A favorable sign."

Peace. Blessed peace.

Epilogue

Melburn Manor, 1196

Never had the great hall seemed so welcoming, Kendrick thought as he opened the door. The air was fragrant with the fresh scent of summer rushes on the floor, mingling with the enticing aromas of a meal in preparation. The large room was so clean from top to bottom that it nearly glowed. Several wall sconces had been lit, their tiny flames illuminating the tapestries hanging on the wall. A hearth fire warmed the room.

"Welcome home!" With a lot of help from Gwyneth, Maida, Chadwick and Humbley, Rowena had worked wonders with the manor.

Kendrick gave himself up to the pure joy of having Rowena's arms around him again. Five months away from her, fighting with Richard on the Continent to recover Plantagenet lands lost to Philip, seemed like a lifetime. But no more.

"Now, at last I can be happy!" Kendrick had fought beside Richard in a war to win back the territory lost while Richard had been in prison. Robin Hood, or the Earl of Huntington as he was now called, had likewise followed the king to the wars. Now, however, Robin and Kendrick were home for good.

"Mmmmm. I'm happy." Rowena snuggled contentedly against his chest.

Kendrick stroked her hair. "I hope that you were not too bored without me."

"Bored?" Rowena could barely stifle a smile. Oh, there were times when she had felt too restrained being the Countess of Nottingham. She had longed for the fresh air of the forest and sorely missed the adventures she had experienced. Could she then be blamed if every once in awhile she had reverted to her old ways and donned lad's attire for a late-night ride? Or that she had practiced her archery every chance that she had?

Kendrick knew his wife well enough to read her mind. "I thought not." He had an intimate knowledge of her adventurous way. She was a free spirit. "But I was. Without you . . ." Slowly he moved his face towards hers, taking her mouth in an urgent kiss. Without her he had been starving, aching, dying. Though he had never believed in love, Kendrick did now. And he had begun to believe in happy endings.

Kendrick and Rowena's wedding had inspired another pair of lovers. Robin and Marian had followed their example a week after the woodland wedding, although they had married in Nottingham Church and not in the forest. The king had given the bride away with Robin's men, the royal archers, in attendance.

Little John had come back to Nottinghamshire where he had achieved great fame as the champion of all England with the quarter staff. Will Scarlet had been given back his property. As to Robin's men, now the royal archers, half of them had been retained in London while the other half had returned to Sherwood and Barnesdale, there to guard the king's forests. Sir William had surprised everyone by deciding to stay at the abbey. Content in his declining years with books and scrolls, he had given the newlyweds Grantham Manor to adjoin to Kendrick's own.

"So that there will be a legacy for my grandchildren, of which I hope there will be many," he had whispered in his son-in-law's ear.

The reminder stirred Kendrick's blood. Now that he was home it was time to start a family. "Rowena . . ." Taking her hand, he led her towards the stairs.

"Are you not hungry?" Nodding her head, Rowena reminded him of the supper that bubbled over the fire.

"Aye." Kendrick nuzzled her ear.

Looking up at him, she saw his look and knew what was on his mind. "Geoffrey!" she whispered.

"What?" For a moment Kendrick was startled.

"If our first child is a boy we'll name him Geoffrey, after your uncle. And if it is a girl . . ."

"Edwina, after your mother."

"Edwina." The image of a woman's face hovered momentarily before Rowena's eyes. Looking up at Kendrick, she felt an overwhelming sense of peace. She had everything she had ever hoped and dreamed of. All was well.

Kendrick's intense gaze clung to her. He ran his hand lovingly over the softness of her shoulder, down to the peaks of her firm breasts. Who could have ever believed that a chance encounter in a forest would lead to such happiness?

"I love you . . ." For just an instant it was as if he had been allowed a look at the future. A stormy one for Richard and for England. But for them? The answer was simple. He could withstand any storm now that he and Rowena were together.

AUTHOR'S NOTE

Richard the Lion Heart won great fame by his quest in the Holy Land and was endeared to most of his English subjects. As for his brother, John, he made his submission to his brother very quickly. Queen Eleanor, mother to both Richard and John, asked of her older son that the trangressions of his younger brother be overlooked. John was forgiven. No doubt Richard felt compassion for John who now seemed like a "plucked" bird and hardly like the ruler who had terrified all England.

For a time there was peace in the land. The remaining years of Richard's life, however, were anticlimatic as he faced the twilight like some vainglorious and rather tarnished god. The actual time he spent in England was infrequent and when he was wounded with an arrow and died, John at last was granted his fondest wish. He became King of England in his own right. That his misrule instigated the Magna Carta tells something about his reign.

YOU WON'T WANT TO READ
JUST ONE—KATHERINE STONE

ROMANCE FROM JO BEVERLY

DANGEROUS JOY   (0-8217-5129-8, $5.99)

FORBIDDEN   (0-8217-4488-7, $4.99)

THE SHATTERED ROSE   (0-8217-5310-X, $5.99)

TEMPTING FORTUNE   (0-8217-4858-0, $4.99)